Ghost of the Gaelic Moon

Carol Maschke

W0006251

Cairn Moon

ISBN 978-1-947593-01-5

Cover design by MadCatDesigns
Formatting by Anessa Books
Editor: Marly Cornell

CairnMoon

Minneapolis, Minnesota
www.cairnmoon.com

Contents

PART TWO—Four Years Later

This is dedicated to my mother, Delores Maschke. Despite having a difficult life, she has always done her best for me and I would be nowhere without her. My thanks will never be enough.

Part One

Chapter 1
The Dream

*S*HE FELT HER breath catch in her throat, as he pulled her close and began to nuzzle her neck. She shivered from the sensation, from the feelings that coursed through her body, both physical and emotional. She saw the pure adoration on his face as he watched her and was amazed that the man gazing back at her was everything she wanted, everything she could never put into words. Compact, but strong, with the grace of a dancer, firm butt, strong back, and hands she instinctively knew would please her when given the opportunity. His wavy red hair was unruly. His intense blue eyes watched her as only he could.

When he placed his lips on hers, she knew he could feel her smile. As they kissed, she felt his smile as well. She was the first to open her mouth, allowing him entrance as their tongues touched, tentatively at first, but with growing ardor.

When they broke apart, they looked at each other almost shyly.

"Where have you been all of my life?" he asked in a heated whisper, the lilt of his Irish accent falling softly on her ears.

"America," she said honestly, and he laughed, a laugh that warmed her heart.

"I've been waiting for you."

"For how long?" she asked as he tenderly stroked her face.

"Forever," he said as he leaned in to kiss her again.

They moaned into each other's mouth. She felt him pressed against her and, God, how she wanted him, how she loved him! *Wait, loved?*

She broke off their kiss and gazed into his laughing blue eyes. Yes, she was sure. Yes, she loved him.

"*Ahh*, Mary, I love you so," he whispered in her ear. "Are you sure you want me in your life knowing what I am?"

"I can't imagine life without you," she answered, and moaned as he kissed her again...

Mary woke up abruptly, trying to clear the cobwebs from her mind and calm her raging hormones. She looked around the airplane cabin, hoping she hadn't embarrassed herself by making any noise, and picked up her book that had slipped onto her lap.

Her traveling companions from work sat with Mary in the airplane. She had the window seat, and her best friend and coworker, Amy, sat next to her. Coworker Paul had the aisle seat, which allowed him to stretch out his long legs.

Thankfully Paul was asleep, but Amy was not. She watched Mary with a gleeful expression on her face. "Good dream?" Amy asked.

"*Uh, huh.*" Mary didn't want to admit anything.

"Anyone I know?"

"Amy!" Mary whispered fiercely.

"You were making the most interesting sounds."

"Drop it."

"Mary?"

"I said, drop it. Let's talk about something else."

"You need a boyfriend," Amy said sincerely.

"Amy!"

"Okay," she said, searching for a new topic. "Sooo... you seem happy to be going to Ireland?"

"Yes! What's not to like? My first trip out of the country and it's somewhere I want to go, courtesy of work."

"Seems like a nice place for a trip," Amy agreed.

"Beautiful countryside, pubs, Druids, Guinness, Irish whiskey, New Grange, Waterford crystal, castles, the Blarney stone, and Irish paranormal. See," she said and flashed the book at Amy. It was about Celtic Druids.

"You're going to check out Irish paranormal?" Amy was amused.

"When I have time. You know I love a good ghost story."

Amy laughed. "Mary, I know you have some psychic abilities... but searching for ghosts?"

"Why not? You do what you want, and I'll do what I want in our down time," Mary said.

Amy gave her friend a sly smile. "I have a better idea."

"What's that?"

"Let's get you hooked up while we're in Ireland?" she whispered.

"Amy! No. I'm not interested in a relationship. You know how my last one ended."

"Who said anything about a relationship? Just a fling, you know, some fun to relieve the stress that you are obviously feeling. I know it's been awhile since Joe..."

"I don't want to discuss this," Mary said firmly.

"I'm not letting you off the hook."

"No flinging!" Paul said as he opened his eyes. "You know I have designs on Mary. I call first dibs."

"But she doesn't want you, Paul." Amy pointed out to the tall, well-built, blond-haired man scrunched in the seat beside Mary. *He may be handsome but he's not good enough for Mary.*

"That isn't true, is it, Mary?"

Mary expelled a long but sympathetic sigh. "Paul, we've talked about this, you know we're just friends."

"So you say, but in the end, you won't be able to resist my charms," he said with an air of confidence. He turned in his seat to face Mary. "My layover isn't long, but perhaps we could find a restaurant and have dinner together?"

"Paul, I don't think there's time," Mary demurred. She did her best not to laugh at the glare she felt from Amy. "We'll see."

Grumbling, the other two settled back against their seats.

The lights of Dublin were just coming into view, twinkling beyond the darkness of the North Atlantic. Mary shivered, but whether in apprehension or anticipation, she didn't know.

AN HOUR LATER the three of them sat in the nicest restaurant at the Dublin airport at Paul's insistence. He had a three-hour layover and was more than happy to be in their company rather than to wait alone.

Mary listened to Paul politely as he talked about his business trip to Germany and the things he was expected to do while there. She suppressed a laugh when she caught Amy making one of her signature eye rolls.

"Something funny?" Paul asked, showing no sign of humor.

Mary coughed on a chip she was eating. "No, Paul, nothing."

"So, Mary, I thought maybe I could convince you to come and visit me in Germany?" Paul gave her his best charming smile.

"Sorry, Paul, but I'm much more interested in exploring Ireland. Besides, you're the hot shot executive with all the money."

"*Hmm*, you have a point. You don't make nearly as much as I do." He nodded as he mused to himself. "All right, I'll do it."

"Do what?" Amy asked, putting down her burger.

"I will come back to visit after I get settled. I'm sure I can clear a few days off my calendar."

"You really don't have to," Mary said, trying to sound convincing.

"It's all right, not a bother at all," he assured her and surprised her by taking her hand in his.

Mary gently but firmly pulled back her hand. "Paul, really. I don't want to put you out."

"Think nothing of it. It will be a present to remind you of my interest."

"Paul, we're just friends," she insisted, "How many times do I have to tell you that?"

"He just wants to check up on you," Amy said with a grin. "He's afraid you might go flinging."

"She wouldn't do that," Paul said, drawing himself up. "She wouldn't take up with a common Irishman."

Amy snorted. "What if she takes up with an uncommon one?"

"She wouldn't waste her time," he said.

Amy regarded Paul in disbelief. "Why? Because she has you? You arrogant, self-serving—"

"Enough!" Mary intervened. "No fighting!"

"Amy needs to fight. She can't pick on her fiancé now. Why he puts up with you I have no idea," Paul said in exasperation.

"Come on, Amy," Mary said, standing and putting her purse over her shoulder.

"And where are we off to?"

"We've rented a flat, haven't we? Let's go see it. I want to sleep."

"But I still have two hours before my flight," Paul whined.

Amy just smirked.

"Fine." He regrouped and said, "I hope you have a wonderful time while you're working in Ireland, and I'll come and visit you as soon as I can."

"Paul! You *really* don't have to."

"It will be my pleasure." He took Mary's hand in his and kissed it, lingering a bit longer than was really necessary, ignoring Amy's blatant eye roll.

"Bye, Paul," Mary said.

"Yeah, bye, Paul," Amy said over her shoulder as she grabbed Mary's arm and they departed, leaving behind an irritated Paul.

BY THE TIME Mary was able to go to bed, the city of Dublin was awakening. She looked out of the window of the flat that the company provided and wondered how those people walking outside could possibly have so much energy? Amazed, she looked over at Amy, her eyes glazing over.

Amy just laughed. "Honey, it's called jet lag. That's why I slept on the plane. I promise, you'll be fine in a couple of days."

Mary only shook her head as Amy took her arm and guided her to her bed, and somehow she was undressed and tucked under the covers. She blinked up at her friend.

"Thanks," she murmured. Convinced her eyelids were now made of lead, she closed them and was claimed by sleep.

THE DREAM FROM the plane was back. Mary relaxed into it as the red-haired Irishman gazed at her in happiness, his blue eyes full of love.

"Who are you?" Mary asked in wonder.

"I'm your lost love, your soul mate," he said and leaned forward and placed a gentle kiss on her lips. "And you've finally come to find me."

"You make it sound like we've known each other before?" She raised an eyebrow.

"We have, many times, many lives." He was now nuzzling her neck, sending all sorts of shivers through her body.

"Have we always been lovers?"

"No, but most of the time. And I like it like that," he said and quietly removed her top, which she willingly let him do. "And I happen to know that you like this," he murmured and fastened his lips onto her breast, teasing it with his tongue, which elicited an unexpected gasp from her.

"Oh, honey." She threw her head back, and he laughed softly, giving her other breast the same amount of attention. "*Umm*" was all she could manage as he traveled down her body, somehow knowing all of her sensitive spots. The feel of his mouth on her again was enough to send her over the edge...

Mary woke up with a gasp, and it took a few moments for her to collect herself. Who was she dreaming about? The dream felt so real. When she thought about him, his face was indistinct, though she was certain of red hair and blue eyes. Her soul mate? Was there really such a thing? Shaking her head, she rolled over in bed, thinking, *Maybe Amy was right, maybe it has been too long.*

Sleep reclaimed her within moments, and she surrendered to it, a contented smile on her face.

"COME ON, MARY, wake up! Rise and shine!" The far-too-cheerful voice woke her out of her satisfying sleep.

Mary decided that being awake was far too much work and pulled the pillow back over her head.

"Mary, wake up." The pillow was yanked away from her.

"What time is it?" She frowned at Amy.

"Well, let's see. Four o' clock. You've been asleep for sixteen hours."

Mary rubbed her eyes and yawned. "It feels like it's still morning."

Amy smiled at her. "That's Minneapolis time, you're on Irish time now." She laughed. "You need to take a shower."

"What? Why?"

"Because we're going out."

She yawned again and sank further into her bed.

"Oh no you don't." Amy grabbed Mary's arm and pulled her up off the bed. "Go get ready. We're meeting people at a pub down the street."

"We are?" Mary stopped and blinked in astonishment. "But we just got here."

"We are." Amy threw a towel at her and pushed her into the bathroom and shut the door behind her.

THE SHAMROCK WAS on a side street off O'Connell, Dublin's main drag. It didn't quite have the status of the Temple bar area, but it was an old bar with a steady stream of regulars and visitors. Located next to several of the city's best restaurants didn't hurt business either.

Inside the pub was an odd mix of contemporary and old world. The tables and chairs that covered most of the floor area were modern and uncomfortable in Sean's opinion—black acrylic material—something easy to clean but unattractive. The old wooden booths on one side of the pub had been replaced with more of the same, along with modern art decor.

The other side was still as it had always been—well-worn, comfortable booths, and tables stained by food and too many beers. The bar was the original, installed more than a hundred years ago. The new owner bought the pub in the middle of renovations over three years ago. He said he would put things back the way they had been, but he had not quite got around to it, despite a profitable business. The new owner was a bit tight with his money, which meant the pub remained stuck in transition.

The place was somewhat crowded, *but not bad for a weeknight*, Sean thought as he climbed onto his usual barstool. Kevin, a friend from work, was already at the bar. Sean sat beside him, placed his order, and drummed his hands impatiently on the bar as he looked around.

"Anything wrong?" Kevin inquired, pulling a long draught from his beer.

"No, why?"

"You seem agitated."

Sean made a noncommittal noise.

Kevin continued. "Say, Sean?"

"Yes?"

Kevin raised his eyes and indicated a group of women across the room. "Some very fine women are here tonight. You should socialize."

Sean shrugged. "Maybe later."

"Maybe now. My guess is it wouldn't be too hard for you to find a lady if you wanted to." Kevin searched his friend's face, looking for some sort of acknowledgment.

"You're assuming I want a woman in my life."

"Don't you? Doesn't every man?"

Sean laughed. "I did once, but not anymore."

Kevin looked at him in disbelief. "You're joking, right? Tell me, Sean. How long has it been since you've been with a woman?"

Sean sighed, turned away from his friend, and ran his finger around the rim of his beer glass. "If I tell you that, how do I know everyone here won't know about it tomorrow?"

"You don't. Just answer the question."

He frowned. "A long time."

"You've been separated for years. You must be as randy as they get! Come on, Sean, go out with a woman. Do yourself a favor."

"It's not that bad, you get used to it after a while," he said, scowling at his friend.

"Yeah, right."

"Stop meddling in my personal life."

"Whatever you say, Sean, but you might want to take a look." Kevin gestured to a small group of people at a nearby table. "I think they're Americans, and they are quite pretty."

Sean watched him suspiciously, but turned to see what Kevin found so appealing and was pleasantly surprised to see two amazingly lovely women. They wore simple knee-length skirts, and form-fitting blouses. The shorter of the two had close-cropped blonde hair, with a lovely oval-shaped face. An air of enthusiasm about her was unmistakable. The other woman had shoulder-length dark-brown hair and a pretty face. Sean watched her smiling at her friend. He was captivated by the warmth and humor of that perfect smile. He found himself wondering if he could get her to smile for him.

MARY LAUGHED AT another of Amy's typical off-color jokes and sipped her drink. She looked unobtrusively around the pub and noticed a cute man with unkempt red hair staring in their direction from the bar. When he saw her looking at him, he offered a genuine, sweet smile, and raised his glass in acknowledgment.

Startled, she focused again on what Amy was saying, but curiosity got the better of her. She stole a glance at the bar only to find the red-haired man was gone.

LATER AT THEIR flat, around two a.m., Amy finally called it a night. Mary was still not sleepy. She sat on the sofa in the living room, looking out the window at the silent street illuminated by city lamps. Mary could hear the faint sound of voices through the open window. The soft lilt of their cadence fell pleasantly on her ears. Without conscious thought, she remembered the attractive man who had watched her from the bar. He had a kind face and a sweet smile. She wondered if he had blue eyes too. After a few moments, she drifted off to sleep.

Chapter 2
Sean

*T*HE PICTURE STARED back at Sean. As always, he wondered why he had been so enamored of his ex. Maggie was an unmistakable beauty—the long, lustrous auburn locks cascaded about her face and down her back. Her green eyes burned with a sultry passion, and she had the sweetest pair of lips a man could want. Her body had curves in all the right places, but her face held a cold beauty that reflected the state of her soul. He touched the photo and marveled at the happy faces of both Maggie and himself and wondered how that moment in time could ever have happened. He didn't remember ever being happy with Maggie. He placed the picture on the shelf, face down. He didn't know why he kept the picture; everything about it was a falsehood, an illusion. He was eternally grateful that part of his life had ended. It served as a reminder that he should not be involved in a relationship again.

His thoughts drifted back to the American woman he saw at the pub. Her dark hair fell in a very appealing way as it flowed about her shoulders, and she had the most amazing smile. That kind of warmth was something Sean had rarely seen of late. With a touch of sadness, he realized he had grown cynical in recent years. He couldn't believe that a gesture as amazingly simple as her smile could touch him in a way Maggie never had.

He turned off the light and left the small study.

A WEEK LATER, the workers from Livingston International went to see their new work place. Mary marveled at Amy's easy ability to drive on the wrong side of the road and find her way around a new city, with only two wrong turns on the way. They showed up at their new place of employment only twenty minutes later, laughing about their mishaps.

The building was small by American standards, clean and compact, with tight hallways and rooms. If employees could manage not to crash into each other during their frantic work periods, everything would be fine. The computer setup was in disarray, wiring and terminals everywhere. If this didn't change quickly, Mary could see the work taking much longer than the projected four months. She wondered if sabotaging their efforts would afford them a longer stay in Ireland? She laughed at her audacity.

Several hours later, Amy and Mary finished for the day. They were far from done, but at least their mess was starting to resemble an organized clutter. They sat back and looked at each other, happy to relax at last.

"I think we deserve a break," Amy said, rolling her eyes and rubbing her sore butt. "This has exceeded my work capacity."

Mary laughed. "The Shamrock?"

"Sounds good. Let's go back and clean up, then we can work on getting you a date." Amy grinned at her friend.

"You're impossible," Mary said as she got up. "Come on, let's go home."

THE JET LAG had finally gone away, and Mary felt better able to observe the city around her. She saw the pub for the first time in the light of day. The building was a basic stone-and-wood structure, much older than the modern buildings only a block away. It was worn with age that only added character. A quaint wooden sign hung over the doorway, proclaiming it proudly as The Shamrock.

Once inside, Mary noted that, although the pub was busy, it wasn't reverberating with the noisy music of a loud club. She decided she liked it. Spotting an empty booth near the bar, she waved Amy over to it. Mary smiled, picked a side, and slid into the booth.

Amy shook her head, laughed, and slid in across from Mary.

"So what's with you?"

"What do you mean?"

"You practically ran in here."

"No, I didn't."

"Yes, you did, but why?" Amy asked suspiciously.

Mary only smiled, but found herself looking over to the bar to see if that Irishman with the sweet smile was still around. Seeing no sign of him, she sighed and turned back to Amy.

"I'll be right back," Mary said, slipping off her coat and leaving it in the booth as she headed for the restroom.

"I'll get the first round," Amy volunteered and went up to the bar.

The bartender was busy, so she waited by the bar as a red-haired Irishman she assumed was a regular stepped up beside her. She noticed how the man's blue eyes twinkled with friendliness.

She greeted him, "Hi, I'm Amy."

"I'm Sean. Pleased to meet you." He smiled, recognizing her from the night before. "You're American, aren't you?"

"It must be my Yankee accent that gives me away."

"Something like that." Sean waved over the bartender. "Will you take care of my new friend, please?"

"I'd be happy to, Sean, but I'm a little busy."

Sean took Amy's order and turned away.

She regarded her new acquaintance with interest. He was on the shorter side of six feet—trim build, pleasant and boyish face, mischievous blue eyes, unruly red hair, and a charming smile. Not too terribly bad of a prospect for only having been in Ireland for one week. She deemed him appropriate for a fling with Mary, provided he was a decent man.

"What brings you to our fine country?" Sean asked.

"Work, lots of work. The company I work for just acquired a company here in Ireland. Mary and I were brought over to help with setup."

"Mary?" he inquired and couldn't help but glance over at the dark-haired woman who was now sitting in the booth waiting for her friend to return.

Amy gestured back at the booth and smiled at him, "Yeah, Mary. Great friend and coworker."

"And what is it you do?"

"I'm with Livingston Incorporated. We're completing a merger with InterTech Limited. I'm a computer consultant for networking."

"I'm in the Domestic Sales Division of Irish Build."

"Oh, a salesman?" Amy arched her eyebrow at Sean, and he laughed.

"Of a sort. Vice-president, actually."

"Congratulations," she said.

"Thanks."

At that moment, the bartender returned with Amy's drink order and placed it on the bar before her. Sean waved off Amy's payment and, despite Amy's protests, insisted that it be put on his tab.

"You shouldn't have done that," Amy grumbled insincerely.

"Consider it a welcome-to-Ireland treat."

Amy was quite taken with his smile. She felt the tendrils of hope as a matchmaker creeping up within her.

"I don't normally ask this, but you've been more than generous, and you're the first native I've actually met here. Would you mind coming over to the table and meeting my friend? Everything is still new to us, and we could use some advice about Irish life, and the touristy things to see while we're here."

"I would be delighted," Sean said.

Sean followed Amy back to the booth where Mary was sitting. He couldn't stop the smile that spread across his face.

"Mary, this is Sean, an actual Irishman. He was nice enough to buy drinks for us. Isn't that great?" Amy was bubbling over, as usual.

"Pleased to meet you," Sean said politely as he felt the two sets of feminine eyes appraising him. He smiled at both women, but his gaze rested on Mary.

Mary saw the most amazing pair of blue eyes. Beautiful, clear as a deep-blue ocean, and full of devilment and curiosity. They were eyes she somehow knew, and she felt a spark of inexplicable familiarity. She responded with a slow, happy smile of her own.

"Sean, please join us," Amy said. She slid unobtrusively to the outside edge of the booth, trying to will the Irishman into Mary's side of the booth.

"Please join us," Mary said, still smiling.

"All right," Sean said and slid in beside Mary.

Mary blushed and moved away to give Sean more room. She hadn't expected her temporary crush to be sitting next to her. It didn't help when she looked across at Amy, who gave her an outlandish grin. Mary knew she had been set up. She kicked her friend under the table and was pleased as Amy smothered a yelp.

"Where is it you ladies from? I mean besides the US."

"Minnesota," Amy said.

"Where's that?"

"The upper Midwest, west of Chicago," Mary said. "Have you ever been to the US?"

"No, I never had the pleasure. I guess I'm a bit of an Irish lad, a homebody I've been called." He rubbed his chin and laughed softly.

"What a coincidence, that's what we're always saying about Mary," Amy said.

"Really?" Sean's gaze was curious. "You seem quite social to me."

"Thanks," Mary said and glanced at him. "But I am kind of a homebody."

"Then what are you doing way over here in Ireland?"

"Work. It was just luck that they sent us here; I've always wanted to visit Ireland."

"Well, I'm glad you've deigned to grace our fair land with your lovely presence," he said, offering a charming smile and, remembering that Amy was at the table, included her as well.

"You're very sweet," Mary said and offered him a shy smile. They looked at each other for a moment. Amy was grinning, but neither noticed.

After a long moment, Sean asked, "How long will you be in Ireland?"

"We're not sure yet. It depends how long the company needs us to be here," Amy said.

"Probably a few months at least," Mary said and looked away from Sean.

"Or until Mary decides to go rogue and start her own business." Amy said, revealing a new topic of conversation about her friend.

"Oh, what's that? You're interested in having your own business?" He seemed genuinely curious.

"Well, yes, maybe." Mary ducked her head, unsure about sharing her aspirations with a stranger.

"What kind of business?"

"I'm not sure. I mean, I work in IT now, and I'm a great manager, but I was thinking maybe something different would excite me."

"I've often thought about having my own business," he admitted.

"What holds you back?" Amy asked.

Sean shrugged. "Guess I'm making too much money doing what I do. It seems I've gotten complacent," he gave a polite smile. "But if you are here for a few months, perhaps I'll have the pleasure of your company from time to time?"

"That would be great. Maybe you could show us around? Mary is interested in history. And movies, especially *Star Wars* stuff, and the paranormal."

"History? *Star Wars*?" Sean smiled at her. "I like those too... but the paranormal? Are you looking for Irish ghosts? Creatures that go bump in the night?"

"Well, not exactly." Mary tried to control her self-conscious smile. "I'm just fascinated with the afterlife, the existence of spirits."

Sean gave a gentle snort in amusement. "Sure you're not Catholic?"

"No, Protestant," Mary said.

"Is that a problem?" Amy asked, hoping her early matchmaking attempts hadn't already derailed.

He shrugged. "No, I was raised as a good Catholic boy, but must admit my behavior has lapsed somewhat."

"So you're a bad Catholic boy?" Amy teased.

"Not exactly," he said, blushing. He saw that Mary was watching him with interest and a warm look that had him reacting on several levels. Steering the conversation to a safer topic, he said, "I would be happy to show the two of you around Dublin."

"That would be nice," Mary said, gazing again into his clear blue eyes.

They stared at each other for another long moment.

Sean cleared his throat. "My apologies, but I think I'd best be going. I'm sure you have things to attend to, and I promised myself to not be out too late tonight."

"Why's that?" Mary asked.

"Early business meeting," he said with a grimace. He reached inside of his jacket and pulled out a business card, which he handed to Mary. "Feel free to call me. I would be happy to give you ladies a tour."

Mary retrieved her purse and dug through it, at last finding her wallet. She pulled out her business card and handed it to Sean.

"Here's where you can find me, though I'm not sure the phones work yet," she said with a sigh.

"Thank you," Sean nodded. "I look forward to our next meeting." He slid out of the booth and gave them a half bow before he returned to the bar. He stopped for a minute, spoke with the bartender, and left the pub.

Amy smiled happily, noting that Mary's gaze followed Sean's every movement until he departed.

Chapter 3
The Tour

ORK WAS CRAZY the next day, too many things to set in order and too little time. The techs were busy trying to get things on track and having varying degrees of success. Issues that came up were put in front of Mary to solve. She prioritized them, instructing her team to work through the most urgent items first. She was contemplating what to do with the current networking problem when Amy opened her door and ran into the room with a huge smile on her face.

"Yes?" Mary asked, amused at Amy's disheveled appearance. Her tattered sweatshirt hung off her shoulder and her T-shirt had pulled out of her pants, exposing part of her midriff. "Something I can do for you?"

"No, it's what I can do for you." Amy was bouncing on her toes.

"What do you mean by that?" Mary inquired suspiciously.

"He's here."

"Who?"

"Your Irish friend."

"What?" Mary's mouth dropped open. "Sean?"

Amy nodded in excitement, her head bobbing up and down quickly. "Did you plan a date with him?"

"No," Mary said, clutching at her casual, well-worn sweatshirt and glancing down at her faded jeans. "I can't see him like this. I wasn't expecting anyone. I mean, look at me!"

Amy briefly eyed her up and down. "I think it will be okay. You have a shirt underneath, right?"

"Yeah, but it's a torn T-shirt."

Amy bit her lip. "Maybe he'll like that. Besides, we're all in our grubbies. "

Mary shook her head. "He'll think I'm gross."

"Not if he likes you. Maybe you should find out."

"No." Mary shook her head and planted her feet. "I won't do it. I just won't."

WITH SOME AMAZEMENT, she found herself being led to the lobby by an all-too-enthusiastic Amy, who, using her best professional demeanor, promised to keep her bouncing to a minimum.

Sean was sitting quietly in the lobby, leafing through a magazine. He was dressed in a casual business suit, no tie, just a dark-green turtleneck. His curly red hair appeared uncombed, but Mary imagined it must always be like that. He set aside the magazine and stood up as the two women entered the room.

"My apologies, I didn't mean to interrupt you at work."

"It's fine, we needed a break anyway," Amy replied smoothly.

"No problem," Mary agreed. Her gaze lingered on the floor for a moment and back to Sean. "I'm sorry about my appearance; we're still setting up and..."

"You look fine," he said, smiling at Mary. Glancing at Amy standing next to her, he added, "Both of you. And I do understand how hard it is to set up a business." He paused. "I remembered where you worked and, since you don't know Dublin, I wondered if you'd thought about my offer as a tour guide?"

Mary couldn't contain the smile that crept across her face. "That'd be wonderful. I mean, if you're certain we wouldn't use up too much of your time."

"It would be my pleasure." Sean bowed to her.

"Amy, isn't this great?"

When Mary didn't receive a response from Amy, she looked over her shoulder and saw that Amy was no longer in the room.

"I think she left," Sean said with a smile. He watched her for a moment, pleased at the blush creeping up her face. "So what do you think? I would be happy to show you around, and Amy, too."

She gave him a shy smile. "I can't speak for her, but I would like that."

"Please call me when you're ready." He stepped closer to her and extended his hand.

"All right." Mary stared into those blue eyes again. As she accepted his handshake, she forgot that she had only met this man a short time ago. He stared back and made no move to leave as they continued to hold hands. There was an unmistakable jolt of electricity between them and memories of her dreams came back to Mary. She dropped her head as she felt the heat rising in her cheeks.

"Call me?" Sean's pleasant Irish lilt fell softly on her ears.

She nodded and watched as Sean turned and walked away.

WHY DID I do that? What has possessed me? Sean hadn't made such an overture to a woman in over four years. He knew to not get involved with anyone. Relationships were painful—Maggie taught him that. But here he was, standing outside the building where this American woman worked, and feeling like a lad trying to get his first date. With a last look back at the building, he put up his collar against the cool, damp day and began walking back toward his office.

I shouldn't be friends with a woman, especially an American woman. He doubted an American would understand the Irish way of things. He was sure that separation must mean something completely different in the States. He knew that couples in the United States had been able to get divorced for many, many years. Divorce was relatively new in Ireland and could be a complicated process, only legally approved a year ago, in 1997. He should have sought an annulment when his marriage ended twelve years before, but given Maggie's mental issues, it had somehow seemed cruel. And since he had no intentions of being in a serious relationship again, he had let things rest, living a life separate from his wife. But why was he thinking such things anyway? It wasn't as if he had any intentions of having a relationship with anyone, not even the lovely Mary. She was only here on a temporary sojourn anyway. But surely she wouldn't mind having a fine Irishman such as himself as a friend?

His steps quickened as he approached the modern office building where he worked.

If only he could stop thinking about her smile, the way that T-shirt seemed to cling to her, the tear that revealed just a bit of her nicely toned abdomen. He'd been a fool about this. Maybe she wouldn't call. Maybe she would. At the moment, he wasn't sure what he wanted...

SEAN RECEIVED THE call the next day at work. He sat at his desk, rapidly adding up a column of sales figures on the calculator, and then ran the total again. He frowned as the numbers still refused to add up correctly. The intercom buzzed, and he regarded it with annoyance for interrupting his concentration.

"Yes, Miss O'Brien?"

"Sorry to interrupt, sir, but you have a call. It's an American, a Miss Kelley. She says she's calling to schedule an appointment with you."

Sean smiled and leaned back in his chair with a tired sigh and ran a hand through his unruly hair, pleased at the unexpected distraction. The curiosity in his secretary's voice was all too apparent. In his current position, he dealt with very few American vendors, or international vendors for that matter. A phone call from an American was most unusual. And a woman besides! The only women who had called him at work over the last three years were his mother, his sister and, unfortunately, his wife Maggie. He could already hear the rumor mills starting.

"Sir? Shall I put her through?"

"Yes, please do." He waited patiently for his phone to ring. When he knew enough time had passed for him to receive the call, he buzzed his secretary again.

"Miss O'Brien? Didn't you send me my call?"

"I transferred the call in to you, Mr. Calhoun."

"I never got it."

"I'm sorry, sir. Maybe she'll call back."

Sean shut off the intercom, surprised that missing Mary's call bothered him. Maybe she had just gotten interrupted at work. Maybe their phone system wasn't working properly. He stared at the phone for all of five seconds before he picked it up and began dialing Mary's number.

MARY HAD JUST replaced the receiver, mentally chastising herself for her actions. She knew she should have talked to him, but she'd panicked. *Damn. Since when did this type of thing start making me nervous?*

"Mary?" a coworker's voice called, and she poked her head around the corner. "You have a phone call. It's a Sean something or another."

"Thanks," Mary said and got up from her desk. "Transfer it here." She took a deep breath, composed herself, and picked up the phone.

"Hello."

"Mary?"

She tried to ignore the feeling of warmth his Irish brogue created within her.

"Oh, hello, Sean." She tried to calm her racing heart.

"Did you just try phoning? It seems we got cut off."

"I'm sorry. We're still having problems with our phone system."

"*Ahh*, I thought as much. No problem. What can I help you with?"

"I was hoping you'd still be willing to be a tour guide?"

"Of course," he said, and Mary could hear the smile in his voice.

"Good. It would be Amy and me."

"Brilliant. When would you like to go?"

They discussed it for a couple of minutes and agreed that the upcoming Saturday would work fine. Sean said, "Grand. Shall I meet you at your office?"

"No, let's not meet here. Let's meet at the Shamrock."

"All right, nine in the a.m."

"I'll see you then," Mary said softly as Amy entered the room without knocking. She watched Mary hang up the phone and gaze off into space, a sweet smile on her face.

CULLAMORE WAS A small, quiet town, nestled among the green hillsides in Ireland about an hour and a half out of Dublin, near the middle of the country, but somehow it remained off the beaten path and its isolation only served to enhance its sleepy beauty. It was small as towns went and could almost be considered a large village, with many old homes built from stone and clay, and only a few buildings that could be termed modern. A small main street ran the length of the town, with many small businesses lining both sides of the street—fabric store, a tailor, a small convenience store, a food store, a gas station, and an antique store. Several other small shops were located throughout the town on roads less traveled. The actual heart of the town was The Gaelic Moon, a pub not too far off the main street. Occupants of the town gathered to discuss their day, complain about what was right and wrong, drown their sorrows, or just relax.

The Gaelic Moon was in the oldest building in town and said to be the oldest pub in all of Ireland. No one could remember when the building hadn't been there. Made of stone and wood, and built around ancient pillars that were said to be druidic in nature, the myth was that The Gaelic Moon was built on the foundation of an ancient druidic temple. Due to its age and mysterious origins, many tales of the supernatural were associated with The Gaelic Moon. The locals took delight in these folk tales and often told them to travelers while expressing their affection for their local pub.

The place was quiet on a Wednesday evening, as a few of the locals argued about their unofficial dart contest. A few men conversed at the bar with Donald. Maggie sat at a table with Patrick.

Maggie studied Patrick for a moment and once again realized that he was a handsome man. Tall and muscular, his dark hair hung into his stern brown eyes. He had a nice smile, but somehow it never seemed genuine. In her mind, Patrick had always been just Patrick, a little slow upstairs, but loyal as a dog, and totally devoted to her. She knew she had only to ask and Patrick would do whatever she wanted. She seldom had to use a spell on him. She liked that.

"Patrick, I know I can win him back," Maggie said.

"Oh, but Maggie, why? It's been years, you should know by now that he doesn't want you," he said, staring at his beautiful companion.

"Patrick, try to think with your brains."

He glared at her.

"Will you help me?"

"You know I'll do anything for you, but why waste your time? Why can't you let this go?"

"It's not a waste of time. He still loves me," she insisted with a glare at him.

"He doesn't. You're separated, for God's sake!" He sighed. "It doesn't matter, I'll change his mind." She insisted.

"You haven't yet, and it's been years," Patrick muttered.

"You're just saying that because you don't like him."

"We don't like each other," Patrick's eyes were filled with a dark anger. "He doesn't love you, Maggie, he never has."

Maggie slapped him, hard. "You shouldn't be jealous," she growled.

Patrick rubbed his cheek and counted to ten as he controlled his temper.

"Oh, Patrick, I'm sorry." She grasped his hand, giving him an apologetic smile. "Forgive me?" She squeezed his hands, using her natural ability and pretty smile to influence him.

He looked at her, knew he shouldn't, but couldn't refuse. "Yes, as always."

"Good." She squeezed his hand, and leaned over and kissed his cheek. "Let's get started, shall we?"

"Whatever you say, Maggie, whatever you say."

THE THREATENING GRAY clouds did nothing to dispel Mary's good spirits as she dressed and prepared for her day. She hummed to herself as she got ready in the bathroom, happy that she'd be seeing Sean again. She was surprised when she got out of the bathroom to find that Amy, the early riser, hadn't emerged from her bedroom yet.

"Amy?" she said, knocking on the door, "are you all right?"

"Come in," said a strange croaking voice from inside.

She found her friend shivering in bed, covers pulled up to her chin.

"I'm sorry. I'm sick," she mumbled.

"Really? You seemed fine yesterday." Mary folded her arms in front of her and regarded her friend skeptically.

"Mary, I'm really sick," Amy said with a miserable, pathetic look at her friend.

Mary took a step toward her, and Amy let go of a tremendous sneeze, causing Mary to retreat to the doorway. "I guess you'll have to go without me," Amy rasped. "Go on, have fun."

Mary regarded her friend with a dubious expression.

"What's wrong?"

"It's nothing. Only that...well...I'd be more comfortable if you came with me."

"But you'll have a better chance to get to know him if I'm not there. That's a good thing," she said with a bit too much enthusiasm and then remembered to cough.

"I don't know..." Her heart was starting to pound, but whether with fear or excitement, she didn't know. This was suspiciously starting to resemble a date. "You're really sick?"

"Terrible. Must be the flu." She sniffled appropriately.

Mary regarded her with suspicion but, with a nod, she closed the bedroom door and left.

Amy lay in bed, waiting until Mary left, shutting the outside door behind her. Throwing back the covers, Amy jumped out of bed, chortling with glee. She stopped, looked at the door thoughtfully, and walked over to the phone in the main room. She picked up the phone and dialed a number that she knew well as she waited for the call to go through.

"Rob?"

"Amy, sweetheart, what time is it?" a sleepy male voice answered.

"Does it matter? I miss you." She held the receiver as close as possible to her.

"Honey, I miss you too, but couldn't we talk about this in the light of day?"

"Oh, the time difference, I forgot."

"What's up?"

"I just miss you."

"I love you, Amy. Better now?" She could hear him stirring on the other end of the connection.

"Yeah. Will you please come see me?"

"I'll see what I can do. All right, since I'm up anyway, why don't you tell me about Ireland..." his voice soothed her and she sat down on the couch recount her latest adventures.

SATURDAY MORNING IN Dublin was anything but pretty. The sky was gray and overcast, and the forecast was for all-day showers. Sean studied the dismal sky before entering the pub and wondered how stout-hearted these Americans were. Rain in Ireland was a normal thing, a good part of the reason it was called the Emerald Isle, and that was all the damn rain! He ducked into the pub, waved at Ginny, the bartender on duty, and looked around. At nine a.m. things were quiet, only stragglers left from the breakfast crowd.

After twenty minutes, he decided he had waited long enough and stood up to take one last stroll about the bar. More disappointed than he cared to admit, he shoved his hands in the pocket of his trench coat and turned to leave.

Just as he was reaching for the door, it opened so suddenly that Sean went tumbling backward to the floor. Mary tripped and fell on top of him, into his arms. As he tried to disentangle himself from the arms and legs that flailed about him, he realized Mary was a shapely woman. Her soft brown hair fell against his face, obscuring his vision. He inhaled her subtle, flowery scent and found himself reluctant to part with the sensations that surrounded him.

After a few more long seconds, they straightened out enough to separate. With some reluctance, Sean let her go and assisted her to her feet.

"I'm really sorry," Mary stammered at Sean. "I'm usually not so clumsy; I don't make a habit of falling into a man's arms..." She panicked, thinking her words felt inappropriate once again.

Sean laughed and gestured to himself. "Mary, it's all right, no harm done."

"You were leaving?" Mary tried to hide her disappointment. "You don't want to do the tour?"

"Of course I do. It's just I didn't think you were coming."

"Oh, because I'm late." She grimaced. "Sorry, Amy's sick and I had to make sure she was all right before I left." She gazed at him uncertainly. "I guess it will just be the two of us. Amy told me to go ahead and enjoy my date."

Sean regarded her curiously. "Date?"

"*Oops,*" she offered a weak smile. "I shouldn't have said that."

He sighed, took one of Mary's hands in his own, and looked into her hazel eyes, now dark with uncertainty.

Mary tried to ignore the fact that a simple touch was making her heart pound fast.

"I have to be honest with you," he said. "I'm hoping we'll be great friends, but I'm not searching for more." He studied her face and was relieved when she smiled at him.

"It's okay, I'd like to be friends."

"Good. Are you ready for the tour then?" He smiled.

She nodded.

Holding the door for her, he followed her out.

The pavement was dry, as the rain stopped midday, but the clouds refused to let the sun shine, so the day remained bleak. Somehow it didn't bother Sean in the least, and he smiled as he regarded the woman at his side.

When the tour was over, it had been a fantastic day. Never in his life had he enjoyed seeing Dublin as much as he had today, through her eyes, nor had he ever viewed it with such enthusiasm. He doubted he would ever regard it with the same blandness again, all because of Mary. How could someone he had known for such a short time have such an effect on him?

They stopped at the bottom of the steps outside of her flat, suddenly awkward in each other's company.

At last Sean cleared his throat and extended his hand. "It's been an incredibly lovely day, and I thank you for spending it with me."

"Despite that too-spicy curry?" She smiled, her hazel eyes twinkling.

"Yes, despite that." He laughed. "*Ahh*, Mary." He opened his arms, and she fell into them. They hugged, and when she moved to leave, he found himself unable to let go. They looked into each other's eyes, and he kissed her, a sweet, gentle kiss that she returned. He kissed her sweetly again, but longer before gently disengaging himself.

"Goodnight Mary," he turned and left before she could say anything. She waved, but he never looked back.

THE RIDE UP the elevator seemed interminably long. Sean waited impatiently for the door to open. He rubbed his temple and tried to get a grip on his unexpected emotions. What was this woman doing to him?

The elevator doors opened, and Sean stepped out into the hallway. With a weary sigh, he dug the keys out of his pocket and put them into the lock, but was surprised when the knob turned and the door opened easily. Cautiously, he reached inside the door and flipped on the kitchen lights.

"Hello... ?" he called and stepped apprehensively into his apartment.

Chapter 4

Maggie

*T*HE APARTMENT WAS quiet as he entered, and a quick scan revealed nothing out of place or missing. Feeling uneasy, Sean carefully opened the closet door, retrieved a handcrafted walking stick he picked up some time ago, and began to check out the rest of his place.

The living room and dining room were clear, but in the kitchen were crumbs and the remainder of a hastily consumed muffin. An abandoned butter knife lay carelessly among the crumbs.

He frowned and tapped the counter with his fingers, trying to remember why this seemed familiar to him. The sudden clarity of it caused him to groan out loud. *How the hell could she have gotten a key?* No, he could guess how that happened. Her sex appeal was enough to undo even the most chaste of men. She had probably given the landlord some sad story, a lie she told so convincingly that the man had no choice but to believe her.

Damn her to hell!

By the time he reached the bedroom door, he was furious. He threw it open so hard that it banged against the wall. He glared at his beautiful wife, who lay on his bed, clad in only a red lace bra and matching panties, leaving nothing to the imagination. She gave him a sultry smile.

"Welcome home, Sean," Maggie purred.

MARY CLOSED THE door quietly behind her as she entered the flat, not wanting to wake Amy. She hung up her coat, removed her shoes, and tiptoed down the hallway to her room. She jumped, startled by Amy's voice as she passed the living room.

"It's about time you got home," Amy teased.

"Do you always lurk about late at night, waiting to scare people?" Mary snapped and put a hand to her heart.

"*Nah*, only you. Come on in," she invited, "I have some hot cocoa waiting."

"*Ooh*, that sounds good. Just give me a minute to change into something warmer."

Mary returned a few minutes later, wearing a comfortable pair of sweatpants, a sweatshirt, and an oversized pair of warm, fuzzy Tasmanian Devil slippers. Before joining Amy on the couch, she punched Amy in the arm.

"*Ow!* What was that for?"

"For setting me up. Again." She smiled and punched her again. "And that's because you're not sick."

"*Ow!*" Amy rubbed her arm. "But it's the first time I set you up with Sean, and it couldn't have been too bad—you're still smiling."

Mary reached for the warm cup of chocolate that sat on the end table but didn't speak, knowing her silence was torture to Amy.

Amy groaned. "Come on, out with it. Tell me what happened."

Mary sipped the warm liquid and sighed contentedly.

"Come on, come on, stop holding back. Tell me."

"There isn't much to tell." Mary shrugged. "He took me around the sights of Dublin which, by the way, are very cool. We had a nice day together."

Amy sat back against the couch, disappointed. "That's it?"

"That's it. He only wants to be friends."

"But he's so cute! And charming."

Mary shrugged.

"And you just want to be friends with him?"

"Why not? He's nice."

Amy looked at her friend as if she had lost her mind. "Mary, you know I have your best interests at heart?

"Yes," Mary nodded.

Amy took Mary's hands within her own, squeezed them, and looked into her friend's face. "Trust me when I tell you this. It's time for you to be more than friends with a man. Have a fling! Enjoy yourself! It's not a crime."

"I know that; I'm just not ready."

"Well, when will you be ready? It's been how long now?" Amy speculated with a raising of her eyebrow.

"None of your damn business," Mary replied calmly.

"Hello! Haven't you heard anything I've said?" Amy threw up her hands in exasperation. "If all this guy wants is to be friends, find someone else."

"But I like Sean." Mary was looking beyond the windows at something Amy couldn't see. "I feel as if I've always known him, like we've been together before." She blinked and looked back at her friend. "But that isn't possible, is it?"

"No, and it's another good reason to find somebody else."

"What?"

"If you like him, you're already forming an attachment. You don't want that for a fling. You want someone whose company you can enjoy, but will have no trouble leaving behind."

"I don't think I'm cut out for this. What's the point of that? What good is a relationship without feeling?" she asked dubiously.

"That's the point of a fling—not to have a real relationship, just to enjoy the benefits. Come on, Mary, you can do it." Amy squeezed her friend's hands, seeing the woebegone expression on her face. "It'll be all right. It's not that hard, and I'll help you."

"Oh, but Amy—"

"No, it's all taken care of. We'll search for your fling partner tomorrow." Amy positively glowed with enthusiasm as she trounced out of the room.

Alone with her thoughts, Mary finished the last of her cocoa and set down the mug on the small table, settling back against the sofa cushions as she stared out the window at the semi-darkness of the city.

Maybe Amy is right. Maybe I should give up my lofty goals of finding the true love of my life and settle for a fling. It did seem more practical to find a man to provide companionship and sex while she was here. The heart didn't need to be involved. The fling would be less exciting that way, but she would also survive it without a broken heart. Joe had nearly killed her when he broke their engagement because he had found another woman. And that was four years ago! It was time to try again, but maybe it should be done in steps. Maybe dating in an uncommitted manner and good sex were all that she needed right now. *Maybe Amy is right.*

But Mary couldn't stop thinking of Sean. She touched her lips where he had kissed her. It had been a soft, sweet kiss, as gentle as the touch of butterfly wings, but with the promise of so much more. And she wasn't totally unobservant; she had noticed his arousal when he hugged her goodbye. She found herself wondering why he only wanted to be friends, and whether it might be possible to change his mind.

"WHAT THE HELL are you doing here?" Sean demanded of his wife. He picked up the clothes she had left lying on the floor and threw them at her. "Get dressed. And get out!"

Maggie's long red hair glowed with the dim light from the candles she had set about the room. Her sultry green eyes raked over him with undisguised desire. Despite his anger, Sean found himself responding to her on the most basic of levels.

She gracefully rose from the bed, and with her best seductive walk, came over to him. He mentally said his prayers and crossed himself like a good Catholic boy and looked into his wife's face. "Get out," he said gruffly.

"Oh, but Sean, aren't you happy to see me?" she asked and wrapped her arms around his neck. "We haven't been together for, oh, how long now?"

"It's been years, Maggie."

"And how long since you've been with a woman?" She played with the hair at the nape of his neck and whispered strange words in his ear that he didn't recognize. The sound of them slipped away along with his self-composure. *What is she doing to me? Why can't I stop myself?*

He shivered and tried to remove her hands from him, but somehow found them about her waist. "Maggie, you have to go." He tried desperately to think of depressing thoughts—of how badly his work had gone all week, how happy his mother would be to see him back with Maggie, how disappointed his sister would be in him, and lastly how much he would disappoint Mary if he did this.

33

Thinking of Mary produced the opposite reaction within him. He had been suppressing his desire for her all night, and now, already aroused, thinking of her only stimulated his need.

"Oh, Sean, it's been so long." Maggie whispered in his ear and led him without protest over to his bed.

She pulled him on top of her. Like a blind man who had finally stumbled across an oasis, he gave in to his natural instincts, and took her, without thought, without recognition, and without love. Raw physical passion that knew of nothing but the moment and wanted nothing more than that. He knew it was wrong, but was unable to heed the small voice within him. He cursed himself, knowing she had won again.

AT THREE THE next morning, Sean woke up with a start, panicked and in a cold sweat. He had dreamt of being with Maggie, of having sex with her, of how she felt beneath him as she moaned his name. It had been a nightmare of unimaginable proportion and the thought was enough to make him sick.

"Oh, my God." He glanced to the opposite side of his bed and shot out of it as if he had been fired out of a cannon. Maggie lay sleeping and didn't stir despite the movement of the bed and his cursing.

Blessed are those without a conscience, he thought, *for nothing bothers them.* He got his robe and left the bedroom, closing the door behind him.

The liquor cabinet was not well stocked, for Sean had little need for liquor. He'd much rather visit a pub and chat with those people he knew, but at the moment he wished that he had an entire liquor store at his disposal. All he had left was an inadequate portion of Scotch. With a sigh of resignation, he poured some into the glass, finished it off in one gulp, and stared at the bottle as if it had betrayed him. One more shot remained, so he poured it into his glass and carried it with him to his favorite chair where he set the glass on the floor beside him, pulled out a cigarette, and lit up.

Oh, God, I've gone insane. There was no other explanation. He'd have to buy a gun in the morning and shoot himself. *Why do I feel so guilty? Why do I keep thinking of Mary and that sweet kiss we exchanged?* That simple kiss meant more to him than the passion he had just shared with his wife.

He expelled the smoke from his lungs and closed his eyes. His stupidity knew no boundaries and now Maggie would never let him alone. *What had changed so much that I was unable to resist her last night?*

Sean rubbed his temple, trying to ease the headache he felt, trying to ease the reality of facing Maggie in the morning and telling her nothing had changed between them. A gun was starting to sound better and better.

SEAN ENTERED HIS bedroom, went over to the window that looked out into Dublin, and pulled the drapes, bathing the rest of the room in the golden rays of the morning sun. The form beneath the covers groaned and blinked desperately against the invading brightness.

"Sean, what are you doing?" She propped herself up on her elbow and regarded him, appearing much more the shrew in the reality of the daylight. He threw her clothes at her.

"Get dressed, Maggie."

"Must I?" she asked coyly, but her powers of seduction had faded with the passing of darkness and the clearing of his consciousness with the light of day.

"You have ten minutes to get dressed."

"Or what?"

"Or I throw you out," he said and ducked as his favorite alarm clock flew over his head. He shut the door behind him. This was not going to be easy.

SHE CAME OUT of the bedroom exactly ten minutes later, quite unappealing without her expertly applied makeup. But maybe that wasn't it at all; maybe it was that he really knew what a cold heart lay beneath her beautiful exterior. She sat down on the couch and stretched her legs out in front of her, smiling up at Sean, who stood halfway across the room.

"What should we do today, Sean, now that we're back together?"

He marveled at her—one act of sex, and she assumed that their years of legal separation meant nothing, that everything between them was miraculously fine once again. She had never accepted that he didn't love her, and he doubted she ever would.

"Nothing's changed, Maggie. We'll not be getting back together. We are still legally separated."

The ticking clock had never seemed louder as he waited for the inevitable explosion, the fury of angry words that would be inflicted on him. But nothing happened. He watched Maggie in disbelief as she quietly got up, reached for her purse, and went to the door.

The smile on her face was that of a cat who had just swallowed the canary. She turned to him, almost purring as she spoke. "You think you can escape so easily, husband of mine? Clutch at the legal separation as hard as you can. It won't change anything. We will be together."

A shiver ran down his back at the confidence with which she uttered those words.

The door remained open behind her as she walked away. Sean went to it, yelling after her, "It's over, woman, do you hear? It's over!"

Maggie's soft laughter was his only answer.

EASY, MAGGIE THOUGHT, *all men were so easy*. Even as strong willed as Sean believed himself to be, she had managed to overcome his objections and seduce him. And the best part was that he didn't understand why he'd suddenly given in to her, didn't understand all of the things she knew, things she had learned since she was a teenager, the special ability the goddess had given her to bend men to her will. She laughed softly to herself because there was so much that Sean didn't know about her.

Sean believed the only reason she had come to Dublin was for him, *foolish man*! She had matters equally as important as him to attend to, matters that would someday give her everything she wanted. She stopped when she saw her destination in front of her.

The run down, ill-kept bookstore was small and tucked away among several side streets of Dublin, but unless you knew what you were looking for, you might never find it. The only entrance was a door at the back of a small restaurant that displayed a menu advertising foul-tasting, authentic Romanian food.

She made her way back to the curtain that hid a door behind it and entered the moderate-sized space packed to the rafters with books and other interesting and unusual items. The bookstore also served as a shop for bizarre collector items as well. Stuffed animals of many varieties abounded, many not in the least native to Ireland. Rabbits, foxes, badgers, snakes, spiders, bats, and even an American eagle were crammed into this small space. More common things included such as antique watches, furniture, glassware, and some crystal from Waterford, and other more normal antiques.

Maggie regarded the shelves that remained in disarray and again found herself wondering how the owner knew where anything was. Piles of books occupied every space that wasn't used by an antique, and the pathways between the stacks were few and only discernible by those familiar with the cluttered environment.

Not seeing the proprietor, she called out and was rewarded with a muffled response from somewhere through a door that Maggie could see but had never entered.

"Lucky!" she called.

A few moments later, Lucky appeared with a scowl. When he saw Maggie, he offered her a calculated smile, displaying a beautiful set of teeth and a mouth that Maggie would like to know better. His face was darkly attractive, with dark unfathomable eyes that masked his thoughts and emotions. He hid his strong, rather impressive body beneath his suit jacket, and that was something Maggie would like to examine more closely. She knew she would ultimately have Sean again, but in the meantime sampling other wares was always a tantalizing possibility.

"Where have you been?" she demanded in a childish tone.

"Trade secrets. I take occasional trips to enhance my collection." He gave her a warm look. "And I have an item that will be of interest to you." He disappeared through the doorway into the room that lay beyond.

Maggie waited patiently, knowing he was remarkable at finding the most useful items. When he returned, he held a book carefully in his hands, the way one does with a collectable of value.

"A book?" She arched an eyebrow. "I have several," she said.

"Not like this." He set it down on the counter and pushed it across to her. "Gently. If you ruin it, I will have your head."

Maggie nodded because she knew he was more than serious. The book was small, and the leather binding was in adequate shape, considering the age of the item in her hand. She carefully opened up the first page and found the paper was in remarkably good shape, just now starting to become brittle around the edges.

She frowned as she tried to read the handwriting on the page, and discovered wasn't a journal at all. A lovely smile spread across her face as she realized what she held in her hands.

"A spell book," she breathed.

"Yes, with many useful items for someone of your current ability," he said.

"What's in it?"

"Stronger charm spells. Basic elemental magic, mostly fire-based. Enough to keep you busy for quite a long while."

"What's this?" she asked, as she had turned to the last few pages of the book and found herself unable to read them.

"Oh, that." He gave her a knowing look, as he understood how her mind worked and the kind of power she truly wanted. "That is a summoning spell."

"What can I use it for? I mean aren't they usually specific?" She frowned, her mind already considering how she could possibly use it in the future.

"They are, but this one is adaptable, or should be once you know the proper way to use it." Again he gave her a warm smile.

"Why would you offer this to me?"

"Why not?" he shrugged. "I have no use for what's in it."

"Because you already know all of this?"

"Of course." His gaze was filled with disdain. "Now I have to find the proper person to sell it to."

"You know I don't have much money," Maggie said, her eyes appraising him openly.

He stepped around the books to her, took her into his arms, and kissed her roughly. She swore she could feel the power contained within him, and she relished that feeling and responded to him with an unexpected eagerness. Their lips found each other, and she parted his lips, seeking to taste him. He allowed it and crushed her to him as if possessing her. Stopping to take a breath, she looked into his dark eyes and saw that his reaction to her was his own; her influence had no effect on him. Lucky was a dangerous man in his own right, and she found that exciting. She had been waiting for this a long time.

"As I'm sure you know, I sometimes accept other forms of payment," he said in a cool voice.

"You mean sex," she said, not at all certain that he hadn't cast a spell on her. But if he had, she simply didn't care. All she knew was that she wanted him, and the sooner the better.

"That and other things."

"What other things?"

"Nothing I sell is free, Maggie. Let's just say I use the bartering system, and since you are now interested in buying things of true value, they will cost you more." He gave her another harsh kiss. When they separated, she couldn't see any emotion except desire in his deep, fathomless eyes, but for now, that was enough. She would make a bargain with the devil if it got her what she wanted.

Lucky brought her hand to his lips and kissed it. When he released it, he gave her a challenging look and motioned for her to follow him. She offered a saucy smile and grasped his hand, knowing that today was only the beginning of the power she would be able to obtain through this man, and she was determined to have it. She would have the power she needed to bring Sean back to her. But perhaps, more importantly, she would be able to punish those who had offended her or stood in her way.

They were in Lucky's back room when he pushed her up against the wall, lifting her skirt and pushing down her panties as he stared into her eyes. She felt nothing but triumph as he pushed himself into her. "Oh, sweet Jesus," she gasped a few minutes later as her climax overtook her and her cool feelings blew up in a hot, all-consuming passion.

"Jesus has nothing to do with us," Lucky grunted and finished.

His eyes only revealed a cooling lust, no inkling of emotions as he stepped away from her and nodded in satisfaction.

"That will do, for now," he said.

"A bedroom would have been nicer." She pulled up her panties and smoothed down her skirt as he stepped away from her.

"But we both know what you are, don't we?" He then added, "Besides, you've already had nice, haven't you?"

"How do you know?"

"I know a great many things about you, things that you don't even know. From here on out, you will be my servant, at least as much as I require."

"And in exchange?"

"In exchange, I will continue to mentor you in the dark arts, that which you so desperately desire."

"And what exactly will I do as your personal servant?" She gave him an appraising smile.

"On occasion I will have needs to be satisfied. And not just of a sexual nature."

"I don't understand," Maggie frowned.

"You really are a bit of a simple wench, aren't you? Slow in some things, but completely astute in others."

"I want to have power," she said.

"Yes, and you shall, but only when I feel you are prepared to handle it."

Maggie pouted, but after a moment offered him a seductive smile. In the end she was sure she would have what she wanted and would be the one in control. Men, all men, were fleshly creatures and weak because of it. She had power over their flesh, knew how to use it, and had no qualms about doing so. Lucky may not know it, but he would be hers, too—she was convinced of it.

Chapter 5
Family Matters

*S*EAN SIGHED AND looked morosely around the pub, glad to be home, but unsettled about what he had done in Dublin. He looked up as Donald stopped in front of him. The barkeep was a man in his early sixties, average height, and in good shape with a balding head and alert blue eyes. He was a good man who had helped to raise both Sean and his sister, Lillie, when Sean's father, Jack, passed away early in life. He was a friend of the family at that time and remained in that capacity over the intervening years, always available for the children when they showed up at home.

"Donald, how are you?" Sean asked, offering the older man a tired smile.

"Better than you, it seems," he said and eyed Sean, who remained pensive.

"What do I have to do to get a drink from you?"

"Just ask," Donald smiled. "Beer or something else?"

"Beer, I think. A Guinness will do nicely."

"All right then, back in a moment." Donald turned away and went to get a beer for Sean.

Sean turned around on his seat to study the room full of people, glad that most of them were friends and neighbors, people whom he had grown up with and had known for most of his life. He loved coming back home for visits, but his work and his life were now in Dublin. He glanced up as a beer was placed in front of him.

"When will you be going back to Dublin?" Donaid asked.

"Tomorrow. Time to get back to work."

"You have good timing, Maggie should be returning here about the time you are leaving."

"Thank God for that."

"There's no chance of reconciliation?"

Sean gave Donald a long look. "After being separated all these years? You know better than that." He took a long drink from his beer. "What's she doing in Dublin anyway?"

"Something about studying," Donald laughed. "I never took her for the type."

"Studying? Maggie?" Sean snorted. "She's not. I wonder what she's about? It would have to be quite interesting for her to take to studying."

"Sean, it's time you went on with your life," the barkeep said, his eyes fixed keenly on him. "I helped raise you, Sean. I know more about your soul than you think, more about the things you can do with your life, and more about the good man you are struggling to be. Don't ever stop believing."

He pulled out a cigarette and lit up. "Believe, Donald? Believe in what?"

"Yourself? God? Love?" Donald shrugged. "One or all are good things to believe in."

"Myself, *hmm*," Sean took a drag from his cigarette. "Well, I'm a successful as a businessman, good at my job, and make a good income. God? I suppose I do believe in God, even though it doesn't seem he's been around when I've need him to be. Love?" Sean laughed. "That one I can't give you. I don't think I believe in love, at least not true love."

"You're wrong, Sean. True love conquers all; true love is the only thing better than magic, the only thing powerful enough to break it."

Sean laughed out loud. "Donald, really? Love? Magic? I think you've had too much to drink."

"Maybe," Donald smiled, "or maybe I know more than you think."

"About what?" Sean studied the older man closely.

"Sometimes I don't understand you, my friend, but I've always been glad you've been in my life. You took very good care of Lillie and me, and mother as she's become more senile. For that I thank you."

"It was my pleasure, Sean. You and Lillie are fine young people."

"Donald, we're grown adults."

"Yes, but you still seem quite young to me."

"You make yourself sound as old as The Gaelic Moon, and we know that's not true." He laughed.

"Then I truly would be ancient." He sighed as someone called for a drink. "Time to wait on the rest of my customers."

"Flock, you mean. I think you take care of us as well as Father Murphy."

"Maybe in my own way. It's hard not to when you own a pub." He regarded the younger man. "Say goodbye before you leave."

"I will. I need to go home and spend some time with Lillie and Mam before I go."

"Don't fight with her. Do your best."

With a grimace, Sean nodded and finished his beer and got up and left the pub.

SEAN STOOD OUTSIDE of a small house in the village of Cullamore. A light breeze ruffled his thick red hair as he stared at the distant rolling hills. The rain had been plentiful, and everything was stupendously green at the moment and damp. He hated the dampness. He took a drag from the cigarette he held in his hand and slowly expelled the white smoke, watching as it dissipated in the air. He turned as he heard the front door open behind him, and his sister came out to join him. Lillie gave his arm a quick squeeze. "Are you all right, Sean?"

He shrugged and gave her a look of casual indifference, studying her quietly. She had long dark hair, a pleasant face, average figure, average height, and deep brown eyes. She had always been the girl-next-door type, and she seemed to be friends with most of the men in the village. They seldom regarded her as more than that. She was a lovely person, and Sean felt bad that she was still alone.

"You know she doesn't mean half of what she says."

"Maybe, but she says it anyway." He gave his sister a lopsided smile. "I should be used to it by now, don't you think?"

"Well, some things one never gets used to," Lille said, searching her brother's face. "And Mam has a sharp tongue, whether she is being lucid or not."

"Don't I know it? Am I such a disappointment to her that she favors my poor excuse for a wife over me, her only son?"

"I think it's mostly that she was expecting a grandchild."

Sean looked away, flicked what was left of his cigarette on the ground, put it out with his heel, and he turned back to his sister.

"I'm ashamed to admit it, but it's true. I never loved her. If it wasn't for the child, I never would have married her." Sean shook his head in sadness. "She murdered it with an abortion. Poor child—it didn't deserve such a fate, though perhaps having Maggie as a mother would have been worse. Mam doesn't understand, but I'm afraid she'll never have any grandchildren, at least not from me." Sean sighed and rubbed his temple; he was getting a headache.

"If you told her what Maggie did, perhaps she'd better understand."

"It depends on the day, doesn't it? Mam mostly seems stuck in the not-so-distant past."

"What about you?" Lilly persisted. "Are you giving up? Will you not get divorce and try it again?"

"Divorce? That's a new concept for us Irish, isn't it? I don't think Mother would ever speak to me if I did that. Besides, it's wrong, isn't it?"

Lillie walked away a few paces and turned back to face her brother. "Normally I would agree, but with Maggie, I think you need to make a final end of things. You've made the mistake of being civil to her the last couple of years. You've given her hope. And as long as you are legally her husband, no matter how far away you are, or how many years separate you, she will think you still belong to her."

Sean ran a hand through his hair. "You're probably right, but it seems cruel somehow."

"Isn't it crueler to let her believe she may yet be with you? For all of your sakes, put an end to it. Shut the door once and for all." Lillie leaned over and kissed her brother's cheek and, with a last squeeze of his arm, turned away and went back into the stone-and-mortar house that had been in the family for generations.

He reached into his pocket, pulled out another smoke, and lit it up, staring again into the distant rolling hills of his childhood.

DESPITE THE BEAUTIFUL, sunny day, Mary was disappointed that she hadn't heard from Sean in well over a week. She had placed a call s few days ago and left a message, but he hadn't responded. He was probably busy with something or other and just hadn't told her about it. To be fair, they didn't know each other very well yet, so she was probably worrying needlessly. She reluctantly admitted to herself t that she found him attractive, and she wondered what it would be like to really kiss him, to open her mouth to his, to taste him like that, to feel his hands on her body as he pressed against her during their kiss...

She laughed at herself, but stopped when she remembered the dreams she'd had about a mysterious Irish lover. The more she thought about it, the more she realized that the man in her dream could be Sean. The phone rang, breaking Mary out of her thoughts. She scrambled to answer it, hoping that the object of her desire was calling her back. She was disappointed when she heard the voice on the other end of the line.

"Hey, beautiful! How's the hottest woman in all of Europe?" Paul asked.

"Hello, Paul."

"Are you okay? You sound tired or something,"

"Fine, and yeah, a bit tired."

"Well, this news will cheer you up."

"What news?"

"I am coming to visit you."

"Paul, you really don't need to... ," Mary said, trying to think of a polite way to discourage him.

"Of course I do. Who else could possibly make sure that you're all right?"

"I'm fine. Amy is here with me."

"That poor excuse for a friend," he began.

"Paul! I will not put up with you slamming Amy."

"My apologies," he said quickly. "I'll be at the Dublin airport by three on Wednesday. You can pick me up there. I'll send you the itinerary. And I will show you how a man treats his woman."

"But Paul... ," she began to protest, but he had already hung up the phone.

Chapter 6
The Rescue

*T*HE SHAMROCK WAS fairly busy for a Thursday night even though the after-work crowd had already departed. Mary and Amy sat at the bar, watching the patrons come and go. Amy looked over to her right and saw a tall, dark Irishman pass by carrying a beer.

"What about him?" Amy nudged her friend.

"Who?"

"The guy with the beer."

"Gee, that narrows it down."

"Smart ass!" Amy turned her around on her barstool and pointed to the man who had just walked by. "Speaking of ass."

"Well, it's nice, but no."

"What do you want? We've been doing this at different pubs for a week, and you still haven't seen anyone you want!" Amy's exasperation was an almost palpable thing.

"I'm just picky."

"Picky? That's hardly the word I'd use." Amy took a drink from her beer. "Come on, look!"

Mary sipped her wine and laughed at her friend's frustration. But to humor her, she looked around the pub. To her amazement, she saw Sean coming in the door. She watched him stop to hang up his coat and take a seat at the bar. He hadn't seen her yet and sat by himself, perusing the menu for something to eat. He took no notice of anyone else, just seemed lost in his own world.

"Oh, no, what in the hell is he doing here?" Amy groaned as if she were being tortured, and Mary saw Paul enter through the main door.

"I told him we'd be here," Mary admitted with a grimace.

"Mary! Why would you do that?"

"Well, he flew here all the way from Germany to see us."

"You, you mean."

"The least we can do is meet him for a drink."

By the scowl on Amy's face, Mary could tell that her friend wasn't convinced.

"You don't like him or something, do you?" Amy gave her a suspicious glance.

"No, we're friends."

"Nothing else?"

"No, Amy, I swear." She saw Paul coming up to them. "Now make nice."

"Must I?" Amy grumbled.

"Yes," Mary said, and her friend expelled the longest put-out sigh she had ever heard.

"There they are, the only things worth looking at in this dreary country and strangely designed pub," he said gazing with curiosity at the pub still stuck in transition.

"Thank you, Paul," Mary said.

"I speak only the truth," he said and took her hand, drawing it up to his lips for a kiss.

"Oh, brother," Amy rolled her eyes, and Paul spared her a brief glare.

"Why don't you join us?" Mary asked, indicating a barstool next to her as she tried to defuse the current situation.

"Thank you, I'd love to," he said and sat down next to Mary.

"WHERE HAVE YOU been, Sean?" Kevin eyed his friend with concern.

"Just busy."

"Yeah, I bet." He paused. "What can I get for you?"

"How about a Scotch?"

Kevin raised an eyebrow and waved to the bartender, ordering another round. The shots showed up promptly. "I'm guessing this will get you off to a good start."

"*Slainte!*" Sean said and took a long drink. He closed his eyes as the liquor made its way down his throat. He enjoyed the warm sensations it produced. "Smooth," he gasped, "really smooth."

"That it is." Kevin grinned.

"What else? Why are you staring at me?"

"I was just wondering if you'd noticed."

"Noticed what?"

"The American ladies are here tonight. Isn't Mary the one you showed around Dublin?" Sean nodded, and Kevin leaned forward to speak in a low voice. "Maybe you should go over and say hello again?"

"Why would I do that? I have no right to be with someone as fine as Mary."

"You sell yourself short, and you shouldn't do that," Kevin said and left to speak with some other regulars of the pub.

Despite his efforts not to look, Sean couldn't help himself and searched the pub for Mary. He saw her, almost directly across from him, engaged in conversation with an attractive man that touched Mary in a casual manner time and time again.

Being here suddenly seemed like a bad idea.

"HOW LONG ARE you stuck in this godforsaken place for?" Paul asked in disdain.

"I'm not stuck at all. I like it here," Mary said.

"You must be joking."

"No, I'm not." She scanned the bar, saw Sean sitting alone at a small table, and found herself wishing that he'd look up and see her.

"What is there to like? The weather is damp, the people are hicks even if they are of a different nationality, and it's next to impossible to find anything that is high end, including hotels." Paul sniffed in contempt and brushed lint from his suit jacket.

"Nice to know some things don't change," Amy muttered under her breath.

49

"In any case, it's wonderful to see you, Mary. You're beautiful as always." Paul leaned forward allowing his fingertips to brush Mary's cheeks.

KEVIN RETURNED A few minutes later, bringing a plate of appetizers to the table with him.

"Sorry, Kevin." Sean said, looking at his friend. "I don't mean to be cross."

"No problem." Kevin quietly regarded Mary and Paul, heads close together. "She seems nice."

"She is."

"And he's quite striking, don't you think? If you like handsome, rugged, muscular, blond American men, that is."

Sean regarded Mary and realized that the man she was talking to was indeed quite attractive. "I guess," he grumbled.

He took a bite of his food and watched Mary and Paul, conversing and smiling now. "Who is he, Kevin? I don't remember seeing him in here before." Sean frowned and realized the food didn't taste good today.

WHEN MARY TURNED to include Amy in the conversation, she realized her friend had once again disappeared. She certainly had a knack for fading into the shadows.

"Amy's gone. She finally figured out that she shouldn't be intruding," Paul said.

"She wasn't intruding," Mary protested.

"This will give us more privacy." Paul shifted his barstool closer to Mary so that their thighs were touching.

She shifted on her barstool as far away from him as she could get, searching for some sort of escape, but finding none. Sean was now talking to another man at his table, oblivious to her presence in the pub. Either he hadn't noticed her, or else he simply didn't care. Miffed at that line of thought, she turned her attentions back to Paul, who reached for and warmly grasped her hands within his own. He gazed at her intently, his dark eyes brimming with desire, and he squeezed her hands.

SEAN DOWNED HIS third shot of Scotch as he watched Mary and

her new distinctly male friend. "I don't know who he is. I've never seen him before."

"Seems like a close friend at least, wouldn't you say?" Kevin goaded Sean as he saw Paul take Mary's hands in his own. "See how smooth he is? A real lady killer, that one."

Sean could almost feel his blood pressure rising as he watched the couple across the pub. "What do you mean lady killer?"

"You know what that means. He has a way with women. Just look at him." And look he did. The other man invaded her space, leaned far too close, and frequently touched her arm. His interest was all too apparent. Sean watched Mary, who suddenly seemed quite defenseless against the tried and true advances of a lecherous, handsome man. He saw Paul smile as he placed a chaste kiss on her lips.

"Shouldn't be long now," Kevin said.

Sean abandoned his barstool and walked across the room to where Mary sat with Paul. He stopped a few feet away from them and arranged his clothes to give himself the disheveled, unkempt appearance of a man who had had too much to drink.

"Come with me, Mary, you won't regret it. I'll show you how you deserve to be treated." Paul dropped his voice to a seductive whisper and squeezed Mary's hand. At that moment, Sean, apparently off balance, collided with Paul, spilling his drink all over the American.

"I'm sooo sorry," Sean slurred and blinked at them in astonishment. "I don't know how this happened."

"You idiot!" Paul yelled. "You drunken, moronic idiot."

"So... sorry," he continued, blinking at them stupidly. "You have no idea..." He stopped, frowned, and looked back at Paul. "What was I saying?"

With a glare for him, Paul turned his attentions back to Mary, who had her lips tightly pressed together to avoid laughing.

"My apologies, Mary. I'll be back. I have to see if I can repair the damage," Paul said, indicating his wet clothes. He leaned over and kissed Mary's cheek, glared at Sean who hovered harmlessly nearby, and headed to the men's room.

When she turned, she saw Sean still standing nearby, clothes askew, seeming like a child who just got caught with his hand in the cookie jar. Unable to contain her laughter any more, it bubbled out of her. "Sean, you look ridiculous."

Damn if it wasn't good to see her marvelous smile and hear her delightful laughter. He grinned at her and began to laugh as well. Soon he was standing next to her, giggling foolishly, and when they calmed down enough to talk, they both wiped tears of laughter from their eyes.

"Thanks." Mary patted his arm. "I really needed that."

"Me too."

"Are you all right?" she asked, her expression now one of concern.

"I am now."

"You're not really drunk, are you?" she asked, appraising him with a calculating eye.

"No."

"Why the charade?"

He looked at her and sighed, the traces of laughter vanishing from his face as he reached for her hands. "I came to rescue you," he said.

"From what?"

"From him. He only wants one thing, Mary. And you deserve better than that."

She bit back the sharp retort on her lips when she saw the earnest expression on his face, and tried to soften what she was going to say. "*Umm*, I'm not sure how to say this." She hesitated and added, "I know that Paul is feeding me lines."

"You're onto him?" He breathed a sigh of relief. "That's good. I thought maybe you were buying what he was selling." He studied her face, as something new occurred to him. "You weren't encouraging him, were you, Mary?"

She found his disappointment in her oddly disturbing, and turned away from him with a small pout. Sean hadn't shown her any attention lately, so she decided to play devil's advocate. "And what if I was? I'm here in Dublin, unattached, available, with no one to go out with. Shall I sit by myself the whole time?"

"No," he scowled. "I didn't mean that. But I know you can do better than him!"

"And how should I find someone better? Can you tell me?"

Irritation sparked in his clear blue eyes, and he glanced toward the men's rest room, only to see Paul emerge from it.

"Blast and damn! Do you trust me?" he asked, squeezing

Mary's hands.

"I guess so," she said with a shrug.

"Come with me."

"Why?"

"We have to talk about this." He got off his stool and helped her off his. "Do you have a coat?"

"On the coat rack."

"Come on," he said as he saw Paul striding toward them. He quickly led her to the exit, where he retrieved their coats, draped them over his arm, and opened the door.

"Hey! Mary, where are you going?" Paul called out.

"What about Paul?" she asked.

"He'll get over it," he said, and hustled her out the door.

Paul stalked to the door, trying to get past the barflies who were entering, but by the time he managed to get out of the pub door, Sean and Mary were gone.

Chapter 7

Flinging

*T*HE DRIVE OUT of Dublin was quiet; Sean had changed from the exuberant man who had hustled her out of The Shamrock to a silent man who appeared to be internally brooding. Knowing he would talk when he was ready to, Mary let him be. She enjoyed the passing scenery, the many different shades of green in the always beautiful foliage of Ireland. She hadn't had much of a chance to explore outside of Dublin, so this unexpected field trip was a pleasant bonus. The further out they got from Dublin, the better she liked it. The sun was out, and the green countryside reminded her of Minnesota in the springtime, which somehow made her feel at home. Trees, grass, and flowers. After being locked in a big city for an extended length of time, she had forgotten how she was normally so used to seeing them. Out here, the air was cool, the grassy hills were green, and the sounds were soft.

Sean parked his small car on a scenic outlook, opened the car door for her, and led her down a hill on a seldom-used path. He had his hands shoved into his pockets and appeared deep in thought as he forged ahead. Mary walked behind him, trying to keep up, but she was dressed for a casual evening in town, not a hike in the country.

Going down the hillside was a bit tricky. Even with short heels, her footwear left a great deal to be desired, but Sean readily offered assistance when she needed it.

At the bottom of the hill were some fallen trees in front of one of the bluest ponds Mary had ever seen. Sean offered his arm and guided her over to one of the trees, which was large enough to support them both. She gratefully sank down on the log and, after a brief hesitation, he sat down beside her. Sean stopped, closed his eyes, and expelled a long breath. Mary watched it dissipate into the cool air and realized that, even with her jacket, she was cold. *Must be the dampness*, she thought, because the actual temperature in Minnesota got much, much colder than this.

"I'm sorry, Mary. I didn't mean to walk so far."

"It's okay. But next time warn me so I can dress for it," she said smiling and took off a shoe to rub her foot. "What's with you, anyway?"

"Believe me; you don't have enough time to hear it all." He rolled his eyes. "But, truly, I have your best interests at heart. I couldn't let you go off with that buffoon."

"That buffoon is a friend of mine from Minnesota," Mary laughed.

Sean gave her a puzzled look.

"Sean, can we be honest?" Mary asked and reached for his hands.

"Of course," but if he works in the US, in Minnesota, what is he doing here?"

"Paul likes me, as in wants-to-have-more-than-a-friendship likes me."

"But you don't feel the same?" Sean asked, a glimmer of jealousy in his voice.

"God, no. I've told him no so many times, but he just doesn't listen." She sighed.

"Why was he kissing you?"

"His idea."

"So I didn't need to rescue you?"

"Probably not, but I'm glad you did. I haven't seen you for a while."

"I went home, had some business to take care of." He finally looked at her again. "Can I ask you something?"

She smiled at him. "Sure."

"Why were you and Amy at the bar? Were you trying to make a new... acquaintance?" He looked her up and down and realized that, despite her outfit being casual, it hugged every one of her curves nicely and the pastel green sweater she wore highlighted her lovely hazel eyes. "And you look nice, like you're..."

"Trying to pick up a guy?" Mary shook her head and sighed. "I kind of am. It's Amy's idea really, but I'm not fighting it."

"Mary!" He was so appalled that she couldn't help but laugh.

"Sean, I'm a woman, and I've been without for a long time." She grasped his hands. "It's okay."

"But you should have feelings for the man!"

"Maybe it's better not to." She shrugged. "Amy says it's what I need."

"She's wrong. It's no good without feeling."

"And sometimes it's no good with it."

He regarded her curiously.

"A failed relationship," she said.

"Go on," he urged.

"What? Tell you about Joe?"

"Was that his name? Yes, what happened?"

Mary scowled and looked away from Sean at the beauty of the emerald countryside and the clear blue of the pond before her.

"His name was Joe, and I was head-over-heels in love with him. We were talking about marriage, but something happened, he got distant suddenly." Her voice dropped and Sean had to strain to hear as she blinked back sudden tears in her eyes.

Sean took her hand in his gently. "Mary, what happened?"

She expelled a long sigh, blowing a stray hair out of her eyes. "I found out why he was so distant. I needed to find him one day— we had to lock down the location of our wedding, or we would forfeit the date. I tracked him down to a bar across town, by his workplace." She brushed away a traitorous tear, her voice angry now. "He was at the bar with the work crowd and with... Corinne."

"*Ouch!*" he said and shared a grimace with her. He reached for her hand and she let him hold it.

"His girlfriend, his very pregnant girlfriend!"

His expression was filled with sadness. "I'm sorry."

"You have no need to be sorry, that bastard, that self-centered, prick! How could he be planning our wedding when he was having a baby with another woman? How could I be so fucking stupid?" She pulled her hand out of Sean's and stalked away from him, stopping at the edge of the pond, staring at it with unseeing eyes.

After a few moments, Sean walked over to her and put his hands on her shoulders, gently rubbing the tenseness he felt. "You shouldn't have been treated like that."

She snorted in contempt. "That's why I'm not overly eager for a relationship." She sighed and turned to Sean. "I don't even know why I'm here with you. Why I find you so damned attractive?"

"Thank you, I think." Sean gave her a guarded gaze. "With what you've just told me I'm not at all certain why you want to be with someone again."

"Because it's been awhile and I want to get past it, and because I miss being with a man. Sean, I appreciate your concern, but I don't want to spend my time here alone. I want some male companionship."

"What about me?" Sean said.

"What about you?"

"I can be your companion. We are still friends, aren't we?"

Mary nodded. "But is that all?"

Sean's blue eyes studied her face intently, and she thought they were far more beautiful than the nearby picturesque pond. "Please, believe me, Mary. I have nothing to offer you but friendship."

"Are you sure?" she whispered and leaned forward to kiss him, a soft, but passionate kiss, full of promise.

He eagerly returned the kiss, his mouth opening as they exchanged breath with one another. When he finally stopped kissing her, he held her tightly as if afraid to let her go.

"Mary. I'm not what you think I am."

"I think you're a cute Irishman who likes me, at least a little bit."

He blinked at her. "Okay, that I am."

"I think we could be good friends."

Sean nodded.

"And I think we're attracted to one another."

"I can't argue," he smiled at her. "But it's wrong."

"What?"

"You deserve someone who will love you, someone interested in more than a fling."

"*Hmm.*" Mary studied his earnest expression.

"Let me ask you this. Have you ever had a fling?"

"Well, no. Have you?"

"Yes. I was young, eighteen or so. I didn't love the woman, and I told her that from the beginning. But she wanted more. It went badly when it ended," he said in a cold voice, remembering his marriage to Maggie. "I don't want to ruin our friendship. How do you know that won't happen?"

"I don't." Mary looked away. "But I know if we're truly friends, if we spend time together and are honest with each other, we'll still be friends."

"I don't know." He shook his head glumly. "It seems dubious at best, and knowing some of your history, I don't want to hurt you."

"Are you seeing anyone else, Sean? If you are, I don't want to interfere."

"What?" he asked, caught off guard. "No, no one. I haven't for several years."

They stared at one another, entranced.

He couldn't stop the attraction he felt for her, and being this close and not pulling her back into his arms was a kind of self-inflicted torture.

"Might we have a fling? Just until I leave Ireland?" Mary asked hopefully.

He sighed and briefly touched his hand to her face. "No, Mary. Friends and sex don't mix."

"Why not? Do you think it was easy to ask you this?" she snapped, her hazel eyes darkened with anger.

"I know it wasn't." He took a moment to recover from her anger, secretly admitting to himself that he liked her fiery nature. She looked damn good when she was mad. "But I don't want to disappoint you."

She started to move away from him, but he reached out and grasped her hand.

"It's not you, it's me…"

"You are not seriously saying that to me, are you? The ultimate of all dumping lines?"

"Oh, Mary," he laughed and clasped her hands. "It's not that at all. You must have noticed my interest." He raised her hand and kissed it. "Trust me on this. Friends will be better for us."

"Will you at least think about it?"

"All right," he said, looking into her sparkling hazel eyes. "I'll think about it. But don't expect me to change my mind. I'm a stubborn man."

Mary only smiled.

LATER THAT NIGHT after they returned to Dublin, Sean dropped Mary off at her flat. Once she was safely inside, he drove away with a last wave of farewell.

She unlocked the door to the apartment and let herself in, not bothering to be quiet since she was sure her roommate was awake. Sure enough, when she stopped by the living room, Amy was sitting on the couch, wide awake, waiting for her. With a smile, she patted a spot on the couch beside her. Knowing it was useless to argue, Mary went took the spot beside her friend. She rubbed her tired feet and winced.

"Where'd you disappear to? Paul about had an aneurism and is madder than hell." Amy grinned. "Did you run off with Sean? He said it was a red-haired Irish man, and though they're all over the place here, I know you're more likely to go off with someone you know."

Mary sighed and held up her hand, trying to quiet her roommate.

"It was Sean."

Amy's sighed. "I didn't think you were going to see him anymore."

"He says he only wants to be friends."

"Seriously, are you back to that?" Amy patted her arm in sympathy.

"There's nothing wrong with being friends," Mary said, springing off the couch to pace restlessly. "It's good to have friends."

"Are you trying to convince me or yourself?"

Mary stopped pacing and regarded her friend with a weak smile. "I don't know."

"Okay so be his friend and see what happens. But be careful," she warned, getting off the couch. "You shouldn't mix friendship and sex. It gets complicated."

"Funny. That's what he said."

"Really?" Amy raised an eyebrow. "Maybe he's smarter than he looks. Goodnight."

"'Night." Mary sat on the couch again, looking out the window, confused by her thoughts of Sean. *Couldn't anything be easy?*

THE NEXT DAY Mary was surprised to find herself going with Sean to see a movie. He had surprised her and asked her out, as a friend, of course, and she had happily agreed. When they discussed movies, he said that one of the theatres in town was showing the original *Star Wars* trilogy back to back to back. Being a fan, she picked that as the movies they should watch. They had a marvelous time together as they binged on popcorn and junk food and emerged from the theatre laughing and happy.

"That was great. I haven't seen those in years."

"Yeah, I was like eight when they came out," Mary said.

"I was twelve, and it was the greatest thing I'd ever seen."

"And what did you think of Leia's slave bikini in *Return of the Jedi*?"

"Do I have to answer?" Sean could feel a blush coming to his face.

"That's what I thought." Mary laughed. "I think she was the fantasy for every male born for several years after that movie. But what an uncomfortable costume to have to wear!"

"It didn't seem so bad."

"Sean, think metal bikini. How would you like to wear a metal cod piece?"

He winced. "Well, when you put it like that. And I'll bet you had a crush on one of the heroes of the story? Was it Luke or Han?"

"Are you kidding me? Han. It had to be Han. Harrison Ford was just as hot for women as Carrie Fisher was for men."

"You just said you were only eight. What does an eight-year-old know about hot?" Sean seemed torn between indignation and bubbling laughter.

"In case you hadn't noticed, Mr. Calhoun, I'm not eight anymore."

"Believe me, I've noticed." As if gauging her reaction, he asked, "You really think Harrison's hot?"

"Without a doubt. He'd be on my short list of five."

"Short list of five? What's that?"

"It's the list." She sighed at his puzzled expression. "People in a relationship always have an exception list. Those are people that you find hot and, if the opportunity of a one night stand arose with them, you are allowed to take advantage of it."

"Okay, I've heard of that." Sean frowned of her. "So if we, you and I were involved, Harrison Ford would be on your exception list?"

"Without a doubt." Mary smiled brightly at him. "But you could put Carrie Fisher on yours. Or anyone else you want. I don't think Mon Mothma is nearly as attractive though." She flashed him a winning smile. "Besides, why would it be a problem? We're not involved, are we?"

Sean watched her for just a moment before hurrying after her, not at all happy that she had an exception list at all.

THE NEXT DAY Mary entered the flat after doing errands and was surprised to find Amy stretched out on the couch, tears running down her face. To say this was unusual was an understatement. Amy took all things in stride, and nothing seemed to get her down.

"Amy, what's wrong?" Mary sat down on the couch next to Amy.

Amy sat up and tried to compose herself. "I didn't expect you home for a while yet." She sniffed.

"Wanna share?"

Amy looked at her in misery. "You'll laugh."

She smiled at Amy. "Probably, but tell me anyway."

"It's Rob."

"Rob? Is he okay? Nothing's happened to him, has it?" Mary was alarmed; she genuinely liked Amy's fiancé.

"No, I just miss him." Amy's expression was so sad that her heart broke a little bit for her friend. "I didn't think I would. I mean, I never have—not like this."

"It's because you love him, you dope!" Mary laughed. "Can you visit him for a week?"

"No, too much to do here. I'm required to stay."

"Why doesn't he come here? He likes to travel and having you here only makes it sweeter."

"You're right." Amy smacked her forehead. "I was so focused on going home that I never thought to ask him here. What a great idea." She laughed. "Mary, you're a genius."

Mary checked her watch. "Can you call him now?"

"No, I won't be able to reach him for a few hours." Amy made a face. "What should I do for four hours?"

"The Shamrock?" Mary smiled at her friend.

"You just want to see Sean."

"Maybe, but it will pass the time."

"You're right. But there's still a problem that you haven't dealt with."

"Paul?" Mary winced and rubbed her forehead. "He's been trying to get me all day, and I've been ducking his calls."

"You know that's only going to piss him off," Amy said, but she appeared gleeful.

Mary couldn't help but smile at her friend's amusement. "You really don't like him, do you?"

"No, and you shouldn't either. With all of your so-called psychic feelings, I don't know why you haven't picked up on it. Something about him just isn't right."

"He can be obnoxious at times, but he can be a good man. I've seen that side of him."

"Well, I think you're the only one. Just do me a favor and please don't get involved with him."

"I don't see that happening anytime soon."

"Good." Amy breathed a sigh of relief. "Sean's much more likable."

"Did you just endorse Sean?" Mary teased her friend.

"Maybe I did. So what?"

"A milestone. Come on, let's go out. I'll call Paul from the pub and we can go back to having fun."

"Sounds like a plan," Amy agreed.

The two women chatted happily as they closed the door behind them.

THE SHAMROCK WAS quieter on a Wednesday night than during the rest of the week, and Mary was quite happy with that. She enjoyed the place much more when she could hear herself talk. She looked around for Sean when they entered and saw him at his usual spot at the bar. He saw them enter and waved at them as he pointed to a nearby booth.

By the time they got to their usual booth, Sean had their drinks sitting on the table for them. He placed a soft kiss on Mary's cheek and slid in beside her as Amy took the seat across from them.

"Missed you," Sean whispered to Mary.

She smiled at him and squeezed his hand.

"You two look good together," Amy said and raised her eyebrow in speculation.

"A compliment? From you? And what is the occasion, my darling Amy?" He finished in a teasing manner, his Irish accent heavy. "Is it a cold day in hell, or have pigs started to fly?"

Amy couldn't help herself and laughed. "You are so full of shit!"

Sean grinned at her and took a sip from his drink. "Blarney, my dear, blarney!" He studied the cute blonde for a moment and realized that she was a bit sad. He exchanged a questioning look with Mary.

"Amy is missing Rob."

"Rob? I don't remember you talking about a Rob."

"My fiancé," Amy said quietly.

"You're engaged? Well, I'll be damned. I would have expected you to shout that from the highest rooftops. You're not exactly the master of subtle." Sean grinned.

"Yeah, well, can't be helped." Amy ran her finger around the rim of her glass. "Rob's a great guy, and I miss him. I can't wait to talk to him."

"You're calling him tonight?"

"Yeah, when we get back. I can't go home because of work but maybe he'll come over for a visit."

"That would be brilliant. If I can help, let me know."

"Could you pick him up from the airport?"

"Me? You'd trust me to do that? My goodness, you have come a long ways, haven't you?" His blue eyes twinkled in merriment.

"You're not bad, I'm just protective of Mary."

"As you should be. She's a fine friend and a lovely woman." Sean raised Mary's hand to his mouth and kissed it. Mary blushed.

"You may be all right, Sean." Amy glared at him. "Just be sure that you treat her well, or you'll have to answer to me."

"With a threat like that, I don't dare step out of line!" he said with a laugh. "How long until you can call?"

"Too long," she moaned.

"Excuse me for a moment, but I have to call Paul with excuses," Mary said.

"Buy us another drink, Sean?" Amy asked.

"My pleasure," he said, but his eyes followed Mary's retreating form.

THE THREE OF them were in the booth, the women giggling in their drinks about a silly, over-the-top story that Sean had just told them. His face was flushed from laughter, too, and he giggled helplessly alongside Mary. They were all surprised to hear someone loudly clearing his throat and looked up to see Paul standing beside the booth, arms crossed and face set in an angry expression.

"Mary? What in the hell are you doing here? You told me you weren't feeling well."

"Did you really? Good for you!" Amy whispered far too loudly.

"I think she was feeling better until just a moment ago." Sean gave Paul a goofy grin and tried not to laugh as Amy caught his eye. Mary bit her lip and tried hard to gather herself together, but it wasn't easy with the other two stifling their laughter.

"Paul," she greeted him, her voice unexpectedly squeaking, causing the other two to laugh harder. She smacked Sean, who once again laughed uncontrollably.

"Oh, Mary, more!" he begged, sending Amy off into another giggle.

Paul was incredulous as he glared at Sean. "You're here with *that* instead of me?"

"Yes, well... ," Mary managed to not laugh, but couldn't stop the huge grin on her face.

"Maybe this will be easier if I get out of here. I don't like him anyway," Amy said quietly to Sean and scooted out of the booth and walked away.

"Paul, I told you I'd talk to you tomorrow," Mary said.

"I came here for a drink. It's only coincidence that I found you here."

"You weren't following me?"

"No! How could you think I'd do that?"

"Maybe she thinks you're jealous," Sean said and draped a casual arm over Mary's shoulders.

"Jealous? Of you?" Paul laughed, a short indignant laugh. "Mary has better taste than to be slumming with the likes of you."

"Paul, stop!" Mary's laughter was gone, as was Sean's, and she felt him tense up beside her.

"You're wasting your time with him when we could have gone out and made a night of it?"

Sean's eyes had narrowed. "Maybe she didn't want to do that, Paul. Maybe she's having more fun with Amy and me."

"Paul," Mary said, "I don't want to hurt your feelings, but I wanted to spend the evening with Amy and Sean."

"And you didn't invite me?"

"I didn't think you'd like it. Tell me I'm wrong," she challenged.

After a long pause, he admitted, "You're not," and glared at Sean, who pulled Mary closer to him.

"Mary's dating me," Sean said, absently stroking Mary's cheek.

Paul glared at Mary. "You are?"

She gave Sean an inquisitive look, and he nodded. "Why, yes, I am. And I've been telling you for a long time that we're friends, haven't I?" she asked Paul.

Paul took a step forward toward the two of them and curled his hands into fists at his side. Sean stood up quickly and planted himself firmly in front of Mary, his actions daring the other man to do something. Paul glared at the two of them, rage apparent in his face as he locked gazes with Sean.

"Is there a problem, then?" Sean asked in a deceptively soft voice.

"This isn't over," Paul said to Sean, hatred apparent in his eyes.

"The choice is Mary's, and she would rather be with me." Sean offered the ill-tempered man a tight smile. "I'm not about to let her go, so why don't you be on your way now?"

"Mary, come with me." Paul held out his hand to her, expecting her to obey the tone of his voice, and was surprised when she stood behind Sean and linked her arm in his.

"No, Paul. Go back to your hotel, and we'll talk tomorrow."

"As you wish." With one last glare for the two of them, he turned and stalked out of the pub.

"Thanks," Mary said, and moved to scoot away from Sean, but he held her in place.

"I wasn't joking, Mary. Will you date me?" His blue eyes searched her confused hazel eyes, which had lightened into a lovely shade of emerald green.

A slow smile spread across Mary's face. "You mean it?"

"Let me show you," he said, and cupping her face with his hands, he kissed her. It started out slow and tender but soon evolved into a passionate, extended lip lock.

Amy returned to the booth only to see them making out, oblivious to her presence.

"About time," she muttered and quietly turned and left them to their own devices.

Chapter 8
Cullamore Ghosts

*T*HE RAIN HAD stopped; the sky was a bright blue with a brilliant sun in the sky, and the Irish countryside had never looked more beautiful. The morning was cool, but once the fog burned off, the sun had done its work and raised the temperature to make it a lovely day. Lillie smiled and waved at her neighbors on her way home from the bakery. She saw Donald, everyone's favorite barkeep, relaxing in a chair outside of his pub. He smiled at her and indicated the chair beside him.

"Lillie, will you come and have a sit with an old man? Help me pass part of my day?"

"Oh, and what a charming invitation you offer." She laughed. "And you're not really that old."

"*Ahh*, my dear, you really don't have any idea."

"You hide it well." Lillie put her bags down, sat beside the man, and smiled. Somehow Donald always seemed to know what was going one with all of those in town, and not for the first time Lillie wondered how he did it. Not to mention that he always seemed to keep his good humor intact despite the sometimes incessant whining of those around him, something she wasn't sure she could have managed without killing some, given the attitudes that people often carried with them.

"And how are you today?" he asked.

"Fine, much the same as yesterday."

"And your mother?"

"Well," she said, "she's in surprisingly good spirits this morning."

"We had a blue moon last night, did you know? Perhaps she's superstitious."

"What do you mean?"

"Surely you've heard the local tale?" His eyes twinkled as he spoke. "On the eve of a blue moon, it's sometimes possible to speak with the dead. Those closest to you can contact you."

Lillie laughed in his face. "You spin a good yarn, Donald, but if that were true, I'm sure I would have spoken with Da by now."

"Maybe you can't hear him or see him."

"Why would you say that?"

"I don't know, only that I've heard some people are more sensitive to psychic things. Maybe you're not." He smiled and shrugged. "Tell me, lass, do you believe in ghosts? Spirits as it were?"

"*Ahh*, there you go again."

"Do you?"

"Being raised with all of those folktales, it's hard not to. And I've witnessed one or two odd things myself."

"It's said that our village is built on the site of ancient Celtic burial grounds."

"Do you believe that, Donald?"

"I do." He smiled at Lillie. "But anything's possible, isn't it? It could help to explain why many of us believe in ghosts." He widened his eyes in mock horror.

"*Pah!* Ghosts are part of the Irish way of things. It's part of our folklore, nothing more."

"Does that mean you don't believe in them?"

"I don't really know," Lillie actually considered the question. "Guess I've never had occasion to question this belief."

"Ghosts exist," Donald said, studying the younger woman.

"Donald? Really?" Lillie smiled at him.

He returned her smile. "I do. They're all around us, don't you know?"

She studied him for a moment. "I don't know if you're serious or teasing. Have you had encounters with ghosts?" she asked, her

68

curiosity rising.

"Yes."

"This is the first time in all of these years that you've told me this." She shook her head. "All the time hanging around with us as we grew up, and you never talked about this before?"

"You weren't ready; neither was Sean."

"Ready for what?" Lillie laughed. "You make it sound, oh, I don't know, like we have to know about them."

"Have to? No. Want to, maybe." He sighed and stood up as Lillie did, opening his arms to give her an affectionate hug.

"Sean and I are fortunate to have you in our lives." She smiled at the older man. "I'd best be getting back to Mother, though. Hopefully, she's still in a good mood."

"Do you think she'll ever forgive Sean?"

"Hard to say. I know that deep down she still loves him, but it's more difficult because of her illness. She has good days and bad days as you know."

"Have you seen Maggie lately?"

"No," Lillie shook her head, "I haven't."

"I heard she went back to Dublin, at least that's what Patrick said a week ago. He's expecting her back today."

Concern replaced Lillie's smile. Lillie only knew of one reason that Maggie would make the effort, and that was to see Sean. Lillie crossed herself in front of Donald. He watched her with a bemused expression.

"I pray for once that brother of mine used his head, and not his... well, what got him in trouble before!"

"He'll find his way, Lillie. He just needs time. And everything eventually works out the way it's supposed to."

"I hope you're right. I love my brother dearly, but he does not always make the wisest of decisions." She gathered her bakery items and left, waving goodbye to Donald.

FUMBLING WITH THE doorknob, Lillie let herself into the house and went into the kitchen, where she deposited the bag she was carrying. She picked up a fresh loaf of bread and brought it with her to show her mother.

"Mother, I got some bread today. Two hours old—it's quite

good. I'm sure you'll like it…" Her voice trailed off as she noticed someone sitting and speaking with her mother. Without seeing her face, Lillie knew it could only be Maggie, the long, dark-red hair was the envy of most women about the county and fueled the desire of many men.

"Maggie," Lillie said coldly.

"Lillie!" Maggie stood up and put out her hand, mimicking great pleasure. "It's good to see you!"

Lillie stiffened at her gesture but offered her hand anyway, releasing Maggie's had as quickly as possible. "What are you doing here?"

"Lillie!" Her mother picked up her hand-carved walking stick and shook it at her daughter. "That's no way to talk to Sean's wife. Apologize."

"No, mother, I won't." A frown of frustration crossed Lillie's expression as she regarded her elderly, white-haired mother. It seemed she had slipped back to the time before Sean and Maggie had separated. "Maggie was a terrible wife to Sean, and you know it!"

"Lillie!"

"Mam, it's true!"

Maggie glared at her sister-in-law, her green eyes narrowed. "Sean is still my husband."

"Only until he divorces you."

"He'll never do that," she hissed. "I won't let him." Maggie glanced over at Geraldine who appeared to have missed her lapse in protocol, put her composure back in place, and smiled.

Lillie clenched her fist and mentally counted to ten, reminding herself that it wasn't a Christian act to hit another person, no matter how awful that person really was.

"Well, I'll be on my way," Maggie said and went over and kissed Geraldine on the cheek, whispering words that Lillie couldn't quite catch into her mother's ear. As she turned to leave, she gave Lillie a smug smile, closing the door behind her. Lillie wheeled on her mother in anger.

"Mother, how can you like her? She's a manipulative, lying woman…"

Geraldine just gave her daughter a patient smile, appearing extremely pleased with the world, enough that Lillie knelt down before her and put a hand to her forehead.

What are you doing? I'm fine," Geraldine protested, her watery blue eyes crinkling with her smile.

"You just don't seem yourself today."

"Why? Because I'm happy?" she snapped, and thumped her cane on the ground. She took a deep breath and relaxed, and the sparks left her watery blue eyes. "Why shouldn't I be? I saw your Da last night."

"You mean you dreamt about him."

The old woman's eyes narrowed again, but she said nothing for a moment. "I saw your Da again, and that made me feel better."

"And how was he?" Lillie asked with a resigned sigh.

"Just fine. He says hello."

"Say hello for me next time you see him."

"I will."

"Does he have anything to say about Maggie?" Lillie asked, remembering that her father was cautious about Maggie, even when she was a teenager.

"Nothing I want to hear," Geraldine said.

With the air of one who is used to humoring the elderly, Lillie patted her mother's shoulder.

"I have more good news," the older woman said.

Lillie went to the kitchen, poured herself a soda, and returned to the living room. "And what would that be?"

"I'm going to have a grandchild."

The liquid in Lillie's mouth spewed into the air in front of her. "What? What? How do you know this? Did Maggie tell you?"

The old woman shook her head.

"Did she say she was with Sean?"

"No."

"How do you know?"

The old woman smiled up at her daughter. "Some things I just know." She sighed contentedly. "There will be a grandchild."

Lillie wiped off the soda still trickling down her chin and regarded her mother with a worried expression.

FEELING JUST A bit ridiculous, Sean found himself waiting inside the departure gate for Amy's fiancé, holding up a silly sign bearing the name Rob Nelson. At least Amy had told her fiancé to look for Sean. That way the poor man wouldn't be introduced to a stranger to drive him to his hotel. The plane was slow to unload, and another hour before the passengers finally began to disembark.

Sean pulled at his collar, feeling a bit awkward and wondered how he'd let himself get talked into doing this, but he already knew the answer to that question. He'd done it for Mary. Amy was Mary's friend, and Amy needed a favor, so he was willing to help. He'd taken some time off from work, but that wasn't really a problem either, as he pretty much ran his own schedule these days. Sometime it was good to be in charge of things.

When most of the passengers had disembarked, and Sean was getting tired of holding up his sign, a man quite a bit younger than Sean and matching Amy's description of brown hair, brown eyes, and six-foot-something, approached Sean.

"Sean?" the stranger said.

"And you must be Rob?" Sean queried, quite relieved to drop the sign.

"Yes, I am." He extended his hand. "Thanks for picking me up. I appreciate it."

"No problem. It's the least I could do for Amy."

Rob said nothing, but glanced at Sean suspiciously.

"Come on, let's go get your baggage."

"Yes, please. I'd like to get out of the airport."

It took another half hour, but Rob's baggage was finally collected, and they made their way to Sean's car. Rob laughed when he saw it.

"What's so funny?" Sean asked. "It's not in that bad of shape."

"You drive a Ford?"

"Yes, and?"

"It's an American car. Why would you drive that?"

"We have imports, too." Sean shrugged. "I don't know. Guess I've always had an interest in America."

"You've never been there?" Rob asked as his baggage was loaded into the trunk.

"No," Sean answered as they got in the car. "Never been fortunate enough to make the trip."

"Why not? I mean if you want to go, why don't you?"

Sean looked at the other man and laughed.

"What?" Rob asked, wondering what faux pas he may have committed.

"No wonder you're with Amy—you both share the same nature." Sean laughed at Rob's questioning look. "You're both quite direct." Sean smiled as he pulled the car out of the parking space and out of the parking garage.

"Oh, that." Rob chuckled. "Yeah I guess you're right. It's just how we are, it's normal for us. Some people get offended, though."

"I can imagine." Sean lapsed into silence.

After a few moments, Rob cleared his throat. "You're seeing Mary?"

Sean recognized Rob was looking for assurance that he himself wasn't anything more than a friend to Amy. "Yes," he said.

"How's that going?"

"Well, I guess," Sean shrugged. "We're still trying to decide what we want to do."

Rob studied him for a few more moments before speaking again.

"Mary's a friend of mine, and a damn good woman, I value her friendship highly. What do you mean that you are trying to decide what to do?" Rob's face was stern.

"Rob, really? You're not her father, and I assure you my intentions are honorable. I think very highly of Mary." Sean's voice was filled with laughter.

Rob laughed. "Sorry. She had a rough time of it in the past. I just want to make sure she doesn't get hurt again."

"You sound just like Amy." He gave Rob an amused look. "What's with you two?"

"Don't know," Rob shrugged. "Guess we're in sync."

"Apparently."

"So, Sean, do you have plans for her?" Rob said but with a smile.

"None of your damn business, Rob."

"Point taken. I had to ask."

"Of course."

They were silent for a while again as they made their way to

Mary and Amy's rental flat. Sean looked over at Rob, who was trying to take in all of the sights and sounds of a new city.

"I hope you're prepared," he said.

"Prepared?" Rob raised an eyebrow, brown eyes curious.

"I think your fiancée has been missing you something fierce and may actually eat you alive when you show up." He smirked.

"*Umm...*" Rob wasn't sure how to respond.

Sean just laughed, and they finished the drive into Dublin.

THEY ARRIVED AT the flat twenty minutes later. Rob retrieved his luggage from the trunk, and Sean led him up to the front door and rang the bell. He was buzzed in and led the way down the hall to Mary's flat but, just as he was about to knock, Amy emerged, glanced at him with a frantic gaze, but calmed as she saw Rob. She indelicately pushed Sean out of the way and threw herself into Rob's arms as Rob dropped the luggage and gathered Amy to him. Mindless of anyone who might be watching them, they locked their lips in a seemingly never-ending kiss.

Sean turned away and saw Mary behind him, watching Amy and Rob with a bit of fascination at their uninhibited public display of affection. Sean picked up the luggage and brought it inside the flat, setting it on the floor. When he turned back to the hallway, Rob and Amy were still lost in each other, touching and kissing. He cast a sideways glance at Mary.

"Should we break them up and drag them back in here?"

"No," Mary shook her head. "They usually figure it out pretty quickly. If they're still at it in five minutes, then maybe." She took a last look at her roommate and turned to face Sean. "Can you stay for a bit? I have tea, or beer."

"Beer? And what kind of beer do you have?" He smiled at her.

"Guinness, of course." She loved the way the corner of his eyes crinkled when he smiled like that.

He nodded in approval. "Good, you're getting used to Ireland."

"I have a good teacher." She smiled at him, and they gazed at each other for a few seconds.

"Well, I appreciate the offer, but I actually have an early work day tomorrow. Regional business meeting." He made a face. "I have to make a presentation."

"Oh, you really *are* a big deal at work."

"Well, sort of," he acknowledged. "It has perks, but it has downsides as well." He took her hand in his and gave it a squeeze. "Can I have a rain check?"

"Yeah, just don't make it too long."

"I won't, I promise." And much to Mary's surprise, he leaned over and gave her a kiss. A sweet, gentle kiss, but she pulled him back to her and opened her mouth to him, and their kiss grew passionate, deep, and breathtaking. When they broke apart, still looking into each other's eyes, he slowly stepped away from her.

"I'll see you later," he said, his eyes still dark with desire.

"Yes," she squeaked out and watched as he turned to leave.

He stopped in the doorway, and saw Rob and Amy in the hallway, still oblivious to the world around them as they continued their kissing. Sean grinned and looked back at Mary. "Don't forget to bring them in. Hate to leave them out here all night long."

They laughed as Sean made his way past the involved couple and down the hallway. Mary sighed as she looked after him and went out to shepherd the pair back into the flat.

LATER, SEAN SAT alone in his apartment, before the television, not seeing nor caring what was on. What was it about Mary that enchanted him so? She was pretty, but in a cute sort of way— certainly no striking beauty, but there was a great deal more to her than to any woman he had ever known. She was compassionate, smart, and had a warm, caring heart. She was also stubborn and determined, which he rather liked. And she was a much better kisser than he had ever expected. Since that was true, what about the rest of it?

He mentally tried to pull himself away from those daydreams, but couldn't. He imagined what it would be like to be with her, to hold her in his arms and to make love to her whenever he wanted, and found himself becoming aroused at the thought of her. It was that damn kiss.

Whatever these feelings were, they were new to him, and he found them rather disconcerting. He had lost control once in his life, in his youth, with Maggie, and he was determined never to make that mistake again. But this feeling was different. He felt lust, passion, to be sure, but there were also deep, overwhelming feelings that threatened to engulf him, and that frightened him. He had felt them building, but had put them aside to be dealt with later. Apparently, later had arrived.

He wanted to be more than friends with Mary; he wanted a full-blown, honest adult relationship with her, a truth he was desperately trying to keep from himself. He didn't want a fling, he wanted the opportunity to know her in every way imaginable, to know her mind, her heart, and body more intimately than he had ever known a woman before; and hopefully, from that, to build a life with her. The cold hand of fear clutched at his heart, but was quickly replaced by the warmth of the growing emotions he was feeling for her. What an interesting sensation it was, a feeling stronger than fear had removed the coldness from his heart.

The image of Rob and Amy's passionate embrace played in his mind and wondered if things could ever be like that for him and Mary. Maybe he needed to be courageous enough to find out, courageous enough to bc thc man he knew he could be.

Sean turned off the television.

Yes, it was time to change things for the better, time to get off the fence and get on with his life and, God willing, Mary would go with him.

Chapter 9
Haunted Places

*T*HE EXPRESSION ON Sean's face was one of amused tolerance as he regarded Mary.

"What?" she asked.

"You really want to take a tour of haunted places in Dublin?"

She gave him a worried look. "Why? Do you think that's weird?"

"Well, let's just say that it's not what I expected to do on a date with you."

"But I told you I'm interested in the supernatural, and as long as I'm here, I might as well check out some of the supposedly haunted places in Ireland." She sat back against her couch and regarded him with curiosity. "You mean you've lived here all of your life, and you've never checked out any of the haunted places?"

"No, I guess it never occurred to me." He smiled and uncrossed his legs as he settled back into the couch next to her. "Besides there were all sorts of ghost stories and folk tales in the area I grew up in. Guess I learned to ignore most of them."

"The town you grew up in has ghost stories?" Mary's hazel eyes danced with interest.

"Yes, but don't get too excited, every town and city in Ireland has at least a couple of ghost stories."

"*Hmm.*" Mary seemed somewhat disappointed.

"Where do you want to go today? A guided tour or go off on our own?" He draped an arm around her shoulders.

"I want to go where we want..."

"You mean where *you* want?" He grinned at her.

"Well, yes."

"And where will we start?"

"At St. Michan's Protestant Church. It's very old and contains mummified remains."

"And that excites you?"

"Yes, that and the fact it's supposed to be haunted. Supposedly you can occasionally hear voices when visiting the mummified remains and sometimes feel a presence."

Sean shuddered. "I don't think that sounds like fun at all."

"It will be a lot more interesting if I pick up on something."

"What does that mean?"

"I sense things sometimes. Like with you."

He chuckled softly. "Me?"

"Yes, you." She took his hand in hers and intertwined their fingers. "Don't you feel a strange connection between us? Like, I don't know, like we've known each other before?"

"Yes, I guess I have," he said slowly. "I thought I was just imagining that feeling, but if you're feeling it, too, what does it mean?"

"I haven't figured it out yet, but I will. In the meantime, will you be my personal tour guide of haunted Dublin?" Her face crinkled in a lovely smile.

"Yes, but on one condition. You have to go to dinner with me after we are done. And I will ask that you dress up, because I would like to take you to someplace nice. I have reservations," he finished with a wink.

"Sean, that'd be great!" She leaned in to kiss him.

They kissed for a few minutes until she pulled herself away from him, stood up, and pulled him to his feet. She took his hand and led him to the door and out of the flat.

THE WORN STONE structure seemed out of place surrounded by the busy streets of Dublin. A modern, structure of steel and glass loomed over it as if to crush it. But still the small Protestant church stood in defiance of the upstart gleaming buildings that surrounded it, serene with its well-established place in the world.

Mary stood quietly, staring at the church, studying its stone exterior, respecting its age and history and generally trying to absorb any feelings she could take in from viewing its exterior. Like many small churches, a cemetery was on the church grounds immediately outside of the church. She found the cemeteries fascinating, not because she was the least bit ghoulish, but rather because the history contained on the markers in memory of the people that had died. It was a way to respect those that had gone before her, and she hoped to talk Sean into visiting the small graveyard on the way out. She glanced over at her companion and saw that he was looking at the church as though he had never seen it before. He caught her watching him and with a smile, gestured her toward the entrance.

They went through the public entrance and made their way into the parish church. Sean was suitably respectful and made the sign of the cross.

"It's not a Catholic church," Mary said as she observed him.

He shrugged. "It's still a church, isn't it?" He chaffed a little under her scrutiny. "I'm still a good Catholic boy, just a bit displaced," he grumbled and she nodded in acknowledgment. "What about you?"

"I'm loosely Lutheran but open to all possibilities."

"So you believe?"

She stopped for a moment and considered, and nodded. "Yes, but probably not the same as you."

"Meaning what?" he asked, not sure this was the time and place for a serious discussion, but letting his curiosity get the best of him.

Mary smiled at him and spoke quietly. "I was raised Lutheran and followed what I was taught, Bible study, confirmation, all of the things I was supposed to do."

"But?" He arched an eyebrow in question.

"But I grew up to be an adult and saw the world was a bigger place than the teachings of how I was raised. I realized that most religions have a common base and that, in my opinion, many similar beliefs. I think fighting because of a difference about these beliefs is incredibly stupid."

"Agreed, and you don't adhere to one teaching?"

"No. Let's just say I'm open to possibilities. I've seen too many strange things in life to discount anything really." She gave him a bright smile.

"Which is why you believe in the paranormal? Have you seen a ghost?"

"Seen? No." She shook her head. "Felt a presence? Known something else was with me? Yes." She considered for a moment before continuing. "I think there's much more than what we are aware of in the physical world, but that doesn't necessarily mean things like ghosts, spirits, are evil."

"No?"

"Is every person you meet bad? Many spirits are humans that have passed from this existence and I believe this carries over into the spiritual world as well."

"*Huh.*" He made a grunting noise as if considering this for the first time.

"You're actually Irish, and you don't believe in ghosts?"

"Not all of us do," he said defensively.

Mary laughed quietly, a pleasant sound in the stillness of the church.

"But I respect that you do."

"You're funny," she replied with a smile and stepped over to the nearby marker, reading more on the history of the church. "Were you aware of St. Michan's history?"

"Some. Let's see what I remember. It was established over a century ago 1090 or something as an early Norse chapel. Later a Catholic chapel was built over the ruins but it became a Protestant church when it was reconstructed in the late 1600s. It's most unique feature is the crypts below with mummified remains." He smiled at her. "How'd I do?"

"Pretty good. Were you reading the marker?"

He grinned and held up his hand, thumb and forefinger indicating a small space between them. "Maybe a little."

"*Hmm.* I thought you were the history buff."

"I am a bit. Are you aware that there's a rare and special pipe organ in this church?"

Mary shook her head. "Somehow that sounds like a joke."

Sean ignored her. "It's a pipe organ that was installed in 1724 and supposedly Handel first played the 'Messiah' on it."

"Impressive and very cool." Mary looked out the entrance they had come in and remembered the signs she had seen. "It seems we have to access the crypt from an outside entrance."

"Probably true."

"You've never seen the crypts?"

Sean shuddered, a ripple of unease working through him. "No, I've never had any interest in it."

"You aren't scared, are you?" Mary teased.

"No. Of course not." He masked his sudden unease and gestured toward the door that led back outside. "Ladies first," he said and smiled at her easy laugh, reminding himself that if she wasn't afraid he certainly had nothing to worry about.

THE LARGE GRAY doors appeared to be planted into the earth protecting what lay within, and Sean found the image quite disturbing. The fact that the doors to the vault had a heavy chain and padlock that had to be unlocked before people could be let into the vault, which were now propped open, did nothing to ease his apprehension. He watched Mary standing at the entrance, her eyes alight with anticipation. He sighed, trying to shake off his strange feelings, and managed to give her a smile as he followed her through the doors. He found himself on a small, weathered stone stairway that led through a narrow cellar and into the crypt area. He pulled on the collar of his shirt, trying to control his breathing.

"Are you all right?" Mary asked.

"Yeah, good," he muttered, reminding himself that it was really only a basement he was in.

"Good, come on." She grabbed his hand and pulled him along. "Our timing couldn't have been better."

"How's that?" He gave her a worried look.

"No one is here but us. At least for a little bit we have the place to ourselves."

"Grand," he said in a dry voice.

"Sean, what's wrong?"

"Nothing, I told you."

Her raised eyebrow and skeptical look demanded an answer.

"It's nothing. It's just... uneasy." So embarrassed was he at his admission that he almost swallowed the last word.

"Is that code for scared?"

"Why would I be scared?" he blustered.

"You tell me." She studied him for a few moments. "Maybe you're psychic too."

Sean snorted and laughed. "Yeah, right."

Mary shrugged. "Whatever, Sean. Come on, let's go," she said and began to make her way through the crypt. She moved slowly, often stopping to close her eyes and inhale deeply.

"What are you doing?" he finally asked, not at all sure of her actions.

"Feeling the area, sensing for spirits."

"You think some are here?" Sean's eyes darted around the area, and Mary laughed.

"Do I expect to see a ghost? No, not really, but it'd be cool, wouldn't it?"

"Cool? Cool, you say? I think it'd be downright creepy."

"Sean, how long have you been afraid of ghosts?" Mary studied him, curious as to his answer.

"Truth?" He sighed. "Ever since I was little. I was out too late once as a young lad, and it got dark before I got home; and I don't mean a little dark, I mean pitch black. There are many, many ghost stories in the town I'm from, some even state that for unknown reasons my hometown is special for them. I was a lad of seven or so, late coming home in the pitch black of a town with nothing resembling city lights. The darkness and the sounds of the night are almost a living entity of their own, especially to a young lad with a vivid imagination who watched too many horror films when he shouldn't have." He grinned at her. "My way home took me past the local cemetery, and that's when I saw it."

"Saw what?" Mary was enraptured by Sean's story.

"The image was... vague, shadowy, but seemed almost human. And it spoke, not words like... well like a voice you know, but... like in my head."

"What did it say?" Mary was completely captivated.

"It said... *boo!*" Sean's eyes lit and he couldn't resist the tease. Justifiably so, Mary hit him in the chest. He made a grunting noise of pain, but grinned at her, pleased with his story.

"It's not true? You just made up a story to scare me?"

Sean gave her a fond smile. "No, it was true enough and it scared the piss out of me."

"You saw a ghost?"

"Yeah, I think. And it told me something I'll never forget." Mary gave him a don't-push-it look, but he held up his hands in surrender. "Truth now, Mary. It said 'find the witch, she is your salvation. Beware the witch, she is your damnation.'"

"That's rather cryptic."

"Right? If these spirits are going to take the time to impart messages, you would think they'd be more direct, wouldn't you? What good is a message if you don't know what it means?" He rubbed his jaw and looked around the crypt as if considering something. "But now that I think on it, I know someone that could kindly be described as a witch."

Mary laughed and leaned in to place a kiss on Sean's cheek. "I think you're brave."

"Thanks. But I've been too creeped out since that time to want anything to do with... this." He shivered before he looked at Mary and laughed. "I ran all the way home, I'll have you know."

She put a hand over her mouth and giggled. "That spirit must have put quite the scare in you."

"Understatement." He sighed and gestured to the next room. "Let's get this over with."

The next room contained the showplace of the public crypts, four bodies who had been exposed to the air in the vault when the coffins disintegrated around them. Three of them lined up in a row next to each other were dubbed with the following identities: a nun, a man with one hand and both feet cut off—either as punishment for thievery or just to make him fit in the coffin, and an unknown woman. At the back of this set of three was a coffin placed horizontally behind them, containing a mummy known as the Crusader.

"Apparently the coffins were one-size-fits-all," Mary observed. "The mummy here with his feet and a hand cut off, that's either because he was a thief or simply because he didn't fit in the coffin."

"Ugh," Sean who had wandered to the Crusader's coffin made a face. "This poor fellow was something of a giant in his day. It says here that he was over six foot tall, and when they put him in the coffin they broke his legs just to fit him in." He grimaced.

"Sean, he was already dead. And practices at that time were

very different."

"It still doesn't make it right."

"No, it doesn't. How did the body of a Crusader get down here?"

"Don't know." Sean stepped back to read the sign and laughed. "Apparently no one else does either, but here he is." He wandered over to the set of three coffins as Mary went back to look at the Crusader. "And this poor fellow, he had his feet and hand cut off." Sean took a deep breath as he suddenly felt dizzy and gently placed his hands on the fencing in front of the ancient coffins.

"Sean, look!" Mary gasped.

Sean opened her eyes to see her pointing at a place just beyond his shoulder. Trying to control the panic he was feeling, he turned around to see a nondescript man with sandy brown hair, calm brown eyes and a winning smile dressed in a dull-brown robe regarding him. Feeling calmed to see only an oddly dressed man next to him, he turned and scowled at Mary whose eyes were still wide with wonder.

"Mary! Stop scaring me! That was payback, wasn't it?"

Mutely she quickly shook her head, her eyes never leaving the man who stood behind Sean.

"Would you stop it already? Do you believe her? She's trying to scare me!" He said over his shoulder and turned to see that the monk-like man appeared a lot more insubstantial than just a few moments ago. Sean realized that he was indeed seeing an apparition.

He shivered and clamped his mouth shut as the spirit only smiled at the two of them and nodded. "Bailey," was the gentle whisper that seemed to echo throughout the crypt, and moments later the vision faded as if it had never happened.

"Christ! I mean bollocks! Mary, what the hell just happened?" He was tightly gripping the fence but when he turned to Mary he saw that with that damned look of wonder on her face as she approached him, or rather the area behind him, hands outstretched as though reaching for the spirit.

Sean couldn't take any more. He let go of the fence and bolted, through the tunnel and out into the world outside of the crypt.

THE DRIVE TO dinner after they had completed their day was quiet, much more than normal. Mary let her gaze wander over to Sean who had remained mostly silent the rest of the day

"Are you okay?"

He gave her a quick, pointed look and nodded.

"Sean, that was amazing! We saw a ghost!" Mary crowed, unable to stay quiet on the subject any longer.

"You sound excited."

"I am. I've waited all my life to see a ghost. That was incredible! And he looked so human!"

"Well, he was once, wasn't he?" Sean muttered in a dour voice.

"And Bailey? What was that? His name maybe?"

"Odd name. Maybe he likes Bailey's Irish Cream."

Mary laughed at him. "You're really scared of ghosts, aren't you?"

"I think we've already established that. I'll leave exploring the paranormal to you. All right?" He finally offered her a genuine smile. "And now we need to change the topic."

"All right. To what?" She settled back in her seat and regarded the street in front of her.

"We're going to dinner, to a nice place and it's on me."

"Really?" Her hazel eyes appeared as a bright green and were filled with excitement and happiness, and Sean sighed at the sight. "A nice dinner with you? Sign me up."

"You're way too enthusiastic, you know that, don't you?"

Mary bit her lip and suddenly seemed uncertain. "Is it a bad thing?"

Sean reached over and squeezed her hand. "No, I like it. Passion is a good thing."

"Passion?" Without explanation, Mary felt herself blushing.

Sean only laughed, delighted by her response.

THE RESTAURANT THEY dined at was nice, with simple white tablecloths and a crystal vase holding a long-stemmed rose adorned each table, candlelight making the setting more romantic. Sean was dressed in a casual dark business suit, which accentuated his attractiveness and made him seem even more handsome. Mary was still wearing the skirt and blazer she had worn to work. Unfortunately, she had no better clothing with her, so it had to do. She looked across the table at Sean, who was just finishing his dessert. After the last few bites of his cheesecake, he pushed the plate aside, and was surprised to see Mary watching him.

"What?" he asked, smiling. "Do I have crumbs on my face?"

"No." Mary shook her head. "But I'm confused. What's the occasion? A bit elaborate, don't you think?"

"Mary, you deserve this and much, much more." He smiled again at her, his eyes twinkling with mischief, and he reached across the table, took her hand in his, and raised it to his lips.

Eyes locked, they became oblivious to all else.

THE NIGHT WAS mild, a warm spring evening to be enjoyed. They had spoken few words between them as they walked the streets of Dublin, but continued to hold hands. She sighed as they approached Sean's car, which he had parked outside of his apartment building. He stopped and smiled at her.

His expression tender, Sean said, "Before I bring you back home, I wanted to thank you for spending this evening with me."

She stepped closer, wrapped her arms around his neck, and kissed him. He drew her to him, deepening the kiss. When they broke apart, Mary felt like she was drowning in his eyes like sparkling blue pools of light. There was nowhere else she wanted to be.

Sean touched her face gently and, with a determined effort, he stepped away from her and cleared his throat.

"I'd best get you home," he said hoarsely.

Mary didn't move, only continued to look at him. He felt as if his heart were going to explode.

"No, Sean. Not tonight." She walked over and took his hand, and led him up the stairs to the entrance of his building. "This is where you live, isn't it?"

"Mary, you're sure? I have nothing to offer you, yet. My life is a mess, though I am working on straightening it out."

"It's a temporary thing," she said. "You know I'll be leaving in a couple of months anyway."

"Yes, but..."

She put a finger to his lips.

"Open the door, Sean. Let me into your life. We've both wanted this for a long time."

Sean looked into her hazel eyes, their golden specks shining with warmth, and saw nothing but determination and confidence in her decision. He put his key in the lock and opened the door.

THE APARTMENT WAS cluttered, papers everywhere, but Mary barely noticed. Sean locked the door behind him and turned to her, taking her coat from her and hanging it up by the door. Their hands touched, and he took her in his arms, lips touching softly as they gauged each other, gently exploring with hesitant touches, seeking permission at this early stage of their new relationship. The kisses deepened as they became more comfortable with one another, and mouths opened and were explored with a sense of eagerness. Their hands removed clothing from one another allowing the touch of skin on skin, the ability to caress places so long hidden from view.

Somehow they found their way to the bedroom; touching one another had become such an urgent need that even pausing long enough to complete their disrobing was an intrusion, as was the necessity of a condom. They fell onto his bed, still kissing. Sean paused long enough to brush a stray lock of hair away from her face, softly kissing her lips before he proceeded to move down her body, touching and kissing until she was groaning with pleasure. When he came up to lie beside her once again, she began leaving a trail of warm kisses on him, starting with his ears. He shivered as she blew into his ear and began to kiss his chest. He gave her a questioning gaze, a last chance for her to say "no" if that was what she wanted. His question was answered with a passionate kiss as she pulled him over on top of her. He gave up any efforts to stop what felt like the most natural thing in the world, and for perhaps the first time in his life, he truly made love to a woman.

THE SUN STREAMED in through the bedroom window the next morning, announcing the arrival of another gorgeous Irish day. Mary awoke to find herself sleeping on Sean's chest, and she sighed contentedly, snuggling against him until she felt him stir. She began to kiss his chest, quickly working her way up to his face. Although his eyes hadn't opened yet, he was smiling. After a moment, he opened his eyes to her lovely face.

"You're so beautiful." He touched his fingers to her lips, and she kissed them. "I feel like the luckiest man in the world right now."

"*Ahh*," she teased, "you Irish men are all alike. You've all got the blarney in you."

"Maybe, but you are beautiful. I've never felt like this before."

"Like what?"

"I don't know. Like nothing matters but you, like I could be here next to you forever, like parting from you will cause me physical pain."

Mary's expression grew suddenly serious. "Sean, this thing between us—it's just temporary, right? I mean, I have to go back home in a couple of months." She studied his face.

"Well, it's supposed to be, isn't it?" He kissed her. "But if I'm not careful, I'll fall in love with you," he teased, but his eyes were somber.

"Me, too," was all Mary was able to whisper d into his sweet face.

"Maybe you should stay longer?"

"That sounds serious," she said, grinning playfully.

"Maybe I am, maybe I'm not." His eyes twinkled mischievously. "Maybe I've only lured you to my bed so that you will have to marry me and have my children."

"I don't think we'll have to worry about that."

"What do you mean? Don't you think I'm virile enough for you?" he asked with mock smugness.

Mary laughed and felt him as he sidled up next to her, and she raised an eyebrow at him. "No, I would have to say it's not that. You seem more than willing to, *umm*, continue." She blushed, and he found it endearing. It only made him want her more. He quietly took her hand, placed it on a strategic part of his anatomy as they talked, and watched her with a playful expression.

"Where was I?" Mary stammered, distracted.

"We were talking about virility."

"*Umm...*"

He smiled at her discomfort.

"Really... I have great faith in you."

"Thank you," he said.

"But I'm an American."

"And? What does that mean?" he raised an eyebrow.

"It means I'm prepared. I'm on the pill. Otherwise we wouldn't have, well, you know..."

"Oh? Well, that's good." Slowly he let a grin spread across his face.

"What?" she asked absently as she continued to touch him.

"I guess it just means I'm going to have to work harder."

"I don't think that's quite how this works," she said with a laugh. "But I suppose we can find out." She gave him a playful look and took him in hand.

"*Ohh*, Mary..." He closed his eyes as her touch created waves of pleasure in him, and he wondered if he could ever let her go.

BY THE TIME Mary showed up for work at ten o' clock, the pile of papers on her desk had tripled from the night before, but it didn't faze her in the least. Humming under her breath, she sat down and cheerfully began sifting through them. When she looked up a few minutes later, she found Amy standing quietly in front of her desk, watching her.

"What?"

"You're late and didn't call in!" Amy said and pointed at the clock.

"I was... detained." Mary desperately tried to suppress the grin that wanted to spread across her face.

"Detained?" Amy raised her eyebrow.

"Yeah, so?" She tried to maintain an air of composure, but a smile crept out despite her best efforts.

Amy came closer and sat on the edge of Mary's desk. "Tell."

Mary realized Amy wasn't going to go away until she talked to her. "There's really not much to tell," she shrugged. "I stayed overnight at Sean's."

"And?" Amy leaned forward expectedly.

Mary frowned at her friend and shook her head.

"You didn't just sleep, did you? Please tell me that's not what happened." Amy sat back in disgust and shook her head. But when she regarded her friend, she saw the smile twitch at the corner of Mary's mouth. "You did it! You slept with him!" Amy got up and did a happy dance.

"A little louder, Amy, I don't think the business next door heard you!" Mary retorted in what was supposed to be an angry voice.

Amy was not about to be put off track. "Admit it, Mary, you got laid. Finally."

Mary grinned foolishly.

Amy leaned forward and dropped her voice. "How was he?"

"Amy!"

"Well, I'm not going to have a chance to seduce an Irishman, since I don't think Rob would approve."

"Amy, please!" Mary felt an unwanted blush creeping up her neck.

"*Ooh*, was he that good? Come on, I'd tell you," Amy laughed.

"You'd tell anyone. You're not exactly a private person."

"Yes, but—"

"Not here. Later, back at the flat?"

"I can't wait. I'll bring the drinks," Amy promised and left as quickly as she'd come.

The paperwork in front of her still needed completing, so Mary set about her tasks, but somehow her thoughts remained with Sean, the night she'd had with him, and what it might mean for her future.

THE SHAMROCK WAS uncrowded on a Wednesday night, and Sean sipped his drink, smiling happily to himself. What a difference a day could make! The only thing that had changed was his relationship with Mary, but that seemed to have made all the difference in the world. Words to describe how he felt, to describe the feeling that had lodged itself in his heart, the joy he felt at just thinking about her lovely smile, and her ever-changing eyes. He was startled when Kevin cleared his throat.

"Something I can do for you, Kevin?"

"Are you all right?"

"Never better. Why do you ask?"

"Well," Kevin smiled at him, "you've been grinning like a fool. Makes a man wonder what's happened to you."

"Nothing, nothing at all."

Kevin grinned and sat down beside him. "And what put you in

such a good mood? Couldn't be work, could it?"

Sean shook his head.

"It must be a woman. Not Maggie?"

"God, no!"

"Your American friend? You two have certainly spent enough time together. Are you more than friends?"

Sean grinned and nodded.

Kevin laughed at his friend and refilled his glass. "And how do you feel about her, Sean?"

"Feel?" He frowned. "I'm not sure. I'm still sorting it out."

"And how much of the day have you spent thinking about her?"

He gave Kevin a sheepish look. "Truthfully? I don't want to tell you."

Kevin sighed and shook his head. "Sean, my friend, I hate to tell you this, but you're in love."

"What? No, I can't be." He looked at Kevin in disbelief.

"Have you ever been in love before?"

"Lust, yes. Love, no."

"Then you should know the difference."

He had to think about that for a minute. At last he pulled out a cigarette and lit one up. "Let me get back to you on this one, Kevin."

"All right, but a word of advice?" Sean waited for him to continue. "Divorce Maggie. And if you love this girl, marry her."

"It's not that simple, Kevin."

"Make it simple." Kevin said.

Sean slowly met his friend's eyes. "I think you may be right. It's time. Time to move on with my life, time to contact a barrister."

"Good God, man. You are in love." He gave Sean an odd look. "You'll do this for her?"

Sean nodded.

"Good enough. I'll have to thank her for her influence on you when you give me a proper introduction. You'll marry her?" Kevin asked, eager for his friend to be happy.

Sean laughed and held up a hand. "One thing at a time, Kevin, don't you think?"

"Right, sorry, you're right. The divorce first."

Kevin patted his friend on the shoulder. "I'll catch up with you later, but right now I've got business to take care of."

Sean nodded and watched as Kevin walked away. Strangely, the prospect of being married again inspired no fear. The thought of waking up beside Mary every morning and sharing his life with her made him feel good. God, he really was in love with her. The first thing he needed to do was to talk to a barrister and find out the procedure to get his divorce started, but that could wait until tomorrow. Tonight, he had a date with Mary, and he wasn't about to let anything spoil it.

He put out his cigarette and wondered what he could get for her that would make an impression. What kind of gift would make her smile?

AFTER DINNER THAT night, in another one of Dublin's fine restaurants, a waiter approached the table where Sean and Mary sat. Sean nodded to him. The waiter disappeared behind a wall for a moment and reappeared, bearing a bouquet of flowers and a small box as he approached Mary from behind.

Mary couldn't see behind her, but saw Sean suddenly smile, his blue eyes twinkling. "What's going on?" she asked.

"Mary, you have such a suspicious mind."

The waiter stopped beside her, bowed, and presented her with the bouquet of fragrant flowers. Just as she was experiencing feelings of happiness from that considerate gesture he placed a small box before her on the table.

Her expression changed from utter astonishment to happiness, and Sean smiled at her.

"Mr. Calhoun has asked that you read the card which accompanies the flowers," the waiter said smoothly and, with a final bow, departed to his other duties.

"Oh, Sean, this is wonderful." Mary smelled the lovely flowers, and reached for the card tucked inside the bouquet.

"Read it out loud." Sean suggested.

She opened the small envelope, pulled out the card, and after a moment, began to read. 'To the finest woman I know. Sean.' *Hmm...* It's not very romantic," she said at last.

"Oh," he said, his expression crestfallen.

"I mean, everything else is, but maybe you need a little more practice with writing."

"Maybe," he sighed. "Okay, forget about my dubious skills with the pen. Open the box."

Obediently, Mary picked up the box in front of her and slowly opened it. A small pair of diamond earrings winked back at her, their brilliance apparent even in such subdued lighting.

"Oh, Sean. They're beautiful!"

"Do you think so? I saw them and know they were for you because of how they shine. But your smile puts them to shame."

Mary wondered at the ease of their transition to such a loving place in their relationship. A man hadn't treated her with such care and tenderness in a long time, and she found her emotions were threatening to overwhelm her, as she reached for his hand, turning it over so that she could stroke his palm. "Sean?"

"Yes. Mary?"

"Can we go home now? I want to thank you properly." Her gaze lingered over him warmly, the desire darkening the golden flecks of color in her eyes.

"Check please!" he said urgently as a waiter passed by them.

Chapter 10
The Problem

THE EARRINGS GLITTERED, sparkling brightly as they bathed in the sunlight from the nearby window. It was midmorning on a Saturday, and Mary sat in her kitchen, staring at the diamond earrings nestled contentedly in their jewelry box of blue crushed velvet. She'd been up since eight, had a light breakfast of toast and coffee, browsed through the paper, and spent the last hour contemplating her marvelous gift.

The look in his clear blue eyes burned bright with desire and love for her, she was sure of it! And despite her words and best intentions about maintaining a temporary relationship, the worst possible thing had happened—she had fallen in love with Sean, and she was finally admitting it to herself.

Mary sighed and reluctantly closed the box. She needed to stop thinking about Sean and face the day. Rob was back visiting Amy, and they wanted to meet up with Mary and Sean for lunch. Since it was already eleven, she'd best get herself in gear if she had any hope of being on time. Still smiling, she carried her prized box into the bedroom with her, setting it down carefully on the dresser as she began to change.

THOUGHTS SPUN AROUND in his head, ideas that were new to him, and he felt utterly clueless as to what to do with these new overwhelming feelings for Mary. Mary was the most beautiful, loving woman he had ever met, and he could hardly believe that she was his. How had he gotten this lucky? A final ending with Maggie had never really mattered before, but now nothing mattered more than being with Mary, than clearing up this mess so that he could spend the rest of his life with her.

This brought about a couple of problems. The actual divorce from Maggie, which he knew would be an ordeal, and telling Mary he was technically still married. He should have told her when he'd first started seeing her, but he'd really thought they would be friends, and nothing more until he had fallen in love with her.

He expelled a long sigh. He needed to get feedback from someone he trusted, and that was a very short list. Within moments, he found himself dialing home, wanting to talk to Lillie.

THE PHONE RANG, and Lillie ran into the house, trying to catch it before it stopped, but missed the caller. She frowned at the phone but shrugged it off, knowing that if it was important the caller would phone back later. Having chores to do she left the house and walked onto the dirt road that ran by their home, on her way to the small church in town. She enjoyed spending her time at the church, working with Father Murphy, the town priest who had been there as long as most of them could remember. It was getting harder and harder for the elderly priest to tend to the church and his flock, so Lillie helped out when she could. It was something worthwhile that filled her days, and something she enjoyed.

The small Catholic church was set back off a small dirt road on the edge of town, its stone façade worn but welcoming. The old wooden door was heavy and starting to stick, but still mostly worked, so it remained as it was. Lillie opened it with a bit of difficulty and closed it behind her. She was surprised when she saw Patrick with a bucket and mop, scrubbing the floor.

"Patrick? I didn't expect to see you here," she said.

"Hello, Lillie," Patrick nodded at her. "How are you today?"

"Fine, and yourself?"

He gave her a small smile. "Fine as well."

"I haven't seen you here for a bit."

"I've been busy. I had some free time today. Maggie's gone." He shrugged. "I come to help out when I can."

"That's nice of you; I know Father Murphy appreciates the help you give him."

Patrick offered her a rare smile. "I like helping him; he's not getting any younger."

"So that's why you've been showing up more often. I had wondered."

"What?" He stopped what he was doing and looked at her. "You're not the only one who sees what is going on in town, how some of our own are aging. They need help once in a while, and sometimes I help. That's all."

Lillie smiled at Patrick. "Will you be here for a while?"

"Yes, and you?"

"For a while, too. I'm going to help him with his accounting. Small though this may be, he still has to report to his superiors."

"That's nice of you, Lillie." He watched her for a moment. "Say, you aren't hungry, are you?"

"Not yet, but I will be when we are finished. Why?"

He dipped the mop in the bucket and began scrubbing for a moment before he looked at her again. "I thought, maybe, since we would both be hungry, well, we could stop by The Gaelic Moon?" He dropped his eyes and began mopping again as if he hadn't said anything.

She waited a long moment until he looked back at her. "That would be lovely," she agreed.

"Stop by when you are done," he said.

"I will. Thank you, Patrick," she said and touched his arm as she brushed by him. She couldn't see the small smile that turned up the corner of his mouth.

THE CHURCH OFFICE was small, and the furniture worn, but it suited the aging priest who sat behind the small desk. He was a small man, with thinning white hair, thick glasses that hid lovely brown eyes, and a sweet smile. He smiled when he saw Lillie enter the office.

"*Ahh*, my dear, good to see you again," he said.

"Sorry I'm late, Father."

"No problem at all. It's not like I'm going anywhere fast, am I?" He laughed at his own weakness.

"Father Murphy, you're only getting better with age."

"You do an old man's heart good," He sighed. "You will help

with the books?"

"Yes, and whatever else I have time for." She reached across and patted his hand.

"You're a blessing, Lillie."

"You're a kind man, Father, and I thank you."

"You need a husband, you're far too good of a soul to waste away helping out an old man like me."

Lillie's answer was a warm, but amused smile.

The old man watched as Lillie took out her calculator and pencils and got ready to work on the rectory accounts.

THE GAELIC MOON was quiet during that day's lunch rush, and Lillie was glad as it would give her a chance to actually talk to Patrick, to see if she could get him to open up a little. He sat across from her, his dark hair spread in disarray across his forehead, silent as he focused on his drink. He had always been a quiet child, and now he was a quiet man. She took a sip from her drink and waited knowing if she were patient, he would eventually look at her and speak. When he did, she gave him a small smile.

"How's the drink?" he asked her.

"Fine, and yours?"

"Fine."

They regarded each other in a comfortable silence.

"Where is Maggie?" Lillie asked.

"Never were one for small talk, were you, Lillie?" Patrick asked, but laughed softly. "She's out and about somewhere with a Scottish fellow by the name McTavish or something. Says he's her mentor, and they discuss the things they learn from books."

"Maggie? Studying?" She gave him a skeptical look.

He shrugged. "It's what she says. She calls this fellow her good luck charm."

Lillie heard the note of jealousy in his voice. "And you're not happy about it?"

"Would you expect me to be? I bend over backward to please her, and she never sees any of it except when it's convenient for her. She does whatever she wants and leaves me behind." He took a long drink from his beer and sulked.

"Patrick?" Lillie said gently and touched his hand.

He frowned.

"Why do you put up with her? Surely you know you can do better?"

"What do you mean? What do I really have to offer anyone? I'm a common worker who has lived here all of his life, not a successful businessman like your brother."

"You have a lot of good qualities," Lillie said.

He huffed. "Like what?"

"Like you have a good heart, you're extremely loyal, and you're helpful to those in need."

He blushed and stared into his beer glass. "Really?" He raised his eyes up and offered her a shy smile. "Thank you, Lillie."

She blushed and decided her beer glass was the most fascinating thing in the world.

THE LUNCH WAS nice, if nothing special—pub grub, but good. In America, Mary had the shepherd's pie, as she wanted something filling and warm, while Sean had the bangers and mash, Rob stuck with a hamburger and fries, and Amy had the chicken curry. It was filling, satisfying, and along with various kinds of alcohol, made for a wonderful midday meal.

Mary felt quite content and leaned into Sean. "I shouldn't have eaten so much," she said.

"No one made you do it, so you have no one to blame but yourself," he said with a smile. "If you get fat, it's your own fault."

"Fat?" She elbowed him in the ribs, and across the table, Rob laughed.

"Don't you know better than to provoke Mary? She's really nice until you cross her."

"Yeah, ask that catcher she ran over," Amy added.

Sean gave Mary a curious look, and she shrugged. "It was nothing, just a softball game."

"Nothing? You called that nothing?" Amy protested. "You ran that poor girl over like a semi against a Volkswagen bug."

Mary squirmed under the attention. "It wasn't that bad!"

"Oh yes it was!" Rob chimed in.

Sean regarded the woman next to him. She hardly seemed lethal. Although with the new information, he realized he wasn't really familiar with this competitive side of her nature and wondered how that figured into her life.

"Should I be afraid now?" Sean asked in mock horror.

"No!" Mary hit his arm. "I was only playing a game and wanted to win."

"Very competitive," Rob said helpfully.

"Yeah, she still has a scar," Amy snorted, "Tell me you didn't hit her hard."

"It's not a scar, it's a deep bruise."

"That never healed?" Sean was curious. "Let me see."

Mary raised an eyebrow and regarded him. "What if it's in a place that should only be shown discreetly?"

He grinned. "Then show me discreetly." Amusement danced in their eyes as they watched each other.

"You could just get a room," Rob chimed in helpfully and the women smacked him as he laughed.

"Just show him," Amy said with a nudge.

"Okay," Mary grinned and bent over, lifting her eyebrow as Sean watched her. She rolled up her pant leg and flashed her ankle at him. "It's there," she outlined what looked like a dark mark and lifted her foot up so it rested on Sean's lap.

He looked at it curiously and frowned as he examined it. "It looks like a deep bruise. Does it hurt?"

Mary shook her head, "No. It stopped hurting a long time ago."

"It's a shape. It resembles a moon. And the bruising makes it almost look blue."

"I guess."

"That's really weird," Sean said.

"Why?" Amy shrugged and looked at her friends.

Sean smiled at them, bent over, and rolled up his pant leg. "I did this in a rugby match several years ago." He put his leg up on Mary's lap and she saw a scar that was nearly a mirror reflection of her scar. If the two pieces were put together they would form a complete circle.

"That's bizarre. Were you two separated at birth?" Rob asked.

"It is odd," Sean agreed.

"I wonder what it means," Mary said with a grin.

"Let's find out," Sean said and pressed his scar against Mary's.

A brief feeling like a static electricity shock tickled them. They laughed as they pulled their legs back and rolled down their respective pant legs.

"That's strange enough to warrant another round of drinks," Amy declared.

"Maybe," Sean shrugged. "So, Mary, besides sports where else are you aggressive? Perhaps in business?"

"No," Mary said.

"Yes," Amy said, and smiled at her friend. "It's how you got where you are and you might as well admit it."

"I like a woman who has drive, who knows what she wants," Sean said.

"Sounds like you found a keeper! One of these days she'll follow through and actually start her own business," Rob said and drained his beer. "I like the same thing, and I've found my keeper, too." He pulled Amy close and gave her a kiss, and another, and one more for good measure before they broke apart.

Sean and Mary looked at each other and laughed.

"As you can see, this is a constant thing with these two," Mary joked.

"How do you stand it?" he asked, bemused.

She laughed. "Ear plugs."

"You could come and stay with me if they get to be too much," he said quietly so that only she could hear.

Her eyes lit up. "Sean, really?"

"Really." He gave her a kiss, but she pulled him in for another and their kiss deepened as Amy and Rob watched them.

"Yes!" Amy said gleefully, giving Rob a squeeze.

"About time," Rob agreed.

They laughed as Mary and Sean finally broke apart and blushed with the realization that they had an audience.

"Come on, Mary, time to go to the little girl's room," Amy said as she got up and grabbed her friend's hand.

"But, Amy..." Mary protested as she followed.

Rob laughed at the two women before looking back at Sean. "You two seem to be getting on well," he said.

"Well, *err*, yes." Sean sighed. "Is this where you're going to ask my intentions toward Mary again?"

"*Nah*, I've already done that. You're both adults; you figure it out. Just don't hurt her."

Sean sighed.

"That was a big sigh. Want to talk about it?"

"Not especially, no," Sean said.

Rob gave him a look that said he'd better talk or else.

Sean sighed again and looked at Rob. "If I talk to you, this has to stay between us."

"A guy thing?" Rob asked, and Sean nodded.

"For now."

"All right," Rob agreed.

Sean nodded and took a deep breath. "I have a problem that I have to deal with; I have a jealous ex who doesn't want to let me go. She hasn't heard about Mary yet, but there will be hell to pay when she does."

"An ex?" Rob gave Sean a suspicious glance. "Why would you still be involved with her?"

"My home town is small, a village almost. Everyone knows everyone and, unfortunately, most everything about everyone. When the rest of my family knows about Mary, they will, too." He sighed again.

"Does Mary know about your ex?"

"No, it didn't seem like the right time to bring it up yet. We haven't been together long and we're still learning about each other."

"But you will take care of it?" Rob said in his best protective big-brother voice.

"*Aye*, I will. Mary means too much to me not to treat her well. I just have some personal business to clean up, that's all." He offered Rob a smile as their new drinks arrived. "*Slainte!*" he said, lifting his glass to Rob's.

"*Slainte!*" Rob said, not quite sure what it meant, only knowing it was Irish and he was in an Irish pub, thus it must be appropriate.

They both took a long drink, and Rob remained thoughtful for a moment before he spoke.

"I like you, Sean, really I do. I hope things work out for you and Mary. I don't know your background, but I have the impression that both you and Mary could use a break. I think you're good for each other."

"Thank you, Rob. I appreciate the vote of confidence." He nodded his head over toward the dart board. "Wouldn't care for a game of darts, would you?"

"Darts? I'm pretty good," he said.

"Not as good as me, I bet."

"Care to put your money where your mouth is?" Rob said in a friendly voice.

"Anytime. What stakes?"

"The loser pays for dinner, for the four of us, tomorrow."

Sean laughed. "I didn't know the four of us had made plans."

"We're making them now." He raised an eyebrow. "Can you make it?"

"I guess I'd better put it on my calendar. Couldn't have the lot of you dragging me away, could I?" Sean smiled. "I hope you have a large checkbook," he added as they drifted over to the dartboard.

Rob just laughed. "Bring it on, Irish boy..."

Later that evening Sean sat in Kevin's apartment, downing drinks and smoking as they watched the television. Sean rubbed his face and looked over at Kevin, who hadn't really said much about Sean's love affair with the American woman. "Well?" Sean demanded at last. "Say something."

"Something," Kevin quipped and smiled.

"You moron, that's not what I mean."

Kevin was silent for a moment. "What do you want me to say, Sean?"

"The truth."

"The truth? Only you know the truth. Do you love her enough to finally end things with Maggie?"

Sean nodded. "It will be hard, but Mary makes everything worth it." He yelped when a pillow bounced off his head. "What was that for?"

Kevin laughed. "It's because you're such an idiot. You are obviously in love, and if Mary loves you even half as much, you should marry her." He shook his head. "Did you really need to hear me say that?"

"I guess not. It's just I've never felt like this about a woman before."

"It happens to us all eventually, or it does if we are lucky," Kevin said. "Congratulations, my friend."

They were a quiet for a few moments before Sean spoke again. "There might be another problem though. *Umm*, well, I haven't exactly told Mary that I'm married."

"What?" Kevin gave him a you've-got-to-be-kidding look.

"Well, I didn't think we'd ever be more than friends, so I didn't see a reason to bring it up."

"And now you're sleeping with her and haven't told her?" Kevin scowled and shook his head. "What would ever make you think that kind of thing was all right? Americans are different, you know. When marriages don't work out, they get divorced, and they don't let things linger as you've done. Most women won't knowingly sleep with a married man. How are you going to get past that?"

A deep frown was now embedded on Sean's face.

"Sean, you're my friend, but apparently you're an idiot." Kevin took a deep breath and collected himself. "No matter what, you have to tell her, and the sooner the better." Kevin sighed. "You need to be honest with her, but she's going to hate it. She'll be madder than hell, and hurt. Unless maybe you had something to prove that you're sincere about ending your marriage?"

Sean sighed. "I've started divorce proceedings."

"Maybe it's enough?" Kevin drained his shot glass and poured another for each of them.

"Thank you, Kevin." Sean grimaced. "Maybe I can salvage this mess after all."

"Well, I hope it works out. You've certainly put both of you in difficult positions."

"I'll do whatever I have to do to be with her." Sean said quietly.

"It will all work itself out. Just have faith."

Sean nodded. With faith everything would work itself out, he only had to believe.

Chapter 11
Marriage

B
Y THE NEXT Friday, Sean still hadn't left for home, but he realized he couldn't put it off any longer. He needed to see how his mother and sister were doing and, perhaps more importantly, make sure Maggie wasn't up to any mischief. Her silence since their encounter couldn't mean anything good, but even that didn't matter because he was finally going to end things once and for all.

A stray hair fell into Mary's face, and he gently brushed it away as she lay asleep in his arms. That he desired her went without saying, but his feelings for her were astounding, so deeply intimate that they scared him.

She stirred, blinked, and smiled sweetly at him. "Morning," she said and yawned. "How long have you been awake?"

"Just a bit. Would you like some tea?"

"Not just yet. I just want to lie here next to you."

"For as long as you want," he said, enjoying the feel of her in his arms. After a few moments, he reluctantly cleared his throat. "Mary, I have to go home."

"To see your mother and sister?"

"Yes."

"How long will you be gone?"

"A few days, I think. I have to do house repairs and tend to some business." He quietly nibbled her ear. "I haven't been home since I met you."

"I wish you didn't have to go."

"I know. I'll be back as soon as I can." He kissed her.

"Sean, what's happening with us?"

He gently caressed her face. "What do you mean?"

"Are we in a temporary relationship? Or is it something different?"

"Mary, do you want more than this?"

"Yes," she whispered. She searched his eyes for answers.

He turned away from her, unable to face the love in her eyes.

"Sean?" She turned his face to hers. "Tell me."

Unable to help himself, he reached out and tenderly touched her face. "Tell you what?"

"What you want. For you. For us."

"*Aww*, Mary, there's no easy answer to that." He searched her face and wanted to drown in the love he saw in her eyes. "I love you." The words had spilled out of his mouth of their own accord, and he found he didn't regret them.

She looked at him in disbelief, trying to still the joy that was leaping from her heart. "What?"

"I love you, Mary. I think I have for a long time, but I didn't want to admit it." He softly kissed her forehead. "But I think I shouldn't have said that. It will give you the wrong idea."

"Wrong idea?" The expression on her face was pure joy, and his heart warmed to know that he put it there. "Oh, Sean, how could that give me the wrong idea?" She leaned forward and kissed him. "I love you, too, but I was afraid to say anything. I was so afraid you didn't feel the same way, but now that you do, oh Lord, now we can be together. Finally!"

She kissed him enthusiastically, and he could do nothing but laugh. To stop her, he wrapped his arms around her and held her tight until she relaxed against him. He sighed, and she was sure something was wrong.

"What is it?" she asked.

"I don't want to tell you. You'll hate me."

He sounded so dejected that she pulled away from him and raised herself up on her elbow to look at him. "How can I hate you when I'm in love with you? Nothing can be that bad."

"I don't think you'll be saying that in a few minutes." He gave her an apologetic look, removed himself from her arms, and began to get dressed.

She watched him quietly, disturbed by his sudden withdrawal after such a serious confession. He dressed without looking at her, and when he finished, he stood up, spared her a glance, and with a smile, brought her clothes over to her.

"Sean?"

"We need to talk, and I don't think we should have this discussion in bed." He brushed a stray lock of hair from her face as he studied her. "I love you, Mary. Please believe me. No matter what you hear from me, please know it's true." He sighed. "I'll wait in the kitchen. Come out when you're ready."

Mystified, she watched as he left the room and got dressed as quickly as possible. She was in the kitchen within moments.

"That didn't take long," he said, a half-hearted smile on his face.

Something was wrong, terribly, terribly wrong. She walked across the kitchen and looked into his blue eyes, questioning him. He gently shook off her arm and walked away again.

"Sean, what? For God's sake, spit it out! You're making me crazy!"

"I don't know how to tell you this. It's very different here in Ireland than it is in the States."

"What is?"

He gave her an odd look. "Marriage."

Her mind froze at his words. Marriage? The thought had never occurred to her. Was he asking her to marry him? Was it possible? Did he love her that much? No wonder he was so nervous! What should she say? How should she react? A million possibilities ran through her mind. Did she love him? Of course she did. Was it enough to marry him? Who was she kidding? Yes, she loved him with her whole heart and wanted to marry him and spend the rest of her life with him. Her smile of love stretched across her face. "Yes," she whispered.

"Yes?" He seemed confused, and she watched as he figured out what she was answering and an expression of surprise and apprehension crossed his face.

He wasn't asking her to marry him. What a fool she was! She turned away from him, embarrassed at her faux pas.

"Oh, Mary, I'm sorry. That's not what I meant. I mean that's not what I'm asking. I mean..." He turned away, muttering some Gaelic oaths Mary didn't understand before he came to stand in front of her. "I see why you jumped to that conclusion, but I'm not asking you to marry me." He grimaced. "I can't."

"What does that mean?" Mary asked as an automatic response, still trying to sort out her internal embarrassment.

"Let me start this conversation over. Do you know how marriage works here in Ireland?"

"Well, I imagine it's much the same as in America."

"No, it's not. In fact, divorce just came in a couple of years ago."

"What happens when a marriage doesn't work?"

"The couple stays married in name only, living separate lives. Sometimes, if certain conditions are met, they can get an annulment."

"They can't get divorced and move on?"

"Oh, they move on. They're just not always divorced." He shrugged. "It's been the Irish way of things."

"That's awful."

"It can be. People are often trapped in a relationship which died long ago, something they no longer want." He searched her eyes and touched her face for just a moment.

"What are you trying to say?" she asked, heart pounding in fear.

"Mary, remember what I told you—remember I love you." He sighed and stepped back from her. "In my youth, I did an incredibly stupid thing that forever altered my life, something I've always regretted." He watched her closely. "I got married."

"Married?" She asked in shock. "You're married?"

He continued to watch her. "Technically, I am."

"Oh my God," she said at last and stared at him in horror.

"Mary, let me explain. Please give me a chance."

"You're married. You lied to me. What else is there to explain?" She turned from him to run out of the room, but he caught her hand.

"It's not what you think. My marriage only lasted a year, and I left her. We've been apart for twelve years. I would have divorced her if I could have."

"But you've had some time to do it now. Why are you still married?" she asked suspiciously.

"I should have taken care of it, but I never seemed to get to it." He sighed. "I wasn't interested in anyone, so it didn't matter."

"Does it matter now?" she asked, starting to cry.

"Yes. It's the only time it's mattered since I left Maggie."

"That's her name?" she sniffed. "Your wife?"

Sean heard the jealousy in her voice and smiled; he went over to her and placed a soft kiss on her forehead. "That's her name. She means nothing to me and hasn't for a very long time, I never loved her.

"Never?" She searched his eyes and saw the truth of his words.

"Never."

"Why did you marry her?"

"She was beautiful, every young man's fantasy, and I was a young man. It seemed the right thing to do." He shook his head and ran a hand through his unruly red hair. "Suffice to say I was coerced into the occasion, and I should have known better."

"But you're married!" Mary shook her head, unable to get over the fact.

"But, Mary, I don't have to be, not anymore." He smiled. "Don't you understand?"

"No, explain it to me."

"I'm going to get a divorce so that I can be with you."

She regarded him through her tears. "Really?"

"Really. I'm not lying to you, Mary. I'm in love with you, and I want to be with you." He watched her. "Please say you believe me."

"I don't know." She shook her head and turned away. "I can't believe this is happening to me again."

"Again?" Sean questioned.

"Yes, again, damn you. You remember me telling you about Joe?"

"*Ahh*, Mary, please don't think that. I'm not Joe, and I'm telling you the truth because I want to officially end my marriage and be with you."

"Why are you sorry? You had nothing to do with it." She glared at him. "It's always my choice of men, I never get it right."

He reached for her hand. "Mary, you got it right this time. I love you; I'm in love with you. My marriage is a technicality."

"A big one! Sean, this is a big deal. Don't you understand?" She glared at him again. "Why didn't you tell me before now? It's not like you didn't have time!"

"I didn't think it would matter. I didn't think I would fall in love with you." He looked into her eyes, and she saw his uncertainty.

"So you lied to me?"

He gave her a long look before answering, and when he did she had to strain to hear his voice. "I guess I did. I lied because I was afraid if you knew the truth you'd leave, and I'd never see you again."

"You mean something like this?" She shot past him to retrieve her coat.

He trailed after her and put his hand on her arm. "Mary, don't. Please. I do love you and want to make a life with you."

She squeezed her eyes tight, trying to contain her tears. When she looked at Sean, he saw the pain and anger fighting for dominance within her now dark eyes. "I don't know what to believe anymore," she said and turned and left his apartment. The echoing slam of the door sounded final.

WHEN MARY ARRIVED at back at the flat she was relieved to find Amy was out for the afternoon. She had a lot to think about and, much as she loved Amy, her constant babble was more than Mary could stand right now. She sat down on the couch and pulled her legs to her chest, hugging them tightly.

What was she going to do? What could she do? How had this perfect romance turned into such a disaster? She groaned as she buried her head against her knees. Dammit all to hell, she loved him. Despite everything he had told her, she still loved him. She should hate him, she wanted to hate him, but she couldn't. Not now, not yet, maybe not ever.

Do something, make a decision, she told herself, but found herself unable to do so. Maybe a drink would help her to think more clearly? She uncurled herself and went into the kitchen, rummaged through the cupboard, and found the bottle of Irish whiskey somewhat hidden in the back of the cabinet. She poured herself a large shot and downed it in one gulp. It burned so nicely down her throat that she poured herself another. She drew a deep breath and began to breathe again.

Sometime later Mary heard the sound of keys in the lock and the door to the flat opening. In her usual careless manner, Amy breezed in, shutting the door behind her. Mary sat where she was, listening to the maelstrom in the hall. She didn't move from her corner, but wondered if she should get up and say something or just remain where she was and let Amy find her.

After a few minutes, she heard Amy calling for her, but chose not to answer, Amy didn't have much reason to be in the kitchen; she never cooked anything. Maybe if Mary was quiet, Amy wouldn't even look for her, and she could just stay sitting on the floor with her surprisingly good bottle of Irish whiskey.

MARY HEARD AMY on her way to the kitchen and swore just a little bit as her best friend entered, took in the situation in a glance, as she saw the tears that welled up in Mary's eyes.

"Mary? Honey, what's wrong?" Amy's face was filled with concern as she knelt down beside Mary.

"Oh, Amy!" Mary collapsed into Amy's arms and wrapped her arms around her friend. "He's married!"

"What?" Amy drew back and looked into her friend's tear-streaked face. "Married? Are you kidding?"

She sniffed and tried to wipe away the offending tears.

Amy frowned, it didn't make sense to her. "He told you he was married?"

"Yes," she said, tears still spilling from her eyes. "It's not fair, Amy. I love him! And worse than that, he said he loves me, too!"

Amy wrinkled her brow in confusion. None of this was adding up to her, but right now it didn't matter because Mary needed a friend more than anything, Amy held Mary and whispered words of comfort as she sobbed against her. When Mary had finally cried herself out, Amy helped her up and tucked her safely into bed for the night. She vowed to herself that come hell or high water, she would straighten this out with Sean the next day.

THE NEXT MORNING, while Mary slept, Amy went over to Sean's.

He politely invited her in, his demeanor restrained and wary; it seemed as if his night wasn't any better than Mary's.

"May I take your coat?" he offered.

"I don't plan to stay long."

"To what do I owe the pleasure of your visit?"

"I'm here because of Mary," Amy said bluntly.

"Is she all right?" He didn't try to hide the concern on his face, and Amy realized his eyes were red rimmed and puffy too.

"Yes, but no thanks to you. She spent half of the night crying her heart out and the rest of it sick in the bathroom."

"She's ill?" His concern was genuine.

"Not so much ill as having to do with the whiskey she consumed when she got home."

"I didn't think Mary was much of a drinker."

"She's not. She was drinking because she was heartbroken. How dare you do this to her?"

His jaw was clenched in anger as he regarded Amy. "I didn't do anything to her. I love her."

"You slime ball, you're married!" Unable to contain her rage, she slapped him. Anger darkened his eyes for a moment before he stepped back and touched his cheek, and she saw the red mark her hand had left behind. "How dare you treat her like that when she loves you!"

"Amy, listen to me. I know you're her friend and you're trying to look out for her, but you must believe I have her best interests at heart."

"Why should I believe you?"

"Did she tell you everything I said?"

She frowned at him. "No."

"Let me enlighten you." He took a deep breath and calmed himself. "I love Mary. I am going home tomorrow to ask my wife for a divorce so that I can come back and start a life with her."

"Anyone could say that."

"I mean it," he said and walked over to his desk to retrieve a paper. He put it into her hands. "Read it."

Amy looked at the paper in her hand and realized it was a legal document asking that divorce proceedings be started for Mr. and Mrs. Sean Calhoun. She blinked in surprise. "Did you show this to Mary?"

"No, she left before I could show it to her." He sighed. "I'm sincere. I've never loved a woman the way I love Mary. I'm trying to straighten out my life so that I can come back and be with her." He ran a hand through his hair. "And just so you know, my marriage to Maggie lasted a year before we separated. That was twelve years ago." He sighed.

Amy studied the Irishman who stood in front of her, and she saw the honesty and love in his expression as he spoke of Mary. Much to her surprise, she found herself believing him. It was the last thing she had expected to come from her visit.

"How can you untangle this?"

"I'm not sure. I only know that I'm trying, and that I will. This is my future, too. What I've wanted all of my life is finally in front of me, and her name is Mary." He felt agitated. "I'll not let you take that from me, you or anyone. Do you understand?"

Amy nodded and studied him closely. "You really love Mary?"

"What have I been telling you since you walked through that damned door?" he asked in exasperation.

The tension between them broke, and Amy smiled at Sean. "If you don't follow through, I'll kick your ass. You know that, don't you?"

"Yes, I do. I'm glad she has a friend like you." He smiled back. "Can I ask you something?"

"Sure."

"Why are you being so forgiving about this? I wouldn't have expected you to listen to my side of things."

Amy was uncharacteristically quiet for a few moments. "Early in the relationship I had with Rob, I made a mistake. Even though I knew I loved Rob, I had an affair with another man."

"You what? Why?" Sean was astounded.

"I don't have a good answer, but I think I was scared. I'd always fooled around, never taken any man seriously, and I somehow met Rob. Incredibly handsome, sexy, and intelligent, he was everything I wanted, and he scared the crap out of me. He told me he loved me, and I bolted. I didn't mean to, but I did. I took an extended vacation from work, and he found me two weeks later living with a guy I'd met a week and a half before."

"What did he do?" Sean was fascinated with this unexpected

side to Amy.

"He punched out the man I was living with and told me in no uncertain terms that I had a decision to make and I had a limited amount of time to do it in. And he left, just like that." She sighed. "I thought long and hard and finally stopped thinking at all, and when I did, the choice was obvious. Rob is my true love. Mary would say he's my soul mate. I had to go back to him; I had to be with him."

She regarded the walls behind Sean lost in her thoughts. "I was lucky to find a man compassionate enough to forgive my transgression and understanding enough to know why it had happened." She looked at Sean, and he saw the tears in her eyes. "And though the two of you may be too stupid yet to realize it, I think maybe it's that way for you and Mary too."

Sean offered her a small smile. "Thanks, Amy."

"She said you're going home?"

"I have to. It's the only way to talk to Maggie. My ex won't make this easy."

"Sean." She placed a hand on his arm. "Be kind to Mary. She's been on the wrong side of this before. I don't think she could live through that again."

"Trust me, please. I will fix this."

"You'd better," Amy grumbled. "All right, I have to go back and see how she's doing. Keep this conversation between us?"

"Guaranteed."

"Thanks." She offered him a brief smile as he escorted her to the door. "You might be all right after all, Sean."

Chapter 12
Quandary

W HEN SEAN ENTERED The Gaelic Moon, he was greeted enthusiastically by the locals at the bar, who hadn't seen him for a few weeks. They chatted and exchanged stories with one another and laughed at the new jokes each had to share. After an hour, all drifted to their own places in the pub, and Sean found himself sitting alone with Donald for company.

"It's always the same," Sean complained with a smile. "Always have to share a bit of nonsense."

"Take it as a good sign. It's because they miss you."

"I know. And it's good to see them, too." He looked around the bar and over his shoulder.

"Looking for someone?"

"Maggie." Sean sighed. "Reluctant as I am, I need to speak with her."

"She's been asking about you, wondering when you were returning home. Besides, I didn't think you two were on speaking terms."

"We have personal matters to discuss."

Donald raised an eyebrow.

"Don't ask," Sean said as Donald opened his mouth to speak. "Suffice to say I've made a mistake of incredible proportions. I only hope there's not hell to pay because of it!" Sean pulled out a cigarette and lit up. He had finished half of it before he looked at Donald again. "When did she say she was coming?"

The door opened behind Sean and he felt the cool draft. He saw the faces of the men in the room and knew it could only be Maggie.

"Is now soon enough for you?" Donald answered helpfully.

Sean shot him a sarcastic look, and turned to face the woman who approached him.

"Maggie," he said flatly with a nod to her.

"Sean," she said, walking behind him, draping her arms over his shoulders. "I was wondering when you'd come home. You've held out longer than I thought you could," she whispered and stepped into his space, lying her hand on his arm.

He resisted her advances and pushed her away.

Confused by his lack of response, she crossed her arms, pouting. "You can't deny what happened."

"No, but it will never happen again."

"You said that before," she smiled at him. "And you still couldn't resist my charms."

"Charms?" He laughed in contempt. "You have about as much charm as a bulldozer." He then tried a more rational approach. "Maggie, I don't love you, and I never have. We've been separated for many years. Let's put an end to it and get a divorce."

"Divorce?" she shrieked. "Is that why you came back? To ask me this?"

Sean nodded.

"You're still my husband, aren't you?"

After a long sigh, he answered. "Technically, yes."

"There will be no divorce."

"But I don't love you!"

"But you will." Maggie put a hand on his arm and met his angry gaze. "Especially when we have a child."

His heart stopped and all of the air escaped his lungs as he gasped for breath. This was a nightmare. How could one man be so stupid as to repeat the same mistake? His eyes filled with cold rage.

"You're lying," he said.

"Did you forget our night together?"

Shame washed over him. No, he couldn't forget that night; it had been nothing but blind lust, and he had used her for that until he'd been spent. Maggie had nothing resembling a maternal instinct in the whole of her body. Though he knew it was wrong, he prayed there would be no child.

"I don't believe you. You lied before and you'd lie again. It's been months so I'm sure there'd be signs by now." His gaze was more than chilly.

Patrick, who had been watching from nearby, stepped over to Maggie's side and placed his hand possessively on her arm. "Maggie, why are you wasting time with him?" He gestured at his table. "Come, sit with me."

"Piss off, Patrick. I'm busy." She turned back to Sean. "Come back to me, Sean. It can be like it used to be. Remember? And we can finally have the family that you've always wanted."

"You're delusional. We never had a happy marriage, and we will never have a family."

"But you married me."

His eyes narrowed in anger. "Because you told me you were pregnant."

"I was."

"Until you had an abortion and murdered the child!"

Maggie glared at him.

"We are separated. I want no children with you." His gaze was cold. "I'll not believe you until I see it with my own eyes."

"You're a cold man, Sean Calhoun." She studied him, trying to read his expression and then gripped his arm tightly, suspicion in her jealous green eyes. "Another woman?"

"That's none of your business."

Patrick broke the angry silence and touched Maggie's arm. "Maggie, darlin', stop wasting your time on this one. Come and sit with me." He gently tried to steer her away from the bar, but she refused to move.

The frost in the air was almost palpable as Sean turned away and ignored her, sipping his drink instead. The fury in her gaze never wavered but, when he refused to respond, she gave Sean a final nasty look and stalked out of the bar, leaving Patrick looking after her helplessly. Glaring at Sean, Patrick left the pub as well, trailing in Maggie's wake.

Sean sat down at the bar and ordered a stiff drink, resting his head in his hands as he tried to ignore the rapid pounding of his heart and the fear that caused it to beat like that...

BACK IN HER small house, Maggie was relieving her frustration by throwing anything and everything that she could get her hands on—if it was breakable, so much the better. After a few minutes and several deep breaths, she calmed herself enough to sit and pull herself together. She surveyed the shattered mess around her and, with a rueful laugh, chanted something under her breath and clapped her hands. The shattered items miraculously put themselves back together in the places where they had been before Maggie's tirade.

"Better," she muttered and sat down at her kitchen table, drumming her fingers on the wood.

What to do now? That was the question. Sean didn't believe what she told him, so she would have to find a way to convince him. She would rather not resort to magic, but she was certainly not above doing so if it would ensure that Sean remained with her. She could cast a spell on him, forcing him to be with her, but it would undoubtedly leave only a remnant of the man she knew now. Perhaps she could still convince him without resorting to magic, or at least not resorting to magic that controlled him. In the meantime, she could visit Lucky again. He had promised her something useful the next time she saw him. Yes, she liked that plan. It would give her a chance to focus on something useful while she figured out how best to handle Sean.

LATER THAT EVENING, Sean sat outside in one of the worn wooden chairs which leaned against his house and stared at the distant green hills. He massaged his temple; the pounding in his head hadn't abated since he had woken up around noon, caused no doubt by the excessive amount of alcohol he had consumed the night before.

The door opened and Lillie came to stand before him. He didn't look up, his eyes were fixed on the distant horizon as she sat down beside him.

He didn't know whether he was irritated or relieved by her company.

"Sean, you didn't eat."

"I'm not hungry."

"Hair of the dog?"

"Partly. But there are other things."

"What's wrong?" She touched his arm. "Like all the men around here, I know you like to drink. But I have not seen you like this since your separation."

Sean turned and gave her a haggard look.

Lillie sighed. "What's she done now?"

"She came to Dublin and let herself into my apartment."

"You escorted her out, didn't you?"

"Oh, yes." He regarded his sister with a pained expression. "But not until the next morning."

"Sean!" Lillie covered her mouth as several implications sank in. "Oh, Sean. How long ago was that?"

He closed his eyes and tried to remember. "I'm not sure... ten weeks ago? I don't remember clearly. I've been trying to block it from my mind."

"*Ohh*, why is it that men are so stupid?" Lillie couldn't help herself—she hit him, and for good measure she hit him again. "Even my own brother, who knows better, has his brains in his pants!"

"I know," he said glumly. "If I had a gun, I'd shoot myself."

Lillie's expression was one of concern. "It can't be that bad."

"Yes, it can! What if she's not lying this time? What if she is pregnant?" Sean got out of his chair and paced back and forth. "Oh, my God, Lillie. What have I done?" He looked at her, and she could see the tears in his eyes. "I'll have to stay married if she is with child."

Unable to do anything else, she hugged him. Grateful, and feeling like a small boy, he hugged her back and tried to calm himself. She studied her brother's face and noticed something else, a deep sadness she'd never seen before. "What else?"

He shook his head. "It's nothing."

"Tell me."

He expelled a long sigh, stepped away from her. "I met someone."

"You've found a woman?"

He nodded. "The finest woman I've ever known. I can hardly

bear it when I'm away from her."

Lillie's mouth dropped open in sheer astonishment as she studied her brother's sad face. "You're in love?"

"Yes. For all the good it does me." He sighed. "I came here to end things, as you and others have suggested—to get a divorce."

"Who is this woman that you're so serious about?"

"She's an American. Her name is Mary." He smiled at the image of her in his mind. "And she's the kindest, sweetest, most beautiful woman I have ever met."

Lillie laughed. "My God, Sean, you are in love."

He nodded miserably.

"Have you told her how it is with you?"

"Yes, I told her I was married."

"How well did that go?"

"Not well." He shrugged. "About as well as I could expect. I was hoping to talk some sense into Maggie so that we could end this farce of a marriage, but she won't allow that to happen."

"Don't tell me you're surprised? You know what Maggie's about."

"No, not surprised, just disappointed, more by myself than anything." He took a deep breath and looked at his sister. "I need to find out if she's pregnant. I don't believe her, but until I have some sort of proof, I can't divorce her."

"Sean, really? You would stay with her for the sake of an unplanned child?"

"Wouldn't you?" He gave his sister a reproachful look. "Come on, Lillie, tell me you wouldn't do the same and stay with someone you didn't love for the sake of a child."

Lillie regarded her brother in silence.

"Can't answer that, can you? Well, it's the same for me. God! To have found the life I want only to ruin it!"

"Sean!" She placed a hand on his arm. "Maggie's lying. What else does she know how to do?"

"Can you help? Can you find out the truth of it?"

"I can try."

"And if Maggie isn't pregnant?"

"I will do whatever I must to end this farce so that I can ask Mary to marry me!" His expression was so honest, so full of love for Mary and full of pain at his current predicament that Lillie had to turn away.

"Won't you be here?"

"I have to go back to Dublin. I need to tell Mary what's happening." He sighed. "I'm going to have to work hard to convince her I'm sincere, especially since Maggie's going to fight me tooth and nail. I can't do any of that until I know the truth."

"I'll help, Sean. I want to see you happy."

"Thank you." Sean caught her in a bear hug and squeezed her until she squeaked. Laughing, he set her down. "I'll never be able to tell you what a good sister you've been to me and how much I appreciate it."

"Well, don't get used to it. I'm not always going to bail you out of your problems. But in this case, the truth needs to be known. Leave it to me."

Satisfied, Sean nodded. If anyone would get to the truth of the matter, it would be Lillie. She had a way of getting things done, and his future, fragile as it was, couldn't have been left in better hands. He turned away from her and clenched his hands, trying to calm himself, but not succeeding. He rubbed a careless hand across his eyes to wipe away the stray tears and turned toward the familiar hills, hoping that the future he wanted so badly was still within his grasp.

Chapter 13
Truth

MARY HELD THE memo in her hand and read it in disbelief. After four months, their job in Ireland was done. They were being called back home to Minneapolis. She had known they'd been doing a great job, but had expected more time. She needed time to settle her personal life. Not knowing what else to do, she went in search of Amy and found her working on her computer.

"Amy, did you see this?" She slammed the memo down in front of her friend.

"You bet your smart ass," Amy commented, attention focused on the computer. "Why do you think I'm working so frantically? I want out!"

"But you like it here."

"I do, but I miss my fiancé! Once a month just doesn't work for me." Her smile faded as she looked over at Mary, who had grown very quiet. "What about you?"

"What do you mean?"

"You know, Sean. Have you worked things out yet?"

"Oh." Mary gave her a sad smile. "I don't know what to do. I mean, dammit, I love him! But he's married."

"It's different here, though; at least that's what I've been told." She tried to comfort her friend. "I think he's sincere."

"This could only happen to me." She shook her head. When she regarded Amy her expression was filled with misery. "I don't know what to do."

"Have you heard from him?"

"No," she sighed. "He went home and hasn't come back yet."

'Oh."

"He's due back tomorrow, I expect I'll hear from him then."

"Well, keep me posted, okay? I'm always here if you need me."

Mary nodded, clearly miserable.

"A piece of advice," Amy offered and waited until Mary looked at her. "Hear him out. At least find out what he has to say, because if you don't, you'll always wonder about it. Okay?"

"Okay, I guess. I want to believe him, I just don't know if I can. And the company wants us back in Minneapolis in two weeks. Two weeks! How can I get all of this resolved in two weeks?"

Amy went over and hugged her friend. "Honey, it will be all right. I promise that somehow this will all work out."

Grateful, Mary let the tears fall. She was surprised when Amy gently pushed her away and wiped the tears from Mary's cheeks.

"What?" Mary asked confusion on her face.

That's when she heard Sean clearing his throat from the doorway behind her.

"You're back," she whispered.

"Yes, I just drove in." He shifted uncomfortably. "Please, Mary, can we go somewhere and talk?"

Mary folded her arms in front of her and glared at him.

She was annoyed when Amy bumped her from behind. "Go," Amy said.

Sean stepped into the room and held out his hand to her. "Please."

She nodded reluctantly but refused to take his hand.

Sean mouthed "thank you" to Amy as he followed along after Mary.

THEY SAT ACROSS the table, looking at each other. The silence was awkward at best. Despite Sean's attempts to lighten the mood, nothing worked. He reached across the table for her hand, and she pointedly withdrew it.

"*Aww*, Mary, talk to me! Nothing will be resolved if you don't."

"What is there to resolve? You're married; resolve that."

"I'm trying," he insisted. "You're not being fair."

"Fair?" she snapped. "Fair? You didn't tell me you're married, and you're talking about fair?"

"A mistake, I see that now, but I did tell you. Give me some credit."

"Credit?" she sputtered, her hazel eyes ablaze. "Credit? You're insane! You've lied to me since I've been here, and you want me to give you a pat on the back for finally telling the truth?" Her voice shook.

Sean frowned, unsure of what to say, realizing her anger was justified.

"Mary, I never expected to fall in love with you. I never knew I could feel this way about anyone." He shook his head. "Once we became close... Well, it all happened so fast." He concentrated on staring at the white tablecloth between them. "I didn't mean to hurt you."

"That doesn't help," she said, but without her previous venom. "It still doesn't make it right."

"No, it doesn't." He looked up from the tablecloth and studied her face, his own suffused with sadness. "Will you please accept my apology?" He reached for her hand again, and she let him take it. "Please, Mary." He searched her face. "Once I realized my feelings for you, I was afraid to tell you the truth." He clutched her hand within his. "I thought you would run from me."

"Well, you were right. I wouldn't have given you the time of day," she admitted honestly.

"Then?" His blue eyes searched hers for an answer, and she made a sound of aggravation.

"It still doesn't make what you did right."

"I didn't say that it did."

"Why is this so complicated?" She glared at him. "Why are you so complicated?"

"I can only say I'm sorry. Again."

"Damnit, Sean!"

"Please," he implored.

"All right, I accept your apology."

"So you forgive me?" His face lit with hope.

"I'm not there yet, one thing at a time."

He gave her hand a brief squeeze and released it. "One thing at a time, and that's a start. Thank you."

"You're welcome," she grumbled. "What happened at home?" she asked, unable to stop herself.

"Nothing."

"What does that mean?"

"Exactly what I said—nothing happened. I went home and talked to Maggie, but she refuses to divorce me." He looked her in the eyes and said, "Mary, this could be a lengthy process. Even if Maggie agreed to it, which she won't, it could take a great deal of time."

"How long?"

"I don't know, a year? Two? Even though it's legal, it's still frowned upon, so no one is in any hurry to approve a divorce." He sighed. "I've made another appointment with my barrister later this week."

"Barrister?"

"*Uh*, sorry. Lawyer, attorney, that type of person. I need his legal counsel on how to proceed. When one party doesn't want a divorce and the other does, it's bound to complicate things."

"No doubt." They studied each other in silence for a few moments. "I'm leaving, you know."

Sean was shocked. "What? When?"

"Two weeks."

"Two weeks," he echoed. "I didn't think you were leaving for months yet. Two weeks! That's not nearly enough time."

"Time for what?" she questioned. "Maybe it's better this way."

"*Ahh*, Mary. Why would you say that?"

"You know why. You're still married, and we both knew I'd have to go home." Her confidence was fading. "Two months would be two more months of closeness and intimacy. Who needs that, right? Besides, I don't date married men."

He caught the uncertain note in her voice and saw the question in her eyes. In another month, he'd know the truth about

Maggie, but he doubted he'd know anything in two weeks. It just wasn't enough time. He regarded her helplessly, words failing him. Mary took his silence as an answer to her question. Trying to hide the pain, she turned away from him.

LILLIE WAS DETERMINED to find out the truth for Sean, and the only person who knew the complete truth about Maggie was Patrick, her confidante for many years. Not finding him at home, she went to The Gaelic Moon and found him sitting in a quiet corner, nursing a drink. She ordered a drink for herself from Donald and went to Patrick's table. As she approached, she saw that he had not only a drink, but an entire bottle of strong whiskey on the table. She knew he drank, but usually not like this.

"Patrick," she asked when he finally looked up, "will you not be asking me to join you?"

His expression was tired and he shrugged.

"I'll take that as a yes," she said, taking the seat across the table from him.

He sighed. "What do you want?"

"Some information."

"About Maggie."

"Yes."

"It's always Maggie," he said drunkenly. "Everything is Maggie."

She hesitated, refilled Patrick's empty shot glass and pushed it back to him. "Is Maggie really pregnant?" she asked gently.

"Why would I know?"

"She tells you everything."

"*Aye*, I suppose she does." He finished half of his drink and looked across at Lillie.

She saw his haggard face. He had a two-day growth of beard, his eyes were bloodshot, and it seemed he hadn't slept in days. His normally handsome face was drawn and pinched.

"Is she?" Lillie pressed.

Lillie could see Patrick was debating with himself. "No, she's not," he answered at last.

"She's lying?"

"Yes, she's lying. Dammit! Lying like she did last time, lying because she wants to keep Sean!" He pounded his fist on the table and squeezed his eyes shut.

This unexpected behavior caught Lillie off guard and, moved by his sadness, she placed a hand on his arm. He started to shake, and Lillie realized he was crying.

She tried to soothe him. "Patrick, it's all right. Really, it will all be all right."

"It will never be all right. Don't you understand?" He looked at her through tear-filled eyes. "Maggie can never have a child. She lost that when she killed our baby, when she went to that back street hack and took the life of my lovely little boy."

"What?" Lillie felt the pieces starting to fall into place. "Sean was never the father?"

"No, it was mine. My poor little lad..." He put his head on arms and cried. "And now she's telling the same lie all over again, and it isn't true, could never be true."

"Oh, Patrick. I'm so sorry. I didn't know."

"No one did, except me, and I couldn't tell anyone."

"Why not? What hold does she have over you? She treats you like dirt, so why do you stay with her?"

"I have no choice! I can't let her go!"

"Why not?"

"I don't know, damn you." His expression was filled with misery. "You think I don't know that I obsess about her? You think I don't know that she tramples my pride? You think it doesn't hurt? I know she doesn't love me and probably never will, but I can't let her go."

She took his hand and squeezed it. "Patrick, you have to. Do it for yourself, stand up to her and do what is right. You know what that is, don't you?"

He hung his head, but nodded after a long moment. She gave his hand a last squeeze.

"You'll be telling Sean?" he asked.

"Yes, he has to know the truth."

"*Aye*, he should. It's past time." He wiped a hand across his wet eyes. "I'm sorry, Lillie. I know you are a good person, and I thank you for your kindness to me. Pray for me if you would; maybe it would help." He offered her a smile edged with pain.

"Patrick, one more question?"

"Sure, why not?" he regarded her again through bleary eyes.

"After all this time, why tell the truth tonight? Why to me?"

"That's two questions." Again the weak half smile. "I don't know. I think maybe it was just time to let go of the secret, or maybe I needed to tell a friend. I don't have many of those anymore." He added, "I think she's doing something to me, Lillie, but I don't know what. I feel better when you are around," he finished shyly.

"I'll check on you later," she said. On impulse she stepped close to him, leaned over and placed a chaste kiss on his cheek.

SEAN WAS ECSTATIC, he couldn't believe the news when Lillie called him and told him about Maggie. He felt like he should be angry, especially since he had been duped so long ago by her, and to a certain extent he was, but more than anything, he was relieved. He would get that divorce come hell or high water, and he would be with Mary. *Damn if things didn't sometimes work out right.*

As his eyes adjusted to the subdued light in The Shamrock, he spotted Mary sitting in what had been their usual booth and made his way over to it. He watched her for a few seconds before she saw him—watched how she moved, how she straightened out an earring that got caught in her hair, just watched her. When she turned, she nodded to him—not the enthusiastic wave he had gotten used to, but at least acknowledgment, and that was good.

He went over, gave her shoulder a brief squeeze, and slid in the booth across from her, grinning. He signaled to a waitress who came around, and she knew to get the two of them their usual drinks.

"Hi, Mary," Sean beamed at her.

"What's with you? You look positively ecstatic." Curious about his wonderfully good mood, she smiled despite herself.

"I had some good news today."

"And what would that be?" she asked as their beers arrived.

"My divorce barrister says I can definitely file for divorce. She may contest it, but it will happen." He reached for and took her hand in his. "Mary, I'll be free to be with you." His grin broadened.

"It's a little early to get that excited." She gave him a dour look, but he saw the small smile at the corner of her mouth.

"Aren't you excited? I can be with you."

"I haven't said I want to be with you."

"*Aww*, Mary, aren't you ever going to forgive me?"

"Ever? You've only told me two weeks ago!"

"Is that all?" he said with a glum expression. "It seemed longer." He took a sip from his beer and smiled at her again. "I love you, Mary."

"Stop it!" She put her hands over her ears. "I don't want to hear it."

"But it's true! I do love you." His regarded her with serious eyes. "Will you live with me here in Ireland, or shall I go and live with you in America?"

"Stop it! I still haven't forgiven you for being married." She glared at him halfheartedly.

"But you will, I can tell you will. Come on, Mary. Tell me you love me." He teased her until she hit his arm.

Mary sighed in frustration. "What's she like? Your wife, I mean."

Sean heard the jealousy in her voice. "You want to know about Maggie? I'll tell you whatever you want to know, all you have to do is ask."

"All right, why did you marry her?"

"Because I was young, and stupid."

She gave him a withering look, and he sighed.

"She told me she was pregnant with my child." Sean watched her carefully, it was as if he had just struck her with his words, and he waited for her to catch her breath.

This was almost too much for her to take in. "You're a father, too?"

"No, it never worked out. Shortly after we were married, she had an abortion and nearly lost her life as well as the child's." He studied the tablecloth and shook his head, still saddened by that part of things. "I don't know why she did it, only that the child died. A backstreet hack took away the child and nearly took Maggie as well. Just that quickly, the only reason for me to be married to her was gone as well."

"Then you only married her for the sake of the child?"

"Yes. After we separated, I couldn't stand the sight of her, knowing what she had done. I moved to Dublin and lived my life here; she stayed home and lived there. Our paths cross occasionally but nothing more."

She sighed. "I'm sorry, Sean, truly I am."

He took a long drink from his beer. "Why should you be sorry? You had nothing to do with it. My own stupidity, I guess. And you know what I just found out? After all of this time?" He ran a hand through his hair. "I found out she lied about the child, too. It wasn't mine. My life has been ruined for nothing!"

He took a deep breath and added, "Mary, I never thought I'd have a life, never thought I'd have a woman to love, because I didn't think I deserved one." He gave her a sad smile. "But I met you and found I wanted all of that again, only this time it was right, this time I am in love." He stopped talking and stared into her eyes.

They sat in silence for a time; their hands caressed each other as he waited for Mary to speak.

"You were supposed to be a fling. I didn't want to fall in love with you! Damn you!" Tears began to seep out of her eyes.

"*Shh*, Mary." He went around to her side of the booth and slid in beside her, putting his arm around her. "It will be all right."

"How can you say that?" She sniffed.

"I say it because it's true. Honey, it will be all right, I promise."

"But you're married, damn you!" she hissed.

"Not forever, not for long, if I have any say in the matter." He pulled her to him and held her until she stopped crying and then reached in his pocket and offered her a hankie. He kissed her forehead and held her close. They sat comfortably together for several minutes until she spoke again.

"I should hate you," she said.

"But you don't, do you?"

She poked him in the ribs, hard. "Stop being so smug."

"That hurt!"

"Good, it should."

"I don't think I want to go to bed with you after all. You'll probably inflict serious bodily injury on me." She couldn't help herself, she laughed. "*Ahh*, better. I wanted to see that beautiful smile of yours."

"You're full of crap."

"Maybe. I've certainly been accused of worse." He sighed. "I think I'd best be getting you home."

"I hate you," she said.

"Yeah, I hate you, too. Can't you tell?" He stopped laughing and quieted, taking her hand in his and tracing little patterns on her palm.

"What are you doing?" she asked suspiciously.

"Touching you, that's all. You don't mind, do you?"

Actually she didn't. She had seen him a couple of times since he had told her the truth about his marital relationship, trying to determine what she felt for him. God help her, she did still love him, but she also felt betrayed. It might be stupid, but the only way she felt she could understand her constantly changing emotions was to see him, to find out if she wanted to live with or without him in her life.

Remaining quiet, she reached for her beer and took a long drink. She didn't remove her other hand from his, and he smiled, understanding the gesture.

Mary set her beer down and watched him. She realized the alcohol was making her feel sentimental, but right now she didn't care. She missed him and wanted to be with him. "Sean, can we go?"

"Of course," he said and helped her out of the booth, draping her coat around her shoulders.

She reached for his hand to stop him, and he looked at her in surprise. "Let's go back to your place."

"My place? Mary?" The joy on his face was amazing, but soon replaced by a more cautious look. "Are you sure?"

"I'm sure. At least for tonight, I am. But I'm not promising anything else."

He reached for her hand, drew it up to his lips, and kissed it. "Let's go home."

Chapter 14
The Necklace

*T*HE BOOK LAY open on Maggie's table. She focused in the page in front of her, mumbling to herself, never quite completing the words. After several minutes of this, she turned to the fireplace and allowed a slow smile to spread across her face. She made a deliberate gesture and saw the fire flare to life, feeding greedily on the tinder and wood, turning into a hot blaze much more quickly than should be possible. And the blue flame was such a nice color, the color of magical fire.

She nodded her head in approval. It was another useful tool to add to her growing arsenal of magic and darkness.

SEAN COULDN'T CONCENTRATE on the newspaper in his hands as he sat by the kitchen table in his robe and waited for Mary to join him. He had prepared toast and tea, coffee for Mary, and also a glass of juice for each of them. And it appeared to be a glorious day, at least weather-wise, as the sunlight from the window brightened his kitchen.

He had believed that he was destined to be alone, and suddenly, here he was, in love and wanting to settle down with this wonderful woman. He sighed and set the paper aside. She was always slow in the morning, but he wished she'd move a little faster today.

When he passed by his favorite jewelry store a month ago he

stopped in his tracks when he saw a beautiful emerald necklace. The bewitching shade of green reminded him of the color of Mary's eyes when they darkened with desire and became the most beautiful shade of green he had ever seen, and he knew he had to buy the necklace for her because he wanted her to understand how much she meant to him, and would always mean to him, no matter what might happen between them.

Restless, he glanced at the jewelry box on the table, at his watch, and out the window. What was taking so long?

MARY LAY IN bed, unable to sleep. Why had she come back to Sean's place last night? No, she knew the answer to that; she'd come back because she wanted to be with him. She could use alcohol as an excuse but, the truth was, she was glad she spent the night with Sean. She had missed him since they had been fighting.

She got out of bed, and started to dress, taking the time to look especially pretty. There was so much uncertainty in this situation with Sean; she wanted to have good memories of their last few days together in Ireland. No matter what Sean said, he would be here, and she would be home in America. God only knew whether such a long-distance relationship could work. She certainly didn't. So she decided to try to make the most of the time they had together.

With a deep sigh, she regarded her reflection in the mirror and began to brush her long brown hair. She had allowed it to grow out during her stay in Ireland, and now it flowed freely about her shoulders. She dressed in a colorful skirt with a bright-green blouse, both of which complemented her figure. Her diamond earrings sparkled and caught every drop of light. Her makeup was subtle, but appropriate, enhancing her appearance and soft eyes. She smiled at her reflection and hoped she hadn't kept Sean waiting too long, but the extra time was worth it. Hopefully, he would agree. She opened the door and stepped into the hallway.

HE WATCHED HER as she entered the kitchen and smiled in appreciation. "Mary, you're more beautiful than ever." He stood up and kissed her.

"Thank you," she said, as he pulled out the chair for her.

"What's the occasion?" he teased. "Do you have a date?"

"It's nothing," she shrugged. "Only that I wanted to look nice for you." She smiled sadly. "I want you to remember me as pretty, and not how I look when I'm in my hiking clothes."

"Mary," he said, reaching for her hand, "don't you know? You're always beautiful to me." He squeezed her hand. "Do you really have to leave in a week?"

"Yeah, I do. Back home to my lonely life." She gazed into the blue eyes she loved so much. "Is it wrong to tell you I'm going to miss you?"

"No, it's not wrong. I'll miss you, too. But only until I can join you."

After a moment, she took a deep breath and tried to lighten the mood. "I can hardly believe I've been here over four months already!"

"It doesn't seem possible. Time passes much too quickly." He grimaced. "I have to go back home and make sure Maggie understands we are getting a divorce. My trip will last two to three days at the most."

"Oh." Her disappointment was all too evident, uncertainty clearly etched on her face. "You'll be back before I leave?"

"Of course I will. And I have your address and phone in my wallet if for some ungodly reason I don't. You will see me again."

"Good." Mary looked as if she were about to cry. Sean decided to cheer her up, and he slid the jewelry box toward her. "Here, I have something for you."

Mary regarded the box with a mixture of suspicion and hope, not understanding what it signified in their relationship.

He nudged the box toward her again. "Go on, open it."

With a curious eyebrow raised in his direction, she pulled the box to her. Even the box itself appeared expensive, so much so that she was almost afraid to open it, but she glanced up and saw Sean watching her expectantly. She cracked open the lid and saw the most beautiful present anyone had ever given her. The gold necklace glittered with a life all its own, the inset emeralds and diamonds reflected the surrounding light so magnificently that it took her breath away. Gently, she eased it out and cradled it in her hand.

"Oh, Sean," she whispered, tears in her eyes.

"The stones matched your eyes. I mean they're the color of your passion with the way they sparkle and all." His voice choked with emotion at her undisguised joy, and he cleared his throat and collected himself. Her tears of happiness blurred her vision as she looked at the necklace. "Well, it's the least I could do since I can't ask you to marry me. Yet."

Mary's tears were now streaming down her cheeks, and he didn't know whether he had made things better or worse.

"Here now," he said, reaching for a box of tissue. "Don't be crying." He bent down in front of her, thrusting the tissues at her as she took one and began to dab at her eyes. Unable to stand it any longer, he took her into his arms, trying to soothe away the tears. "I just want you to know I love you." His eyes were suspiciously bright as she buried her head against his shoulder and cried.

BOXES ONCE AGAIN made the office seem the center of organized chaos. People wandered to and fro as they collected their belongings for packing. But despite the activity around her, Mary took little notice. Instead she sat at her desk, numbly staring at the jewelry box that sat in the middle of it. She wiped at another tear running down her face and reminded herself that crying at work was very unprofessional. She looked up as Amy playfully bumped her.

"*Oops*, sorry!" Amy's grin faded when she saw Mary's face looking bleakly back at her. "Hey! What's wrong? then remembering, "Oh, yeah. Sean." Amy noticed the jewelry box. "What's that?"

"A present."

"From Sean? Cool. Can I see?"

Mary nodded and watched as Amy opened the box. Her friend was stunned into silence except for the sounds of admiration that escaped as she gently touched the necklace.

"What are you going to do?" Amy asked.

"About what?"

"Sean! The guy's in love with you."

Mary touched the necklace and gave Amy a miserable look. "He said he wanted me to have this because he couldn't marry me."

Suspicion marred Amy's features. "He said that?"

"He said, 'Yet.'" Mary shrugged. "He says he's going to get a divorce so we can be together."

"He's serious." Amy smiled. "Congratulations."

"Don't congratulate me; nothing matters until he gets his divorce." She sighed. "And he went home to do that."

"Go after him," Amy blurted out.

"Amy, why on earth would I do that? It's like chasing him."

"Okay, chase him. Go after him. See if what he says about his wife is true."

"Why can't I just wait here?" Mary scowled at her friend. Go after him? What an idea. Part of her wanted to run out the door right this minute, but the other part of her recoiled, scared to death of what she might find.

Without warning, she clutched at her chair, feeling dizzy.

"Mary?"

She felt the familiar nauseous sensation she'd been experiencing for the last week, and with her hand over her mouth, she ran to the bathroom.

Amy followed her down the hall and into the bathroom, locking the door behind her. She waited until Mary was done being sick, and leaned against the wall by the sink. "Mary, you've been sick a lot recently."

"You noticed?" She shook her head. "Stress. Nerves. Just a really bad week."

"Honey, how long have you been sleeping with Sean?"

"Amy! That's none of your business!" Mary tried to be indignant, but failed, still too weak from being sick. She offered her friend a weak smile. "Are you going to make me answer?"

"Yes." Amy smiled. "Make it easy on yourself."

"Exactly? I don't know. A couple of months, I guess. Why?"

"Were you using protection?"

"Of course." She frowned. "He used condoms, and I'm on the pill."

"Did you ever miss taking them?"

Mary frowned. "Maybe once?"

"Did his condom ever break? Did he ever forget to use one?"

Mary eyed her friend. "I can't be pregnant!"

"It only takes once, and you two have been busy." Amy sighed in sympathy.

"Pregnant?" Mary leaned against the sink. "No."

"Tell you what, let me take you to a doctor, and you can find out for sure. I'm thinking you'll want to know before you go to see Sean?"

"Yes, of course," she mumbled, her mind in chaos.

"Come on, Mary, time to go." Amy opened the door and led her down the hallway.

HOSPITAL GOWNS NEVER *improve*, Mary thought as she sat on the edge of the exam table, waiting for the doctor to return. They were always cold and drafty. She shivered. She had never quite adjusted to the lower temperature setting here in Ireland. Why was the doctor so damned slow? Mary checked her watch. It was getting late, and she was anxious to be on her way. She had already gotten dressed and was now only waiting for the results.

Almost as if on cue, Dr. O'Connell entered. She was a middle-aged woman of average stature, with graying hair and thick glasses. Warm was not the first word Mary would use to describe the woman who had done her exam.

"Your test results are in," the doctor said. "Congratulations, Miss Kelley, you are going to have a baby. You're pregnant."

Chapter 15
The Gaelic Moon

*T*HE LITTLE BLUE car made its way along the narrow passages that passed for roads, Mary carefully navigating her way along them. How in the world could anyone drive like this, in a tiny car on the wrong side of the road? God, even the shift was for the wrong hand!

She frowned, trying to concentrate on the road in front of her, but she couldn't help speculating on Sean's likely reaction to her completely unexpected news. Would he be happy? That was the best of all possibilities. Ideally, he'd profess his undying love for her, again, and he'd still want to marry her. She sighed. Somehow that sounded too much like a romance novel, complete with a happy ending. Nothing had ever been that easy for her.

Would he be mad? She didn't want him to be with her because of an unplanned pregnancy; she wanted him with her because that's where he chose to be—because she was the woman he wanted to be with, not because she was the woman he had to be with.

She gave up and found a safe place to pull over and park. When she looked at her hands, she realized her knuckles were white from gripping the steering wheel so hard. She closed her eyes and massaged her temples, trying to calm herself.

No matter what she said, it wasn't going to go well. She unclenched her fists and tried to alleviate the tension she felt. Deep breaths, she reminded herself, take deep breaths.

As Mary drove into Cullamore, she looked for a suitable place to park her car and pulled into the parking area for a lovely guesthouse. Rather Victorian in appearance, two-storied and well-kept-up, despite the worn brick facade. The porch outside was neat and clean, with weathered wooden chairs sitting on the gray deck. It seemed like a nice place to stay.

She got out and surveyed her surroundings, trying to etch the place in her mind—anything to distract her from the task at hand.

The town was almost too picturesque for words. The green, gently rolling hills that surrounded the village left no doubt as to why Ireland was referred to as The Emerald Isle, and even from here, she could see a turquoise blue stream cut its way through the valley leading to the village, it was all quite beautiful. The small shops that lined the street were made of stone and wood and looked to be several decades old. It added an air of quaintness without the undercurrent of being a tourist attraction. Yes, she was impressed. It was no wonder Sean sometimes expressed his distaste for Dublin, a large, noisy city was like hell when she compared it to the serenity and solitude of this place.

She nervously looked down the street at the Lake View Guesthouse and wondered if she should reserve a room. She was more fatigued from the drive than she wanted to admit, but she attributed a great deal of that to stress. Driving back to Dublin tonight wasn't something she cared to do, but if things didn't go well, she had no desire to stay, so reserving a room probably wasn't a good idea.

She got out of her car, wondering where she could ask for directions, and saw a pub sign at the end of the road. The local gathering place seemed a good bet, she thought, and walked down the street to The Gaelic Moon.

The pub inside was remarkable, woodwork lining the walls, a fire providing heat to a small group of people sitting on the chairs around it. It was a comfortable place, providing a kind of inner warmth to the people who visited here, and with something of a start Mary realized that she felt drawn to this place, just as she felt some sense of unknown power as soon as she stepped in the door. She took a deep breath, gathering herself together, and realized the local patrons had been staring at her and were just now resuming their conversations. She approached the bar, and saw Sean was casually dressed in his favorite form fitting jeans, as he sat on a barstool smoking a cigarette.

Hesitating only for a moment, she took the seat beside him. "You wouldn't care to buy a girl a drink, would you?"

He looked at her in astonishment. "Mary! What in the world are you doing here?"

"I couldn't bear to be away from you," she teased, her voice pitched higher than normal.

"Now that sounds like blarney to me," he replied with a smile. "What's the real reason? Following me here? What could be so important?"

Mary remained quiet and bit her lip, not sure what to say.

After a long moment, he asked, "Would you like a drink?"

"Sure cider, non-alcoholic."

"You don't drink that often." He shrugged and motioned Donald over. "Donald, I'd like you to meet Mary," he said and grinned at the barkeep.

Donald extended his hand. "Pleased to meet you."

Mary took his hand and felt an immediate jolt and, when she searched Donald's kind face, she found he was watching her intently. She tried to shake off the feeling that she knew him from somewhere and, even more than that, the sudden, overwhelming feeling that she and Sean had been lovers over several lifetimes. She let go of Donald's hand with a questioning gaze and turned her attention back to Sean.

"Donald here is the best barkeep in all of Ireland, and we'd all be lost without him."

"*Ach,* don't buy that load of rubbish! He's pullin' your leg, he is."

"So you say." Sean smiled at his friend. "Donald, this is the most beautiful woman in all of Ireland, and she's visiting here from America. I was fortunate to meet her while I was in Dublin, and she's forever changed my life." He took Mary's hand and kissed it and, much to his delight, she blushed.

"And that would be in a good way, I gather," Donald said with a wink. "It's easy to see that you two are fond of each other."

"Fond?" Sean grinned at Mary. "Yes, at the very least." He leaned over and kissed her cheek.

"Do you feel the same?" Donald asked.

Mary felt she was looking into the eyes of an old familiar soul and was comforted by a feeling of serenity, compassion, and peace. He saw the curiosity in her eyes and gave a slight nod in acknowledgment.

"Yeah, I do" she answered at last.

"*Aye*, 'tis obvious to all but one who is blind." He smiled at the two of them and passed along their drinks. "I'll let you be. Call me if you want anything else." With a last smile for the couple, Donald turned away to assist his other patrons.

Sean studied Mary for a few moments and realized she was uncomfortable. He reached out and took her hand. "Mary, what's wrong?"

"What?" She frowned. "Oh, nothing."

"You don't seem yourself. Is something bothering you?"

"I already answered that," she snapped. "I'm fine."

"All right," he said, "What shall we talk about?"

Anything but what she really had to tell him, she thought. She looked around the pub and found part of her mind thinking about historical things, wondering how old the pub was, when it was first built, what was built here before it? She was always interested in historical things and found that to be a good distraction.

"How about this place?"

"The Gaelic Moon? Sure, what do you want to know?"

"Tell me its history."

"*Ahh*, folk tales then. Why not?" He surveyed the building around him. "The Gaelic Moon is old, very old—some say the oldest pub in Ireland. Though old, this is not the original building. It's been built and rebuilt many times over the centuries. Legend has it that it has always been called The Gaelic Moon, and it will always be called that, something about it being a tribute to the restless souls of murdered Druids."

"That sounds frightening."

"Not really but it is good story telling. See those beams over there?" He indicated what appeared to be a set of ancient wooden beams just a few feet away.

"Yes." There was an odd tingling in the back of her mind when she regarded them. "They're special, aren't they?"

"It's said they have survived since druidic times, part of an ancient druidic alter." He leaned in as if to whisper a secret to her. "And they are supposed to be magic."

"Magic?" Mary wrinkled her brow, taking in his words, and gave him a curious smile. "Magic? Do you believe in magic?"

"Guess I've never given it much thought. Being Irish, I suppose I should believe in such things, at least a little bit, but I don't know."

"But, magic?" Mary got off her barstool and walked over to the beams, scrutinizing them closely. She put her hands on them, touching them tentatively, studying the blackened wood, wondering what stories the beams could tell if they could talk. "Where's the magic?" she asked, giving Sean a daring look.

"Oh, like that, is it? Think I don't know what I'm talking about?" He walked over to her side, took her hand, and led her around to the back side of the large beam; which was big enough to hide them from sight. "I can show you magic," he said and pulled her in his arms and kissed her. She kissed him back, enjoying the feel of being in his arms. "See, magic."

She could feel the smile on his lips.

"I don't think that's what was meant in the story."

"And why not? There's no better kind of magic than a strong love between two people."

She put a hand to his cheek. "You still love me?"

"Yes, now and always."

"Good." She nodded and seemed to get some confidence back, pulling herself out of his arms she returned to her study of the ancient beams, her fingers tracing the carvings in the wood. "Now, what about the real magic?"

"The magic is an artifact that ancient Druids fought over centuries ago—called Gaelic Moon. They needed to possess it so badly that they fought a bloody civil war and killed everyone but a few survivors. When they went to retrieve the artifact from the altar, they found only an empty box with traces of blue paint."

"Which means their war was pointless?"

"Totally. They sought to own a dangerous power that never existed. Or at least, one they didn't find."

"Which means what?" she looked at him suspiciously.

"Many years later, it was rumored the relic, the Gaelic Moon, still existed. That its special power belonged to those long-dead Druids, and only they could channel it."

"What power?"

"No one knows."

"Where is the Gaelic Moon relic?"

"There are many rumors—one is that it's right here, that it's part of the pub."

"It would make sense," Mary agreed and saw the twinkle in Sean's eyes. "You know, don't you?"

He put a finger to his lips, took her hand, and gently placed it on the pillar. She felt the inlay and found herself tracing a circle. Sean picked up a candle from a nearby table and brought it close to the beam and that's when she saw the faint traces of blue paint, the pattern so dark and worn it could hardly be seen.

"It's said that if you trace the pattern three times and wish your fondest wish, it will come true."

"Did you?" she asked.

"Once in my youth." He shrugged. "I haven't noticed it works." He gave her an odd look and rubbed his chin. "But now that I think about it, maybe it has."

What did you wish for?"

"To find the love of my life, settle down, and have a family with that very special woman."

"Did anything else happen when you traced the figure? Anything obvious?"

"Well, now that I think about it, I may have seen a brief blue glow, a slight tingle in my fingers, but it could have been my imagination or alcohol." He laughed at his youthful self.

"Is that normal? Did it happen to anyone else?"

"I don't know, I doubt it means anything," Sean said with a shrug.

"*Hmm.*" Mary bit her lip and turned away from him, studying the pillar instead. "I'm going to try it," she said and began tracing the pattern three times. She thought carefully about what she wanted most. "Sean, I want you with me forever, no matter what may happen between us," she said as she finished tracing the pattern. She noted a definite tingling in her fingertips but nothing else.

"Nice wish," he said with a smile. "I'll do my best to comply."

They turned away, and neither noticed the faint blue light over the pattern, light that quickly disappeared.

THEY STOPPED OUTSIDE of the Guesthouse later that evening. The night was lovely, and the stars shone brightly as she held Sean's arm. Mary sighed in contentment; everything was almost perfect. Now, she just had to find the courage to tell him what had caused her to take this trip in the first place.

"What's wrong?" he asked, hearing her sigh.

"Nothing. At least I think nothing."

"I'm assuming you'll be staying here at the Guesthouse?"

"If they still have room. I haven't checked in yet."

"That will not be a problem. Let me take care of it." He offered her his arm again and escorted her up the set of steps. After a room had been assigned to her, he went out and retrieved her overnight bag and led her up to her room.

Once inside, he set down the bag and just looked at her, he could never get enough of just watching her. She moved about the room checking out her accommodations, and he saw her smile with delight at the warm, cozy room.

"This is lovely," she said when she turned back to him.

"I'm glad you like it. It's a nice place for our quaint little town." He cleared his throat uneasily. "I should be going then."

"Sean?"

He heard the question in her voice and, stepping close to her, he touched her elbow. "Mary, what is it? I know you came here for a reason, but so far you haven't told me what why. What's bothering you?"

"I don't know how to say it."

"Say what?"

"Sean, do you like kids? I mean, if we do end up together, do you want children?"

"Oh, is that all?" She looked so worried that he had to laugh. "I'm Irish, my love. We all love children."

"But do you?"

"Of course I do. By this point in my life I expected to be happily married and have a whole houseful of children, but as you know that didn't happen." He sighed and put a tender hand to her face. "But if you'll have me as soon as I get my divorce, I'll marry you and give you as many children as you want." He smiled and leaned forward to place a sweet kiss on her lips. "Would that please you?"

She nodded and tried to stop the tears that were falling from her eyes.

"Mary, please don't cry. Why are you upset? I'm going to get a divorce and marry you, and we will be free to live our lives together."

Mary suddenly reached for him and pressed her face against his chest, trying to stifle her tears.

"Mary?" he draped his arms around her, holding her close.

"What if we started early?" she asked so softly that he had to strain to hear her.

"What?" he asked and she couldn't tell if it was disbelief or if he just hadn't heard her.

"I'm pregnant!"

He stared at her in shock.

She continued, "I didn't mean for it to happen. I mean we both used protection..."

"And it still happened." A slow smile began to spread across his face, one of wonder and joy. "Don't you see, Mary? This is supposed to be. It's another sign that we're supposed to be together."

"You're not mad?"

"Mad? Hell no! Mary, I love you. This is wonderful!" He pulled her to him and swung her around in glee.

He began to shower her with kisses until she succumbed to his affection and began to return them in earnest. They undressed each other quickly and fell on the bed in each other's arms, lost in their passion for one another. For the rest of the night, no more words were needed as they joined and fulfilled each other in ways no one else ever could.

THE FEELING OF Sean's arms wrapped around her as she awoke was comforting in a way she hadn't dreamed possible. She pressed back deeper into his embrace savoring his nearness. The feel of his skin against her and his rhythmic breathing calmed her as she struggled to wakefulness.

All of her worry had been for nothing as Sean's reaction to the news of impending fatherhood was everything she wanted, everything she had hoped for, and she knew he would make a great dad. She smiled and, unable to help herself, turned her head just enough to place a soft kiss on the corner of his mouth.

"Mary," he mumbled, "what time is it?"

"Don't know, I didn't look."

He raised his head just enough and squinted at the clock. "It's four in the a.m.! Why are you awake?"

"Not sure, just counting my blessings, I guess."

"Am I among them?" His tone was a bit querulous.

"Of course you are!" she rolled over to face him and kissed him.

"*Hmm*, that's nice," he let his hands gently trace a pattern down her side. "Are you happy, Mary? I will make this work, I promise you."

"I want to believe you."

"You still have doubt?" He leaned forward and nibbled gently at her ear.

"A little. You still have a long way to go before you get a divorce."

"I'll make it happen." He stopped as he felt her tense up and pulled back to look into her eyes, now filled with worry. "What? What is it?"

"What if something goes wrong? You aren't lying to me, are you? I mean you really want to divorce her, don't you?"

"Mary! Of course I do. I've told you that since I came clean."

"You mean since you stopped lying to me."

"Well I wouldn't put it quite so indelicately, but yes."

"No more lies?" Her eyes, now dark green with distress searched his almost desperately.

"No more lies."

"I want to believe you."

"Believe me, Mary. I've never loved another woman the way I love you."

She looked at him for what seemed forever, but was probably only a few seconds, and finally nodded. "Okay."

"That's it, okay?"

"Isn't that enough?"

He leaned forward and kissed her, a sweet kiss of promise. "It's plenty."

"Will you move to America?"

"If that's what you want, yes."

"And until the divorce is taken care of?"

"I will come and visit you as often as I can."

She made an accepting noise and laid her head back down on the pillow, still watching him. "I want a boy and a girl, you know."

"Twins?" he grinned at her and she paled at his words.

"No! No, that's not what I meant at all. Just one at a time."

Sean laughed at her horrified expression. "It's all right, my love. It's all fine."

"And I want a dog. You like dogs, don't you?"

"I do as a matter of fact. Big dogs."

"Terriers. I have to have a terrier, preferably a Cairn terrier."

"Cairn terrier?" Sean wrinkled his brow, trying to remember what they looked like.

"Think Toto from the *Wizard of Oz*."

"That scruffy little thing?" He chuckled. "Why would we want a dog like that?"

"Because they're a big dog in a small dog body, and because they have attitude." She sighed as she turned over and settled back against his chest. "I like attitude."

"I see. So just one dog?"

"Maybe more, we'll see. Depends on how many kids we have," she said as her breathing evened out and she fell asleep.

Sean sighed and pulled her close, content with the simplicity of holding her in his arms as his eyes closed and sleep claimed him once again.

Chapter 16
Manipulations

*T*HEY STOOD BY Mary's car the next morning, Sean holding her hand in his as their eyes remained locked.

"Do I really have to go? Can't I just wait here? She can't be that bad."

"Maggie?" Sean laughed. "I told you she was part banshee, didn't I? I'm not exaggerating. I'd rather know you were safe and out of her line of fire." His lips drew together in a grimace. "Let me deal with her."

"If you're sure," she said doubtfully.

"I'm sure." He squeezed her hand. "As soon as I've had my say with Maggie, I'll return to Dublin. I'll be back before you go."

"Do you promise?"

"I swear you will see me again."

"All right," she said, but made no move to go. Mary was thrilled by the future laid out in front of them and she held his hand tightly, not wanting to let go of him, nor of this moment.

MAGGIE FROWNED AS she made her way to the Guesthouse; the word about town was that Sean's lover was there. For him to bring his mistress home to where his wife lived was unpardonable. If he'd had affairs during their extended separation, she was unaware of it, and she was sure she would have found out. The fact he so openly flaunted his relationship with the woman, an American, if the rumors were true, was not a good sign.

Armed with no real plan, only righteous anger at Sean's behavior, she stormed out of her house in search of her wayward husband.

He really thought he could be unfaithful to her? Well, she would show him how ruthless she could be when cornered. By the end of the day, he would regret ever bringing this American to town. She would remind him who he really belonged to!

Maggie stopped to concentrate on her appearance, on how she wanted to look. Putting her illusion in place, she patted her stomach in satisfaction.

"Sean, there you are," she said, putting a pleasant smile on her face as she walked up to him and touched his arm.

The spell between Sean and Mary was broken with the touch, and he recoiled as if burned.

"Maggie," he said with barely concealed contempt, and she struggled to hide the building fury within her. She reminded herself to smile sweetly as she watched him drop a protective arm around the other woman.

"Where have you been? You never come home anymore," Maggie said.

"I come home when I need to, and never on your account." His face suddenly lit with a smile. "But on this particular occasion I'm glad to see you. In fact, I have something for you."

Sean reached in his jacket pocket and handed an envelope to Maggie.

"What's this?"

"Go on, open it."

With a wary eye for him, she did so and nearly spit glass when she read what was in her hand. "Divorce papers?"

"Preliminary ones, yes, but we will get a divorce," the conviction in his voice was unmistakable.

For a few moments, she gazed at Sean and Mary, deciding which course of action would suit her best. When her decision was made, she looked at Sean and smiled at him.

"Who is this? Is she why you are being foolish?"

Sean, tight-lipped, said nothing. Mary glanced at his stoic face and decided to remain silent as well.

"You poor child, he's got you brainwashed. Did he tell you he was married?"

"He did," Mary said, bristling at the other woman's treatment of Sean.

"Really?" Maggie's surprise at this revelation was confirmed by the smug look on Sean's face and her blood boiled at his confidence. "How unusual. He usually just finds his mistresses, uses them, and discards them."

Mary glared at Maggie. "I'm not his mistress!"

"Oh, lass, of course you are. I'm his wife, so what does that make you?" She watched as her words sank in, and she saw Mary give Sean a questioning look "Sean, have you told her the rest of it?"

"The rest of what?" he growled. "There's nothing to tell."

Maggie stepped forward and placed a hand on Sean's arm. "But, Sean, didn't you tell her about the child?"

"Stop talking nonsense. There is no child!" He stepped away from her and dropped his arm from around Mary.

Mary looked from Maggie to Sean. "Child? What child?"

"My child, and Sean's child," Maggie said, placing her hands on her small, slightly rounded stomach.

Mary glared at Maggie with growing horror as the implications set in, her mind screaming in pain as she looked at Sean in shock.

"Mary, it's not true! I swear it!" he implored Maggie, as he saw a roundness to Maggie's belly that alluded to a pregnancy. *But how it could it be possible?* Had Patrick lied to Lillie when he told her Maggie was barren? Was this some sort of cruel joke? His expression grew cold as he stared at his wife with disdain. "She's lying. She's barren."

"Sean, how can you say that when the evidence is growing right here?" Maggie rubbed her stomach, clearly showing the small bulge to Mary. "Didn't you tell her about our night of passion? And the result?"

"No, it can't be true. It can't," Mary muttered to herself, shaking her head. "It can't be." She gathered her courage and, through the tears that were filling her eyes, looked at Sean. "Tell me it's not true. Tell me you weren't with her."

Before he could speak, Maggie sneered at Mary, saying, "He

was with me. What further proof do you need?"

"Just because you're pregnant doesn't mean it's his."

"That's right, that's absolutely right," Sean shouted. "Because it's not!"

"Who else would it belong to, my darling husband? Besides, I haven't heard you deny our night together."

"You haven't, Sean." Mary crossed her arms in front of her. "Were you with her? Did you... have sex with her?"

"Mary," Sean sputtered, unable to answer her. He saw the tears running down her cheeks.

"You slept with her, you made love to her, and the child is yours."

"There is no child!"

"How can you say that? Look at her!" Mary shouted as she pointed at Maggie.

"Yes, Sean, dear, look at me. Look at your child."

"Maggie, shut the hell up!" He turned from her only to find Mary had removed the beautiful emerald necklace he had given her. She opened his hand, placed it there, and closed his hand around it. Heart pounding in wild panic, he met her devastated eyes with fear in his own. "Oh, Mary, no. Please don't."

"I believed you. Damn you! I believed you." She was crying openly now, and Sean tried to take her in his arms. But she pushed him away. "Stay away from me. You lied to me. You lied to me!" She backed from him.

"Mary, please!" Sean grabbed her arm, but she shook him off. Without moving a muscle, tears streaming down her face, she reminded him of a crystalline figure, delicate and fragile, as if the wrong move would shatter her into a million pieces. Her normal warmth and enthusiasm were dying within her, the bright coals destroyed by the cold reality of a twisted truth.

"You lied to me and took advantage of me," she said in a voice shaking with emotion. "You told me you loved me and that I could always trust you." She swallowed with difficulty, tears flooding her face. "And you're starting a family with your wife?" She shook her head in disbelief. "What's left to say?"

Mary backed toward her car, much as any cornered animal expecting another attack. "Damn you! I love you, you lying bastard!" She screamed with all of the tragedy of a breaking heart and dove into her car to escape from him, slamming the car door and pressing the locks.

"Mary! Mary!" Sean pounded on the window, pleading with her. "Please listen to me! It's not true. I swear it's not true! She's not pregnant! I love you!"

He could see the gut-wrenching pain in Mary's hazel eyes. She closed her eyes for just a moment, gathering her strength, gave him one last cold look, and put the car in gear.

"Mary!" he yelled as the headlights were turned on. Breathless, he ran beside the car as it began to pull away. He pounded on the door and stopped in front of it, his hands spread apart in a pleading gesture.

"Mary, please," he said, blinking back his tears. "Give me a chance! Let me explain!"

They exchanged a long look through the windshield, and the misery in her eyes nearly ripped Sean in two. At that moment, he would have done anything for her, anything to make her pain go away.

The car moved again, and Sean was forced to move aside or be run down. As she accelerated away from him, he stared numbly at the empty road, his breathing labored.

After a few moments, Maggie approached and touched his arm, and he turned around. With a satisfied smile, she linked her arm in his. "I told you, you're mine."

"Get away from me!" He removed her grip, his voice filled with a dark fury she had never seen before. "I never want to lay eyes on you again!" He shoved her away with such force that she stumbled and fell to the ground, and with a last look of hatred for her, he stalked off into the darkness.

Lillie had come upon the Guesthouse and silently seen the scene unfold before her. She shook her head sadly, her heart going out to Sean and the poor woman with the broken heart. That was when she noticed the glint of light that reflected from the ground. Curious, she went over and picked it up. Although covered with dust, there was no mistaking the elegance and expense of the jewelry, it was a gift to someone's beloved. The emerald necklace seemed to sparkle with its own inner fire; it was the prettiest necklace she had ever seen and knew only something completely devastating could cause a person to give it up.

MARY COULDN'T THINK. Not now. All she could do now was flee. Run away and deal with the fallout later. Leave this country that felt like a second home to her, leave the man who was the father of her child. God, the thought made her ill. She had been taken in by a married man, by a married man who was starting a family with his wife. She'd trusted him and loved him. How could she have been so blind?

Tears clouding her vision, she found a place to pull off the road and bent over the steering wheel, grief shaking her body with sobs.

Chapter 17
Vengeance

*T*HE GAELIC MOON was quiet, with only a few locals inside. Sean sat by himself, the table in front of him cluttered with empty glasses. Nothing mattered but the shot glass in his hand. Unshaven, his chin was covered with stubble, and lines of fatigue etched his face, highlighting his bloodshot eyes.

Lillie entered and saw her brother at the same place she'd left him the day before. He didn't even look up when she pulled out a chair and sat down across from him. After a moment, she shoved his shoulder, trying to gain his attention and he blinked at her in surprise.

"Sis, it's you."

"Sean, you've been here for the better part of three days, and you've refused to talk to me. I have to talk to you, now. It's important."

He shook his head. "No."

"You don't have to stay married to her, she's lying to you."

After a long silence, he finally spoke, but his voice sounded lifeless. "Yes, I'll divorce her no matter what. What reason to be civil anymore?"

She leaned across the table and took his hand. "You'll be free, Sean."

"It doesn't really matter," he said with a shrug.

"Free to go to America. Free to bring her back. What is her name?"

"Mary," he whispered.

Lillie squeezed his arm and was surprised to see her brother close to tears. "You broke her heart. I've never seen such anguish."

Miserable, he nodded, and finished his current drink in one gulp.

"Go after her, Sean."

He held his head and tried to focus on her face. "You just said I broke her heart," he slurred. "Why would she talk to me? I wouldn't."

"Maybe because she still loves you."

"How can she?"

"Hearts don't heal in three days, nor do you fall out of love so fast."

"She'll never believe me," he mumbled.

"You'll never know if you don't try."

He squeezed her hand and offered her a grateful smile.

THE DAY WAS gray and overcast—dreary, but typical Irish weather. It didn't bother Maggie in the least; she had more important matters to attend to, matters that would end things once and for all.

Patrick, who stood by her side, frowned and looked anything but happy.

"Something wrong?" she asked.

"There must be another way."

"No," she said in an icy voice that would frost even the warmest of summer nights. "I won't give him any more chances. He wants our marriage to be over, and now it will be."

"Please, Maggie. Don't do this."

"But I want to." She gave him a sultry look, and went to him, kissing him as she pressed her body against his, knowing the promise of being with her always convinced him to do her bidding, but much to her surprise, he didn't respond. In fact, he pushed her away. What was wrong with him?

"Please, Patrick, just this last little favor."

"And what do I get in return?"

"Sean will be gone, and I'll be yours forever." She brushed her lips over his cheek.

At one time he would have done anything for her, but as she regarded him now, she saw an uncharacteristic coldness in his deep brown eyes, he felt as if he had never seen her before.

"Patrick, will you help me?"

"To kill Sean? You're talking about murder." He paused. "I don't like him but this is wrong!"

"No! If I can't have him, no one can!' she hissed and clamped her hand tightly on his forearm. "Now will you help me or not?"

"Not," he said, and gave her a small smile as if unsure of himself. "No, I won't." He gave her a full smile, confident of himself and his decision. "I've done many things for you, but I'll not kill another man." He regarded her with disdain. "You won't do it either; I don't think you capable of murder."

"I'm capable of a great many things that you know nothing about!" With a last glare of disgust she turned on her heel and left.

THE SILENCE HAD lengthened between them again, and with a note of false cheer, Lillie tried to engage her brother in small talk.

"Did you now that the O'Leary's had their child? It's a fine young boy; they're going to name him Robert."

"That's a nice name." Sean smiled drunkenly for a moment. "I wanted children. Did you know that?" He closed his eyes in pain. "Just not with Maggie. *Ahh*, Lillie. I've made such a mess of things."

She patted him fondly. "You can't help it, you're a man." He focused enough to glare at her. "I found something after Mary left, and I'm guessing it belongs to you." She pulled out the beautiful emerald necklace and put it on the table in front of him. His expression grew more depressed as he reached for it and held it up in the light.

"I gave this to her. I didn't think I had anything else to give her, so I found the most beautiful necklace I could find and got it for her." He held up the necklace, and even in the dim light, it shone. "See how it sparkles! Just like her eyes."

Lillie sighed, got up from her seat and kissed the top of her brother's head, and he clung to her like a little boy. When he finally let go, she wiped the tears from his face, and after a moment, he held out the necklace to his sister.

"Sean?"

"Take it. Keep it safe. If I have need of it, I'll get it from you."

With a reluctant nod, she back the necklace. "You'll be coming home tonight?"

"Yeah. Just let me wallow a while longer."

She hugged him again and, with a last concerned look at him, she departed. Sean's new drink arrived, and he breathed a sigh of relief. He didn't want to think. He didn't want to feel. He didn't want to remember the pain in Mary's face. So he drank and, when he knew he'd drunk too much, he drank some more, knowing oblivion would soon follow. He put his head on the table and closed his eyes in relief. He had nearly reached his destination of alcoholic stupor.

EVERYTHING WAS IN disarray. The things Maggie had wanted were disappearing, dissolving like shadows in the mist. Sean had finally found enough courage to ask her for a divorce, no doubt due to the influence of his American girlfriend. That bitch! How dare she take Sean from her?

And what was wrong with Patrick? She'd thought that if all else failed, she would always have Patrick to fall back on, but for once in his life, he'd stood up to her. How could they both be escaping her spells? Sean had always been a bit problematic, a bit resistant to her, but Patrick had always been easy to manipulate. What could be interfering with her control of him?

She expelled a deep sigh, and shook her head sadly.

She was being forced into the actions she was now taking, forced by a husband who no longer loved her. It was all his fault, so she would do what she must.

The storage area for the pub was seldom used by anyone, and she unlocked the door with ease and entered the small room where cases of alcohol were stored. Yes indeed, that should be enough for a nice consuming fire. Quietly, but slowly growing louder, she chanted to herself, her eyes closed in concentration. She continued this for about a minute and opened her eyes and pointed to the dry wood of the door frame, the blaze from her finger sending hungry flames licking at the dry wood. She reviewed her work—the blue tinge of the flames was slightly abnormal, but she doubted anyone would notice. She used a few more words and gestures to place a cloaking spell over her magical fire. That was when she realized the small room was already growing warm, and the fire was progressing much more quickly than she had anticipated. She needed to get into the front of the pub to complete her plan, to lure out Donald and the others before the fire was out of control; there was no need to sacrifice the whole bloody town. She had to hurry though, before the fire was discovered, and they tried to save the pub.

THE PUB DOOR opened, and Maggie entered. Thoughtfully, she assessed the current situation in the pub. Donald was over by the dart board, throwing a friendly game with Ian, another local. And except for Sean, who was dozing quietly, his head on the table, there was no one else in the pub.

Maggie chuckled as she watched Sean sleep restlessly. She had never seen him in such a stupor. this would be far too easy.

"Gentlemen, could you help a woman in distress?" she asked, approaching Donald and Ian after they finished their dart game.

The two men exchanged a knowing look and turned to face her, politeness masking their features. "And what is it that you'd be wanting?" Donald asked.

"My car," she said embarrassed. "It's stuck in the mud, and I can't get it out. I'm afraid I'm not a good driver." She put her hands on their backs as she walked up behind them, they didn't hear her whispered words.

"Well," Ian offered reluctantly, "I suppose we could help you push it out."

She smiled at them prettily. "Oh, would you? Could you? I'd be ever so grateful." Ian returned her smile, but Donald only sighed. "Donald, will you help too?"

"Of course, I'd be happy to," he said with a pleasant smile, but he felt a sudden rush of uneasiness. He felt blocked somehow and eyed Maggie suspiciously.

"Are you sure that you need two of us?" Donald asked.

"Yes, I'm afraid I'm really stuck. You will help, won't you, Donald?" She put her hand on his back again and rubbed it lightly.

"All right," he agreed with a frown.

"Thanks so much," she gushed, leading them to the door.

"What about Sean?" Ian asked.

Donald looked over and saw Sean sleeping, his head on the table as he snored softly. "Leave him be."

The sound of the door shutting woke Sean, but only for a moment. He blinked in confusion, and closed his eyes, welcoming the darkness of oblivion as he passed out again. A vague noise reached his ears but he paid it no mind; he remained unconscious, unaware of the smoke filling the bar.

DOWN THE ROAD from The Gaelic Moon, Donald and Ian tried to move Maggie's car, which was stuck to its hub in mud. They exchanged heated words with each other and with Maggie, who expressed her displeasure with them.

Hearing the commotion, an old woman came out of her house, sniffed the air and looked down the road toward the pub. She shrieked in alarm. Donald and Ian turned to see the building in flames and, despite Maggie's efforts to detain them, they broke away from her and ran toward The Gaelic Moon. The town erupted into chaos, shouts of "Fire!" filling the air. The antiquated fire truck arrived, but its supply of water wasn't enough to stop The Gaelic Moon from burning in the hot, all-consuming fire.

Lillie ran into the crowd, searching desperately for Sean. Not seeing him, she ran toward the pub, but Patrick wrapped his strong arms around her.

"Let me go!"

"Lillie! It's too late, there's nothing you can do," he whispered and held her tightly as she fought against him.

Donald and Ian, glancing at each other and quickly about the crowd, realized the last place they had seen Sean was alone in the pub, just a few minutes earlier, and he hadn't come out. They yelled to the others who had gathered nearby, and other locals ran into the burning pub with them.

Patrick watched with a strange expression on his face as the flames reached toward the sky. His face was etched with sadness as The Gaelic Moon died before them, the agonized cries of those within piercing the dark night. He saw the crazed look on Maggie's face and, clear of her manipulations, he hissed at her, "It's your fault!"

"He's going to die," Maggie said as if realizing the truth of her actions for the first time. Confusion marred her features as if she were fighting some sort of internal struggle and losing. She broke her gaze from Patrick and looked at the inferno of blue flames, her face full of conflict. Without warning she ran out of the crowd and into the blaze.

"Maggie, no!" Patrick's desperate attempt to grasp her as she flew by failed miserably.

SMOKE. FLAMES. HEAT. Fire. Fire. Fire. The word echoed through his mind as Sean struggled toward consciousness. He coughed, breathing in the smoke that saturated the pub, and awoke.

He broke the surface of his unconsciousness to wake to some sort of horrible nightmare. The Gaelic Moon was in flames, smoke obscuring his vision and filling his lungs. He coughed again and fell to the floor, his legs unable to support him.

He heard a noise as the fire roared louder, heard Donald's voice calling to him. He raised his head and tried to call, but could only cough. Weakly, he tried to wave at Donald. And miraculously, Donald saw him.

"Let's get you out of here. This damn fire is magical," the barkeep said and began to help Sean off the burning floor.

A large beam, flaming and blackened, gave way, and Sean screamed as it fell on Donald, pinning both of them to the floor. The heat was unbearable. The flames licked his body, and he smelled burning flesh and knew it to be his. Excruciating pain covered him, blanketed him with searing agony.

He didn't want to die.

Oh, Mary! I love you! Don't forget! Don't ever forget!

The roar of the flames sounded like a train. He covered his ears and tried to escape the burning beam that trapped him, and when the noise became unbearable, he said his last prayer, and his world ended.

PATRICK AND THE others watched in disbelief as the building burned with an intensity that none of them could really explain, an intensity that somehow ignored that much of The Gaelic Moon was made of stone, and the fire busily consuming it shouldn't burn so hot, or so bright. The onlookers could only watch the tragedy before them, knowing that the rescue of those inside was impossible now, knowing those beloved people would never be seen again. Unable to turn away, they watched the historic, mystical building burn to the ground.

Patrick wrapped his arms around Lillie and held her tight, holding her as she cried against him, heart-rending sobs that broke his heart. When he looked up again, the pub had collapsed on itself, flames of red and blue still hungrily feeding on the structure.

Lillie wrenched free from Patrick's arms and fell to the ground seeing what was left of The Gaelic Moon. "Sean!" she cried, "Oh, God! Not Sean!"

Wails of grief filled the air, and they clung to one another in sorrow, unable to bear the tragedy of their loss as The Gaelic Moon died before them. As one, they fell to their knees and began to pray for their lost family and friends, knowing that only God could help them now.

Chapter 18
Reawakening

*S*MOKE! FLAMES! THE fire consumed him, ate his soul and his body, keeping him from the one that he loved above all others. The flamed burned intently until there was nothing left of him but... ashes.

Sean bolted upright from where he lay on the floor of the local pub, The Gaelic Moon, trying to calm himself. He rubbed the back of his neck, trying to ease his sore muscles from his impromptu sleep on the floor.

Dear Jesus! What kind of dream did he just have? And just what in the hell was he doing on the floor?

"*Ahh*, Sean, we were wondering when you would join us." Donald said as he extended a hand to Sean and helped him up from where he sat.

"Donald?" He blinked in confusion as he looked at the man. Clearly his brain cells were not working coherently yet.

"You really are out of sorts, aren't you?" Donald said in a voice filled with sympathy. "No matter, you'll come around. It just takes some souls longer than others."

Sean staggered to his familiar barstool and sat down. "My head hurts," he complained and rested it in his hands.

"Maybe this will help." Donald slid a glass of Guinness across the bar to him.

Sean wrapped his hand around the cool glass and some level

of his mind noted that the glass didn't feel as smooth and substantial as usual. "What's going on?"

"What do you mean?" the bartender asked with far too much innocence.

Sean looked around the quiet pub and only saw a few other patrons. The building was filled with sunlight, so Sean gathered it must be early afternoon but why did everything seem off to him? He drummed his fingers on the bar before turning back to Donald. "Something isn't right. What is it?"

Donald gave him a long look but said nothing.

"Don't keep me in suspense, spit it out."

"What do you remember?" The barkeep asked.

"You mean besides waking up on the floor?"

Donald nodded.

Sean concentrated and immediately felt the fire licking at his skin, and he shuddered. He poked further into his memories and remembered being completely inebriated and in such a bad way that he wasn't even able to stand. He saw himself slouched over a table in a drunken stupor, cheek pressed against the tabletop.

What the hell? He seldom got that drunk, so what had happened?

"I remember a fire," he said at last, rubbing his temple. "The Gaelic Moon burning, and you were trying to save me. But here we are. How can it possibly be true?"

Donald still remained silent.

"Christ! Would you say something? Normally you won't shut up."

"A lot has happened. I'm not sure where to start."

"Pick a spot, any bloody spot."

"You have to ask me the questions as you remember things. I can't force your memory."

"Just brilliant! What is that? Some weird vow of silence?" Sean yelled at Donald, who only shrugged.

"Fine." Sean took a deep breath trying to calm himself. "I remember a fire burned The Gaelic Moon, but it sure as hell doesn't seem burned," he said looking around him. "Was it just some bizarre dream?"

"No."

"So the pub burned?"

"Yes.

"Can you please elaborate?"

Donald crossed his arms in front of him and regarded Sean. "What do you remember?"

"Again?" Exasperated, Sean ran his hand through his unruly red hair. "All right, fine." He closed his eyes and concentrated, really concentrated and tried to remember all of the events that had led him to this point.

He had been drinking in the pub because he felt miserable, because something had upset him so much he got dead drunk and didn't care about what happened to him. He searched his mind and found an unexpected pocket of grief that was almost enough to knock him off his stool.

Mary. The name resonated through him with overwhelming love but laced with far too many layers of a sharp, unbearable pain. Hesitating, he pulled at the memories, not sure he wanted to dredge up what was currently eluding him.

He closed his eyes and was assaulted by memories of a lovely, shapely woman with dark hair that fell softly to the middle of her back, hazel eyes that sparkled a lovely shade of green when she teased him, and a wondrous smile that caused his heart to melt when it lit her face. She meant everything to him, and he'd fallen in love with her despite his best intentions. And the best news of all—she was pregnant with his child. He almost cried as he remembered the love and passion that had led to such a treasured turn of events, but like the wind from a tornado, Maggie had blown his world apart.

Then the pub was on fire, and he couldn't escape, and he...

"Died?" He looked over at Donald. "We're dead?"

Donald leaned over and wiped a tear from Sean's face. "Sorry, lad."

"But I can't be... I have too much left to do. I have to find Mary..." He wiped tears from his face. "She left and... and I haven't fixed things..."

"Sean, it will be all right."

"No! I have to find her, I have to make amends."

"It's too late for that," Donald said in a gentle voice.

"But she's pregnant!"

"I know. She'll be fine."

"How do you know? How in bloody hell do you know that? I was going to marry her!" Sean lurched off his barstool toward the door that led out of the pub.

"Sean, don't!" Donald cautioned.

"I have to find her. I will find her!" His hand was on the door handle, but the handle seemed to burn into his hand. He flinched and glared at the handle as if it were an enemy.

"Don't go out," Donald said in a calm voice.

"Why the hell not?"

"It won't do you any good. Please sit down so and we can discuss this."

"Discuss what? The fact that I'm dead and everything I ever wanted has gone to hell?" Sean screamed at him in rage. "I'm leaving. I have to find her!"

He reached for the door again, ignoring the burning of his hand and flung it open.

He found himself looking out on the street of Cullamore. He tried to take a deep breath, but the air hurt his lungs. He felt Donald's hand on his shoulder and wrenched himself away, throwing himself out on the street. It hurt, his entire body hurt, like he was being pulled apart into a billion pieces.

"I have to find her," he gasped, all the while wondering how a ghost could feel white hot slivers of pain through what now passed for his body.

"Sean." Donald was surprisingly strong as he gripped Sean's shoulder and hauled him to his feet. "You need to come with me."

"I can't... " He tried to wrench free from Donald but fell to the ground on his back. He was shocked to see not The Gaelic Moon that he knew and loved, but instead the scorched and burned remains of what had once been his favorite pub. Most of the structure had collapsed into an indistinguishable pile of rubble, and all that remained was part of the stone walls and a few thick square beams which reached beseechingly toward the sky.

"Oh my God," he muttered and winced as the pain returned. He felt as if he had to concentrate to hold himself together.

"Sean, come back inside The Gaelic Moon, or you will suffer so much pain and weakness that you will not be a viable spirit."

"How can a ghost die?" he gasped, sagging to his knees.

"Not so much as die as cease to exist, but it's not pleasant, I'll give you that. Come on, lad, enough of this nonsense." Supporting Sean, he assisted him back inside The Gaelic Moon and sat him back on his barstool.

"You need a moment to recover, I'll be right back," Donald said and went to assist another patron

Mary. He had to find her, he had to be with her. It was the only thing he could think about.

He closed his eyes and brought the image of her and her warm smile to his mind, the light in her eyes as she teased him, and the soft sound of her voice as she told him that she loved him. He concentrated on her and, for just a moment, thought he touched her mind and felt all of the things that uniquely made her the person she was.

"Mary," he whispered, but the feeling was gone.

THERE WAS A chill in the air when she opened her eyes. The window was open to the cool fall air, and her covers had fallen off, but it was the dream that woke her. The dream of the man she loved more than she could admit, the man who had torn out her heart and run after her car as she had driven away from him.

She was still coming to terms with his betrayal, her mind insisting that everything his wife, Maggie, had said was true, and her heart insisting that she should give her love another chance to talk to her. The best she could manage was that if he called, she would talk to him, and she desperately wanted him to call.

She rubbed her growing belly, aware of the life contained within, the life she had created with Sean. She was torn between joy and grief at the child's impending birth, but couldn't deal with those thoughts right now. All she wanted to do was to shut the world out and go back to sleep.

Mary closed her eyes and winced.

Smoke! Flames!

The sound of screams.

The snapping of fire.

The bright blue flames and smell of burnt flesh.

Ashes.

She sat upright, breathing hard.

She'd had those dreams since she had returned from Ireland a month ago and wanted them to go away. Trying to push them away, she allowed herself a painful indulgence, a few moments to remember the comfort of her time with Sean. A time not so long ago, when everything had been wonderful and they had been cautiously planning a future together, a time when she could believe in him.

"Mary." As she neared sleep, she heard him whisper her name, knew her mind was playing tricks on her, but didn't care.

"Sean," she murmured and closed her eyes squeezing out her tears as she let sleep claim her.

Part Two

Chapter 19
Nightmares

Four years later

SMOKE. FLAME. HEAT. Fire, fire, fire. Mary coughed and opened her eyes only to find smoke clouding her vision. The building was an inferno, but as she tried to find a path out of it, flaming debris fell from the ceiling and onto her clothing. The pain was instant, unbearable, and she grabbed her arm, trying to quell the heat that now seemed to burn from within her. The flames crackled, dancing as they seared her flesh and the building collapsed around her!

Help! Oh, please help! Oh, God! She didn't want to die... not like this. *Oh, God! Oh, God! Oh, God!*

She cried out as the fiery beam exploded and trapped her beneath it, brutal heat melting her skin. And as the darkness of oblivion overtook her, a whisper, so faint she had to strain to hear... "Don't forget... don't ever forget..."

Her eyes opened and she looked around the room wildly, expecting flames and smoke to engulf her, but there was nothing. No smoke, no fire. Her heartbeat slowed to a bearable level, and she told herself to breathe normally again, to not be so affected by a dream. But she couldn't prevent the sobs that escaped her because she felt as if she had lost part of her soul.

That damn nightmare! Why did she still have it? She closed her eyes and saw a fire, heard the screams of people dying within it, and shivered. The nightmare was always the same—so real that she sometimes felt as if she had died in the fire. And always, after she woke, she cried as if she had lost some part of herself.

The most frustrating part was that she didn't know why she cried, only that it felt like something precious had been taken from her. She never knew who died or what building had burned to the ground—those images remained vague. But dying in the fire was vivid, as was the overwhelming feeling of things left unfinished. Knowing sleep would be impossible for the rest of the night; she picked up the book on the nightstand and wandered into the living room. Despite her best effort to avoid sleep, she found her eyes getting heavy as she struggled to stay awake.

The flames licked greedily at her skin, and when she looked up, she saw Donald trying to save her, his face grim as he reached his hand down to her, and the beam collapsing which made escape from the inferno impossible for both of them. She suddenly realized that it was The Gaelic Moon burning, succumbing to the hunger of ravenous blue flames...

Mary gasped as she bolted upright into a sitting position, heart pounding, the images in her mind moving almost too rapidly for her to keep up as she finally recognized the setting of her dream: the Gaelic Moon. Her heart thumped hard in her chest as she thought of Sean. *What happened to him?*

"Crap," she muttered, and got up off the couch. She knew a drink was inappropriate since she had to go to work in the morning, but she was shaken by her nightmare and felt in need of one. She went into the kitchen, opened a seldom-used cupboard, and reached to the upper shelf for the bottle of Irish whiskey she kept there—Tullamore Dew, her favorite. Her young son wasn't the only thing she had brought back from Ireland with her due to Sean's influence.

She pulled herself a healthy shot and drank it down in one gulp, managing to not quite cough, and she poured one more shot for herself and replaced the bottle in the cupboard, shutting the door. She took the shot glass with her and wandered back into the living room to a bookshelf. She pulled out a small photo album that was hidden from sight and brought it with her to the couch. Taking a large sip from her glass, she swallowed the whiskey, enjoying its warmth as it slid down her throat, appreciating the term "liquid courage." Her hands only shook a little bit as she opened the photo album and saw the first picture—herself and

Sean, arms around each other and staring at one another as if no other person existed in the universe. Amy had taken it at their flat when she and Sean hadn't been looking. Mary traced the outline of Sean's face in the photo.

It had never crossed her mind that maybe Sean wasn't able to contact her; she had always assumed that he had chosen not to contact her. What if she had been wrong?

She threw back the rest of the drink and curled up on the couch with the small, but highly treasured photo album, staring sadly at the photo that she had once believed was her future.

THE INFORMATION ON the computer screen burned into Mary's memory, and she had to remind herself to blink, and look away from it. She closed her eyes and rubbed them, wondering when this job had stopped being fun. The long hours, difficult problems, and tedious work had never used to bother her, there was no mistaking she was still capable of both—such qualities had resulted in a promotion giving her more money, this comfortable office, and more responsibilities. This type of promotion would have been ideal a few years ago, but with the arrival of her son, her priorities had changed. Now she treasured the time spent at home with her son.

Even with a good job, being a single mom was hard, and she always felt like she didn't spend enough time with her son. Getting out of the office was the highlight of her day. When the clock hit four in the afternoon, she could hardly stand the last hour. *Just like now*, she thought, and watched as the clock rolled over to 4:05 p.m.

She heard a knock on her door, and she looked up to see Paul enter, blond as ever, but now sporting a mustache. Four years had given his face more character, and he was even more handsome. He made sure no one was looking, smiled at her, and closed the door behind him. Stepping over to Mary, he pulled her out of her chair and into his arms, kissing her softly.

"What's that for?" she asked.

"Only because I haven't seen you all day, and I missed you." She smiled, but withdrew from his arms. "Something wrong?"

She sighed as she thought of her four-year-old son waiting at home for her. "Nothing. Too much work. And a blasted headache."

"Are we still on for tonight?"

"I don't know." She bit her lip. "Can you get a refund for the tickets?"

Paul stepped away from her, frowning. "Yeah, fine."

"Maybe someone else will go with you?"

"I don't want to go with anyone else." His body language reminded her of a small child who has just been told he can't have what he wanted.

"I'm sorry." She winced and rubbed her temples. "It's this stupid headache."

He frowned in concern. "Another bad one?"

"Yeah. I'm going home before I'm completely incapacitated."

"Let me drive you; you know you're not supposed to drive when you have a migraine."

"It's okay, Amy volunteered."

He grimaced. "Amy."

"She is my best friend, you know. You're going to have to accept that."

He snorted in contempt. "Yeah, I bet. Just like she's accepted me."

"Paul!"

"What? Tell me it's not true. "You haven't spent much time with me lately"

She heard the suspicion in his voice.

"Sorry. Stupid migraines, and taking care of my son."

"Are you sure you're not avoiding me?" The tone was casual, but something in his voice made her shiver.

She rubbed her temple again and sighed. The drums in her head were beginning to bang loudly, and she just didn't have time to deal with a pissy boyfriend. "Why would I do that?"

Paul took her hands firmly within his own. "Mary, you need someone to take care of you, to look after you. You need to start a new life for yourself. Start it with me."

"I told you, I haven't made up my mind yet."

He offered her a charming smile. "But we're good together. You know I love you and treat you far better than Sean ever could," he said, making a definite point.

"You are never to talk about Sean like that again!" she hissed and closed her eyes, trying to soothe away the ever-increasing pounding in her head and the pain the light was causing to her eyes.

"Mary, don't you think it's time we settled this?"

She opened her eyes and regarded him through the slits she now used for vision. "We can't have this discussion now, Paul."

"Why not?" He seemed genuinely surprised.

"Because my frickin' head is about to fall off!"

He frowned, his lips compressed in a thin line, but shut up and, without another word, turned and left her office, stalking past Amy in the doorway.

Amy glared after him but quickly turned her attention to her friend. "Mary, is everything okay?"

"No. Get me home," she said through gritted teeth.

"I will, honey, but put on your winter gear so that we can brave the cold."

"Thanks, Amy." A weak smile was the best she could manage as she shrugged into her coat.

IT TOOK A little persuasion but within a few minutes of Amy getting Mary to her small house in St. Paul, she convinced her that she would be no good to anyone until she took her medication and went to sleep for a while. And while she was sleeping, Amy promised to go and pick up Mary's son, little Sean.

When they returned, Amy opened the door and led the boy into the house, putting a finger to her lip to indicate that he should be quiet.

"Why, Aunt Amy? What's wrong?"

Amy bent down and took off the boy's hat, mittens, and his jacket, hanging it up in the hall. He smiled up at her and wrapped his small arms around her leg, hugging her.

"You're mom isn't feeling well, so we have to be quiet."

"Again?" The boy's brow creased in concern. "She gets a lot of headaches lately."

"Yeah, I know it seems that way. Sorry, buddy. If we let her sleep she can get better."

"All right." He gave his adopted aunt a charming smile and, for just a moment, Amy saw his father in that smile, and the blue eyes that looked up at her. "Can we play until she gets up?"

"Yes, we can, but not until you get supper. Go wash up and then into the kitchen."

"Do I have to?"

Amy pointed to the bathroom. "Yes, now go. The sooner we have supper, the sooner we can play."

"Okay," the red-haired boy grumbled, and trudged to the bathroom.

Amy somehow managed to hold in the smile that threatened to escape onto her face.

THEY WERE BUSY coloring two hours later when the door to Mary's bedroom opened and she emerged, the pain gone from her face, although she still seemed pale and tired.

"Mommy!" The small boy launched himself from Amy's lap at his mother, who caught him and swung him around, hold him close. He giggled gleefully until she set him down on the floor again. "Do ya feel better?"

"Yes, my little one, I do." She nuzzled his neck, and he laughed once more. "And I hate to ruin your party, but it's almost time for bed."

"But you just got up, and I haven't seen you all day!"

Amy laughed. "Smart kid, he knows how to push your buttons."

"All right, half an hour, and then it's off to bed."

"Deal," he said. "Can I play with my squirt gun?"

"No, it's too late for that."

"Tomorrow?" he asked hopefully.

"We'll see, but since it's a weekend, so maybe."

He bounced up and down enthusiastically. "I want a water rifle!"

"We'll talk about it tomorrow. I'm not at all sure winter is the right time for that kind of present." She ruffled his hair. "We'd better get playing if you're going to bed soon."

Her son squealed in delight and ran back to his coloring book. Mary and Amy sat down on the couch behind him.

AMY RETURNED TO the living room, with two glasses of water and handed one to Mary before sitting down on the couch beside her.

"I said I wanted coffee," Mary tried to complain through her yawn.

"Not good for you when you need to get hydrated again. Shut up and drink your water."

"*Umm.*" Mary sipped her water.

"So what brought this headache on?"

Mary exhaled and bit her lip, not wanting to share that bit of information.

"Mary, tell me."

"Fine. I had that dream again."

"The fire?"

"Yeah, except this one was different." Her gaze drifted away from Amy.

"How?"

"This time I recognized the building that was burning."

"You did? What was it?"

"The Gaelic Moon," Mary whispered.

"The Gaelic Moon?" Amy tried to laugh it off. "Come on, Mary, you were dreaming."

"It was real, and much more intense than usual. And you know how I always feel like I'm the one trapped? Like I'm the one caught in the fire?" She gave her friend a somber look. "That's because I'm seeing it through someone else's eyes. I'm seeing it through Sean's eyes."

"Sean? That's impossible."

"Is it?" Mary got off the couch and paced back and forth. "I always thought I had been blind and fallen into the same trap again. And the reason he never contacted me was because he had settled down with that bitch of a wife!" She nearly spat out the words before collecting herself once again.

"Are you finally open to other possibilities?" Amy asked.

Mary gave her a short nod. "What if he didn't contact me because he couldn't?"

"I don't follow."

"What if there was a fire, and he was trapped in it? Oh, Amy. He could have been hurt, or maybe he's so disfigured that he thought he shouldn't see me again? I don't know, anything!"

"Honey, do you believe this, or are you reaching for straws?"

Mary stopped and crossed her arms, regarding her friend. "What do you mean?"

"When I've suggested there may be a reason he didn't contact you, you've always shot me down. And now, suddenly, you're willing to believe?"

She nodded. "I've never felt the pain like this... Oh, my God!" Tears prickled at the back of her eyes.

Fighting with her skepticism, Amy asked, "This is psychic?"

"It has to be, and I've been ignoring it all this time because I was so mad and hurt."

"Then what does it mean?"

"It means that I have to go back to Ireland to see if he's all right."

Amy gave her an exasperated glare.

"He needs to meet his son, and my son should at least know who his father is."

"God, you should have had this dream years ago." Amy gave her an exaggerated eye roll.

"I did. I've had this dream ever since we left Ireland four years ago, but I was so upset I ignored them, thought they were just anxieties working themselves out. And I've gotten headaches. I never used to get headaches when I would see things."

"So do you still hear his voice in your head? You said that happens sometimes. . ."

"Stop looking at me like I'm crazy."

"I'm not, but maybe Sean's trying to tell you something?"

"Like what?"

"Oh, I don't know, maybe, 'talk to me'? From what you told me, he was begging you to do that when you drove away."

Mary dropped herself onto the couch and curled up against it. "I should have stopped," she whispered. "But all the letters I sent came back with no forwarding address, and when I called his workplace they told me he was no longer there. And his apartment phone was disconnected."

"I think there's more to this story. I still think he loves you," Amy said.

Mary scowled at her. "Why are you on his side?"

"Because we had a couple of talks, and I decided he was one of the good guys."

"Oh," was all Mary said as they settled into a comfortable silence. "Do you think I should go?"

Amy smacked the back of her head just enough to get her attention. "What do you think?"

"Fine, I'll go. And after all of this time, I think the sooner the better."

"Great!" Amy grinned at her. "Rob and I will go with you. We really liked Ireland and are in need of a vacation as well."

"Aren't you moving a little fast? I've just barely said yes." But Mary felt the smile creeping across her face. She had fallen in love with Ireland.

"Fast? Nonsense, when the time is right you have to act," Amy declared.

"Oh? If that's true, why are you and Rob still engaged? Five years later?" Mary arched her eyebrow at her friend.

Amy shrugged. "We're just not ready."

"I think Rob's ready. You're the one who's not ready."

Amy pouted. "How can you say that? I love Rob."

"I believe you. I just think you're afraid of commitment."

"Me?" Amy feigned indignation at the suggestion, but Mary stared her down. "All right, all right, I am, kind of."

"Why?"

"I guess I'm afraid of being tied down."

"You've been tied down for over five years," Mary said. "You love the guy. Just do it."

"This part of the discussion brings us to our next topic," Amy said and Mary gave her a frustrated look. "Our next topic is another man."

"Another man?" Mary frowned. "Who?"

"Paul. What about Paul?"

"Honestly? I'm not sure. He was wonderful when I was such a wreck after returning from Ireland. He held my hand, gave me a shoulder to cry on, listened to me rant and rave and cry, and I'm grateful and want to feel more than I do, but. . ."

"You don't love him," Amy said.

Mary shook her head. "No, I just don't feel it, Amy. I'm not sure how to tell him that, either."

"Could you ever love him? I mean, if you settled your past with Sean and got past it, would it be possible for you to love Paul?"

Mary had given a lot of thought to of late and try though she might, something about Paul never sat quite right with her.

"I don't think so," she finally said after a long silence.

"It seems you have a lot of things to take care of. Which of the men in your life are you going to deal with first? The Irishman or the American?"

Mary put her face in her hands. "I don't want to deal with either of them, truth be told. But, I'd rather face up to Sean first. That problem has existed longer, and when I come back, I can let Paul down gently."

Amy gave Mary an encouraging smile. "I don't envy you, but if you need me for anything, you know I'll be there for you. How about we forget this serious stuff for a while and get some food? Chinese?"

"You're not seeing Rob tonight?"

"*Nah*, he's out of town." Amy grinned at her. "You and little Sean have me all to yourself. Good thing I'm here too. How else could you possibly get your life in order?"

"All right, we're having Chinese. Get the Kung Pao chicken for me, and whatever you want. You order, and I'll buy."

"Deal." Amy went to grab the nearby phone.

THE RESTAURANT THE next night was a very nice place in a Minneapolis suburb, set up with a bar side and a more formal dining room. It was well known for its own brewery and also hosted a wide variety of Scotch malts. Mary loved the place and was happy that Paul had chosen this particular restaurant for their dinner.

Despite what she had told Amy, she was fond of Paul and felt she owed him a lot. After her return to the States, she had been a wreck. Somehow she had managed to go to work and keep focused on her job, but she didn't remember much of those months before her son was born. Paul and Amy had taken care of her when she'd had no interest in looking after herself. And after several months, the devastating sense of grief and loss became livable. Though her thoughts of Sean lessened, they never went away. How could they? She was having his child.

The man across from her had been with her the entire time, holding her hand and looking after her and little Sean. Whenever she needed him, he was there, and she was grateful. She finally consented to date him, but it never felt quite right to her. He persuaded her to be exclusive and here they were.

Paul took her hand in his, and she gave him a wan smile.

"It's been a nice evening, hasn't it?"

"Yes, it has, though I worry about you plying me with all of these drinks..."

He laughed quietly and gave her a warm smile. "You have a wonderful sense of humor. Has anyone ever told you that?"

"I think you may have mentioned it once or twice." She paused. "Paul, I need to talk to you about something."

"Why such a serious expression? You aren't breaking up with me, are you?"

"No, of course not." Mary shook her head, knowing that she should do it—now was a good moment to do it—but she had decided she wanted to deal with the Irish problem first. "I'm going to be gone for a while."

"Gone?" He frowned. "Where?"

"To Ireland." She took a deep breath and waited for his reaction.

"Ireland?" He let go of her hand and sat back in his chair. "It's not a pleasure trip?"

"Hardly. I've decided it's time that my son met his father. And Amy is coming with me."

"What about me?"

"What about you?"

"Wouldn't I be a better choice to go with you than Amy?"

"I can't ask you to take time off from work."

"I'd be happy to. I need a vacation anyway."

"No. I want Amy to come with me."

"What about Sean?" The jealousy in his voice was unmistakable.

"What about him?" She made a sound of anger as she saw the jealousy on Paul's face. "The only reason I'm going is because of my son. He deserves to know who his father is."

"Sorry." He sighed and studied her for a few moments, taking her hand in his. "You're right. It's just that I worry about you. I don't want to see him hurt you again."

"He won't. He can't. It's been over between us for years." She smiled and said, "You're sweet. Thanks for looking out for me."

"How long will you be gone?"

"I don't know, two, maybe three weeks."

"I'll have to make this a night to remember!" he said with a possessive look for her.

Mary wondered who he wanted to make it a memorable night for, her or himself, and realized that tonight he would be disappointed as she would send him back home.

Chapter 20
Relearning

A WEEK LATER, Mary found the streets of Dublin hadn't changed a great deal in the four years since Mary had last seen them. A large, noisy city that was just as she remembered it, although somehow the already bad traffic seemed to have gotten worse. Even the flat they had stayed at before was available and seemed to welcome her as the three of them got out of the taxi and walked up the stairs.

The inside hadn't changed much either. A fresh coat of paint, somewhat different furnishings in different positions, but that was all. It was still the same warm cozy flat she remembered, complete with a fireplace. Little Sean let go of his mother's hand, and ran to the window overlooking the Dublin street, his blue eyes were wide with wonder as he took in his new surroundings. Finally, he turned to look at his mother, his expression serious.

"Mommy, is this Ireland?"

"Yes. It's a country across the ocean from where we live."

"Daddy lives here?" His small voice was filled with hope, and Mary hoped she wouldn't disappoint him.

"Yes, he does. In a small town."

"Can I see him?" The innocent blue eyes were filled with such trust that Mary found it difficult to answer him. "Please, Mommy, can I?"

"Not right now." Mary bent down and kissed his cheek.

"Mommy has to see your daddy first."

The boy began to pout, disappointed at his mother's words, but smiled again after she hugged him. "I promise, you will see your father," she said, shrugging off the concerned look that Amy gave her.

MARY TOOK ONE last look where her son lay asleep on her bed and shut the door. She entered the living room and found Amy waiting for her, a cup of cocoa on the coffee table.

"Just like old times," Amy said with a smile.

"Thanks." Mary squeezed Amy's arm as she sat down.

"Oh, the cocoa? It was nothing."

"No, I mean, thanks. For everything. You're a great friend. I don't know how I would have survived these last few years without you."

"No problem." She grinned. "And neither do I."

Mary remained silent but after a few moments let out a long sigh.

"Mary?"

"You were the one who said I should have a fling. If you hadn't pushed me, maybe I wouldn't be in this predicament." Her lips tightened into a thin line, and she glared at Amy.

"Sorry, sorry, sorry. I can never apologize enough for that one." She grimaced. "But have you noticed how I've kept my mouth shut since then?"

"Oh?" Mary raised an eyebrow. "Since when?

"Hey, I haven't tried to set you up with anyone lately."

"No, but you haven't exactly kept your mouth shut either." Mary glanced toward the bedroom

"Are you sorry to be back here?"

"Back in Ireland? No. I love this place." She slid the coffee cup away from her on the coffee table. "But I don't know what's going to happen tomorrow. Being here reminds me of everything I lost."

"I know, hon." Amy came over to her friend and dropped an arm around her neck and hugged her. "Do you have to go so soon? Maybe you should put it off for a day and rest."

"No, I can't. It's hard enough to do it now. If I put it off, I'll never get to it. I'm afraid I'll talk myself out of seeing him." She shook her head in dismay.

"Do you want to see him? I mean, you really loved him once."

"I did, I really did." She shook her head. "Lying son of a bitch!"

Amy raised a questioning eyebrow. "I think you still care."

"I deserve better."

"But, do you still love Sean?"

"No. How could I?"

Amy studied her friend with a knowing smile. "I don't know. But you're different than me. You're much too forgiving, and take too long to get over things. I would have killed someone before I walked out of town like you did that day, probably his bitch of a wife but, hey, that's me." She laughed. "I prefer violence. It's so much more direct!"

"Believe me," Mary said with a laugh, "I've thought about killing her... and him."

"Have you?" Amy's eyes were filled with concern.

"Oh don't look at me like that, I'm not some homicidal maniac. My reactions are normal." Mary's expression changed and the anger left her face, replaced by sadness. "If it wasn't for those damn dreams."

Amy searched her friend's face. "I know the fire dreams bother you."

Mary shivered, her gaze distant, seeing things Amy couldn't comprehend. "You have no idea—the pain, the longing, the sadness..." Damn, now she was crying, she could feel the tears rolling down her cheeks.

"*Aww*, honey, it'll be okay." Amy pulled her close and let Mary cry against her.

"I don't know," she mumbled in the comfort of her friend's embrace, "I guess I'll find out tomorrow."

DAMN! MARY SWORE under her breath the next morning as she tried to navigate the narrow roads of the Irish countryside. She still hated driving on the wrong side of the road, she had never gotten used to it. Maybe she should have brought Amy. She had said goodbye to Amy and little Sean that morning, with them scheduled to take the train to Cullamore in two days, where Mary would pick them up at the train station. They had both wished her well, and her son had hugged her tightly, whispering in her ear how happy he would be to see his father.

What had happened to Sean since she left? Did he have a happy marriage after all? How many kids did he have? Did they all look like him? Her son certainly did, and it was one of the reasons she couldn't completely hate him; he had given her a child that meant everything to her.

She glanced out the window at the overcast day and found the gray, gloomy weather to be strangely appropriate to the mood she was in.

And in all of this time, did he ever think of her? Did he miss her at all, or wish things had gone differently between them? With a sigh, she dismissed those useless thoughts and concentrated on her driving. Only the present mattered. The past was gone. And all she had to do was tell Sean he had a son, and somehow convince him to see the boy. How hard could that be?

THE GAELIC MOON was always the same—same people, same problems, and the same places to go. Sean wondered how they found peace with themselves; it was something he had never achieved. He ran a hand through his thick, curly red hair. He never had been able to do much with it, no matter how neatly he combed it. He surveyed his reflection in the mirror, and saw that he looked just as he always remembered himself. Was that an illusion? Was he actually some hideously charred representation of a man? He didn't know. This being dead was a tricky business. He still didn't understand it, but he was learning more every day.

He inhabited The Gaelic Moon, as did those who had died with him, but while most of them had settled into this new existence, he hadn't. He was restless. The first few times he had journeyed out of the pub, it had taken all of his energy to do so, and it had been a long time before he could go out again. The Gaelic Moon gave him strength somehow, perhaps it was because he had died here; at least that was his theory.

Donald had made him go see his family, forcing him out of the pub—or he guessed, the illusion of the pub. It had been a very difficult transition. His mother was a bitter old woman, and his sister was still grief stricken. It broke his heart not to reach them, to tell them he was all right despite his death. That was a sad bit of irony, he thought.

The most he could manage for a long time was a whisper, and

not everyone could hear it. When he tried whispering to Lillie, she complained about the flying insects that were bothering her. Insects! On the evolutionary scale, he'd been demoted to a bug! The thought appalled him. He was now able to stroll about the village when he liked. No one saw him. Once or twice his mother looked right at him and bitterly complained she'd never have grandchildren. Startled, he realized he was standing in front of Lillie, and surely his mother was talking to her?

So he struggled and practiced, trying to make himself heard and seen by those in the material world. Gradually his abilities increased, but it was difficult for him. Frustrated, he retired to the pub until Donald booted him out again.

He practiced every day until he was exhausted and could only slump over the bar in The Gaelic Moon to rest and regain his energy until his next foray into the real world. Donald continued to offer support and encouragement, telling him he'd need to be strong because he still had tasks to attend to, and people to take care of. Sean wasn't sure what he was talking about, but agreed to the assignments Donald had for him. It was certainly better than fading quietly into eternity. And truth be told, he liked having things to do, he liked being a friendly ghost.

Certain people in the village began to be aware of a certain oddness to things, a sudden good luck in regards to small things. A reminder for a doctor's appointment when a misplaced note suddenly reappeared on the table, a prized vase falling to the hard floor but landing softly without harm.

And Sean kept busy, because being busy kept him from thinking about Mary. He still wasn't over her and, right now, doubted he ever would be. How long since she had left in tears? A month? A year? More than that? He simply didn't know. Time passed differently here, wherever here was.

But he knew he couldn't go after her. He was forever tied to this village and his final resting place. So he prayed for her and her recovery from the pain he had caused her, and prayed her pregnancy had gone well and that the baby was healthy. And he knew it was wrong and selfish, but most of all he prayed he could see Mary again, that she would return to the village and he could somehow make amends. With a sigh, he wafted out of The Gaelic Moon and found himself standing on a small hill some distance away from the Guesthouse, the place he had last seen Mary, the place where she had driven off and left him behind. Despite his promises to the contrary, he had never gone after her, and he could never marry her. On the upside, he supposed that in God's eyes his marriage to Maggie was officially over—"Till death do you part." There was more than a bit of dark irony in that scenario, and he wasn't sure he appreciated it at all.

He lit up a cigarette and watched with mild interest as a small gray car pulled up in front of the Guesthouse, and a lone occupant, a woman got out. She stretched and looked at the lodging and around the front of the place nervously. Her long, brown hair had reddish highlights and Sean idly wondered if she had some Irish background. He frowned, thinking that something about her was familiar, but he dismissed the thought and put out his ghostly cigarette. Time to get back to work. He was sure Donald would have something new for him to do.

TIRED, SEAN RESTED against the bar. It had been a busy day, and he had spent most of it trying to get Lillie's attention. His efforts had gotten him promoted from an "insect" to a "whisper." And she had felt the kiss he had placed on her cheek because she had brushed at it with a strange look on her face. Perhaps, finally, after all of this time, he was getting through to her! It would be so much easier if she were psychically sensitive, but she wasn't. Any contact with her would be hard won.

"A beer?" Sean asked as dark ale was placed in front of him, and he looked into Donald's smiling face.

"Why not? It's still enjoyable," Donald said.

"But it isn't real. We're not real."

"If you believe you will enjoy, you will enjoy, so believe." Donald sighed and drank from his glass. "*Ahh*, that goes down well." He looked at Sean and said, "You seem tired."

"I am. Busy day." Sean took a long drink. Donald was right, it did taste good.

"Have you noticed?"

"Noticed what?"

The bartender opened his mouth to speak, but stopped and held up a hand to Sean. "Just a moment."

Sean watched with interest as the bartender spoke to thin air for a couple of minutes, and then without batting an eye turned back to Sean.

"Who're you talking to?"

"Oh, that." Donald shrugged. "I forgot you're still new. There are many souls here you can't see yet."

"But all of the locals are here."

"Well, in a sense, we're all locals. But there are many you can't see, those who have gone before us."

"And they can see you? You can see them?"

"Yes, I can."

"Care to explain?" Sean asked.

"*Hmmm*, what would the short version be?" he mused to himself. "I have been and always will be the keeper of The Gaelic Moon."

"The pub?" Sean looked around him.

"It hasn't always been a pub."

Sean studied Donald for a long moment, his mind working over the words Donald had just spoken. "You're saying those druidic legends are true? There was a civil war for that relic and it still exists today? And that you look after it?"

"Yes, and the pub." Donald smiled at him.

"What are you, Donald? If this is your vocation, you are certainly more than a mortal man. And since I am now a ghost, I know there is more to the world than I ever believed."

"I am more than a mortal man, Sean, much more." He leaned across the bar and stared into Sean's eyes. Sean felt the power radiating off him, but strangely, he wasn't put off by it, just more curious than ever.

"What are you?" he asked.

"I can't completely answer you," Donald smiled.

"Why not? It's not like I can tell anyone. I'm dead."

"Look at all the other spirits around you. Though they may appear so, not all can be counted as good. I have found it best to play things close to the vest."

"What things?"

"Rules exist in the spirit realm as well, my boy, and I disseminate information only as needed. I am much more than a spirit, but let's just say I'm an agent for good and leave it at that. And I will help you with your new journey." Donald laughed.

"Why are you laughing? What journey? Care to share?" Sean

couldn't help laughing himself.

"No, need to know information, remember?"

"*Hmm*, guess I'll figure you out later." He took a long drink and looked around the pub. "You help them out as well?"

"Always. I do what I can." Donald leaned across the polished bar toward Sean. "But right now we need to discuss you."

Sean sipped his ale. "Me? Why?"

"Concentrate."

"On what? Donald, I'm tired. Let me be."

But the bartender's expression was stern, so with a sigh, Sean closed his eyes and did what was asked of him. He searched within himself, searching for—what? He cracked an eye open and peeked at Donald, who still regarded him with a stern look.

"Concentrate, my lad."

"On what?"

"On the task at hand."

"What task?"

"I can't tell you. You must find it within yourself."

Sean opened his eyes to give Donald a look of annoyance. He mimicked the bartender's voice in a mutter, far too tired to play with this. With his eyes closed he began to block out all else, searching within himself for some undetected awareness, some sort of change, something his subconscious knew that he didn't. He felt a glimmer of something familiar, and it niggled at the edge of his mind, it was something he should know. He pushed further and found a connection that he believed had died within him at the fire. His eyes flew open in astonishment, and his heart opened with hope again.

"Mary," he whispered, "she's here." His mind immediately focused on the stranger that had just arrived at the Guesthouse, and he knew without doubt that, although her appearance had changed a bit, it could be no one except her.

Donald only smiled.

MARY'S ROOM AT the Guesthouse was a fair-sized bedroom with an old-fashioned double bed, complete with a yellow quilt and comforter. Bright wallpaper adorned the walls, and a large window overlooked the village and the lovely Irish landscape. The small town was in a large valley, surrounded by green hills, and further in the distance, a rocky countryside.

Mary turned away from the window and back to the business of unpacking. She placed her clothes in a dresser that was in the room, then sat down on the bed and reached for one of her favorite sweaters. A warm, wool sweater, dark green which highlighted the green in her hazel eyes. But it was the picture wrapped inside of it that she was after. She removed the small frame, looked at it, and smiled at the picture of her and her precious little son Sean.

He was all smiles, his blue eyes dancing with devilment, and all Mary could do was grin. She set it on the nightstand and unzipped a compartment inside of her suitcase. She removed a smaller photo. Tears formed in her eyes as she regarded the picture of her with Sean taken during her visit almost five years ago. They held one another in laughter, their joy and togetherness apparent in the picture. Briefly, her fingertips grazed his cheek on the picture. She quickly put the photo away from her, setting it behind the other one on the nightstand.

SEAN LOOKED UP at the corner room on the second floor of the Guesthouse, where he knew Mary was sleeping. She was like a beacon to his soul, and he could feel her presence from where he stood, longing for her, willing her to wake up and see him. Mary. She washed over his battered self like a soothing balm, extinguishing the pain of the fire, the pain of her leaving, and the pain of his death.

HEAT SCORCHED HER skin, fire seared her flesh, she cried out as the building exploded and the fiery beams trapped her...

She woke up, heart pounding wildly, and put hand to her chest to try to calm down. She shivered, the sweat cooling on her skin in the chilly room. Wide awake, knowing she wouldn't be able to get back to sleep any time soon, she got out of her bed and went to the closet for her dark leather coat. After bundling herself into it, she quietly let herself out of the room and out of the Guesthouse, hoping that a short walk might be just the thing to calm her down.

Lost in thought, she left the inn, unaware of a lone figure standing in the shadows, watching her. After a few paces, however, she stopped and looked into the darkness.

"Sean?" She couldn't see anything in the dark, but inexplicably, felt him nearby and stepped toward him.

Startled, he flinched. Mary had moved toward him without error, and now stood a few feet in front of him, calling his name. Did she actually see him? He cleared his throat, hopeful, and afraid at the same time. "Mary?"

"Sean?" She heard him but didn't see him and peered into the deep shadows. "Where are you?"

"You can't see me?"

"No," Mary shook her head.

"Perhaps it's better that way."

"I need to talk to you!" she whispered in an angry voice. "Stop playing games!"

"Mary, I'm sorry," he said, aware she hadn't forgiven him yet. "I can't stay."

"This is important. Don't put me off."

"You don't know, do you?" he asked, stunned as he realized she had never found out about the fire, stunned that she didn't know he had died. He didn't know how to deal with this revelation, what to say, how to tell her, so he backed away from her.

She whirled about, trying to see him in the darkness. "Know what?"

"I'm sorry, Mary. I have to go." It was true, the energy that sustained him and kept him in the physical world was dissipating much more rapidly than he had anticipated.

"Sean! You bloody bastard! Don't you dare disappear on me!" She stomped into the darkness, but he was already gone.

How could he have disappeared so quickly? Angry, she found herself rapidly making her way down the road toward The Gaelic Moon. She couldn't believe he'd left like that. *Ooh*, when she caught him she'd let him have what for!

She slowed as she finally approached The Gaelic Moon. The night was dark, and she didn't remember how far off the road it was located, but she spotted its dark silhouette, visible against the night sky only because of the lights from within. She stopped and realized that she couldn't confront Sean. Not now, not yet. With a shake of her head, she turned away. Time enough for this conversation tomorrow. She turned away, taking the well-traveled road back to the Guesthouse.

Chapter 21
Hatred

*P*ATRICK, WHERE HAVE you been?" the shrill voice demanded as he entered the small house where Maggie lived.

"Out."

Four years had changed Maggie tremendously, and not for the better. In that terrible fire, Maggie had been badly hurt when she ran into the burning pub. Her legs were injured, she had several painful burn scars, including one at the corner of her mouth and another that began at her temple and ran down the left side of her cheek.

When she was recovered enough to leave the hospital and return home, Patrick had stepped in and volunteered to help take care of her because she had no one else. As time went on, he found he no longer loved her, the passion that had once burned so bright now couldn't even light a cigarette. Once he couldn't have lived without her; now he could hardly stand to check in on her.

"How was your day, Maggie?"

"My day? How the hell do you think my day was? Stuck in this house, in this wheelchair, with no one but the cat for company?"

"Of course, Maggie. Of course. What else would you say?"

Her green eyes glared at him. "What is that supposed to mean?"

"Nothing, Maggie, nothing." He looked around and saw the small house was a mess as usual, clutter everywhere, only the sink and the cat pan had been cleaned. Maggie could do a lot for herself from her wheelchair, especially since she could walk for limited distances, but usually she refused to, instead leaving a mess for him to clean up. "How do you feel?"

"Feel? How am I supposed to feel? Crippled and stuck in this house with only you to take care of me." She snorted and glared at him. "Poor excuse for a man, you are."

"I guess I am. I must be, to put up with you for all of this time."

"Of all of the nasty things to tell a poor, crippled woman, a woman you love..."

"Loved." He shook his head, and focused on a painting of a ship going down in a storm, he'd always found it vaguely disturbing. "I don't love you anymore, Maggie, and haven't for years."

She laced her tone with venom, asking, "Is it because of that bitch, Lillie? Are you still dating her?"

Patrick drew back his hand in anger, as if to slap her, but instead took a deep breath and gathered himself together. "You will not speak of Lillie in such a manner, she is a good, kind, loving woman, something you have no idea of."

"Maybe not, but you haven't slept with her yet, have you?" Maggie snorted in contempt as the look on Patrick's face answered her question. "Should have known you weren't man enough to do that."

"I was man enough for you."

"You were never man enough for me. Why do you think I always wanted someone else?" she asked sweetly. "You think after all of this time I don't know what a coward you really are?"

"I'm going out," he said abruptly.

"Again! How dare you leave me here alone?" she screamed at him.

Her screams followed him as he went down the small hallway and out the door, slamming it shut behind him.

A SMALL PUB called The Emerald Isle served, more or less, as the substitute for The Gaelic Moon. It seemed a poor excuse for a pub to Patrick, but beggars couldn't be choosers. The town had lost much when The Gaelic Moon was destroyed, the ancient pub that seemed as though it had existed forever and was the unofficial meeting place of the town. So many friends and family members had perished in the unforgiving flames that engulfed the structure; nothing could ever be the same in Cullamore. No one could completely explain it, but it seemed as though the heart and soul had been ripped out of the town with the death of The Gaelic Moon. With no plans to rebuild, the remains of the beloved pub stayed as it had died, a brutal reminder of the fire that had ravaged it and destroyed so many lives.

The Emerald Isle was a dive compared to The Gaelic Moon. Cheap furnishings, cheap building, and leaky roof, but they served alcohol. That was cheap, too. The bartender was a pale imitation of Donald. His name was John, and he was as boring as his name. Still, Patrick and several others sat in the old chairs and drank. People talked, but very little laughter and few smiles, things that had been standard fare at The Gaelic Moon. No one laughed anymore.

Patrick glanced up in surprise as the door opened to admit another patron to the somber bar, and he saw Lillie. Once she shut the door behind her and her eyes adjusted to the light, she looked around the bar. When she saw Patrick, she made her way over to him.

"Lillie," he said when she stopped in front of the table. "Would you care to sit down?"

She nodded and took the seat across from him.

"The usual?"

"Yes, please."

Patrick signaled to the bartender, who nodded, acknowledging his order.

"What can I do for you?" Patrick asked, and Lillie saw a small smile touch his face.

"I'm not sure." She studied him. "Are you all right? You seem upset," she said and placed her hand on his arm.

He sighed and placed his hand over hers. "I just saw Maggie. It makes for a bad day," he muttered. "And nothing will change as long as things are the way they are."

"Then change them." She offered him a small smile. "Let go of Maggie."

"I can't. Don't you understand? They'll put her in a home!"

Lillie waited for a few seconds before she spoke. "Perhaps it would be for the best."

"How can you say that?"

"Maybe she needs more help than any of us can give her. You more than anyone should know how erratic she is, how unstable her emotions are. Many of us in the village think that she's needed help for years, even before the fire. Being in a care facility would help her. Surely this isn't the first time you've heard this."

"I'll not listen."

"But you have to; you're throwing your life away by taking care of her. You don't owe her anything. I wish I could convince you that Maggie's dangerous."

"To who?"

"To everyone."

"And what can she do from that chair?"

"I don't know." She bit her lip. "But I'm willing to bet she's not as helpless as she seems."

He snorted in contempt.

"Be careful, Patrick. That's all I ask of you—just be careful." She searched his face, waiting for his eyes to meet hers. "Can't you find something better to do with your life?"

"Like what?" he asked, his breath catching in his throat when Lillie looked at him this way.

"Like this," she said and gave him a sweet smile before she leaned forward to kiss him.

The kiss was soft, tender, and conveyed a pureness of feeling that he had often felt from Lillie, an honest feeling that humbled him when he thought of all of the cheap, illicit kisses of passion he had shared with Maggie. When he compared the two, he was always surprised to discover that he would rather share Lillie's sweet honest kisses than Maggie's dark, impassioned ones. The kiss lasted only a few seconds, but when he opened his eyes, he gave Lillie a genuine smile filled with his love for her. He brought her hand up to his lips and kissed it. He was delighted when Lillie blushed. Someday he would find the words to tell her how he really felt, if he could ever convince himself that he was deserving of her.

"That is a good argument," he said, offering her a shy smile.

"I hope so." She still held onto his hand and gave it a squeeze.

"Tell me you'll at least consider not taking care of Maggie anymore?"

He saw the uncertain expression cross her face as she asked, "You don't still love her, do you?"

"No, Lillie, I don't love her, and I haven't been with her since well before the fire. Does that make you happy?"

"Yes, actually, it does," Lillie said, and a smile spread across her face, crinkling in the corners of her mouth.

"Good. Maybe one of these days I will find a way to make you even happier?" He winked at her, and she blushed. He laughed. "Care to join me for dinner tonight? We can drive up over to Tunnagh."

"I'd love to. It would be nice to get away for a night."

"Good. I'll be by at seven."

"Another date?" She smiled at him, her eyes twinkling.

"Yes, is that a problem?"

"No, not at all. I like dating you."

He offered her a heartfelt smile, and she melted just a little as he took her hand.

Patrick watched her leave. Her looks were pleasant enough, but compared to Maggie and the passions of a young man who was too blind to see anything but that placed before him, Patrick had never given Lillie a second thought.

But as Lillie had grown older, her girl-next-door features had become more of a refined elegance, a stately way of carrying herself with grace and dignity that Maggie could never aspire to have. Lillie had turned into a lovely lady that Patrick was pleased to know. Such a fine woman. Patrick felt ill-deserving of her friendship, let alone anything else that could ever be between them.

They had both been apprehensive at first because they were coming from opposite sides of a battlefield which had been defined by Maggie and Sean. But soon they were friends and, after a year, Patrick worked up enough nerve to ask Lillie out on a date. He wanted more, oh so much more with her, but he didn't want to rush her into anything, he was happy to be in her company and have a stolen kiss or two. When and if she brought it up, they could talk about it, but until then, he would leave things alone and adore her in silence.

THE DOOR TOOK a beating as Maggie continued to throw items at it. She watched the vase shatter against it, water spraying in all directions. The violence somehow calmed her and she took a deep breath, realizing her anger wasn't getting her anywhere.

She wheeled her chair around to look out the window. Nothing had been the same since Sean died, since they had all died in the fire. Where Patrick had once hung on her every word, now he tried to ignore everything she said. Where once there was slavish devotion, now only sarcastic indifference remained. She continued to use her magic on him, but somehow he seemed immune to it; he completely resisted any and all spells and suggestions that she used on him.

What in the hell was wrong with him? What was wrong with everyone? With the exception of Sean and Patrick, everyone still saw her as the beautiful woman she was before the fire, but she couldn't change her injury and she was sick of the looks filled with pity, so tired of people feeling sorry for her. Sometimes she wished she could kill them all—that would remove the sympathy from their faces.

Her goals had changed after the fire, but she supposed that was normal, as a person's life was constantly in a state of change. Magic consumed her—the more she learned, the more she wanted to learn, and the more powerful she wanted to become. She spent a great deal of time learning on her own, but had no qualms about visiting her mentor, Lucky, when there was a need for it, nor for giving him what he wanted, whatever that may be.

She had two short term goals for the use of her magic. The first was simple, something she had always wanted, and that was Sean. She planned to summon him to her. Even Lucky wasn't certain if those spells would work on a ghost, but she wasn't above experimentation. Though she might not have Sean in the way she had originally planned, it would be oh so satisfying to have him under her control, to finally make him bend to her wishes, whatever they might be.

If it was the last thing she ever did, she would track down the American woman and kill her. Sean falling in love with her had ruined all of Maggie's plans—the plans for her and Sean. It didn't matter that her performance had broken the other woman's heart—that woman deserved to die for her transgressions, and Maggie would make sure she received her just reward.

Soon, she would be walking again. Lucky had some amazing

spells at his disposal, and Maggie was more than happy to do whatever was necessary to achieve her goals. It may be at a cost of another's life, but that didn't bother her in the least—she had nothing to apologize for.

With the closest thing to a smile she could manage, Maggie pulled herself out of her wheelchair and clumsily made her way around the room, hanging onto things as she went. Out of breath from her exertions, she opened what appeared to be a decorative door and pulled out a book; an old codex with a worn binding, faded blue color, and barely discernible words on the binding. She pulled it to herself and held it tight.

Her salvation was here—she knew it. She could feel it. This would let her walk and give her so much more. Only a few more sessions, and she would be up and about. Pity Lucky hadn't found it for her sooner. One fine day, she would show them all the knowledge she had amassed, as well as the power. They would all be sorry they had treated her so badly!

She hugged the book to her as she made her way back to her wheelchair where she set the book down on the table in front of her and began to read.

THE UNEXPECTED RIPPLE of sheer hatred Donald felt from somewhere within the town was giving him a headache. He was always aware on some level of the emotions of those around him as not all humans were kind people, but usually it was more of a dull ache, a subtle headache instead of a blinding migraine. What he felt was a focused hatred that emanated from Maggie. Poor girl—he had always been afraid she would become a lost soul.

He leaned on the bar of the pub, lost in thought, and didn't even notice when Sean took a barstool across from him.

"Donald, why so glum?" Sean asked, lighting a cigarette. "You look like your best friend just died."

Donald offered him a weak smile. "Do I now?"

"What is it? Something must be really bothering you."

"I think maybe you're starting to know me too well," he said and favored Sean with a sharp look which Sean ignored.

"What can I say? I have time on my hands and nothing better to do."

"There is a disturbance in the force, Luke." Donald smiled.

"Yeah, very funny. Try again."

"My joke isn't that far from the truth. There is a disturbance in the way of things, and that never bodes well." He shook his head. "It's Maggie. I'm afraid she'll do something to get herself into further trouble."

"Great! Burning down the pub and murdering people wasn't bad enough?"

"Don't worry, I'll figure it out," said Donald.

"You'll let me know when you do. I'll be happy to do what I can to put a stop to her games." Sean's expression was grim and filled with anger.

"Sean, you've been out and about since you became a spirit. Have you become aware of the nuances of people? Of distinguishing between good and evil intent?'

"I'm working on that, but if you're asking whether I know Maggie is a bitch, then, yes, of course I know that."

"Well, bitch isn't quite the right word. I mean, unfortunately, yes, she is, or can be, but..."

"Donald! You're rambling. Spit it out, man."

"She's a witch."

"What?" Sean was unsure whether he had heard Donald correctly. "A witch? You must be joking. Witches don't exist."

Donald gave him a pointed look. "Sean, think about what you are and tell me again?"

Sean still felt so human most of the time, especially when he was sitting in the pub talking to Donald, that he forgot he wasn't a physical person anymore. "*Err,* you're right, sorry." Maggie as Maggie was bad enough, but adding in black magic—and with Maggie, what other kind could it be—was a disaster waiting to happen.

"You will need to keep an eye on her," Donald said.

"Me? Why me? I don't want anything to do with that poor excuse for a woman."

"Because she will undoubtedly get herself and others in trouble if you don't keep an eye on her, and I'm sure that trouble will involve you."

Sean let out a string of expletives under his breath. When he looked up again, Donald was gone. Sean shook his head. "I hate when he does that," he muttered.

IT HAD BEEN a long day and Paul was tired. It was one o'clock in the morning on a Friday night, now Saturday morning. He had gone out clubbing with some friends, flirted, danced, got laid, and just returned to his apartment a short time ago.

He hadn't engaged in that form of stress release for a while; but since Mary wasn't around, he didn't see the harm in it. What she didn't know wouldn't hurt her and the way she had been acting lately did nothing to endear her to him. He had gone out of his way to prove how much he cared about her, how much he desired her. But lately all she did was push him away. He couldn't imagine what was wrong with her to refuse him and his advances. He had his pride after all, and knew that he was an extremely good catch.

He looked onto the balcony of his elite apartment in downtown Minneapolis and scowled into the night, unsettled because he was distracted by Mary.

He had everything—money, health, good looks—most women would kill to be with him, but not Mary, and he didn't know why. That was what had first caught his interest, her lack of interest in him despite his amazing attributes, and he was determined to win her, he took it as a personal challenge. Given some time, he had wormed his way into her affections, and he had been well on the way to becoming a trusted friend when she had been assigned on the business trip to Ireland. That's where she met that Irish bastard who ruined her life! All of Paul's carefully laid work shot to hell because another man had come in and claimed her affections.

The only good thing to come of it was that the Irish bastard had broken her heart and left her pregnant. He had used both elements to his advantage and slowly rebuilt a relationship with Mary. She had finally accepted him as a lover within the last year— not nearly as often as he would like, but he could work on that. Exclusive was what Mary insisted on, and he was, except when she was out of town.

He went into his bedroom, closed the vertical blinds, and removed his clothes as he got ready for bed.

Ireland wasn't a good place for Mary to be, and he supposed he would have to go and retrieve her and the boy after giving them another day or two. She was his now, whether she realized it or not. He would allow her some indulgences, but she needed to realize he was serious and that now was the time to settle into a life with him.

He climbed into bed and gazed up at the ceiling, the

circulation of air created by the ceiling fan felt good on his bare chest as he drifted into a contented sleep.

Chapter 22
The Plea

*B*REAKFAST THE SECOND morning for Mary in Cullamore was quiet, a welcome relief from the maelstrom of emotions in her mind. Whatever made her believe that discussing this with Sean would be easy? His disappearance from her life only confirmed the fact. She got up from the small table where she sat, put her purse over her shoulder, and picked up Sean's business card, which she had been staring at for the last hour.

When she arrived in the lobby of the Guesthouse, she rang the bell and waited for someone to appear. After a short time, the hostess, Mrs. O'Malley arrived and smiled at her guest.

"Good morning, I'm hoping you can give me directions?" Mary said.

"Of course, my dear, I'd be glad to. Where would you be going?"

"I'm looking for the residence of Sean Calhoun. His address is at 80 Glengarry."

Mrs. O'Malley's smile faded and she regarded Mary. "And why would you be wanting to go there?"

"I have business with him."

"You do?" The older woman shook her head. "Well, he's been gone from the town some four years now. You'll not be getting any answers from him."

"I don't understand," Mary said, knowing she had spoken to

Sean the night before.

The older woman saw Mary's look of frustration and took pity on her. "But maybe I can tell you something that can help since you won't be seeing him."

Mary regarded her hopefully.

"His mother and sister still live in the family home. Maybe they can help you."

Mrs. O'Malley warned her to avoid the old woman if she could, as it seemed that Sean's mother was a formidable woman who harbored a grudge against Americans. But she said Lillie, Sean's sister, was very nice. So Mary left the Guesthouse and with a pounding heart, as she convinced herself to go and visit Sean's family.

SOMETHING WAS DIFFERENT, Maggie could feel it. Every time she thought of that woman, it seemed as if she could feel her, as if she was somewhere nearby.

She glanced out the window and her jaw dropped in disbelief.

This was far too wonderful. That bitch had come back of her own accord; Maggie wouldn't have to hunt her down after all.

She watched as the American homewrecker walked past her small house up the road.

Sometimes life went in an unexpected direction, and she couldn't help but smile at the new turn of events, everything would now fall into place and she could exact her revenge on the woman who had stolen Sean from her. Pleased, she turned from the window as Mary disappeared from sight.

AS SHE APPROACHED the small house, Mary noted that this area of town seemed to have much older houses made of some kind of stone masonry. An old woman sat in a rocking chair in front of the house, her expression a sour one. A younger woman with pleasant features, brown hair piled on top of her head, watched as Mary drew closer. She stopped between them and looked from one to the other. Sean's mother ignored her, but his sister watched curiously.

"Excuse me," she said to Lillie. "I'm Mary. Mary Kelley. I'm visiting from America. I don't mean to intrude, but I'm looking for Sean's family."

"Mary." Lillie smiled as she recognized her. "Of course. I remember you now."

"You do?"

"Yes. I saw the aftermath of your discussion with my brother."

"Oh." Mary suddenly found the ground fascinating as memories of that night came flooding back to her, and she had to take a moment to control the sudden outpouring of the emotions she had so carefully locked away. She looked back and saw the woman was still watching her.

"Hello. I'm Lillie. Sean's sister." She extended her hand and Mary shook it gratefully. She watched as Lillie stepped over to her mother and put an arm around the old woman, who was regarding her with a sour expression. "And this cranky old woman is my mother, Geraldine."

"Who is this?" his mother asked suspiciously.

"I'm Mary. A friend of Sean's."

"Who is this?" the old woman asked again.

"You'll have to forgive her, she doesn't always hear very well." Lillie bent down in front of her mother, and spoke loudly. "This is Mary. She is a friend of Sean's."

The old woman gave her a daggered look. "Are you an American?"

"Yes, yes I am," Mary said loudly.

"Have you been here before?"

"In Ireland?"

"No! Here! In this town!"

Lillie reached out and patted her mother's hands, addressing her in a soothing voice. "Now Mum, don't get all worked up."

Mary fidgeted under the direct gaze of Sean's mother, suddenly wishing she were somewhere else, anywhere else but here. "Have you been in this town before?"

"Yes. Once."

"Mother," Lillie cautioned, and Mary wondered why.

"When?"

"Almost five years ago."

Geraldine looked at Mary in anguish and clutched at her heart as she emitted a cry of pain. Alarmed by the woman's actions, Mary saw that Lillie was surprisingly calm.

"Come on, Mam," Lillie said stepping up to her mother. "Let's go inside."

"It was you!" The anguish on the old woman's face changed to one of hatred as she glared at Mary.

"I don't know what you mean," she said, seeking some sort of help.

"You killed my son! You led him astray!"

"What? Killed him? What do you mean?" Mary asked, unprepared for such an accusation.

Geraldine got out of her chair, fists balled up in rage, and Mary stepped away from her. "You ruined his marriage! You vile, wicked woman! You took him from his wife and home! And you killed him in that awful fire!"

"Fire? What fire?" Mary began to shake as she closed her eyes, the memories of her dreams overwhelming her, the memory of dying in the smoke and flames.

"My brother," Lillie said in a neutral voice, "died in a fire in The Gaelic Moon shortly after you left."

Mary staggered under the weight of those words, the color draining from her face.

"You didn't know?" Lillie asked in amazement.

Mary shook her head and blindly reached for the nearest chair.

"I'll be right back," Lillie promised. "Come on, Mum, let's go inside," she said, leading the crying woman into the old house.

Mary watched them leave and, as the door closed behind them, buried her face in her hands trying not to give in to her tears. She had expected some sort of news about Sean, but not that he was dead.

Her heart ached knowing she would never gaze into his mischievous blue eyes, never feel her hand in his, or share another sweet kiss with him. But that couldn't be right because she had spoken to him the night before—how could he possibly be dead?

BRIGHT SUNSHINE DISPELLED any shadows that lingered in the daylight, as Lillie and Mary walked side by side down the road toward the pub, Mary's expression was one of shocked confusion as she trudged along, eyes focused on the ground beneath her.

Lillie stopped when she reached the gutted exterior of the

burned-out pub. Ashes, rubble, and some charred ancient pillars were all that remained of the once welcoming building. She surveyed it sadly and realized Mary was still walking along, head down, unseeing what was before her. Lillie gently reached out and put a hand on her shoulder.

Startled, Mary looked at Lillie, her expression one of shocked disbelief. "I don't understand." She stared at the remains of the building in shock and shook her head. "I went for a walk last night and came here and it looked the same as the last time I saw it. The Gaelic Moon, lights shining from the windows."

"You were seeing things."

"When did it happen?" she choked out between waves of grief.

"The fire, you mean?"

Mary nodded.

"About a week after you left."

"I really don't understand." Mary looked at Lillie with a confused expression. "I saw Sean last night," she said slowly. "Or at least I heard him."

"How can that be?" Lillie shook her head. "No, you were imagining things."

"But I talked to him."

"He's dead! Now let him be!" Lillie turned away from Mary and tried to control her anger.

Mary blinked and took a step back, startled by Lillie's hostility. "I'm sorry," she stammered, "I didn't mean anything..."

"It's all right, and I'm sorry, it's just I'm still so angry that it happened. Will you accept my apology?"

She nodded and saw the deep sadness in Lillie's face. "You really miss him, don't you?"

"Yes. He was often stupid about his own life, but he was my brother, and I loved him." She studied the American woman. "How are you?"

"I don't know." Mary turned toward the charred remains of The Gaelic Moon; a deep grief settling in her soul. In an attempt to gather herself together, she studied the distant hills before speaking. "I loved Sean with all my heart. When I found out the truth—what Maggie claimed was the truth—I wanted to die."

"If you didn't know about the fire, why'd you come back here?"

"I finally wanted to find out why I'd never heard from him." She closed her eyes trying to squeeze them shut before the tears escaped once again. "Why do you leave it like that?" Mary whispered, looking at the burned-out building and black rubble.

"I guess we think of it as a memorial, we buried our people that had died that day in the cemetery up the hill." She walked over to a charred beam that still stood as a tribute to the dead and placed a hand on it, and with a sigh, she turned back to face Mary. "But this is where they died. We can't forget about them."

The ruins of The Gaelic Moon were suddenly ominous, black beams helplessly reaching for the sky, along with the souls that had perished. She staggered as the images of the fire flooded her mind. She felt the heat, watched people succumb to the flames, and felt herself die as the huge, burning beam crashed down on top of her.

"My God!" She fell to her knees, finally understanding the dream and what it meant. It had been The Gaelic Moon she saw burning and Sean's death she re-lived in those nightmares. She looked up at Lillie in horror, but Sean's sister was staring at the charred remains, her expression filled with melancholy.

THE SMALL CEMETERY at the top of the hill was well kept up, the grass cut short, and areas around the markers neatly trimmed. Colorful flowers adorned all but the oldest graves. The two women walked past many small markers to the modest one with Sean's name on it. A large bouquet of fresh cut flowers was placed at the site. Mary looked at Lillie, who shrugged.

"Mam or I come here every couple of days. It's the least we can do. I know he loved you, Mary. You should have let him explain."

Staring at the marker, Mary knelt down and touched his name in the stone. "How could he?" Mary's expression was suffused with sadness. "He lied to me."

"But you still love him, don't you?"

Mary shrugged. Her feelings were a tangled mass of sadness, loss, grief, and some unexpected, unnamed emotions buried deep within her for the man whose grave she now regarded.

"Will you let me tell you what happened? I know that he would want you to know."

Mary regarded her through a tear streaked face. "Yes, I would like that. Very much." She gathered her courage. "And there's something you should know too, perhaps a bit of hope amongst the tragedy..."

Lillie regarded her with sad curiosity. "Hope? That would be a welcome thing."

"I have a son, Sean's son..." she could no longer control the tears, and began to break apart in front of this woman's eyes.

Lillie stepped over to her and pulled her close in a comforting embrace. Mary hung onto her as if she were drowning. They clung to each other until Mary straightened up and wiped the tears from her face.

"I'm sorry, I'm normally not like this."

"It's a lot to take in," Lillie eyed her in concern, "Are you all right then?"

Mary nodded. "Yeah, I will be," she said, but didn't move away from Lillie.

"You have Sean's son? I have a nephew?" The smile that spread across Lillie's face was filled with joy. "What's his name?"

"Well, I wasn't original. It's Sean. Sean Murray Kelly."

"It's a fine name, a grand name for the lad." Lillie beamed at her and they looked at each other and laughed. "Sean should have told me."

"Well, he just found out before..." Mary gestured back at the town.

"No matter, it's wonderful!"

"You're not mad at me?" Mary's voice was hesitant.

"Why would I be mad at you? You just told me I have a nephew, that part of my brother still lives." She stopped and studied Mary for a moment. "I'm sorry everything has been so hard for you, but I'll do what I can to make it better."

"Sean was right..."

"About what?"

"You are an exceptionally kind woman. Thank you for that."

"*Pssh*, nothing to thank me for; you're family now. We will have to tell mother, of course." She grinned at Mary. "When can I meet the lad?"

"Well, he's not here right now, my friend Amy will bring him here tomorrow. I felt I needed to talk to Sean first, so..."

"I understand. Just let me know when we can meet him. Oh, I can hardly wait!" Lillie clapped her hands together in happiness and Mary grinned.

"Will you walk back to the Guesthouse with me?"

"Of course," Lillie said and fell in step beside Mary.

THE TWO WOMEN walked along the road that led to the Guesthouse, each remembering the past and Sean's place in their life.

There was an unmistakable change in the air, and Mary suddenly felt a familiar presence that could only belong to one person. She looked over Lillie's shoulder at the surrounding hillside, but didn't see anyone, and then the feeling vanished as suddenly as it had appeared.

"What will you do now?" Lillie asked as she and Mary came to a stop in front of the Lakeview Guesthouse.

Mary shrugged. "I don't know. Go home, I guess."

"Well, I wish you well. No matter what Mum thinks, I believe you're a fine woman. Much better than the witch Sean married." Despite herself, Mary smiled at the anger in Lillie's voice. "It's a pity Sean didn't meet you first. He would have been happier, and so would we."

"How can you be sure? You only met me this morning." Mary's smile was filled with warmth.

Lillie took Mary's hands and squeezed them, and smiled sadly. "When he caused you all that pain it almost killed him."

"What do you mean?"

"After you left, he spent three days in the pub and refused to leave. He passed out just before the fire started. That's why he died." She sighed. "If only things had been different, I think we'd all be very happy."

In the daylight, a few feet from the women, Sean suddenly appeared. He watched them converse for a few moments, his gaze intent.

"Are you all right?" Mary asked as Lillie shivered, feeling his presence again.

"Fine, fine." She hesitated. "It's only that, well, sometimes I feel as if... Sean has never left, I feel like he's still around," she said with a shrug, looked at the air around her, and laughed. "It's nothing, just my imagination."

Mary concentrated, trying to find him but saw nothing.

Sean studied them with a smile, and glided over to stand beside his two favorite women. Then with a soft sigh, he leaned over and kissed each of their cheeks in succession. Lillie's eyes darted around nervously, but Mary just expelled a soft sigh as she touched her cheek.

The two women regarded each other and shared in uneasy laughter, as Sean grinned happily.

A SOFT BREEZE blew in through the window, ruffling the curtains. A suitcase was open on Mary's bed, half packed. Mary knew she should finish packing, but instead, she looked at the pictures on the nightstand. She picked up the picture of herself and her son, hugged it to her for a moment, and replaced it where it had been sitting, then her gaze fell on the picture behind it, the one of her and Sean, happy and smiling. Quietly, she picked up the picture and began talking to it.

"You bastard! How dare you treat me like that? And how dare you die on me? What the hell is wrong with you?" She wiped at a stray tear. "Bastard!"

Outside, on the dark night, Sean gazed up at the window. He closed his eyes and concentrated, and her curtains moved with a gentle breeze.

It seemed to be a still night. Mary looked over at the curtains in mild surprise and back to the picture she held in her hand.

Contacting her was something he shouldn't do, he knew that. He should let her accept him as dead, let her move on with her life; after all he had put her through, he owed her some peace. But he couldn't do it, he owed her an explanation, didn't he? Didn't she deserve to know that he truly loved her? And that he wanted to apologize for the depth of his stupidity? Yes, he told himself, he owed her that much. And he wanted to know that she was all right, that her life was going well, that she and their child were healthy and happy. What else could he do but contact her? And, bless the saints, she could hear him. He looked up to her window, and called softly to her.

"Don't go, Mary, don't go. Don't go, Mary, don't go..."

A sudden gust of wind blew into her room, and Mary yelped in surprise and dropped the picture in her hand. It crashed to the floor, the glass shattering on impact. She bent over it, and shook her head sadly.

"Oh, Sean," she sighed.

"Don't go, Mary, don't go. Don't go, Mary, don't go." The whispered voice echoed within the small room, but Mary knew that voice—she would recognize it anywhere.

"Sean?"

He stood as before, eyes closed in concentration, his voice no longer a whisper, but strong as he projected it into Mary's room.

"Don't go, Mary, don't go."

She ignored the broken glass and ran over to the window to look outside. Somehow, she saw the dark figure, and despite the fact that darkness hid his features, she knew who it was.

"Sean?" she called out. "Sean?"

Her voice startled him out of his trance, and he saw her peering out of the window at him.

"Mary? Can you hear me?"

"Yes. And I see you, too. Wait there!"

"Oh, God." He almost sank to the ground in relief, but instead, laughed joyfully. "She can see me. Oh, thank God, she can see me!"

Chapter 23
Reunion

*M*ARY RAN TO where she had last seen Sean, but he wasn't there. She turned around, surveying the shadows and finally called out to him.

"Sean, where are you?"

He stood ten feet away, shrouded in blackness, watching her. Her hazel eyes sparkled with excitement as she searched the darkness for him. After a brief hesitation, he stepped toward her, hoping she could still see him. "Mary?"

"Sean?" She looked at him, and knew the man before her could be no one but him, but it couldn't be him, could it?

Confusion marred her pretty features as Sean slowly opened up his arms to her. She hesitated, but unable to help herself, ran to him and threw herself into his arms. As she reached for him and his embrace, however, she fell through him and to the ground.

Sean looked at himself, surprised, and over to Mary, who regarded him in shock. He reached out to help her, but slowly withdrew his hand. Shrugging helplessly, his hands dropped to his side. She dusted herself off and struggled up.

"So you're a ghost?"

"Yeah."

Tears welled up in Mary's eyes.

Sean reached to put his arms around her, but again realized

he couldn't do it. Frustrated, he spoke to her—at least he could still do that. "Mary, don't cry. Please don't cry."

"But you're dead! Damn you!" He recoiled from her, surprised by her anger, and blinked at her change of tone. "Damn you! How dare you leave me!"

"Excuse me," he said, "but last time we saw each other, you left me."

"Because you cheated on me!"

"Technically, I cheated on my wife."

Mary screamed in frustration and clenched her fists. "You bastard!"

Sean bowed his head in shame. When he looked back to Mary, she was gone, walking toward the front door of the Guesthouse. He closed his eyes, concentrated, and disappeared. She was almost to the door when he suddenly appeared in front of her, and with a shriek, she stepped away from him.

"Get away from me!"

"No."

Whenever she tried to step away from him, he appeared before her. Exasperated, she glared at him. "Get out of my way!"

"No. You have to hear me. It's been too long."

"You lied to me. You betrayed my trust."

"And I fell in love with you."

Mary looked at him, searching his face for truth, and some of her anger faded.

"Please. Let me explain. Let me tell you what I should have said before." His gaze implored her to listen. He extended his hand, but again realized that he couldn't touch her and let his hands fall limply to his sides. "Please, Mary. Give me a chance."

Mary pinched the bridge of her nose, closing her eyes. With a large sigh, she opened her eyes again, but Sean was gone.

"Sean?"

"Over here." He watched her from ten feet away, smoking a cigarette.

"Why are you doing that?"

"I don't know." He shrugged. "Habit, I guess. It certainly can't hurt."

She sniffed the air and gave him a curious look. "I can smell it.

The cigarette." He regarded the cigarette with interest and ground it out under his heel. "How is that possible?" she asked.

"I don't know. Maybe some things are tangible between the two realms. Maybe that's why you can see me." He looked her in the eye and said, "Mary, she wasn't pregnant."

"She was! I saw her!"

"You saw an illusion. She wanted you to go away, so she pretended to be pregnant."

She regarded him with suspicion. "She didn't have your baby?"

"No, Mary, she didn't. She couldn't have if she'd wanted to—she's barren."

They exchanged a long look, and Sean watched as Mary's expression grew calmer. She walked away from him, stopped and collected herself as Sean waited patiently. After a couple of minutes, she turned back to face him. "You're telling me the truth?"

"Mary, I swear it. I swear it on my somewhat tarnished soul."

"Your soul? Why would you swear on that?" Mary asked him curiously.

"It's all I have left, isn't it?" He said, a wry smile on his face.

"I forgot," she said. "You seem so real."

"Right now I feel real, except I can't touch you, I can't hold you. All I can do is tell you how much I love you." He shook his head. "It just doesn't seem to be enough."

The two of them looked at each other, their faces suffused with sadness.

Mary felt her resolve melting as she searched his blue eyes so filled with love and pain. For the first time, she realized that the way she had reacted, leaving before they had a chance to sort things out, may have been part of what ultimately led to his death. She gasped and stepped away from him, feeling as if she had been shot in the chest.

"My God," she said, and felt the tears filling her eyes. She had visions of him in The Gaelic Moon, completely inebriated and talking to Lillie, some of the words were unintelligible, but the meaning was clear—without Mary in his life he didn't have a reason to go on, and he had buried himself in an alcoholic stupor within the safe walls of The Gaelic Moon.

"Mary, what?" He watched the emotions flash across her face—acceptance, realization, pain, terrible regret, and now tears. "Honey, what's wrong? Please, let me help?"

"Oh, Sean." She only cried harder. "It's my fault, isn't it?"

"What?" He was truly confused by her words, not sure of where she had gone with her thoughts. "Mary? Please talk to me?"

Mary shook her head and ran from him.

With a sigh, Sean disappeared and reappeared before her. "Mary?"

She stopped running but couldn't look at him. "No, I can't."

"Can't what?" he asked softly.

"It's my fault," she said. "Sean, I'm so sorry!" She looked up at him, and he saw the tears streaming out of her hazel eyes now tinted with green.

"Sorry? For God's sake, what do you have to be sorry about?" He was trying to be patient, but he didn't know what could be bothering her this much. What was she trying to blame herself for?

"I'm sorry," she repeated through her tears. Mary watched as the edges of his form began to get indistinct. Unable to help herself, she reached out to touch him, but touched nothing.

"Mary, one question before I go?"

"What?"

"The baby. Did you have our baby?" He was starting to fade away but she saw him swallow a large lump in his throat and knew how much it meant to him. "I'll be back soon..."

Seeing the emotion on his face, she couldn't find her voice to give him an answer, so she nodded.

He closed his eyes for a moment and saw relief wash over his now indistinct features. When he looked back at her, she saw the tears in his eyes. 'Thank God," she heard him whisper, and he was gone, as if he had never been there at all. She turned around, but he was nowhere to be seen.

AMY SAT ON the bed beside young Sean, the boy nestled comfortably beside her. She finished reading the children's book she had in her hand, closed it, and looked down at the small boy smiling up at her.

"I like that. Read it again."

"No, my sweet. I've already read it twice."

The boy frowned in disappointment, and Amy kissed his forehead.

"Aunt Amy?"

"Yes?"

"Do you love me?"

"Of course I do." She leaned forward and gave him a big wet kiss, then nibbled on his ear until he giggled. Still laughing, they grinned at each other.

"You're silly!" he said, pointing at her.

"No, you are."

He laughed, but his expression became serious. "But what about Daddy?"

"Oh, honey, he'll love you more than you can ever imagine."

"Okay." The trusting blue eyes looked at her and smiled. "Can I see him soon?"

"Very soon," Amy promised as she tucked him in and pulled the covers over his shoulders. "Goodnight," she whispered and shut the door behind her.

THE OLD WOMAN, Geraldine, watched her daughter in silence as she worked between the stove and the kitchen table, placing breakfast on the table for the two of them. She carefully picked up a piece of toast and examined it critically. After tasting it, she made a face and set it down on her plate.

"It isn't any better.

"Too much butter!"

"And yesterday too dry. Face it, Mam, you're never happy anymore. Can't you be happy because we have a new, bright day before us?"

Geraldine gave her daughter a dour look as Lillie finished pouring her tea and sat down at the table. Lillie stirred her tea and set down her spoon, watching her mother pick at her food.

"Mam, we have to talk." The old woman went about her business, seemingly deaf to her daughter. "Mam, it's important." Her mother continued to pick at her food. "It's about Sean."

Geraldine looked away from her breakfast, slowly raising her sharp eyes and staring into her daughter's face, regarding her with disapproval. "What about Sean?"

"I think he was doing the right thing."

"What do you mean?"

Lillie took a deep breath, preparing for the argument she knew would follow. "I mean that he should never have married Maggie."

"She was a fine girl. And she was his wife."

"No. She was a manipulating, evil woman. And he only married her because he couldn't control his desires."

"Lillie! How dare you speak of Maggie that way!"

"Mother, it's true. And it's long past time for you to face facts."

"Maggie is a good girl," Geraldine insisted to Lillie, who stood before her mother with a scowl.

"Maybe as a girl, but she isn't a good woman. Sean made a mistake. He married the wrong woman."

"And since you're so wise, who is the right one?" The old blue eyes flashed with anger. "Certainly not that American!"

"You should give her a chance. She's really nice."

Her mother made a sound of disgust and turned away. Lillie shook her head in frustration at her mother's stubbornness.

THE SUITCASES SAT packed by the door of the small Dublin flat. Little Sean played on the floor with his toy car, making screeching and zooming noises as Amy looked around the apartment, trying to make sure she had not forgotten anything. Looking around she saw a set of his beloved water pistols and picked them up to pack them away. The phone rang, and she went over to answer it.

"Hello. Hello! I can hardly hear you. Paul? Is that you?" She tried to listen, putting a hand over her other ear. "Yes, we're fine. Mary's fine, Sean's fine, we're all fine." She listened carefully, trying to hear through the bad connection. "No, she's not here. Yes. Looking for... adult Sean."

Young Sean walked over to Amy, bored with his toy, and hugged her. She ruffled his hair in affection, but listened to the phone again.

"What do you mean you think it's a bad idea? It's a good idea. You said so yourself." She ran a hand through her hair, her voice irritated. "For God's sake, stop being paranoid. The man's married. No, that is not a good idea. Paul, no! Stay home! Don't come here! Paul!"

Amy rolled her eyes. How could he do such a thing? The man was losing his mind, and his jealousy and possessiveness were all too apparent.

The boy tugged at her pants, and Amy looked into his sweet young face. "Can we go now, Auntie Amy? I want to meet my father."

"You bet we can. And I'm sure your father will be happy to see you," she said, bending down to hug him. She only hoped she was telling the truth.

A FEW MINUTES later Amy was on the phone again. Paul showing up in Ireland was a really bad idea, and nothing good could come from his trip. It would only serve to make a difficult situation that much worse, Amy was sure Mary coming here to face her ghosts was hard enough without throwing in the complication of a sometimes lover. As far as Amy was concerned, that's all he was and all he would ever be to Mary.

The only time she had ever seen Mary in love—truly, deeply in love—was here in Ireland, with Sean. She had never figured out why Sean hadn't gotten back in touch with Mary, but she was sure there was some good reason other than one named Maggie. Maybe now that Mary was back in Ireland, the two of them could sort it out and get back together, because despite her usual protectiveness over Mary, she was hoping for a happy ending for the two of them.

Which was why she was on the phone calling her fiancé, Rob, hoping she could convince him to either stop or delay Paul's trip to Ireland. Much as Rob loved her, it was still a lot to ask, but she was confident he would do it for her. Rob had never liked Paul and thought Mary deserved much better. She was sure he'd be happy to stop him.

Come on, darling, pick up, Help me out here, and pick up the damn phone...

THE TABLE SETTING was sparse, a plain white tablecloth on the small kitchen table, a place setting for two, with a single red rose in a vase set in the middle. Dinner was basic, with lamb stew and soda bread, but the fact that Patrick had taken the time to put it together and invite Lillie to his place for dinner spoke volumes to her. He had escorted her to his solitary couch, brought her a tea, and was busy cleaning up in the kitchen for longer than was necessary.

"Patrick?" she called. "Leave that for later. I thought the point to my coming over was for us to spend some time together."

He didn't answer her directly but continued to bustle about the kitchen, finding things to do. Was he nervous to be here with her? They had shared dinner before.

"Patrick, please. Don't make me come and get you."

Muttering under his breath Patrick took the few steps across his kitchen to go into his small living room. He sighed as he regarded Lillie with a look of adoration.

"Lillie, would you like some more tea?" he asked.

"No, I'm fine." She frowned at him and patted the couch beside her. "What I'd like is for you to sit down."

"I don't want tea, would you mind if I had a drink?"

"I'd like one too, please." Lillie set down the tea cup and pushed it away from her.

"But it's whiskey," he said in surprise.

"You know I drink whiskey on occasion," she reminded him.

"Uh, okay," he said and poured them both a partial glass. He approached close enough to hand her a glass, but hesitated when he looked at the spot next to her on the couch.

She laughed. "What is wrong with you tonight? Sit."

"All right." He took the spot next to her and sat down, his back stiff.

"What's wrong?" she asked after a moment and put her hand on his arm.

"What d'you mean?"

She shook her head and downed her shot in one fell swoop. Somewhat impressed, he did the same, then got up and poured himself another. He looked at her, and she nodded, so he poured her another one, too, and went back to resume his seat on the couch.

"That was lovely, thank you for dinner."

"You're welcome."

"I didn't know you could cook," she said.

"I've made food for you before," he appeared offended.

She smiled at him. "Sandwiches, microwave food—not the same thing as cooking."

"I suppose."

A silence fell between them once again. Granted, Patrick wasn't always the most talkative soul, but usually he did better than this. Lillie eyed him with concern. "Are you feeling all right?" she asked.

"Fine, why?"

"You're quiet tonight, even for you," she said.

"Thinking," was all he said, but for the first time that night, he looked directly into her face, and Lillie was amazed by what she saw. His brown eyes were open to her, and she saw his emotions—anxiety, nervousness, desire, and love. Wait, love? Did she really see that? Or was it only her hopeful imagination?

"About what?" Was all she could whisper as he moved closer to her, his lips meeting hers eagerly. They had kissed before, and there had been moments of passion, occasional sparks. Patrick had always been quick to step away, much to Lillie's dismay. She opened her lips to his and found that with just a little encouragement, Patrick was kissing her with abandon.

"Oh, Lillie, I'm sorry! I didn't mean to take advantage of you. I didn't mean to..." Patrick appeared mortified by his behavior.

"Stop it!" she reprimanded him. "I'm not made of glass, and I won't break. Why do you treat me like I will?"

"I just don't want to..." Patrick stammered.

"Don't want to what? Kiss me? Hold me? Love me?" Much to her surprise, Lillie pushed him back against the couch, angry with him for not treating her like the real woman she was. "Why can't you love me?" She shook her head as her emotions veered in a different direction and she was suddenly overcome with tears. "You loved her, why can't you love me?"

The "her" in question was obvious to both of them—Maggie.

"Are you still not over her, Patrick?" Tears were running down Lillie's face.

"Oh, Lillie, how can you think any of this?" He drew out a handkerchief and gently wiped away her tears until she stopped crying. "I haven't loved her for a long time now." He hesitated for just a few moments, took a deep breath and plunged ahead anyway. "I love you."

"You what?" Lillie gasped in surprise.

"I love you, Lillie, but I've been too afraid to say anything." He searched her face. "I treat you the way I do because I cherish you, because I want to do this right." He reached out and ran his fingertips over her cheeks. "You deserve so much better than me, and I know that. I didn't want to ruin your reputation by soiling you," he finished quietly.

"Soiling me? What do you think I am?" She smiled shyly. "An angel?"

"You are." His eyes met hers, and she saw he was serious. "And I shouldn't soil an angel with my desires," he whispered.

"You love me?" she whispered, still trying to take in his words.

"Yes," he said, looking away as if ashamed.

"Patrick." She touched him under his chin and turned him so that he had to look into her face. "I love you, too," she said softly.

"*Ahh*, Lillie," he said and pulled her into a fierce hug. When he let her go, they stayed on the couch together as they began new explorations of one another. It was some time before Lillie went home.

Chapter 24
A New Reality

THE MORNING LIGHT streamed through the open window, and a soft breeze caressed Mary's face and woke her from a sound sleep. She yawned, and opened her eyes, blinking at the sudden brightness. Not quite ready to get up, she rolled over on one side and saw Sean lying on the bed beside her, grinning like the devil himself.

"Good morning," she murmured, not yet awake.

"Morning, love."

With sudden clarity, her sleepiness vanished, and she shrieked. She rolled away from him off the bed and got to her feet, as he laughed in delight.

Sean and Mary faced each other, a few feet apart. She glanced out the window and saw the bright morning light, and looked back to him, her brow wrinkling in puzzlement. "How can you be here?"

"What do you mean?" he asked, still smiling.

"It's daytime."

"Yes, and?" He waited for an explanation.

"You can't be out in the daylight!" she said.

Sean laughed loudly. "Why on earth not? I'm a ghost, not a vampire!"

She tried to shush him.

"Mary, no one but you can hear me or see me."

"Not even Lillie?" she asked sadly.

"She can't see me, but I think she's starting to hear me." He moved toward Mary, thought better of it, and instead glided over to sit on her bed, grinning. He patted a place on the bed beside him. "Come, sit down."

"How're you doing that?" Mary asked, indicating the bed, which appeared as if the weight from a real person was on it.

"I guess I've been learning a lot. Now come sit down."

"What're you up to?" she asked suspiciously.

He grinned again and patted the bed. She hesitated, not trusting the look on his face, but overcome by curiosity, she went to sit beside him.

"Good. Now turn to me." She did so, but avoided looking in his eyes. "Look at me, Mary."

After a long hesitation, she did. He brushed a stray lock of hair away from her forehead as he continued to gently touch her face. "Will you listen to me please?"

She nodded and gazed into his blue eyes as he spoke. "I am telling you the truth when I say that I love you, and not just as a friend. I am completely, totally besotted in love with you. I have been ever since I first laid eyes on you."

"Even now?" she asked.

"Even now. You are the only woman that I have ever loved, the only woman I will ever love. You gave me a reason to change my life, to want something again, to hope again for those white picket fences and five children."

"Five?" Mary laughed.

"I was open to compromise," he said and gave her a wicked smile.

"I gave you hope?"

"More than I could ever have imagined. I had become rather jaded, you see."

"You, jaded? Really?"

"So you noticed?"

"We did spend a lot of time together. I think I picked up on a thing or two."

"Yes, you would have. You certainly knew me better than Maggie ever did."

"Maggie." The name dripped with loathing, and Sean was rather surprised by Mary's tone.

"She's a witch, you know?" Sean added.

"You mean bitch, don't you?" Mary was really pissed, Sean noted.

"Well, yes, that too, but she really is a witch. As in casting spells, creating illusions, those things."

Mary's brow wrinkled in skepticism. "A witch? Does she have a broom, too?"

"Honestly, I wouldn't doubt it. She'd be a perfect recast as the Wicked Witch of the West from the *Wizard of Oz*; the trouble is, she'd eat that cute little dog."

Mary couldn't help herself—she covered her mouth and giggled.

He gave her a sad smile.

It had been a difficult four years, believing that the man she had loved had betrayed her, had lied to her about their relationship, had never really loved her. It had never occurred to her that something might have happened to him, that he might have died. And the hardest thing of all was that he was a ghost, spirit, apparition, and that he was sitting next to her on the bed talking to her as if it was the most natural thing in the world.

"A guilt-ridden ghost?"

"Yes. One asking forgiveness from you, if you will grant it." His blue eyes searched hers, and she saw tears in them.

"You can cry?" she asked and reached out to touch him, but felt nothing.

"I guess so," he said softly.

"Yes, I forgive you," she said and saw the love in his eyes.

"Thank you," he said in the most sincere voice Mary had ever heard. "Now I have something else to ask you?"

"What?" Mary began to squirm under his intense gaze.

"Why did you run from me last night?"

"Oh, that," she said and turned away from him, trying to hide her guilt.

"Yes, that. Tell me what's wrong."

She regarded him with sad eyes. "I should have believed in you." She searched his blue eyes, amazed they looked just as they had when she had first met him so many years ago. "I always wondered why I never heard from you again. The only thing I could believe is that what Maggie had told me was true, that you had gone back to her and had a child with her," she finished in a small voice. "I never thought that there might be some other reason that you didn't get in touch with me. That it could have been because something had happened to you."

"Mary, The Gaelic Moon burned shortly after you left Ireland." He shrugged. "How could you know that?"

"No, don't you see, the point is that I know you. Despite what had happened, I knew that you would come looking for me if you were sincere."

"But instead you believed I wasn't sincere, that I was back together with Maggie?"

"Yes." Her expression was laden with guilt. "Would you have come looking for me?"

"Yes, once I was done wallowing in my self-pity, which I did very well, I may add." He said sincerely, "Mary, don't make yourself responsible for what happened to me. That's what this is about, isn't it?"

"But if I believed you, you wouldn't have had any reason to drink like that, and you wouldn't have died in the fire! So it's my fault that you died," she whispered, a tear running down her cheek.

"Don't be ridiculous! We are all responsible for our own actions. I'm the one that made a mess of things. It's my own fault I died. If I hadn't been inebriated, then I wouldn't have died. My fault," he said with certainty.

"But, Sean..."

Sean stopped and looked at her, a slow smile spreading across his face until he began to chuckle. "Mary, this is silly."

"What?"

"We're arguing over which of us is more responsible for my death. It's a bit late for that, don't you think?"

She cracked a smile at his observation.

"That's better. Let's just accept it happened and that I believe you to be blameless in any way, shape, or form."

"But," she began to protest, and he held up a hand.

"Blameless, my love. It's time to go on."

"Go on to what?" she asked, her brow wrinkling in puzzlement.

He extended his hand, wordlessly asking her to take it.

Puzzled, she stretched out her hand and felt him take it in his. He caressed her face with his other hand, and it felt like the softest of flower petals against her skin. She regarded him with amazement, feeling his tender caress, and instinctively, reached out to touch him. But her hand passed through him, and she looked at him in frustration.

"Mary, isn't it wonderful! I can touch you! Well, sort of!" He gave her a lopsided grin.

"But I can't touch you!" She clenched her teeth in frustration.

"*Ahh*, well. I don't know what to do about that. But this is good!" He caressed her face again, and she shivered.

"I don't know, Sean. It's kind of creepy."

He stopped and dropped his hand, giving her a reproachful look. "Creepy? I've never been called such a thing in all my life!"

"You're dead."

"But I'm not creepy."

"All right." She rolled her eyes in exasperation. "But you're still dead."

"I am." He sighed, but suddenly his expression changed and he gave her a hopeful look. "Mary, did you have the baby? Our baby?"

She sighed, looked into Sean's beloved face, so much like that of her son, and wished she could at least squeeze his hand. "Yes, I did. He's a lovely little boy."

Sean grinned. "Is he healthy? Is he well?"

"He's beautiful. He looks just like you."

"Ouch, I'm sorry for that," he said. "I was a hellion as a child, or so my mother always told me."

"Well, he's not a hellion, but he does have his moments. I should have known that's where he got it from."

"Because you were never a bad child?" Sean arched an eyebrow at her. "I seem to remember a couple of stories you told me about growing up in Minneapolis. Like the time you broke the gumball machine by tipping it over because you wanted the gumballs, or the time you scared your parents to death and the whole time you were hiding in a tree..."

She tried to keep a serious expression but couldn't stop a smile from escaping.

"Just as I thought," Sean said with a smile. He brushed a stray lock of hair off her cheek, and she shivered at his touch. She saw the twinkling in his eyes and briefly wondered how that was possible. "Mary, I can still touch you."

Mary's mouth dropped open in astonishment as she took in the suggestive tone of his voice. Shocked, she asked him, "Really? How much? I mean, how real are you? I mean..."

"Ah, you're curious? Me too. Truth is, I don't know." He gave her a wicked smile. "We could find out."

"Sean!" She tried to imagine how he would feel as a ghost and found herself intrigued by the possibilities. "You couldn't, could you?"

"Well, not... that. But you can feel my hands. Maybe my lips."

"But you're a ghost!"

"That doesn't mean we can't have a bit of fun, and I so want to touch you again."

She was about to protest when she was softly pushed down on the bed. When she struggled to get up, he enthusiastically nuzzled her neck, and she giggled. She really could feel the touch of his lips on her neck, and the sensations were like nothing she had ever experienced before. As soft, feathery caresses began to cover her body, she surrendered to the feeling.

THE GENTLE BREEZE blew over Mary's face and hair, and Sean watched, utterly content. After a moment, he pushed the hair back, not wanting anything to spoil the perfection of her face. He was still completely in love with her; apparently becoming a ghost hadn't changed that in the least. He didn't understand, but that was all right, too.

"Mary, I love you so," he murmured as she blinked and opened her eyes, still regaining her composure after his spirit hands and lips had done amazing things to her naked body. He had given her the satisfaction she had been lacking since he had disappeared from her life. "Was it good? Are you happy?"

"Oh, Sean, that was... amazing," she whispered, her eyes filled with happiness. "I felt things I never felt before." She raised an eyebrow. "Something to do with your ghostly abilities?"

"I don't know." He shrugged. "Just glad I could make you happy." He smiled at her, but an odd expression suddenly appeared on his face.

"Sean?"

"I feel funny," he said.

He was being pulled in several different directions at the same time. He didn't really feel pain anymore, but still the feeling was most disconcerting and seemed to be getting worse. What was happening to him? With a final confused look at Mary, he disappeared.

"Sean?" Now where in the hell did he go? Damn it! Why did he leave so abruptly? Quietly, she got up and began to get dressed.

HE WAS IN a small house, a dark room where he hadn't been before. Frowning at his sudden unexpected appearance here, he expelled a deep breath and took a step forward. That's when he saw the shadowy figure in the corner, he didn't know who or what it was until he heard her laughter.

"Maggie," he growled and tried to take a step forward but was stopped by an unseen barrier. "What the hell?"

"*Ahh*, it does work. An interesting experiment," she said, coming out of the shadows and looking at him.

"An experiment? Maggie, what in the hell are you talking about?" Sean asked.

He was struck by her unexpected appearance. What had once been so vividly striking, so breathtakingly beautiful was now disfigured; a long scar ran from her right temple down her cheek, and the skin there remained wrinkled and discolored. He knew the scars were from the fire but thought perhaps it was also a physical manifestation of the ugliness of her soul.

"I summoned you, and you came to me." She smiled at him. "Are you a ghost, Sean?"

He glowered at her. "I died in the fire, what do you think?"

"Still the same caustic personality, I see."

Sean tried to walk over to her but was thrown back on his ass and landed with a thud on the hard floor. He glared at her. "Maggie?"

"My experiment, Sean. I summoned you. I not only summoned you, but I drew a protective circle for ghosts. And since you are a ghost, it seems to be working." She gave him an self-satisfied smile. "I didn't know if I could summon a ghost, but demons come when they are called."

"Demons?" Sean's brow wrinkled in apprehension. What was she getting herself into? "Maggie, you shouldn't be doing anything with demons. Or ghosts for that matter." He looked at her and asked, "How is it that you can see me?"

"Because I called you." She sighed. "I can't keep you for long this time, but I will work on that small detail." She smiled. "I will see you again soon, my love."

"Your love? Maggie, how many times... ?" A sudden blackness surrounded the place where he stood, and in an instant it lifted, just as he finished his sentence, "have we been over this?"

DONALD LOOKED AT him from behind the bar with a raised eyebrow. "Sean, that was a rather spectacular entrance. Care to tell me about it?"

Sean took a deep breath and calmed himself. How in the hell did he get to The Gaelic Moon? He regarded Donald with a somber expression. "Damn it, Donald, we have to talk! In private."

"I'm right here, Sean. Please keep your voice down and stop being so impatient. No one can hear us if we wish to have a private conversation. Private rooms are only illusions anyway. You know that."

Sean leaned back and gave him a wary look. "You are certain of this?"

"Yes."

Sean took a long drink from his beer. "Maggie. She's a witch."

Donald gave him a patient "I know that" look.

"She seems to be doing awful things, evil things. It worries me. What are we going to do?"

"You mean what are *you* going to do?" Donald gave him a bemused smile.

"Me? Isn't this your problem, too?"

"In a manner of speaking, yes. But as spirits, we all have tasks to perform, and this is one of yours."

Sean frowned. "What is? Dealing with Maggie?"

"Yes, because it concerns your life, both past and present. You need to take care of it."

"You won't help?"

"No. But I can give you information. That's something."

Information? Sean was actually hoping for some assistance from Donald, but he guessed something was better than nothing. Donald did seem to be a font of knowledge, so it might be enough. "How do you kill a witch?"

"The normal way you would kill a person, I would think? Maggie, though growing more powerful, is still a mortal witch. She hasn't made the transformation."

"What transformation?" *This is sounding worse and worse,* Sean thought to himself.

"When a person becomes a witch and dabbles in the black arts for long enough, their soul becomes tarnished and eventually unsalvageable. When that happens, the person transforms into something darker, something that appears as their human form, but is evil and much harder to kill."

"Maggie's not there yet?"

"Not yet."

"But she will be?'

"Given the road she has chosen, it seems that it's only a matter of time," Donald said sadly. "Are you sure you want to kill her?"

"I don't want to kill anyone, but I'm afraid it may come to that, given her tendencies."

"You will have to find a way past her spells before you could physically attack her. And you may have a problem with that as you have not learned to make yourself corporeal yet."

"Can I learn to defend myself from her spells?"

The barkeep gave Sean a serious appraisal. "I believe you could."

"Can I learn spells to attack her?'

"Not spells, per se, but you could shape some of your abilities, some of the things you already know." Donald nodded to himself. "But do you have enough time to prepare properly?"

"You can show me?" Sean asked eagerly.

"Yes, either myself or another spirit I can trust this task to. Give me a day to decide what would be best for you."

"Deal!" Sean pounded the bar with great enthusiasm. Maybe he could finally give Maggie what she so richly deserved.

Chapter 25
The Witch

PITY MARY WASN'T hungrier than she was, as the food set before her looked delicious. She was distracted by everything that had happened last night and this morning; everything having to do with Sean, the now dead love of her life and ghost extraordinaire.

Mary concentrated on buttering her roll. When she set down her bread and looked across the table, she saw Sean sitting across from her.

"Mary," he said.

Irritated, she ignored him and concentrated on eating lunch, but when she reached for her fork, it moved away from her. She reached for it again, with the same result. With a glare at Sean, she tried to grab her spoon, only to have it move away from her. She quickly managed to snatch the fork, but he held onto the other end, suspending it in mid-air as she pulled against Sean's hold on it.

"Let go of it."

"All right."

He did, and with a glare at him, Mary set her fork down on the table.

"That was completely uncalled for," she whispered.

"We need to talk."

"No we don't," she said, and offered a weak smile as the proprietor, Mrs. O'Donnell, clucked in sympathy at the American woman speaking quietly to thin air.

"Why are you so mad at me?" Sean asked.

She buttered her roll, using more force than necessary.

When she raised her head he saw tears glistening in her eyes, and he glided over to her. He placed his hands on her shoulders and squeezed them gently.

"Mary, I didn't leave you because I wanted to. I'm new at this... ghost business and I was quite literally pulled away." He paused as a new thought occurred to him. "Are you afraid I'll go away for good?"

She dropped her eyes, unable to look at him.

"*Shh*, it's all right. I promise you that I will do everything I can to remain by your side as long as you're in Ireland."

"Ireland?" She blinked in confusion. "Can't you go anywhere else?"

"I haven't tried to, but I don't think so. It's where I died."

"Oh," she said.

He took the seat next to her and held her hand between both of his. A silence fell between them, and they gazed into one another's eyes. Mary's expression softened. She watched as he reached out and tenderly touched her face, a look of understanding finally present on his.

"I'm sorry, I'm just so afraid..." she said.

He smiled at her and squeezed her hand. "Of losing me again?"

"Yes, you confident bastard, I don't think I could stand that."

Sean dropped her hand, turned away, and cursed under his breath. "I never meant to be such a fool, you must have hated me."

"I did, for a long time. But when I had our son, Sean, I saw you in him every day, and since I love him so much, it was hard to completely hate his father."

He reached out again, took her hand between his, and felt the oddest sensation as if her hand was being tickled from the inside out. His blue eyes regarded her with a somber expression.

"Will you give me another chance?"

"I wish I could. I wish things were different."

"What do you mean?" he asked, trying not to sound too disappointed.

"I hate to remind you, but you're dead."

His face was glum, and he began to play idly with the place setting, the utensils bouncing up and down without any means of support. "I keep forgetting," he said, and sighed. "There's another problem, Mary."

"Of course there is." She waited. "What now?"

"It's Maggie. Remember I told you she's a witch? It seems she has learned some new spells."

"Okay," Mary said, still not sure how to process this information. "What does that mean?"

"She summoned me, called me to her. That's why I disappeared." He shrugged. "It seems there are some things I have no control over."

She tried to smack his arm, but her fist disappeared through it. "Why didn't you say so?"

"It's not something to casually bring up, is it? Oh, by the way, my ex-wife summoned me with a spell, and being a ghost, I had no choice but to show up as called."

Mary was appalled. "She can do that?"

"So it would seem."

"Why can't she leave you alone? I so want to kick her ass!"

"That's my girl." Sean grinned. "I don't know that I've ever seen this side of you. I rather like it."

"She's not like you, is she? I mean she's still physical, still mortal?"

"Far as I can tell. Why?"

Mary gave him a wicked smile. "Because it allows for the possibility of me kicking her ass."

Sean laughed. "I want to see that. She deserves a good ass-kicking."

"With any luck at all, I'll be able to accommodate that request. You're my ghost, damn it!"

"I am?" He liked the sound of that. An unusual relationship to be sure, but maybe there was hope for him and Mary after all.

She expelled a long sigh and looked back at him. "But first I have another problem to deal with."

"What's that?"

"How do I tell a little boy who's come all the way to Ireland to see his father that his father's dead?"

Unable to answer, Sean could only shake his head.

THE DRIVE TO the nearby town of Daghloonagh was a short one, but it was always nice to get away from things for a while, Patrick mused as he concentrated on the narrow road in front of him. He glanced over to the passenger side where Lillie sat, quietly watching the countryside. The sun was bright, the sky was blue, the breeze was cool, and he had Lillie at his side. He was content.

They pulled into a local restaurant that had a good reputation for serving exceptional food. Patrick went around to Lillie's door, opened it for her, and gallantly offered her his arm as he escorted her inside.

The restaurant was nice, but smaller than Patrick expected. Several neat, clean tables had white tablecloths spread across them in the medium-sized room. Each table had a small vase in which a single red rose was placed. The woodwork in the building was warm and polished, in good shape, despite its age. Patrick pulled out the chair for Lillie and got her seated before he took the chair across from her.

After waiter came and took their order, they regarded each other in a comfortable silence.

"Did you know Sean's girlfriend is in town?"

"Do you mean Maggie?"

"No, of course not." Lillie grimaced. "Patrick, you know her better than anyone. What else is going on with her?"

He was silent again for a while as he thought things through—instances where he caught her reading old books and muttering to herself, instances in which he had walked in on her doing something she quickly tried to hide.

"Well, I caught her lighting a fire once," he said at last.

"Why is that unusual?"

He frowned. "She didn't use a match, or a lighter, she just pointed and... poof! Fire."

"That didn't strike you as strange?"

"Well, yes, but I thought maybe I had imagined it. You know, wishing she was in hell and all of that." He gave her a wry smile.

Lillie covered her mouth and laughed. "Oh, Patrick, that's wonderful. Not Christian, but wonderful nonetheless." She frowned and leaned across the table. "Did you catch her doing anything else?"

"Well, she reads a lot, a very old book."

"Did you ever see it?"

"Once or twice when she wasn't around, it was written in a language I didn't understand, with lots of unsavory pictures. Dark pictures..."

"Dark?"

"You know, demons, witches, things like that." He frowned and looked at Lillie. "Lillie, this is going to sound silly..." He took a deep breath before continuing. "Do you think she could be a witch? I mean, a real witch? I mean, she does spells. I think she cast a spell on me long ago to make me her lap dog."

She frowned. "How did you break it?"

"I don't know. But it seemed the more time I spent with you, the less her words and manipulations affected me." He smiled at her. "I guess you saved me."

They sat in silence for a few moments. "Well," Lillie said at last, "I guess we have our work cut out for us, don't we?"

"But how can we stop her?"

"I don't know, but we'll have to find out. I don't trust her not to stir up trouble."

"I can't argue that," said Patrick as their lunch arrived and was placed in front of them. The waiter quickly left them to their conversation. "But you said Sean's girlfriend is in town?"

"Yes, a lovely young woman, named Mary, a far sight better than Maggie."

"Why is she here?"

"She came looking for Sean, she didn't know that he died. Poor thing. You should have seen how brokenhearted she was. She cried when she saw The Gaelic Moon, or rather, what's left of it."

"I miss that place," Patrick said. "The town hasn't been the same without it or without Donald. I bet he'd know what to do about a witch."

"What makes you think so?"

"Didn't you ever notice all of the odd things Donald knew? All of the legends, folklore, and things about the people from this town? And he knew a lot of it without anyone saying anything to him. It was weird."

Lillie laughed. "I would never call Donald weird but yes, he was a font of knowledge in that area and many others. Too bad he's not around to talk to, to help us with this," Lillie trailed off sadly, and Patrick squeezed her hand.

"I guess we'll have to do it on our own, because it's time she got what she deserves. She's caused pain for too many people for too long." He smiled at her. "Now let's eat our lunch and talk about more pleasant things."

She lifted her eyebrow. "Such as?"

"You and me," he said.

"I'd like that," she agreed.

He didn't answer but offered her his most charming smile and took her hand. Love was grand!

Chapter 26
Old Friends

*I*T WAS MIDMORNING the next day and many people milled about at the small bus station, cluttering Mary's vision as she searched for her son. In a few moments, she spotted him holding Amy's hand and regarding the busy world around him with wide blue eyes. Her heart skipped a beat, and she realized how much she had missed her little boy.

Mary made her way to them and, as a space cleared between them, she bent down and called out her son's name. The smile on his face was instantaneous as he let go of Amy's hand and ran to his mother, arms spread wide. She caught him and pulled him close, picking him up and spinning him around in her arms, kissing his neck until he laughed out loud, and gave his mother a soft kiss on her cheek as he nestled against her in contentment.

"I missed you, Mom."

"And I missed you. Were you good for Amy?"

The boy's eyes slid over to Amy, and he gave her a questioning glance.

Amy stepped up beside them and ruffled the boy's hair. "He was great as usual."

"Glad to hear it." Leaning back to regard her boy, Mary asked him, "Do you like Ireland?"

"I don't know. We haven't gone out much."

"We'll go out more while we're here because it's a smaller

237

town and it's safer for little boys. Okay?" Mary rubbed her face against his until he giggled.

"Okay." He sighed. "Where's Daddy?"

Oh. Mary hadn't thought they would be addressing that issue so soon, but in the mind of a four-year-old, the most important thing always won out. She looked over at Amy, who appeared equally curious.

"He's not here," Mary replied, shrugging at her friend.

"Will I get to see him?" the boy asked, placing his small hand on his mother's cheek and staring intently into her eyes. Mary cursed inwardly that her son had his father's eyes.

"We need to talk about this, but not at a train station, all right?"

The child sighed with great patience and replied in a serious voice. "All right, Mommy, as long as you promise."

"You have my word; we will discuss your father back at the hotel."

The boy nodded and wanted down, so Mary put him back on his feet. Once she had helped him straighten up his clothes, she extended her hand, and he took it eagerly, happy to be off the train and walking again.

A SHORT TIME later, Mary pulled the rental car up to the Lakeview Guesthouse, and the three of them got out. Both Amy and the boy looked at the countryside around them. The Guesthouse was off the main road, set back on the property, with a tarred drive with a small parking lot that offered a short walk to the guesthouse itself. The rolling hills in the countryside behind the guesthouse with their various shades of green were dotted with the ruins of stone fences, and numerous sheep. The sun was out on this particular day, and the landscape was lovely.

"This is where Sean lives?" Amy asked, and she spun in a circle, trying to see everything at once. "What a lovely little town. No wonder he escaped from Dublin to here."

"This is all Ire-Ireland?" the boy questioned, imitating Amy's spin as he tried to take it all in.

"Yes." She smiled at her son, who grinned back at her. "It's a different country than we live in. Do you like it?"

"Yes! It's beautiful!"

Amy turned away, hiding her smile.

"Come on," Mary said, "let's go to our rooms."

They went to the trunk, pulling out two suitcases and a carry-all, and they chatted happily amongst themselves and walked to the front door of the building.

LATER THAT DAY, Sean returned, leaned against the small stone house, arms folded in front of him as he watched his mother sit on a chair on the porch, rocking quietly, her eyes on the distant horizon. Lillie came outside, took a seat beside her mother. She took the old woman's hands in her own and waited for her mother to turn her sharp gaze on her.

"Mam, I want you to talk to Mary."

"Why?" she asked, pursing her lips in disapproval. "Why should I? She took Sean away from us."

Sean made a sound of disgust and walked over to stand in front of his mother. "For God's sake! Maggie's responsible, not Mary. Damn it, I love Mary! Do you not know that yet?"

"She didn't take Sean; Maggie was responsible," Lillie continued.

Geraldine regarded her daughter with a cool stare and looked over her shoulder to where Sean stood. He looked back at his mother, surprised by her gaze.

"Mam, can you see me? Can you hear me?"

There was no reaction to his words but, feeling he had nothing to lose, he bent down before her. "If you can hear me, please give Mary a chance. She needs you, and she's a good woman." He searched his mother's face for some sign of recognition, even waving a hand in front of her, but nothing. "Please, Mam."

Geraldine turned her attention back to Lillie, who was watching her quietly. "You don't think the American is responsible?"

"No."

The old woman resumed rocking and was quiet for a long time. "Bring her to me."

Sean sighed in relief, straightened up, and disappeared. Slowly, his mother turned her head, and regarded the now-empty space with a knowing gaze.

LATE AFTERNOON SUN filtered into Mary's bedroom as the door burst open and Mary entered, her son squirming in her arms. Without ceremony, she dumped him on her bed, and laughing, began to tickle him until he finally begged her to stop. They laughed until tears ran from their eyes, and Mary collapsed on the bed beside him. When the boy finally stopped laughing, he rolled over on the bed and touched his mother's face.

"I missed you," he said.

"And I missed you."

"Good." He smiled and kissed Mary's cheek, but noticing the photos on Mary's nightstand, he crawled over her and looked at them. He saw the one of him and his mother and clapped happily. Then he saw the one of Mary and Sean and pulled it onto the bed to inspect it more closely.

"Is that Daddy?"

She watched him intently as he studied the photo, his small face scrunched up in concentration. "Yes, it's Daddy."

"He looks like me."

"Very much. But you're more handsome."

"I know." He was quiet for a moment, touching the picture. "Mommy?"

"Yes?"

"Is he here? Can I see him?"

The blue eyes that looked into hers regarded her with such trust and innocence that she had to look away for a moment. "He's not here right now."

The boy dropped his head in disappointment.

"But you have a new Auntie and Grandma. Would you like to meet them?"

"Okay." He offered her a shy smile. "But I want to meet Daddy most of all."

"I know, but you've had a big day and you need a nap now."

"No!"

"Yes, my boy, you do."

"All right," he grumbled and pulled off his small pants and set them on the nightstand before he climbed into bed and settled under the covers.

Mary placed a soft kiss on his forehead. He put his hand on

her cheek and gave her an angelic smile. With eyelids too heavy to keep open, he gave a happy sigh and drifted off to sleep.

THE DOOR TO the adjoining bedroom was open, and with a parting glance at her sleeping son, Mary stepped back into Amy's room, and found her friend sitting comfortably on a chair.

"Poor little guy," Amy said. "He's pretty tired. But he's been a real trooper."

"Any problems?"

"No," Amy smiled, "though he did decide to take me out with those damn water pistols of his. And he locked himself in the bathroom."

"He did?" Mary frowned. "Why?"

"He said he wanted some privacy."

She laughed. "That's my boy. Where do kids that age come up with stuff like that?"

"I don't know." Amy gestured to the bed. "Would you please sit?" After a brief hesitation, Mary complied and sat on the bed. "So tell." Amy leaned forward in her chair. "Did you find him? Is he here? What did he say?"

Mary frowned before she turned to her friend. "I guess you can say I found him. And yes, he is here."

"But there's more?" Amy didn't like the troubled look on Mary's face and wondered what could have happened.

"He has a headstone at the cemetery up the hill." Mary regarded her friend sadly. "He died shortly after I left."

"He died?" Amy stood up, shocked at the news. "How?"

"A fire at The Gaelic Moon trapped him and several other people in it. They all died."

"How horrible! Poor Sean." She shook her head in sadness. "I thought he was the real deal, I thought he really loved you, but it explains why he didn't come after you. I'm sorry, kiddo."

They exchanged a long look of understanding, and a sad silence fell between them.

"You never got over him, did you?"

"No. I guess I didn't realize that until I came back here." Mary offered Amy a wan smile.

Amy squeezed her friend's hand in encouragement. "Are you

all right?"

"As well as can be expected."

"I'd hate to be in your shoes now."

Mary's brow crinkled in puzzlement. "Why do you say that?"

Amy gestured to the next bedroom, where the child's quiet snores were barely discernible. "How're you going to tell the little guy?"

"I don't know." Mary shrugged. "It's not going to be easy. But at least I can introduce him to the rest of Sean's family."

"How're they?"

"His sister is wonderful. A warm, kind woman, very loving. But Grandma is rather formidable." Mary grimaced. "She blames me for Sean's death and the break-up of his marriage."

"How can she do that?"

Mary shrugged, ignoring Amy's outburst. "I don't know. And I have no idea how she'll react to having a grandson, or if she'll even accept him."

"Damn. That's unpleasant." Amy watched as Mary got up off the bed and began to pace. After a few minutes, she interrupted, startling Mary with the sound of her voice. "Mary, what else?"

"I'm sorry, what?"

"What aren't you telling me?"

With a deep sigh, Mary resumed her spot on the bed and sat down. "You're going to think I'm nuts." Amy waited patiently until her friend appeared ready to speak. "Sean's still here," she said at last.

"What?"

"His ghost still lives here. Wait, that's not quite right, is it?"

"His ghost?" Amy regarded her friend with concern. "It's the shock, isn't it? Maybe your imagination's gotten the better of you because you don't want to let him go. She offered Mary an encouraging smile. "It's okay. I understand. And I'll help you through this. What are friends for, anyway?"

Mary gave her a long-suffering look.

THE GAELIC MOON appeared the same as it always did, warm and welcoming to those who still inhabited the place. Inside, at the bar, Sean sat quietly, having a drink and a smoke. A short distance away, Donald conversed with some of the regulars, sharing a bawdy joke. Sean smiled at their antics.

Sometimes being here didn't seem so bad. It was tempting to stay in this realm, to disconnect from the material world and explore the call of the spiritual world, a call which he chose to ignore in favor of the world he had left behind. The spiritual world seemed peaceful, alluring, and would give him the rest he so longed for these days—at least that's how it seemed to him. The desire to leave this physical plane of existence was tempting, and the door was open to him—had been open to him since his death—but he still chose to cling to the semblance of physical life that he had. He still had business to attend to on the material plane, business important enough to keep him there.

Mary had come back to him, and once again he had disappointed her. But this time, there was no going back because he was dead. It was a situation that couldn't be reversed.

"Sean, you're thinking loudly," Donald said with an amused smile on his face.

"What?" He hissed in frustration. "I can't stand it, Donald. They're my family, and I can't be part of their life. They'll go on living a marvelous life together without me. I'll not be able to love Mary as she deserves, and I'll not be around for my son as he grows up." His head bowed in grief. "I can't fix this."

"And why would you say that?"

"Because we died in the fire." He regarded Donald with disdain. "And because we're here." He looked around. "You've never been quite clear on that either. Where is here, exactly?"

"It's The Gaelic Moon, lad. It's a special place. Surely you've heard that there is none other like it in all of Ireland?"

"Yeah, but those are just stories, aren't they?'

"Sean?" He cuffed the side of Sean's head with his palm. "Where are we, and what are you? Think about your answer."

Sean laughed at the scolding. "Donald, I know all of that. Obviously this place has some significance, but how much? Stories have existed for years, but I'm sure you know many stories are embellished, at the very least. What is the truth about this place? What is it really?"

Donald rested his chin on his hand and gazed across the bar for a few moments before he turned his attention back to Sean. "I haven't been asked to describe it in a long time. The Gaelic Moon is old, at least as old as the ancient Druids, probably older."

"You're not talking about the pub, now are you?"

"What do you think The Gaelic Moon really is, Sean?"

"I don't know, that's why I'm asking you." He ran a hand through his hair in exasperation as Donald straightened up, crossed his arms, and regarded Sean with great patience. "What do I think The Gaelic Moon is?" Sean looked around the room at the few spirits who lingered there in this apparently ghostly pub and actually gave the idea some thought. "It's a place for spirits to be, though I doubt The Gaelic Moon is actually an ancient pub?"

"Well, the pub—it's a representation of the physical world, a place that's comfortable to spend time at. But the Gaelic Moon is an ancient relic, one that's quite powerful. It assists with our being here; it helps us to interact on the material plane."

"The Gaelic Moon?" Sean got off his bar stood and made his way over to the ancient pillars, with Donald following close behind. He walked over behind the one where he had, just as a lark, made a wish on the ancient drawings of a blue moon. "Is this it?"

"*Aye*," Donald nodded. "And not everyone realizes that it's right under their noses. Some simply don't care."

"What can it do?" Sean looked at the embedded relic, barely discernible in the wood of the old pillars.

"It depends on who utilizes the power of the Gaelic Moon. For certain people who can channel its energy, it can do great good."

Sean raised a skeptical eyebrow. "And who would those people be?"

"I think it would be you and Mary," Donald replied a matter-of-factly.

"And why would it be us?"

"Because you have things to accomplish."

"Care to share exactly what those would be?"

"Not at the moment, no," Donald replied. "The two of you will have to take one thing at a time."

Sean frowned. "What is this power and why is it here?"

"The power changes and it must stay here." Donald frowned. "If it was taken, or corrupted, it could create a great many problems

"And what is your job?" Sean persisted.

"To be the guardian of the Gaelic Moon until the rightful people claim it." He smiled at Sean. "And I am here to mentor spirits that do not pass on, either to heaven or to hell. I provide guidance to those the earthbound ones, to those that have missions of one sort or another. Whether they be personal tasks to complete before they move on or something greater." Donald waggled his eyebrows at Sean.

"And just what does that mean? Are you suggesting I'm still here because I am to serve a purpose beyond completing things I left unfinished?" Sean regarded him with suspicion.

"My lad, you are just beginning to learn your abilities, and your true purpose. You are meant for great things." Donald regarded him with a fond smile.

"What the hell does that mean?"

"It's what you make of it, a place from which a great deal of good can be accomplished if you want to do so."

"Why can't you ever give me a straight answer?"

"Not in my nature, I guess." Donald patted his arm. "Don't despair, Sean. Many things are still in store for you—you only have to believe." He finished his statement with such conviction that Sean looked into his earnest face and felt himself believing.

"Right now the thing I want most is to be part of their life and find a way to help them."

"Surely you want to do more than that?" Donald chided gently.

"What else is there?"

"Don't you believe in anything else?"

"Like what?"

"I don't know." The barkeep shrugged. "Maybe God. Have you ever thought about the fact that we still exist despite the fact that we are dead?"

"Oh, that conversation." Sean shrugged. "I don't know. I guess it's possible, but I'm not sure why God would have saved my sorry ass."

"You're a good man, Sean. You only have to believe in yourself and great things will happen."

Sean snorted. "Great things, huh? Why couldn't great things have happened while I was alive?"

Donald regarded him with a disapproving expression, one

that reminded Sean of a father reprimanding his child. "Apparently you weren't ready," he said and turned away from Sean, leaving him to his drink.

"Ready for what?" he asked, but Donald had already disappeared.

THE EXPRESSION OF concern was still etched on Amy's face, and Mary wanted to rip it off.

"Amy, you don't understand," she said. "I'm not imagining anything."

"*Uh-huh.*"

"I've seen him! I've talked to him! He's real!" She paused. "Well, as real as a ghost can be."

Amy stood up and crossed her arms in front of her. "All right, prove it."

"Prove it?" Mary was taken aback at the request. "How do I do that?"

"I don't know." Amy shrugged. "Have him do something unusual."

"Like what? He's not a circus pony. He doesn't do tricks."

"This really has been too much for you, hasn't it?" Her friend shook her head in sympathy as she went over to give her a big hug. "It will get better, honey, I promise."

Irritated, Mary broke away from her friend and went to the open window. She stuck her head out the window, and yelled. "Sean! Where are you? I need you!" Nothing happened. Mary glanced over at Amy, who stood watching, arms crossed in front of her, studying the room. Nothing seemed unusual or out of place.

"Well? He's not here, is he?"

"No." Mary had a stubborn set to her jaw. "But he's real. I've talked to him."

"*Uh-huh.*"

The back of Mary's neck tingled, and she felt his entrance in the room before she saw him. She turned to look at the corner of Amy's room and saw Sean had appeared.

"Why did you call? Are you all right?" he asked, a frown marring his features.

"Can you show yourself to Amy?"

246

"I could get arrested for that," he said with a raise of an eyebrow.

"Not anymore. Besides, that's not what I meant." Mary felt a blush rising in her cheeks.

Amy watched Mary talk to thin air. "He's here?"

"Oh yes, he's here." She threw a glare at Sean.

"Where is he?" Amy asked. "I don't see him."

"He's right here, beside me." Mary watched Sean who had come over to stand beside her, and inclined her head in his direction.

Amy looked, but saw nothing. She stretched her hands out, finding nothing but thin air.

Sean watched with a bemused expression as Amy's hands went through him, somewhere just around his navel. He rolled his eyes at Mary, who was frowning. "Do you really want her not touching me there?" he asked.

"Amy, stop!" Mary said more sharply than she intended.

"Mary?" Amy's expression was one of total confusion.

"It's just that—well—you put your hand through Sean, right around his..."

"Private area?" Sean supplied helpfully with a grin.

Mary flushed, and Amy, not hearing the interchange, but seeing Mary's reaction, quickly brought her hands to her sides.

"I'm so sorry; it's just... I can't see him. Sean, you bastard, are you really here?"

Sean laughed. He and Amy had actually gotten to be friends, and he rather missed her. Amy couldn't see him, which meant he would have to find another way to communicate with her that was when he noticed the pen and notepad on the desk. He smiled as he picked up the pen and began to write a message for her.

"Tell her to go to the desk," he told Mary.

"Amy, Sean says to go to the desk; he left a message for you."

Amy gave her a strange look. She clearly hadn't decided whether her friend was insane from grief or on the level, but she walked over to the desk and found a note scribbled on the top piece of paper. She picked it up, read it, and covered her mouth as she began to laugh.

"What is it?" Mary went over to Amy's side, curious as to the cause of her laughter.

Amy thrust the note at her. "Here, read it."

"If you reach for my unmentionables again I will have to inform Rob that we are having an affair. *Shhh*, don't tell Mary!"

Mary covered her mouth as she began to laugh.

Sean, who was still beside her, grinned.

"Now does she believe me?" he asked.

"He wants to know if you believe him yet?" Mary asked.

"I don't know. What else can he do besides leaving lewd notes?"

They both turned as they heard the scribbling of a pen on paper, and Amy gasped as she saw the pen move by itself and set itself down on the desk. The top piece of paper floated over to her. Amy took it and read it and laughed again.

"Now what?" Mary asked.

"It says, 'That's for Mary to know!'"

Amy gasped as her imagination began to run wild. "Is he your lover? How can he be?" Amy's eyes widened as she started to imagine possibilities. "What can he do?"

Sean laughed as Mary turned a lovely shade of red.

"Sean, I'm glad you're still around, I think," Amy said to the air around her. "I just wish I could see you."

"Me, too," he said, the humor leaving his face.

"This is amazing! I'm so glad he's still here, he's such a better choice for you than Paul." Amy's expression changed to one of annoyance, and with a pained expression she looked at Mary. "*Umm*, Mary, you need to know something else."

"What?" Mary wondered what else could possibly go wrong.

"Paul called. He's on his way here."

"What?" she exploded. "What in the hell does he think he's doing?"

"I tried to talk him out of it, but he wouldn't listen. You know how he gets."

"Paul? Who's that?" Sean asked, not remembering the man he had met only briefly in life.

"Damn it!" she swore.

"Who the hell is Paul?" Sean asked, and Mary stopped and

blinked at him, unused to hearing anger in his voice.

"*Umm*," Mary was suddenly at a loss for words as she turned to Sean.

"Mary?" Amy questioned as she watched her friend turn to face thin air.

She gave her friend a "please help me" expression. "Sean wants to know who Paul is."

"I think I need to go downstairs so that you can talk to Sean alone." She retreated to the door, but turned before exiting to add, "But just so you know, Rob is coming with Paul. He wanted to come back to Ireland, and I thought he could keep Paul from getting into too much trouble. I really tried," she said and quietly disappeared out the door.

"Who is Paul?" Sean asked again.

"Paul is someone from work. You met him once when I was here before."

Sean's face darkened as once-forgotten memories came flooding back to him. "Him, your American friend that kissed you in The Shamrock." He gave her a suspicious look. "If he's still only a friend, why is he flying all the way to Ireland to check on you?"

Mary turned away from Sean to look out the window. "We may have dated a little," she murmured.

"You dated him? How dare you?" Sean rumbled.

"Sean! It's been almost four years since I was here last. I thought we were over!" She turned to face him, her anger turning to tears. "I was lost when I returned home. I was devastated. You were the one true love of my life, and you were returning to your wife and starting a family with her."

"That's not true," he reminded her in a tight voice.

"Will you shut up and listen to me? I didn't know that at the time. I was about ready to kill myself. I didn't know how I would get from one day to the next, and on top of it I was pregnant. Pregnant with the child of the man who had betrayed me, who had broken my heart and not even tried to repair it." She was unable to stop the tears that now trailed down her face as she remembered her despair from that earlier time.

"I'm sorry, Mary," he said and stepped forward to move in front of her.

"Paul was—is my coworker. He helped me when I needed help

and I owe him a great deal. We became friends and, after a long time, started to date."

"I suppose I should be grateful to him," Sean said with reluctance. "He did what I should have done for you, he was there for you when I couldn't be." He gently wiped her tears from her cheeks.

She felt the gentlest of tingles along her skin, as she felt his ghostly touch. She closed her eyes and allowed herself to enjoy the moment before it vanished.

"Do you love him?" Sean asked, his voice filled with dread.

Her hazel eyes met his blue ones, and he saw the truth in them as she shook her head. "No," she whispered. "There was this man in Ireland I could never quite get over," she said.

He cupped her cheek in his hand. "*Ah*, Mary."

Mary realized that now would probably be a good time to tell him everything, to confess she had not only dated Paul, but had slept with him as well, but she just couldn't bring herself to do it. Hopefully that part of this discussion would never rear its ugly head.

Sean looked past Mary and, noticed the door to the adjoining room was open, and he suddenly realized they weren't alone—that his son was in the next room, the quiet broken by his gentle snoring. Mary saw the uncertainty in his face and offered him an encouraging smile as motioned for him to follow her.

"Come on, Sean. It's time you saw your son."

Chapter 27
A Son

*T*HE SOFT SNORING continued as the boy lay stretched across the bed, his face scrunched into the pillows. Sean entered the room, glided over to the bed, and bent down over his son. He watched the small chest with its quiet breathing, saw the small eyelids flutter as the child dreamed, and marveled at the perfect features, knowing no child could ever be as wonderful as his son. With a wry smile, he realized that all fathers must feel like this. He reached out to touch the soft cheek, amazed at the smoothness he felt. He turned to Mary, his eyes brimming with tears.

"He's beautiful," he whispered.

Touched by the emotion in Sean's voice, she reached out without thinking and wiped a tear away from his very substantial cheek. She looked at him, her fingertips still wet with his tears. "How is this possible? I didn't feel this before!"

"Maybe only for something special."

Curious, she reached out to touch his shoulder. He was again insubstantial, but her hand passed through the space he occupied with difficulty, as if forcing its way through some unseen substance.

"Sean, you're different."

He didn't hear her, his eyes on the boy as he leaned over and kissed his cheek. Little Sean stirred, blinked sleepily, and looked at his mother.

"Mommy?"

"Yes, Love?" She sat down on the bed beside him. He smiled at her, his little cheeks rosy as he rubbed his eyes.

"I had a good dream."

"You did? What did you dream about?"

"Daddy. You found him, and we all went home."

Sean moved away from the bed, bowing his head sadly.

"Will Daddy come home with us?"

Mary leaned forward, kissed her son's forehead, and settled him back against the pillows. Soon, he closed his eyes and drifted off to sleep, but when she turned to speak to Sean, he was gone.

THE MOONLIGHT WAS bright, although it was not a full moon yet, and it bathed the grounds outside of the Guesthouse in its lunar light. Mary wondered where a distressed ghost would go and found her gaze resting on the road leading out of the village, past the pub, and up to the small cemetery. She shivered as she realized that if he went anywhere, he probably went there.

For years, Mary had been secretly superstitious, and visiting a cemetery at night was not her first choice of things to do. But she had to see him, so she gathered her courage and walked out of town.

She didn't know what to do. How does one comfort a disturbed ghost? He couldn't return to them, and they could never be a real family, no matter how much any of them wanted it. How could she tell him everything would be all right, when from his viewpoint, it never would be again?

Still contemplating this, she marched up the hill to the town cemetery.

THE SPELL BOOK was explicit. The dried parchment gave Maggie the ability to summon a demon to her service, all she needed was the proper ingredients to cast the spell, and she already had those. There was also a variation of the spell that would allow a demon to possess a human, thereby taking its form until it left, which could be quite useful. It would give her the ability to control people in the village, make them do things she wanted, and that would be a wonderful thing indeed.

She tapped her fingers against the tabletop. Who could she start with? Not Sean, because he didn't have a physical body anymore. His mother Geraldine was too old and frail. Lillie? It would be extremely gratifying to put that bitchy sister of Sean's in her place. And there was Mary, and tempting as it may be, Maggie wanted the pleasure of torturing Mary in front of Sean.

A satisfied smile spread slowly across Maggie's face as the perfect candidate came to mind.

The traitor Patrick would be ideal. It would be a way to make him pay for his dalliance with that poor excuse for a woman! Lillie was so pristine that they probably hadn't done the deed yet. She was no woman at all!

Maggie nodded to herself, happy with her decision. Yes, Patrick would be a lovely servant. She would take the time to teach him a few lessons and she would break Lillie's heart in the process.

She smiled. Things were looking up.

AT THE TOP of the hill, Mary spied a lone figure standing quietly, went over to him, and touched his arm. She was again surprised to meet resistance in the air where his arm should be and gave him an odd look. He didn't acknowledge her presence.

"Sean?"

"I can't give my son what he wants, what he deserves. We can't be a family."

"Maybe not, but you can tell him that you love him."

"But he can't even see me!"

"Maybe he can feel you like Lillie seems to, maybe he can hear you."

"I don't know, Mary." He shook his head. "I hope you're right." He raised his gaze from the marker, and a slow smile spread across his face. "He's beautiful. You've done a fine job with him. I bet he's a good lad."

She smiled at him, "Most of the time, but sometimes he's naughty."

"Oh, Mary, I can't wait to take him with me around the town..." His words faded along with his smile. "But that's not the way of things, is it?" He turned back solemnly to the headstone. "I want to be a true father to him, but I can't." He sighed and stalked away but his voice still carried to her. "It's so damned unfair! I finally have everything I want, and it's all for nothing!"

"I don't think your son and I are nothing, do you?" Mary's reply was crisp, and he looked at her, hearing her despite his sorrow.

"I didn't mean it like that," he grumbled.

"But you said it. I need you to say what you mean."

When he turned to her, Mary saw the tears in his blue eyes that he was trying to blink away, and all she wanted to do was to wrap herself around him and hold him tight, offer him what comfort she could.

"I'm lost, Mary... Without you I'm lost..."

"Sean..." Damn. Now she felt tears in her eyes.

They stood silent for several moments.

"Ballocks!" he said in frustration. "Do you see how difficult this is? Do you understand how impossible it is for us to be a family when this is what I am?"

"Maybe we can do something..." she ventured in an uncertain voice. "We haven't done any research..."

"Mary, I don't have a disease. I'm dead. We can't cure that."

"Cynic," she groused.

"Unrealistic optimist!" he growled.

"Pessimist!"

"Dreamer," he retorted.

Suddenly she stopped, shook her head, and grinned at him.

"What?" he asked.

"We're doing it again," she said.

"Doing what?"

"Fighting about the fact that you're dead, which is pointless."

"Yeah," he said, a glum expression on his face.

"Sean, you have to meet your son, you have to try. He wants so badly to see you." Mary implored him with her pleading hazel eyes.

Sean looked like a puppy that had been hit with a stick. "What if I scare him?"

"You won't. You're not a very frightening ghost," she said, a smile in her voice.

"Says you. I'm not trying hard."

"You're not trying at all, and why would you frighten your son anyway?"

"I wouldn't," he seemed offended.

"So we have nothing to worry about. I'll bring him up here to tell him about the fact that you died, and that... you didn't." She shrugged.. "I guess that's how I'll have to explain it. You'll be here with me, won't you?"

Sean watched the distant hills for a moment and turned back to Mary, nodding. "Yes. I have to try to meet the lad; I already love him so much."

"And he'll love you. Thank you, Sean," she whispered, and leaned into him, once again surprised to feel a brief resistance where his arm should be. She gave him a curious look but he didn't notice.

THE NEXT DAY, Mary sat in kitchen of Sean's house with Lillie and Geraldine. The ticking of the clock was abnormally loud, or at least that's how it seemed to Mary as she sat at the small kitchen table The women sipped their tea in silence, and Mary wondered how she could ever tell this old, intimidating woman that she had a grandson. They had made some small talk, but Geraldine had remained noticeably silent, leaving Lillie and Mary to talk about the weather, the town, and nothing else of importance.

Mary searched for something else to say.

"Did you visit with one of your neighbors yesterday? When I walked by yesterday, I saw you visiting with one of your neighbors," Mary said to Geraldine.

"Oh, and what did he look like?" the old lady's sharp eyes studied her.

"He was a middle-aged man with dark hair and eyes. He had a kind face, "Mary said.

"Mary, that could be anyone," Lillie said with a happy laugh. "It even sound a bit like Da, doesn't it, Mam?"

The old woman gave Mary a thoughtful look, but remained quiet.

"Well, I guess I should be going," Mary said when it seemed Geraldine had nothing more to offer.

"I'll walk you back." Lillie said getting to her feet. "But don't you have something to tell Mam first?"

Mary hesitated under Geraldine's suddenly intent gaze, but gathering up her courage, looked back into the sharp blue eyes. She might fool some people, but Mary knew this woman was well aware of much that went on around her, despite her progressing senility.

"I don't know how to say this, but you need to know. I can only hope it will make you happy." She took a deep breath. "When I fell in love with Sean, I didn't realize he was married. We were together in every sense of the word, and before I left, I found out I was pregnant. I came here four years ago to tell him that."

The old woman remained silent, her expression unchanged.

"You have a beautiful grandson who wants to meet his grandmother." She studied the old face that watched her. "Will you meet him?"

Geraldine finally turned back to Mary. "Bring him here tomorrow."

Lillie grinned broadly and gripped Mary's hand in joy, as they shared a happy smile.

Chapter 28
The Family

*S*EVERAL HOURS LATER, Mary and her son slept quietly, their gentle snoring a comforting, though somewhat erratic sound. Or at least that's what Sean thought as he sat in a nearby chair and watched over them.

They were his family, or at least they should have been. He briefly mused over the possibility of the fact that he might still be alive if he had never met Mary, but the idea of not loving her, of never having known her love, caused him a sensation that felt like pain, every cell he had left tingled in distress. A love-sick ghost— *now that was something you don't run into every day*, he thought with a wry grin.

It still amazed him that all of those who had died in the fire with him seemed at peace with what had happened. They were content to go about their business in their new realm and leave the world of the living behind, but not Sean. Maybe, he mused, he just wasn't very good at being a ghost. Or maybe he refused to move on as long as Mary was alive, as long as he was needed to watch over her and his son. Right now, he just wanted to memorize their faces as they slept and, for a night, pretend he was real to them. Real enough to be the husband and father they both deserved. With a soft sigh and a smile, he settled in for the night with his dreams and continued to watch as the people he loved most slept the night away, oblivious to his presence.

THE NEXT MORNING, Lillie went in search of Patrick and was pleased to find him at his house, working outside as he cleaned up his yard.

"Lillie." He grinned warmly at her.

"Patrick," she greeted him with a warm smile.

"What can I help you with today, Lillie?"

"Can we go inside and talk?"

He gave her a concerned look but, with a nod, agreed and gestured to the house.

They walked into his house, and he held the door for her and followed her in. The living room was still mostly tidy. The worn gray fabric of the couch contrasted against the cream wall behind it, and the green, well-worn carpet had seen better days. A TV inhabited a small stand in the corner, and a rocking chair was near the end of the couch. It was a small, lived-in room, but a place where Lillie felt comfortable.

She took a spot on the couch and waited for Patrick to join her.

"Would you like some tea?" he asked.

"No, I'm fine. Sit down, please."

"All right," he said and sat down beside her, keeping a small distance between them. "I'm almost afraid to ask, but what do you want to talk about?"

"Maggie."

"Maggie? Why do you want to waste a perfectly fine day talking about her?"

"Because I'm worried about her—what she can do, what she might do. Were you telling the truth when you said she was a witch?"

"Well, she certainly thinks she is, she practices some sort of nonsense."

"We have to stop her."

He was silent for a long moment. "If she really is a witch, why do we have to be the ones to stop her?"

"Because we know what she's doing, and because I think she's the one who burned down The Gaelic Moon."

Abruptly, Patrick stood up and went to look out the small window at the surrounding hillside.

Startled by his strange behavior, she went over to him, resting a hand on his arm. "What is it?"

"I don't want to tell you. I think you will hate me, but you need to know." Patrick took a deep breath and turned to face Lillie. "She set The Gaelic Moon on fire. She wanted to get back at Sean for betraying her."

"That bitch! That unprincipled, unscrupulous, mangy, unwanted, ignorant, horrible, ruthless, wanton, selfish, meddling, slutty..."

Patrick listened in amazement, stunned by Lillie's vocabulary.

" ...unspeakable, unwashed, unclean, spoiled whore!" She stopped to catch her breath, and began to cry. "She killed Sean. She killed my brother." Lillie stopped and glared at Patrick. "And you didn't tell me?"

"We weren't involved at the time."

"But we were still friends."

"I was under her influence, but she asked me to help her and I refused."

She said nothing for a moment. "You couldn't stop her?"

"I didn't think she would really do it. I can't believe she did." He swallowed the lump in his throat. "I'm so sorry. I understand if you want to go now." He sighed and looked down at her feet.

"Why didn't you tell anyone?"

"Because I was afraid of her... the things I saw her do. I know that's no excuse, but..." He shrugged helplessly.

"Why would you help me fight her?" Lillie asked him, her voice sad.

"Because I don't want anything to happen to you." His bright eyes met hers, and she saw his love for her shining through his gaze.

"It won't. I won't let it." she said and gave him a reassuring smile and let him pull her into his warm embrace.

SOMETIMES SHE WISHED the mirror did lie, Mary thought as she surveyed herself with a critical eye. Although the forest-green peasant skirt and black silk blouse she wore were nice, they seemed plain to her, almost drab. Helplessly, she regarded the closet. She didn't know what else to wear because it was either this or the jaw-dropping dress that she had brought along on a whim, thinking if she confronted Sean she would make him regret letting her go.

Little Sean tugged at her skirt impatiently as the boy was anxious to be on his way. He looked quite handsome in his best jeans and warm dark-blue sweater.

"Mommy, can we go? We had lunch."

"Just a minute, Sean." Mary ran a brush through her hair one last time, and sighed.

"Mom! I want to meet Grandma and Auntie!"

"Why the rush?" she asked with a laugh.

"Cause we see Daddy after! You said!"

"All right," she said softly, smiling at the little boy, who pulled hard on her hands.

The locals smiled at them in curiosity as they walked by, the boy proudly leading his mother down the road. His blue eyes danced happily, trying to take in everything around him, and as they approached Sean's house, Mary saw Lillie and Geraldine sat outside, enjoying the day. Lillie waved as she saw them, and her eyes never left the boy leading his mother to the house.

With a large smile for the small face that regarded her so seriously, Lillie bent down and extended her hand to him.

"I'm very pleased to meet you," she said.

"Are you my Auntie?"

"Yes, I am. I'm your Aunt Lillie."

First giving his mother a questioning look and getting a nod of approval from her, the boy went to Lillie's outstretched arms and hugged her. When Mary glanced over at Geraldine, she saw the old woman was watching them with interest.

Behind her, Sean leaned quietly against the house. He nodded to Mary, who regarded him curiously as he went to stand behind his mother.

"Mam," he said, "that's my son. He's a fine lad, isn't he? I want you to welcome him, and Mary, too. They're my family." Hesitating for a moment, he stood up and stepped away from his mother as Lillie brought the boy over to stand before her.

"Do you see what Mary has brought us? Your grandson," Lillie said.

Geraldine inspected Mary with a critical eye, and then turned her gaze to the young boy. Fearing the worst, she watched the old woman, daring her to say something out of place. No matter that this woman was his grandmother, she wasn't about to let her son be harmed.

"Pleased to meet you, Grandma. My name is Sean." He extended his small hand and smiled slowly as he looked into her lined face.

Unable to resist the impish grin of the young boy, Geraldine ever so slowly began to smile. And to everyone's surprise, she extended her hand.

BACK AT THE Lakeview Guesthouse, a new model, mid-sized car pulled into the parking lot, dust showing evidence of a long journey. With an irritated sigh, Paul got out of the car and surveyed the area, pausing to comb his thick blond hair. He glared across at his companion, Rob, who had all but forced his way into Paul's trip with the flimsy excuse that he wanted to visit his fiancée, who was with Mary in Ireland.

"What kind of country is this? Only one place that can actually be called a city and we had to leave it to come here! Here! In this backward local area that calls itself a town."

"Irish towns are different than America. I think it's a beautiful country,' Rob said in a relaxed voice, staring blandly at his agitated companion.

Paul gave Rob a long look before speaking. "Yes, but what do you know? You grew up on a farm in Minnesota."

"And you're from New York City and grew up with money." Rob snorted. "What do you know of the people that surround you? You're a snob, and I'm surprised Mary's put up with you this long."

"Leave Mary out of this," Paul snapped.

"Gladly. What she does with you is up to her, anyway. You're a comedown from Sean, that's for sure."

"Her Irish lover? The one that left her pregnant with no one to turn to? Yes, do compare me to him, and I'll come off splendidly." He smirked, and it took all of Rob's self-control not to wipe the smirk off his face.

"He must have had his reasons," Rob muttered.

"Mary doesn't believe that, and I'm here to rescue her from this godforsaken country."

"You'd best be careful, Paul. I'm not sure the people that live here would enjoy that comment."

"What do I care?" He eyed Rob and the area with disdain. "I'm only passing through." With that remark, he opened the trunk and retrieved his bags, and stalked up the front steps of the Guesthouse and past Amy, who was just coming out. He offered her a curt nod, his form of courtesy, and continued past her and through the door.

"Well, nice to see you, too," she said to the air left in his wake and turned to see Rob muttering to himself, his focus on retrieving his bags from the trunk.

"Rob!" She ran the short distance to him and threw herself at him.

Caught off guard, he grunted as she landed in his arms. "Ames!" he snapped. "Give a guy a little warning, will you?"

Amy drew back and looked into his face, seeing a tenseness that wasn't usually there. Rob was one of the most laid-back people she knew. She put a hand up to his cheek and let her fingertips brush it until he turned her. "What's wrong?"

"That," he said, a curt nod of his head, indicating the doors where Paul had disappeared, "is what's wrong! The man is nuts! He thinks he's God's gift to everything. Why in the hell does Mary go out with him?"

Amy grimaced. "That bad?"

"Worse. If I didn't love you so much, I wouldn't have done it. And having said that, I doubt I will ever travel anywhere with him again." Rob's eyes were still angry. "He insults everyone and seems to think Mary is incapable of a rational decision. How has she put up with him?"

"Well, believe it or not, he actually behaves better around her."

Rob snorted as he finally pulled his bags from the trunk and shut it.

"Really he does. I don't understand it, but she has a way about her. She settles people."

"Well, I'd really like to settle him!" Rob gave the door a final glare and expelled a long breath, closing his eyes.

From long experience, Amy knew he was trying to get a handle on his emotions, to collect himself and calm himself, so she gave him his time, leaning against the trunk of the car until he opened his eyes. She saw a smile touch the corner of his mouth, and he pulled her close once again.

"Now I should greet you properly, shouldn't I?" He kissed her, slowly, tenderly and they melted into each other for the next few minutes, unconcerned about anyone or anything else.

"See, I am happy to see you,' he said when they finally pulled apart.

"And I bet that's not a flashlight you're carrying around either, is it?"

"Hardly." He laughed, a sound filled with warmth and love. "I plan to show you just how glad I am to see you after I settle in." He looked at the Guesthouse. "Is this where you and Mary are staying?"

"Yes."

"Did she find Sean? Is he here?"

"Well, yes..." Amy didn't quite want to blurt out that the man was dead, and in all probability a ghost, as Rob had just arrived and he and Sean had been friends of a sort.

"That's great! Maybe she can finally offload that piece of crap and get back to the man she was meant to be with." He grinned at her.

"Yeah, maybe." Amy bit her lip, and Rob saw her uncertain look but decided to let it go for the moment.

"Come on, let's go in. I need to check in and get settled and get used to Irish time again. And I'm hungry, and we'll have to keep an eye on Paul. Who knows what he's going to do. He's hell bent on finding Mary."

"This is going to get very interesting," Amy muttered as Rob took her hand and they walked into the Guesthouse.

LATER THAT AFTERNOON, Patrick stood in the doorway of his small house and watched as Mary and her son walked past the house on their way up the road. Unaware of it, Patrick smiled as he watched the boy who held his mother's hand with such trust; he seemed such a good lad. He sighed, wishing he had such a son.

He was surprised to find that Maggie, unannounced, was suddenly beside him, appraising him with slitted green eyes, and he felt like a bug under a microscope.

"What do you want?" he growled at her and with a start

realized her wheelchair was gone. "And how is it you're walking?"

"Told you I would walk again. It's magic, Patrick."

He couldn't think of a thing to say since he knew it was probably true. He tried not to appear frightened.

"You know I have powers." She looked down the street at Mary and the boy. "Such a lovely child, who knew that Sean had it in him?"

"I'd say that's none of your business."

"Really? After all that he and I shared? The fact he married me and never had a family with me? That's none of my business?" Her tone was silky, mesmerizing, and Patrick blinked away the tranquility of it.

"The fact you can't have children is your own fault. We were going to have a child together; we should have had a child together."

"With you? That was an unwanted complication, nothing more." She shrugged it off, and Patrick felt the fury building in him. He clamped down the tears that threatened him whenever he thought about this subject.

She touched him, and he saw her mumbling things under her breath, and suddenly he felt unnaturally calm. He backed away from her, fear in his eyes. "I'll not let you do anything to me. I have a good life now. Leave me alone!"

"Do you really think it's that easy?" Maggie laughed, and it sounded like bits of glass falling on a hard surface. "I can have you for my use whenever I want, and there's not a damn thing you can do about it." She smiled sweetly.

Patrick willed himself to stand his ground and not run away from her.

"I've broken your spells over me," he said.

"Maybe for the moment, but it won't last. I'm always learning more, and soon I'll be able to do whatever I want." She walked across to him and laid her hand on his chest, and he had to fight off waves of desire as she kept murmuring words he couldn't understand. He saw her in his mind the way he used to see her—her sensuous red hair that cascaded over her shoulders, her green eyes that burned with desire, and her sensuous lips so meant for kissing. He fought against the feelings, closing his eyes as he desperately turned his thoughts to Lillie.

"If I want you, I will have you," she whispered in his ear. "Or I could give you to a demon, and you would have no choice at all. Would you like that, Patrick? To be a prisoner within your own body?" Again the brittle laughter. "And I can do that to anyone. I'll soon be able to get back at everyone that has wronged me."

Patrick shivered even as his body was beginning to respond to her. She was right—she was stronger. He clung to his images of Lillie, of how her brown hair felt as he lay with his face next to hers, looking into her loving and accepting brown eyes...

"See, you are mine," Maggie said as Patrick leaned forward to kiss her. After a moment, feeling only air and not the soft lips she was used to, she opened her eyes in surprise and saw Lillie standing before her, arms crossed and her face furious. "Ah, the whore returns."

"You home-wrecking bitch!" Lillie closed the distance and punched her in the face, knocking her to the ground. Patrick quickly snapped out of his stupor and grabbed Lillie from behind, restraining her.

"Not now," he whispered in Lillie's ear. "Later. There will be time for it later." He had his arms full as Lillie was hell bent on making the other woman suffer.

Maggie picked herself off the ground and rubbed her jaw, all the while staring at Lillie. "I'll not forget, Lillie. You always were too much of a saint for your own good. I will take special pleasure in your demise." Maggie smirked. "Curses are wonderful things. I'll make sure to think up a special one for the two of you." With a short nod, she turned her back on them and walked away.

Patrick held onto Lillie tightly as they both regained their composure and calmed down.

"I hate her," Lillie said.

"I know. I do, too." Patrick shifted uncomfortably. Whatever Maggie had done had left him with some undesired after effects, and he felt a definite need to relieve his stress. "Um, Lillie, perhaps you should go," he suggested.

"Go? I just got here." She gave him a puzzled look. "What did she do to you?"

"She was trying to get me to... well... you know." He felt ashamed and avoided her eyes.

"Patrick, it's not your fault."

"I still think you'd better go," he growled and gently pushed her away from him.

"What in the hell is wrong with you?" Concerned, she stepped up to him and reached for his forehead, wondering if he had a temperature. As she leaned against him, he groaned, and his problem was easily surmised. "Oh, and I'd like to help you with your problem," she whispered in his ear.

"Lillie!" He was shocked, and his expression told her so.

"Stop being such a lout; it's time you understand, completely understand that I am a woman and not some glorified angel."

"This isn't a good idea," he stammered.

"Why not?" She took his hand and led him back into his house.

"I might not be able to control myself," he said.

Lillie only smiled as the door shut behind them.

THE BURNED OUT remnants of The Gaelic Moon were more depressing than usual on this fine sunny day, but perhaps it was because Mary was so dreading what she had to tell her son. She knelt down beside him and watched his young face as he studied the blackened building. After what seemed an eternity to Mary, he looked back at her, his small mind trying to understand. With a brief glance over his shoulder, she saw Sean standing in the burned out doorway watching them.

"Are you going to tell him, Mary?"

She nodded as her son began to speak. "Something bad..." He pointed to the building. "A fire?"

"Yes, Sean. A big fire. Do you see all of the black pieces around here, and over there?" She pointed around her, and the boy nodded, a serious expression on his face. Sean came over and joined them.

"Well, they're all part of the building that burned."

"That's bad."

"Very bad, but it's really sad because there were people inside."

"Did they get hurt?"

"Yes, they did. Some of them died. Died and went to heaven."

The boy looked up at the sky and back to his mother. "Are they okay? Is it bad to die?"

Mary pondered the question thoughtfully, trying to find a simple answer. When she looked at Sean, she found his pained expression heartbreaking, but was unable to take her eyes off him as she answered her son.

"Living is better than dying. But those people are in a good place because they're with God."

"Does everyone go to heaven?"

Sean shrugged. He was still here.

Lord, she thought, putting a hand to her head, this was getting complicated. "No, sometimes, but not often, a person who has died stays nearby. They become a ghost."

"Oh." He was quiet as he tried to process the information. "Are ghosts good or bad?"

"Well... " Again, she looked at Sean. "There are both good ghosts and bad ghosts, just like people are good and bad."

"Okay." He squirmed and turned about impatiently. Finally, irritated, he looked at his mother. "Where's Daddy?"

"That's the saddest part of all." She took a deep breath and made sure the boy was paying attention to her. "Your Daddy was in the building when it burned. He died in the fire."

The boy's shocked expression slowly turned to one of horror, and he broke away from his mother and ran to the blackened ruins, yelling at the rubble. "No! Daddy! Where are you? Daddy!"

Tears welled up in Mary's eyes as he continued to call for his father. Standing nearby, Sean could barely manage a whisper. "Tell him I love him. That I would do anything to be with him right now."

"Daddy! Daddy, where are you?" the boy cried at the building, unwilling to give up on his father.

Unable to stand his cries any longer, Sean stood in front of the boy, but the child didn't see him. He bent down so that he was at eye level with his son and softly reached out and touched his cheek.

Little Sean stopped yelling, his grief and anger replaced by uncertainty and fear. He gave his mother a frightened look.

"Sean?" she questioned the child, worried by the fear she saw in his face. By the time, she reached him, tears were running down his face.

"I love you, son. I love you," his father said quietly and kissed the boy's cheek.

The boy took a sharp breath and gasped, excited. "He's here! Mommy, he's here!" He jumped up and down, grabbing her hand. "I heard him!"

Stunned by the strange turn of events, Sean and Mary turned to each other in surprise.

Chapter 29
Nemesis

MARY BENT DOWN, wiped the stray tears away from her son's cheek and hugged him. After a long moment, he regarded her with a serious expression.

"What did you hear?" she asked.

"A voice." he looked around nervously. "A man's voice."

"What did the voice say?"

"That he loves me. Daddy loves me, doesn't he?"

"Of course I do," Sean said.

"Daddy?" The boy spun around too quickly and, off balance, began to fall. Sean put a hand out to steady the boy, and was surprised to feel, actually feel, his small son's arm. Little Sean reached out to regain his balance and touched Sean's hand.

"Mommy, I feel him. Is he here?" Astonished, she nodded. "Is he a... a ghost?

Mary wasn't sure how to answer her son. She didn't want to scare him. The truth seemed best, but this was such a strange thing to tell a child. She felt Sean's blue eyes fasten on her, acknowledging that he would accept her decision. She took a deep breath and looked down at her son, who was watching her with such a hopeful expression on his face.

"Would you be scared of a ghost?"

"Maybe. Is it a good ghost or a bad ghost?"

"Good question," Mary muttered to herself and decided to just tell the boy. "Well, when your father died, he decided not to go to heaven. He decided that he wanted to wait for us and make sure we are all right. So he came back as a ghost."

"Cool!" The small boy grinned from ear to ear.

Sean burst into laughter at the unexpected approval and was soon joined by Mary. Hearing warm laughter all around him, the little boy added his high giggle to the mix of merriment.

SEAN WALKED THE streets of his hometown, so preoccupied that he hardly noticed when a child's ball bounced through him. He stopped and laughed as the child ran by, almost feeling the air that circulated around him.

God! He didn't know if he was blessed or cursed to still be around as a ghost. It was fortunate in the sense that he still existed, and it made him amazingly happy because Mary could see him. But he was dead. He knew Mary loved him and that he loved Mary but, in the end, was it enough? Would Mary consider him man enough to stay with him despite his distinct lack of a body? That one sounded iffy even to him. *Damn!* Some sort of existence was still better than none at all, and he knew he could never really be alive again, but there had to be something more than this.

His path had led him to the Guesthouse and as he glanced at the picturesque building, he was surprised to see Rob wave and walk toward him.

"Hey, Sean," Rob called, stopping before Sean, smiling. "How the hell are you? I was wondering when you'd come around."

Sean gaped at him. "You can see me?"

Rob regarded him with a strange expression. "Why wouldn't I be able to see you?"

"You don't know?" Sean laughed. This was priceless.

"Know what?" With a grin, Sean opened up his arms to give his old friend a hug. Rob laughed, stepped forward with open arms, and passed right through Sean.

"What the hell?" Rob spun around to face Sean, who was laughing. "How'd you move so fast?"

"But I didn't move."

"What do you mean?" Rob asked in a suspicious voice.

"I can't believe you can see and hear me. Of all people, why you?" Sean shook his head.

"Sean, what the fuck are you talking about?"

"Can't you figure it out?" Sean extended his hand. "Here, try to shake my hand."

"Okay." With a smug look, Rob reached for his hand to encompass it within his strong grip, but found only air where his hand should be. "Sean? You don't seem to be all here, and I mean that in the kindest way."

"Ah, Rob. It's good to see you, and I hate to be the bearer of bad news, especially for me, but I'm dead." He offered the other man a pained smile.

"Dead? Oh, come on." Rob laughed, but Sean's expression remained serious. "You can't be dead, that would make you a... a..."

"A ghost?" Sean widened his eyes and raised his arms and took a step toward Rob, who seemed briefly alarmed. "*Boo!*"

"Sean, you bastard! What kind of trick is this?" Rob did a quick search for mirrors or wires but didn't see any. "It's a damn good illusion."

"Rob, my friend, it's not an illusion. I only wish it were." He sighed sadly.

Rob studied Sean for a long moment and stepped toward him. Sean stood quietly as Rob poked and waved his hand through him several times. "Do you feel that?"

"Only a little, like the softest touch of a breeze."

"Wow, I guess you really are dead." Rob looked at him with concern. "Are you all right? I mean, don't most people die and go to, you know, heaven?"

"I can't say, I haven't been there," Sean snapped.

"Sorry." Rob wasn't sure what to say. "*Um*, does Mary know?"

"That I died? Yes, we've talked."

"So she can see you?"

"Thank God, yes, she can. And my son can hear me, so I'm grateful for that." He studied Rob with a curious expression. "Why you are aware of me, I have no idea."

"This is so damn weird!" Rob laughed. "Well, I'm about to join Amy for lunch. I don't know that it matters, but do you want to join us?"

"It could be amusing, as Amy can't see or hear me."

"Does she know what happened?"

"Yes, I've left her a few notes; she accepts that I'm around as a ghost."

"Could be fun?" Rob raised an eyebrow. "And Mary and your son are joining us as well."

Sean mulled it over. "All right."

"Great, let's go. I'm starving." Rob turned to return to the Guesthouse. "I should warn you, a friend of Mary's is here. His name is Paul."

"Paul?" Sean felt his hackles rising. Why in the hell was he joining them for lunch?

"Oh, you remember him?" Rob asked as they got to the front steps.

"Unfortunately, I do," Sean said, tightlipped.

"Yeah, well, he's an ass as far as I'm concerned, and I think Mary knows it, too."

"Paul," Sean muttered as he clenched his teeth and followed Rob through the front doors of the Guesthouse.

IN HIS ROOM, Paul hesitated, looking from his suitcase to the dresser with skepticism because he didn't like it here. A small room, no amenities, and a shared bathroom was not something that he relished, four-star hotels were much more to his liking. He shuddered at the thought of a shared bathroom and closed his suitcase, clothes still inside.

Well, he would deal with that later. Right now, he had to be sure his appearance was immaculate. He wanted to remind Mary that he was an attractive man, surely much more handsome than the Irish lowlife she had fallen for.

He surveyed himself in the mirror and, with some reluctance, decided to discard the tie and go with somewhat more casual attire. He pulled a dark-blue sweater over his dress shirt, examined his reflection, and decided the sweater went well with his tan pants, so the combination was acceptable. After combing his hair, he put on some fresh cologne, the one that Mary had always favored.

Paul regarded the picture of Mary and the boy and allowed a fond smile to touch his face, one that he rarely showed. With a last look in the mirror for any imperfections, he went to join them for lunch.

THE LUNCH RUSH was quiet, Amy thought, as she sat at a table alone, waiting for Rob, Mary, and young Sean to join her. She hoped it went well with Sean's family and that they welcomed the two of them. Mary had been through a lot and deserved to be happy.

She hated to spring a probably unwanted surprise on her in the form of Paul, but she had no choice as he planned to join them for lunch. Hopefully, now that Mary seemed to be back together with Sean—at least as much as a person could be together with a ghost—she would tell Paul to take an extended hike off a short pier.

She smiled and waved as Mary and her son came in through the door, the boy bounding along happily.

"You two certainly are in a good mood."

"Amy! Amy! You know what?" Little Sean ran over to Amy and gave her a hug.

"What? Did something good happen?"

"Yes." The boy bounced up and down with excitement. "I found my Daddy."

Amy exchanged a concerned look with Mary, who just shrugged and smiled. "Did your mother tell you what happened to your Daddy?"

"Oh, yes." He dismissed it with a wave of his hand. "He died in a fire."

"He did. And what do you think he is now?"

"He's a ghost," the boy said proudly. "It's cool. He's still here, and he loves me."

Amy frowned at Mary. "You've seen him?"

"No, but I can hear him." The boy smiled happily and went over to his mother, who helped him into a chair.

"Well, that's good, I think." Amy made a funny face and peered around the table.

"He's not here," Mary said with a laugh.

"Yes, he is," the boy said, as Rob and Sean walked through the door into the dining room.

Startled, she looked up from her son and saw Sean standing beside the table, a scowl on his face. Now what had happened?

"Sean? What's wrong?" she said as Rob took a chair beside Amy.

"That's what's wrong," he snapped, as Paul entered the room.

The dining room doors opened and Paul entered, doing is best to make a grand entrance, his appearance as handsome as ever. He saw Mary and started over to their table.

"Mary..." Amy said.

Mary heard the note of anxiety in her friend's voice and gave her a questioning glance. Amy helplessly pointed over Mary's shoulder at Paul, who without warning, turned Mary around, pulled her into his arms, and kissed her. The silverware on the table rattled noisily and the table began to move. Flustered, Amy scooted away from the table and cast a nervous look around the room as Paul continued to hold Mary close.

"Easy, Sean," Rob murmured to his friend, causing Amy to regard her fiancé strangely.

"I'm so glad to see you. I've missed you," Paul said, letting his hand drift down to rest on her shapely derriere.

"But I've only been gone a few days," she said and pulled away from him.

"Is that all?" He squeezed her again. "It seems like more." He gave her a quick kiss, let her go, and held out his arms to the boy, who shook his head, and stayed seated in his chair.

"Hello, Paul," said the boy.

"Well, hello to you, too. Have you had fun? Do you like it here?" Paul had a pleasant smile on his face that Sean was seriously thinking of removing.

"Yes, I like it here." He looked at his mother, the empty space where he felt his father to be, and back to Paul. "Mom and I found Daddy."

"You did?" His eyes narrowed ever slightly.

"Yes, we did," Mary started, but before she could continue, her son interrupted.

"He died," the boy said sadly.

"He what?" Paul turned to regard Mary, and she couldn't miss the way his eyes lit up with happiness. He was glad that the love of her life had died.

"He died," the boy said again, but slowly the impish smile returned. "But that's okay."

"It is? Why?" Paul looked at Mary curiously.

"Because he's a ghost. I can hear him. That's why."

"Sean, you know there are no such things as ghosts," Paul tried to reason with the little boy.

"Want to bet?" Sean muttered, as a glass of water flew off the table and spilled all over Paul's backside. "Just like old times," Sean muttered under his breath.

Rob coughed to smother his laughter as he put his napkin up to his face.

The boy clapped happily. "See, Daddy's a ghost!"

Paul took a moment to compose himself and decided that since he wasn't soaked he could put up with the momentary discomfort, but his expression told everyone that he was running out of patience. "Okay. But can you see him?"

"No." The boy bit his lip. "But I can hear him."

Impatient with the boy's answers, he turned to Mary, his expression filled with disapproval. "Why are you letting him believe this?" She remained silent and looked at Sean, who ignored her but was staring daggers at Paul.

The people at the table ignored Paul and his question, and he couldn't control his growing anger. "Do you believe this, too?" Paul demanded of Mary.

Mary shrugged. "Could be."

"Could be?" Sean fumed. "I'm right here, and you're telling him that maybe you believe I'm still around?"

"*Shh.*" Mary tried to shush him.

"He can't hear me, so don't bother shushing me! Tell him I'm here," Sean demanded.

"I can't, not right now," she hissed at him.

With a concerned expression, Paul grasped Mary's hands in his and offered her a look of deep sympathy. "Mary, I'm sorry he's dead."

"I'll just bet you are," Sean muttered, jealousy oozing from every ghostly pore.

"I know it's a terrible loss for you." He again offered her that comforting smile. "But maybe now you can finally put this behind you and get on with your life. You and your son deserve a good man, a man who is still alive, to take care of the two of you."

Mary fidgeted uneasily and removed her hands from Paul's.

"Paul, we're good. We don't need anyone to take care of us. We're doing just fine."

"Really? How can you possibly think that?"

"What do you mean?" Mary felt her anger rising.

Paul's sympathetic voice was filled with condescension. "I understand how hard this is for you. You're back here in Ireland— a sad excuse for a country I may add—but Sean's homeland. It's stirred up memories for you. You're nostalgic, remembering when you were happy here. But it's time to get over those feelings and move on with your life." Paul reached out, grasped her hands again, and gave a dismissive look to the rest of the table, moving closer so that he was talking only to Mary. "Marry me! I'll never walk out on you like that Irish bastard did!"

"Paul!"

Sean couldn't take it anymore; he grabbed Paul by the shoulders, ripped him away from Mary, and punched him, dropping him to the floor. Little Sean looked at Paul, who was now sprawled in a undignified pile, and laughed. Amy grinned, and Rob had his head buried in his arms on the table, his body shaking with laughter.

"Sean!" Mary reprimanded him and he stopped mid-gesture as if his hand hit a wall. He gave her a startled look. "How'd you do that?"

"Do what?"

"Stop me?"

"I didn't do anything," she said quietly.

He glared at her and then turned his attentions back to his adversary.

"I like him better down there, don't you?" Sean's blue eyes glowed eerily, and Mary realized she had never seen him really angry as a ghost. She briefly wondered what he could do and realized that she didn't want him killing Paul. God forbid she was haunted by him as well.

"No more," she told him with a "don't argue with me" expression.

"What do you mean?" He turned his anger on her. "You're not

taking him seriously?"

Paul scrambled to his knees, wincing as he turned his neck about, looking from side to side. "What the hell just happened?"

Seeing no answer was forthcoming, he got to his knees and surprisingly smiled at Mary. He gave her his patented, devastating smile, the one that always got him his way with women, reached into his pocket and drew out a ring box, and looked at Mary. "This isn't the way I planned to do this, but as we've discussed this before, during an intimate exchange, as I recall, it shouldn't matter where I ask you. Mary, will you marry me?"

"Mary! You've been... on a... special date with him, too?" Sean modified his words, remembering his small son was in the room, and found his anger fading to be replaced by a growing sadness. He'd been wrong to be hopeful. How could he think to offer anything to her when what she needed was a living, breathing man in her life? As objectionable as Paul was, he was a living, breathing man, one who could do all of the normal things in life that he could no longer do. How could he have ever believed anything else? How could he ever be that to them? He had messed up his life and Mary's life, and this was his punishment.

"Sean?" She reached out a hand to where he stood and saw the sadness etched in his face.

He bowed his head and quietly faded away.

As THEY WALKED along the peaceful country road, Paul regarded Mary with annoyance. She hadn't said anything since they had left lunch a half an hour ago, and even now, had her arms crossed in front of her, her stance was anything but friendly. So he fell silent, waiting until she was ready to talk, knowing he would get an earful, though he wasn't quite sure why. Finally, with no one in sight, she stopped and turned to him, angry.

"How dare you come here without warning and intrude in my business!"

"Intrude? I'm your fiancé, remember?"

"I never said yes. Just because you asked, you think you have the right to tell me what to do?"

"If it involves being here, then yes, I have every right to tell you what to do. You've obviously lost your grip on reality." He moved forward and grabbed her roughly. "I know it's hard, but accept that he's dead. Let him go, as you should have done four years ago. Stop imagining things! A ghost? Really?" He scowled at her.

"Who do you think knocked you down in the dining room?"

"Oh, that." He dismissed it with a gesture. "I must have slipped."

"Why do you have a bruise on your jaw?" With a glare, she pulled herself out of his grasp. "Don't you ever tell me what to do! Or what to believe! Is this how you would treat me if we were married? Why would I marry you?"

"Why wouldn't you marry me? I've been by your side through everything, thick and thin. I've taken care of you when you needed it and have been a father to your son." He ran a hand through his hair. "How dare you treat me like this, after all I've done for you? And the excuse you're using is unbelievable. A ghost? You'd rather stay here in Ireland with a ghost than marry me? How can you be so ungrateful?" He pulled her roughly to him and kissed her, bruising her lips. "Mary, I'm real. Marry me, let go of Sean. You know it's the right thing to do."

She slapped him, incredulous that this man she'd known for years as a friend, and more recently as a boyfriend and a lover, would treat her like this. With a noise of disgust, she stalked away, leaving Paul to rub his sore jaw and ponder his rash words.

THE BOY FIDGETED, his attention wandering away from the story book Amy was reading to him. She closed the book and watched as he looked around the room, oblivious to her gaze.

"Sean, what's wrong?"

"Nothing."

"What are you doing?"

"Looking for Daddy."

"But he's not here."

"Maybe he is." The boy smiled at her. "You can't see him either."

Amy eyed the room with a worried expression, remembering their lunch earlier in the day.

"Forget about that," she said. "He's not here, and I know a very special little boy that needs to get his sleep."

"Me?" The laughter that bubbled out of him melted her heart, and she hugged him.

"Yes, you."

"Okay." He obediently climbed under the covers. "Aunt Amy?"

"Yes?"

"I don't want to go home with Paul. I want to stay here with Daddy."

She took his hand as she sat down on the bed beside him. "*Shh*. Go to sleep. You have to take a nap."

"I don't like Paul anymore. He made Daddy go away."

Amy cautiously glanced around the room. "You don't hear him anymore?"

"No, I don't," he said sadly.

Amy leaned forward and hugged him again, holding him tight. "It'll be all right, Sweetie, I just know it will.

Chapter 30
Allies

*T*HE EMERALD ISLE was a miserable excuse for a bar, but at least they had a good supply of cheap liquor, Paul thought as he sat at the bar, drowning his sorrows. In all of the time he had known Mary, she had never been this angry with him. What was wrong with the woman, turning down his offer of marriage? Didn't she know what she was throwing away? Didn't she know how many women wanted him to be theirs? And out of all of those women, Mary was the one he was willing to commit to, willing to give the title of his wife, the fact that she would turn down such an honor was appalling.

He finished his shot and ordered another. Godforsaken country, backwater land filled with sheep, short people, and leprechauns, or so he'd heard. Why did she act like a different person here? She seemed much more docile at home in Minneapolis—except when she played sports, but he was sure that, given time, he could break her of that unladylike habit too. She had such potential, she just needed him to mold her into the perfect wife so that she could have a great life with him. He had to find some way to get her and her son back to Minneapolis. He didn't especially care how he managed it; he just needed some time to formulate a plan. A ghost, my ass! He snorted in contempt as his next drink arrived.

At midday the dark bar was nearly empty, so it was easy for Maggie to spot the stranger. That was the lovely thing about small towns—it didn't take long to learn of new things that had happened, and the gossip always traveled quicker than anyone thought it could.

Maggie had heard some version of what had happened at lunch, how it had ended with Mary and her American boyfriend leaving the Guesthouse in utter silence after exchanging angry words. Maggie had played a hunch that Mary's head was filled with thoughts of Sean and was ready to give her American boyfriend the heave ho, and if that happened it followed that he would be trying to assuage his anger and hurt through drink. Something so typically male that she didn't expect less. What she didn't expect to find was an exceptionally attractive man, with thick blond hair, ruggedly handsome good looks, a strong jaw, and brooding brown eyes. And not a clue as to who she was in this town. Yes, she could work with this.

"Excuse me," she said and placed a warm hand on his bicep.

Paul turned to see who had the audacity to bother him was greeted by the sight of an amazingly beautiful woman. Long, wavy red hair cascaded from the top of her head, over her shoulders and onto her back. Her face was a lovely heart shape, with blazing green eyes and luscious lips that begged to be kissed.

"Hello," he said, dropping into his alluring voice as he flirted with her.

"Hello," she replied in an equally seductive voice.

"You're the best thing I've seen all day. Care to join me?" he asked, gesturing to the empty barstool next to him.

"I will, but not here." Maggie pointed to an empty booth. "Over there."

"And what are you drinking?" he asked.

"Whatever you're having is fine," she said.

He ordered two more shots of whiskey from the bartender and slid into the booth across from Maggie. "And to what do I owe the pleasure of your most enticing company?"

"I needed to speak with you,' she said, and moved around the booth to slide in next to him.

"And how would you know who I am?" Paul was a bit surprised, but it wasn't the only time he had dealt with aggressive women. Mary was being foolish at the moment, and taking advantage of an opportunity that was placed before him was only sensible. He leaned forward and brushed a stray lock of red hair away from the woman's beautiful face.

"It's a small town, word travels fast."

"I see," he said and let his hand fall to her knee. He smiled when she didn't resist. This would be all too easy. "And what is it that I can do for you?"

"A lot, and I can do things for you as well."

"So, a trade?" He sighed and leaned forward to kiss her lips and was rewarded with a more-than-willing response from her. He was picturing how marvelous it would feel to make love to her, to feel her ample, voluptuous body under him.

"Of sorts." Maggie offered him a genuine smile. "I know you came here to see Mary.'

"Her!" he said, the anger apparent in his voice. "I'm here to forget about her."

"Why?" she asked.

"That's not really any of your business," he said.

"Oh, but you're wrong. It is my business. I want nothing more than to see her out of Ireland."

"I want nothing more than to take her out of Ireland. Back home where she belongs. With the man she belongs with."

"You?"

"Me. I'm the best thing for her," he said in an sure voice.

"I can see that. What would you say if I could help you to achieve that? Would you be interested?" Her hand rested strategically on his thigh.

He drew in a breath. This woman knew what she was doing, and he was more than willing. "Do you have a place we can go to discuss this further?" he asked, as he discreetly removed her hand.

"I live nearby." She leaned forward and they exchanged a long passionate kiss.

"Please, lead on," he said as they got out of the booth.

Taking his hand in hers, Maggie led them out the door. Neither of them realized that Patrick had been sitting in a dark corner the entire time, and he regarded them thoughtfully as they left the pub.

As THEY LAY in bed together in the aftermath of their coupling, Paul was extremely pleased with himself. He had managed to nail a desirable single woman during his unexpected sojourn in Ireland, an unexpected bonus, and soothed his ruffled ego after Mary's rejection of him.

"You're beautiful," he whispered to Maggie. "An amazing lover."

"Thank you. You are skilled as well," she said in the way of a compliment, and offered no resistance as he nuzzled her neck. "So you'll help me?" she asked.

"Anything you want." He was starting to lose himself in the feel of her body next to his and the stirrings of desire.

She whispered something in his ear that he didn't understand, and when he pulled away from her, her green eyes had an unnatural sheen to them, Curiously, he gazed intently into them.

"I want you to make love to me again," she said in a sultry voice that he couldn't resist.

His eyes filled with desire. "My pleasure."

"I am hosting a demon for a short time," she said, her lips trailing kisses down his nicely sculpted chest and to his abdomen. "When we make love again he will enter you. You will not be able to refuse me anything once he in within you. His reward when I am done with him will be you."

"Of course," Paul whispered as her hands stroked him and their tongues played together. Why did everything with this woman feel about ten times better than with any other woman he had ever had? If all he had to put up with was a little dementia, the sex was definitely worth it.

"You agree to this?" she purred when she removed her mouth from around him.

God, he was so hard, his head was swimming. He had to take her. He rolled her over placing her underneath him, needing to have her.

"Do you agree?" she asked, her green eyes eerie in the dim light of the room.

"Yes, woman, I agree," he all but shouted, and sighed in relief as she opened up to him. He felt so basic, so feral in his needs that it was freeing. The sex was rough but satisfying in a way he had never experienced before. Sated at last, he passed out.

Maggie sighed, content to lie in her bed for a few moments. Rough sex didn't bother her; in fact she often found it stimulating.

She stroked the face of the man beside her, knowing that when he woke, he truly would be hers to do with as she willed. The demon was bound to her until it fulfilled its obligations and would not be released until she had exacted her revenge. Yes, she was content. The day was turning out extremely well.

THE CHURCH OFFICE was quiet, the aging priest retired to his quarters, leaving Lillie to do the accounting for the week. She was surprised to hear a knock on the office door and even more surprised when she got up to answer it and saw Patrick on the other side.

"Patrick? What are you doing here? If you're looking for Father Murphy, he's gone for the day."

"No, that's not it at all." He fidgeted as if someone might be listening. "I think Maggie's up to something."

"She's always up to something." Lillie scowled. "What happened now?"

"You know about the American woman, Mary?"

"Well, yes. She's sort of my sister-in-law."

"Yes, I guess she would be, wouldn't she?" Patrick frowned. "Well it seems she has an American friend in town."

"Yes, Amy. She's very nice."

"No, a man."

Lillie frowned. "Really? Who would that be? She never mentioned expecting another friend to come here."

"I don't know what happened, only heard that they got in a fight, enough of one that he went off by himself to drink at the pub."

"How do you know that?"

"*Umm*, I was having a few myself. While he was there, Maggie showed up, and the two of them got... friendly."

"So what else is new? She's such a slut." She sighed.

"I think she was using spells."

Lillie realized that Patrick seemed really scared. "What's wrong?" She closed the distance and took his hand in hers.

"Lillie, do you remember when I ran into her the other day? The conversation you walked in on..."

"I know she was trying to lure you to her bed again." The

anger was evident in Lillie voice and her eyes.

"Yes, well that's not all." He bit his lip for a moment before he spoke again. "I didn't tell you what she said before you came because I didn't want to believe it, but now I'm wondering if there might be some truth to what she's saying."

"And what's she saying?" Lillie tried to still the sudden pounding of her heart.

"That she could summon demons, that she could control someone else by putting a demon in them!" Patrick eyes filled with fear, and Lillie squeezed his hand. "Lillie, what if she can do this? That American man was really angry at your friend. What if Maggie did something to him? How do we stop her?"

"Let me wrap things up here. Shouldn't take more than a few minutes, and then we'll talk about it and let Mary know so that she's at least aware of what Maggie is up to. *Tramp*," she muttered under her breath as she walked back to the desk to finish her work.

Content to wait in Lillie's quiet company, Patrick took a seat in a nearby chair, feeling calmed by Lillie's presence.

AN HOUR LATER, young Sean suddenly woke up. He opened his eyes, rubbed them, and saw Amy was still sleeping beside him. Frowning, he looked around the room, but didn't see anything.

Paul stood in the doorway of the room, watching the boy.

"Sean, your mother sent me to get you."

"Why?" the boy asked the older man suspiciously.

"She wants the three of us to go on a walk together, just like we did back in Minneapolis."

"Why?" the boy asked again.

"That way we can all be friends again," Paul replied smoothly, his eyes brighter than normal.

The boy frowned at Paul. "You're not going to try to take me away from my dad?"

"No, I only want to be your friend. Now grab your jacket, and we'll go to meet your mom."

He watched Amy, who continued to sleep. "What about Aunt Amy?"

"She's tired, so we'll let her sleep."

"Okay," the boy said. He scrambled off the bed and shrugged

into his small coat.

Paul extended his hand, and the child took it in his.

"Paul, I'm glad we can be friends," Sean's small voice said as he left the room with Paul.

"So am I," Paul said and, with a simple gesture at Amy, pushed her into a much deeper sleep.

Chapter 31

Gone

*T*HE CHARRED BEAMS of The Gaelic Moon reached out beseechingly toward Mary, and again, when she closed her eyes, she felt glimpses of the fire and winced at the pain connected to it. She knew now that, somehow, she felt this because of Sean and the intimate bond that existed between them.

And ridiculous as it was, she'd still rather be with Sean than Paul, even though Sean was a ghost. What kind of life would she have spending it with a ghost? Oh, Lord, she'd gone insane. That was the only explanation. But even as a ghost, Sean was all too human, otherwise he'd be beyond being jealous of Paul, because he simply wouldn't care.

Though she thought he was overreacting to Paul, here she was, looking for him, wanting to see if he was all right. The burned-out remains disturbed her, but she knew it was where her ghost resided so she sighed and closed her eyes, calling to him. It worked before, shouldn't it work now?

"Sean, where are you? Please talk to me." She stomped her foot in annoyance. "Sean!"

INSIDE THE GAELIC Moon, Sean sat at the bar, doing nothing in particular besides sitting there. He was startled by the sound of Mary's voice.

"Sean? Where are you? Come back. We need you."

Donald went over to where Sean was sitting and regarded him curiously. "You're being called, lad."

Sean shrugged.

"Aren't you going to go to her?"

"No."

"Most of us don't get called at all. We're simply forgotten."

"Leave the living to those alive."

Donald cuffed him on the side of the head and glared at him in disapproval.

"*Oww!*" Sean rubbed the side of his face, surprised that the blow had actually hurt.

"What kind of ghost are you? You have unfinished business. Go and take care of it!"

"They don't need me. They need someone alive. Someone like..." He made a face and forced the words out, "someone like Paul.

"No wonder you died! It's because you're so damn thickheaded!"

Sean gave him a look of annoyance as they both heard Mary's voice again.

"Sean?" she called. "Sean? Where are you?"

"Can't we talk about something else?" Sean asked.

"For a minute." Donald leaned on the bar. "You need to do a favor for me and for yourself."

"What's that?" Sean lit up a cigarette.

"Put that out!" Donald snapped his fingers and Sean's cigarette disappeared.

"Hey!"

"When I ask you to pay attention to me, you will pay attention to me, is that clear?"

"Donald, you're acting like my father again..."

"And why shouldn't I? I all but raised you and Lillie, didn't I?" He paused for a moment. "Let's switch to another important topic... are you aware that a witch, a Druid of The Gaelic Moon, has special powers?"

"And that matters how? Wait, are you saying that Maggie is..."

"God help us, no, not Maggie."

"A witch or Druid of the Gaelic Moon? As in to help fight Maggie?" Sean snorted. "Where are we going to find one of those?"

"You know her well," Donald said quietly.

"Mary?" Sean's eyebrows arched so high they almost met his hairline. "Mary's a witch? A Druid? No, she's not! I would know." Sean saw the somber expression Donald had on his face. "Wait, you mean she doesn't know?"

"Not yet."

"And why are you telling me this?"

"Because it will be important. Just tell her to believe in herself and everything will work out. We can deal with the rest of it later."

"What the hell does that mean?" Sean asked, but was interrupted by the sound of Mary's voice once again.

"'Sean, please! Where are you?" Mary's voice drifted over their conversation.

"Lad, you should go to her. Settle your differences; she needs to talk to you."

"I can't. Don't you see? I can never be what she wants, what she needs."

"Shouldn't you leave that up to Mary?" Donald gave him a significant look, but Sean turned away, ignoring both him and Mary. Muttering under his breath, the bartender walked away.

OUTSIDE, MARY FINALLY stopped calling. Wherever he was, either he didn't hear her, or he didn't want to see her. Maybe she should just leave well enough alone. She could deal with Sean later. He wasn't going anywhere.

As she walked back to the Guesthouse she was surprised by the unusual amount of activity on the grounds and wondered what had happened to cause such uproar. She walked up the steps to the front door, and was almost run over by Amy who came to a sudden stop and flushed guiltily.

"Amy? What's wrong?" she asked.

"I hardly know how to tell you." Amy fretted, afraid of Mary's reaction. "Sean's gone," she blurted.

"I know. I was out looking for him."

"You were?" Amy's jaw dropped. "But how could you know?" Understanding crossed her features, and she realized they were talking about two different people. "Oh." She went over to Mary and put an arm around her shoulders. "Mary, honey, little Sean is gone. We're all looking for him. That's why all these people are here."

"What?" Mary frowned, trying to understand what Amy had just said. "But he was with you."

"Yes, he was. We took a nap together, but when I woke up, he was gone."

"Gone? But how? Why?"

"I don't know. But he can't have gone far. We'll find him."

"I don't believe you," Mary said and pulled away from Amy. She ran into the Guesthouse and up the stairs, looking for her little boy. She started in their rooms and searched every inch for a clue but found nothing. Growing frantic, she went down the hall and opened every open door, even the rooms with guests, muttering a short apology when they told her they hadn't seen him. She stormed down to the front desk and demanded that they take her upstairs to open the empty locked rooms. Amy trailed after Mary, trying to smooth any feathers that her friend was ruffling. The rest of the Guesthouse was inspected again in record time, but there was no sign of her beloved little boy.

"Oh, Sean." As she sank down on the porch steps, she felt the catch in her throat and the tears that had been building threaten to spill onto her cheeks.

Lillie, with Patrick in tow, arrived at the Guesthouse at that moment, wondering what all the commotion was about as they made their way up the steps and stopped by Mary and her friend who were quite tense.

"Are we interrupting something?" Lillie asked.

"My son's gone!" Mary said, the realization of Amy's words sinking into her numb mind. She turned back to Amy. "What happened? Tell me exactly what happened."

"Honey, it's just what I said. We took a nap together. When I woke up, he was gone. I haven't been able to find him anywhere." Amy was miserable.

"When did you wake up?"

"Half an hour ago."

"When did you go to sleep?"

"Two hours ago."

"He could be gone for up to two hours and a half or else not even half an hour. Either way it's not very long." Mary was already trying to convince herself that everything would be all right.

Rob came running up to Amy's side and, seeing Mary, stopped to include her in the conversation. "I just got done speaking with the police. They say it's far too early to call this a missing person case, a person has to be gone a day, but because it's a child they will try to get a couple of officers to look for him."

"That's it?" Mary was appalled. This was her son, her only child, and they weren't going to search for him? *The hell with them!*

Amy saw the look on her friend's face and knew what was coming.

"I'll find him myself." Mary's jaw was set in a stubborn line that Amy knew all too well.

"Mary, how will you know where to search?" Amy pointed out gently.

"We'll help," Lillie said. "We live here, after all."

"Yes, happy to help," Patrick agreed.

The group turned and gave Patrick an odd look. Mary had only seen him in passing and the others hadn't seen him at all before now.

"And you are?" Rob asked at last.

"I'm sorry, I should have introduced you a long time ago," Lillie said and flushed. "This is Patrick."

Mary did notice that Lillie took his hand as she introduced him.

"Glad to have your help, Patrick," Rob said and extended his hand. There were murmurs of assent from the rest of the group. "Since the police are pretty much worthless at this point, where do we even start looking? Since you two are local, do you have any ideas?"

"I know where I have to start," Mary said with conviction and practically leapt off the stairs as she began to move away.

"Where are you going?" Amy called, though she was sure she knew the answer.

"To find Sean. He can do things we can't. He'll find his son," Mary called and broke into a jog as she moved away.

"What did she say?" Lillie said as she and Patrick exchanged a long look before turning back to face Rob and Amy. "Did she say she was going to find Sean?"

"Yes, she did." Amy said with a tenuous smile.

Lillie gripped Patrick's hand tightly. "But how can that be?"

"It would seem Sean is still here as a ghost," Rob said with confidence.

"A ghost?" Patrick laughed. "You're daft. He died in the fire."

"Died, yes. But he's still here," Rob said. "I can see him and talk to him, and so can Mary."

"You can? You have?" Lille turned to Rob. "How is he?"

"Well that's kind of hard to answer. I guess he's as well as a ghost can be, but he's most definitely around. Mary's not crazy."

"Should we go with Mary?" Amy moved toward the porch.

"Leave her for now; I imagine they'll let us know what's going on. In the meantime, let's sit down and plan where to look. Since you two know the area, we'll need your input," Rob said.

"Let's go back to my house," Lillie said. "It will give us a quiet place to make plans."

The others nodded their assent and made their way down the road to Lillie's house.

IT SEEMED AS though no time had passed at all before Donald was back, bothering Sean again. Sean ignored him, but at last he couldn't take it anymore. "What do you want, man? Why don't you leave me alone?"

"Don't forget about tonight."

"Tonight?"

"It's the blue moon."

Sean shrugged. "And? I don't understand the significance."

"I forgot. You haven't gone out on a blue moon before. They don't happen often."

"What happens on a blue moon?"

"Go back to Mary. Resolve the crisis and find some peace between the two of you. God knows, you both deserve it." Donald smiled at him. "The blue moon is a special night for us, you'll see. Our abilities change."

"Change? How?" Sean's brow wrinkled in puzzlement.

"It's different for each spirit, but a good change. Trust yourself. Be smart, listen to your instincts, and you'll all be fine. And be sure to spend tonight with Mary." With a wink, he turned and walked away, leaving Sean to look after him thoughtfully.

Just what in the hell was Donald talking about?

THE MAP OF the local area was on the table as the four of them scrutinized the map as if doing so would provide them the answers they were looking for, as if it would somehow tell them where the boy was.

"We should split up," Rob said. "We can cover more ground that way."

"Sounds like a good idea," Lille agreed.

"Sure, why not?" Amy shrugged.

Patrick remained quiet because something didn't seem right, he didn't feel that the boy had wandered off by himself, and he could think of someone who would go as far as to kidnap the child. In fact, it made a great deal of sense to him.

"Patrick? Earth to Patrick," Rob said, watching the face of his new acquaintance.

"Patrick, are you quite all right?" Lillie said and squeezed his arm.

"What if the boy hasn't wandered away? What if he was kidnapped?"

"Oh, Patrick, who would do that?" Lillie started to scold him, but covered her mouth with her hand as she quickly followed his line of thought. "Oh no, she wouldn't go that far, would she? To hurt an innocent child?"

"She has before, hasn't she?" Patrick said with great bitterness.

"Kidnapped? You think he was kidnapped?" Amy stood up and glared at him. 'What would make you think that?"

He gave her an annoyed look. "Do you know who Maggie is?"

"Do you really think she would have gone as far as kidnapping Mary's son?" Rob asked.

Patrick scowled. "What better way to get back at the two of them?"

"But Sean's a ghost!" Amy said. "How can you take revenge on a ghost??"

"By destroying that which he loves most? From what you say, he still has very human emotions."

"He still loves them," Rob said.

"If that's what happened, what do we do?" Amy said at last. "How do we find her and stop her?"

"That might be a better question than you know," Lillie said in a grim tone.

"What in the hell does that mean?" Rob asked.

Patrick and Lillie exchanged a long look before Lillie spoke again. "Maggie's a witch," Lillie said.

"A bitch or a witch? Both are equally applicable," Amy said.

"That's always been my opinion as well of that slutty, horrible, classless, fish mongering slut!"

"Fish mongering? That's a new one," Patrick murmured quietly to her. "Concentrate, Lillie, task at hand and all of that."

"My apologies, but I don't think much of Maggie," she grumbled.

"I'm impressed," Rob said with an easy smile. "Some day when we have more time, I want to hear the rest of your comments. I get the feeling you were just getting warmed up."

"She really is a witch," Patrick said. "She's been playing with spell books for some time now. I never thought much of it because, ever since we were all little, Maggie has been going on about magic and spells and power. I stopped hearing it a long time ago."

"What makes you think it's anything different than that?" Amy was just starting to wrap her mind around the fact that Mary's lover was dead and a ghost. Now she was supposed to believe Sean's ex was a witch?

"I've seen her put spells on people; I've felt her put a spell on me," Patrick said, his voice grim.

"What kind of spell?" Rob asked.

"I'd rather not say, thank you very much," Patrick said, unwilling to admit his stupidity to others.

Lillie came to his rescue. "I guess it would be considered a... I don't know, an influence spell? It seems she is able to charm other people?"

"That can't be a good thing," Amy commented. "So we have to

fight a witch? A real witch?"

"Is she working alone or does she have help?" Rob asked.

"I don't know," Patrick said. "She might have help. I think she influenced someone visiting the town."

"Visiting? Who?" Amy asked.

"He thinks it could be that American man who came to visit," Lillie said, "the one who was dating Mary."

Amy blinked in surprise. "Paul? How does she even know him?"

"Your friend seemed quite put out yesterday," Patrick said, "and went to the pub for several drinks. Maggie did her best to seduce him, and I think it worked."

"Paul went off with Maggie?" Amy all but spat, her dander up now. "What a slimeball!"

"I can see him going off with her," Rob commented, "but why would he help her with a kidnapping? He's arrogant as hell, but that would be an international crime, and he's not stupid."

Patrick gave them a long hard stare. "I doubt it would matter to a demon."

"Demon? Are you kidding me?" Amy shouted. "Why the ghost is starting to seem like the normal one in this scenario? That's screwed up!" She turned to Rob. "Rob, I'd like to go home now, please."

"Come here, my angry darling," he said, and Amy stepped into his embrace. With a smile and some soft words whispered in her ear, he got her to relax against him and after a few moments she stepped away from him and turned to face the others.

"Sorry, but this is all just a bit overwhelming for me. I'm not even sure I believe in this shit."

"Let's figure out where Maggie could be and get there," Patrick said in a grim voice.

DAYLIGHT WAS SLIPPING away, the sun just starting to set, but that didn't matter, nothing mattered except finding her son. Mary was on her way back to the remains of The Gaelic Moon when she heard a noise from the alley she was passing. She stopped mid-stride and realized that it sounded like a child, a sad child. Maybe her lost son? She turned and made her way down the alley, calling out his name.

"Sean? Where are you? Can you hear me?"

Startled by an odd noise in a dark corner by a dumpster, she saw an indistinct darkness form in the corner.

"Sean?" she asked, but had a feeling of dread in the pit of her stomach. He had never appeared like this. He had just always been there. She wondered if something was wrong with him.

"Sean?" she called again and saw Maggie step out of the shadows.

THE BUILDING WAS abandoned and condemned, and with good reason, Paul thought as he surveyed the holes in the ceiling and the gaps in the wall where the wind blew through. A small cot sat in the most intact corner of the room. Tucked comfortably on the cot was little Sean.

Funny, he had always believed that he had liked the boy, but after being with Maggie, things were so much clearer for him. The boy's life had ceased to matter to him; he was only the means to an end, a way to get back at Mary. And if he had to be sacrificed in order to hurt Mary, well, Paul was surprisingly comfortable with that. When all this was done, he would be with Maggie—she promised him —and that promise would make it all worthwhile because she had shown him the way. He knew something was different about himself, but truth be told, he didn't much care. He felt stronger and more powerful than he had in years. He relished the feeling. He would show that bitch Mary he was not to be trifled with, and he would, along with Maggie, exact his revenge in the form of the small boy sleeping on the cot.

He glanced at the chloroform-filled rag on a nearby table, knowing the boy would be asleep for quite a long time yet. More as a curiosity than anything else, he wondered if perhaps he had used too much on the boy? He shrugged and stretched back against the chair he was sitting in. No matter. One less thing to deal with.

MAGGIE'S EXPRESSION WAS so cold that Mary expected the air around her to turn to snow, and she couldn't suppress a shiver. Nothing good could come from having a conversation with Maggie.

"What do you want?" she asked the red-haired woman, who watched her with satisfaction.

"I'm only here to deliver a message."

Mary eyed her adversary warily. "What message?"

"You took what I loved most in life, so it's only fair that I return the favor."

Mary felt an icy grip of fear encircle her heart. "You took my son!"

"Now you're getting it."

Mary's eyes narrowed. "Where is he?"

"Do you think I would tell you, really?" Maggie laughed, a chilling sound that only hardened the ice now gripping Mary's heart. "I just wanted you to know I have him. I can tell how much you and Sean love the little boy. He's sweet, isn't he? Full of love and hope, a truly lovely child that you produced. I can see why Sean would be so taken with him. It's obvious how much you love him; I can see the anxiety in your eyes." Maggie smiled. "I want you to know your sweet boy's suffering will match my own. Only then will I be satisfied."

"You're going to kill him." Mary tried to keep a grip on the fury that was ready to explode from within her.

Maggie walked over to Mary, standing mere inches from her and glared into her eyes, but with a quick move Mary slapped Maggie as hard as she could, hard enough to send Maggie reeling back, the back of her head connecting with the brick of the building behind her.

When Maggie straightened up, she glared at Mary, wiping the blood from the corner of her mouth. "You will be sorry for that."

"Not if you can't get away, I won't!" Mary launched herself at Maggie, and smashed her against the wall again, fighting her with every ounce of strength she had. "Give me back my son!"

Maggie was caught off guard by the unexpected assault and did her best to fend off the furious American. She finally connected with a blow to Mary's jaw that dazed her for just a few seconds; but it was enough time for Maggie to escape from her grasp. Mary shook her head and tried to recover, but before she could move, Maggie raced down the length of the alley and disappeared around the corner. Mary ran after her, just steps behind her, but Maggie was gone.

"Oh, God." The implications of everything that Maggie had said were lethal, and Mary knew she was running out of time, and that Sean was her only hope. She ran out of the alley pushing herself to get to The Gaelic Moon in record time.

Chapter 32
N'ight of the Blue Moon

*T*HE REMNANTS OF **The Gaelic Moon** were somehow brighter due to the light of the full moon that was just now rising into the night sky, with the black beams outlined against a starry sky. She walked closer to the building and looked at it; the beams seemed to be glowing strangely and she stepped back and watched in amazement as the outline began to take shape, particles of light highlighting the building against the blackness of the night, and before she knew it, The Gaelic Moon Pub had solidified.

The moon cast a pale light on the pub which now stood before her complete as it had been in life, so she reached out her hand and touched it, feeling the weathered wood beneath her hand. Startled, she jumped back as light abruptly shone through the windows of the dark building, and she clearly heard sounds of drinking and laughter from inside. Not knowing what else to do, she reached for the handle of the front door and opened it.

INSIDE THE GAELIC Moon, Sean sat at table playing cards with Bailey, a fellow patron at the pub. Bailey offered him a grin when he won yet another hand of cards. "Too bad we can't really make this interesting," he said.

"Gambling, you mean?"

"A good gamble is always worth it, don't you think?"

He studied Bailey and wondered if his words held a hidden meaning. He had just recently met this spirit and still wondered at his choice of clothing, a long floor-length brown robe made of a nice linen material, but nothing fancy, and it came complete with a cowl which Bailey seldom had up. It was rather monkish. Sean frowned as he tried to puzzle this out once again knowing this was the same spirit he had met at St. Michan's Church with Mary but so far his new friend had not been forthcoming about his origins.

When he looked over at the bar, he saw Donald coming over.

"What's it that you'd be wanting now?" Sean asked.

"Just to give you a reminder."

Sean glanced at Donald over his cards. "And just what would that be?"

"Don't die tonight."

"It's too late for that," Sean said and laughed.

"I mean, don't die tonight. If you die a second time, you're damned."

Sean set down his cards and grumbling, Bailey got up, shook his head, and ambled away. Sean turned back to Donald. "What are you talking about? I'm not going anywhere."

For the first time in a long time, Sean heard—actually heard— the squeak of the front door to the pub, and surprised, he turned to see Mary standing in the doorway.

"It's time for you to go, Sean," Donald said. "I think your ride is here."

Mary stood inside the pub and looked all around her in amazement.

THE BOY WAS just now starting to stir, obviously groggy, but fighting the effects of the chloroform, he twitched and groaned, occasionally uttering a cry for his mother. Paul watched the child, a strange expression on his face, studying the boy as if he were something new, something he hadn't seen before. He felt funny, dazed, almost like he was falling asleep despite the fact that he was awake. What was happening to him? If he closed his eyes for a moment, only a moment, he knew he would be all right.

The lanterns cast an odd light, and the shadows moved strangely as a sharp breeze blew through the rickety building. Paul frowned. But seeing the moon outside the window, he smiled a smile full of confidence. A sound echoed from the shadows, and he felt the boy stir.

"Maggie?"

A figure emerged from the blackness, and Paul saw that her eyes shimmered with a silver light when she turned her gaze on him. "Paul," she said with satisfaction when she saw the red sheen to his eyes.

"My mistress," he said in a voice not his own and bowed his head in reverence.

WARY AND UNSURE of her apparently real surroundings, Mary made her way over to Sean, who watched her with a startled expression on his face.

"What're you doing here?" he asked. A panicked look crossed his face as a horrific thought occurred to him. "You're all right? Nothing's happened to you?"

She dismissed his question. "I'm fine."

"You're not dead?" he gasped in astonishment. "How is it that you're here?" He gingerly reached out and touched her.

"I need your help," Mary said.

"What's wrong?"

"Our son, he's gone!"

"What?" he blinked in surprise. "What do you mean gone?"

She tried to control her anger. "Maggie has him!"

"Oh, my God."

Forgetting his state of being, she reached out and grabbed his hand, pulling him along with her. They both stopped after a few steps, when they realized they were touching, and gaped at each other in shock.

"MY MISTRESS, ALL is going well?" Paul asked, his face glowing with an unnatural light.

"Very well, thank you. There is so much natural power here, and these fools aren't even aware of it." She laughed in contempt. "And tonight, the night of the blue moon, is even more intense. The veil between the worlds is weak."

"Magic." Paul took in a deep breath as though he were inhaling magical fumes.

"Yes, magic. It's all around us, and it always has been, but everyone here is just too blind to see it." She stepped around Paul to look at the sleeping boy. "Wake him. I want you to work on him."

"Torture?" Paul asked in a happy voice.

"Yes. Eventually I will take him away from his parents, but first I want them to know how much he is suffering. They may have brought him into the world, but I will take him out." She gently laid her hand on the boy's cheek.

The boy woke and blinked at them in confusion. He looked at Paul and slowly became aware of the figure standing beside him. He cringed into his blankets and whimpered.

Maggie allowed a cold smile to seep across her face.

UNABLE TO TAKE in her current reality, Mary grasped Sean's hand within both of hers and felt her way up his arm to touch his chest and face. As if afraid to touch her, he stroked her hair and cheek, amazed by her softness.

They shared an urgent kiss filled with long-denied emotion and then, with Mary still holding his hand, they went to the door.

Sean stopped, bowed his head, and concentrated. When nothing happened, he regarded Donald in confusion.

"Donald?"

"You're real, my lad. You have to act that way."

"My ghostly abilities don't work?"

The bartender shrugged. "Some will, some won't. You'll find out as you go. It's different for all of us."

"Brilliant, just brilliant."

Impatiently, Mary rushed him to the door. Sean called over his shoulder, "How long will this last?"

"You've got the night, until the blue moon sets," Donald answered.

"What happens then?"

Mary pulled him out the door before he could hear Donald's answer, but Donald surprised them and followed them out into the cool night.

"Donald?"

"I thought you might like a few tips on how to fight a witch?"

"Yes, please!" Mary nodded enthusiastically.

"First she will undoubtedly have some sort of help, chances are they will be some type of demons. Holy water always works well against demons."

"Okay, we'll come up with something," Sean said, but looked uneasy.

Donald laughed quietly. "Don't worry, Sean, it won't affect you."

"I knew that," Sean muttered under his breath.

"And Maggie is susceptible to physical attack. If she can be distracted from spell casting long enough to allow a physical attack..."

"I can kick her ass!" Mary all but shouted, clenching her fists in anticipation. "Thanks, Donald!" She leaned across and gave him a quick peck on his cheek and looking over at Sean who was standing still, lost in concentration.

"Oh, and here." He shoved two pieces of paper into her hand. "A list of items that might help you, and as for the other one; when it's all over, read this to Geraldine. It will remove the spell that Maggie has placed on her."

"Will do." Frustrated by his silence, she looked over at her ghost. "Sean?"

Sean put a finger to her lips to silence her. She watched nervously as he closed his eyes and concentrated, trying to feel the location of that which was most precious to him, his beloved son. But after a long few moments, he turned to Mary, his eyes sad, and shook his head.

"Sean, let's get help! I'm not sure we can do all of this alone."

After a long moment, he nodded and grabbed Mary's hand. They ran into the darkness.

THE CHILD LOOKED at the hard features of the two adults who stood before him, and he stepped toward Paul, who put a comforting hand on the boy's shoulder. The boy didn't see the look of understanding that passed between Paul and Maggie.

The boy watched Maggie with a guarded expression and pressed closer to Paul. Little Sean didn't like Paul, but he had never hurt him. His mother had trusted this man, and his mom knew best, so he pressed against him for protection.

Maggie stepped toward the boy, and he quickly ducked behind Paul, peering at the stranger from behind his back.

"All right." Maggie glared at the boy. "Have it your way. Tie him up and start cutting him."

The boy knew what cutting meant and staggered to his feet, but still suffering from the effects of the chloroform, tripped after only a couple of steps. Paul stepped over to him and roughly hauled him up, holding him in a vise-like grip. He returned his attention to Maggie.

"Is that all?" Paul seemed disappointed, a strange reddish tint to his eyes glowing oddly.

"To start with. Make sure to cut the scalp. I want to start by giving them some bloody locks of his hair and progress from there." Her smile was filled with ice.

Paul inclined his head to her. "It shall be as you say."

"Finally, someone I can work with," she said in a satisfied voice. "I know you're not entirely Paul anymore, but I will still reward you when we are done." She stroked his face in a seductive manner.

Paul offered her a warm smile filled with gratitude. "Thank you, Mistress."

With a last look over her shoulder, Maggie walked out the door.

MUCH TO HIS surprise, Mary ran to Sean's house and waited for him to catch up before she opened the door. He trailed along behind, wondering what kind of help she was looking for, who was around that would be willing to help them with this situation. Mary threw open the door with a resounding thud, and five sets of eyes regarded her. Lillie, Patrick, Rob, Amy, and sitting quietly in a corner chair, Geraldine.

"Mary, thank God you're here," Amy said.

Sean regarded the others with great wariness, wondering what their reaction to him would be.

"Oh, my God, Sean?" Lillie put her hands to her face as she burst into tears. "How can it be? How are you here?" She ran over to him and threw her arms around him crying against his shoulder.

"Lillie, it's all right, I've missed you, too," he said, tears in his eyes. After a moment, he set himself away from her and walked over to where his elderly mother sat in a corner smiling happily, her eyes misted with tears as well. "Mam, are you all right? I've missed you."

"About time you got here," she groused, but placed a kiss on his forehead as she leaned into him.

"You sound like you were expecting me," he teased.

"I was. It's the night of the blue moon, after all." She drew back and gave him a knowing look.

"You know about the night of the blue moon?"

"Yes."

"Then you know more than I."

"No time for this, we need to find our son. Now!" Mary interrupted, trying to control her agitation.

"You're right," Sean said and turned to the others. "What have you come up with?"

THE SYMBOLS AND patterns were drawn on the floor, the candles were lit, and Maggie's hex bag was in place in the run down excuse for a house where they held the boy captive. With a sigh of anticipation, she knelt down in front of the circle and began to chant, words murmured at first and rising in clarity as her voice grew more powerful. She finished her spell with Sean's name and looked up, smiling. It would only be a few minutes at most and he would appear before her.

"I'm waiting my love," she whispered. "Come to me."

SEAN STOPPED, SHIVERED, and brushed at his ear as he heard Maggie's voice whisper in his ear. "Mary," he called.

She turned around and noticed that Sean's appearance was odd, as if he were ill. "Sean, what's wrong?"

"I don't know. I feel funny." He grimaced as he remembered when he felt like this before and that he had ended up with Maggie, unable to escape until she released him. "Blast and damn!" he swore before he disappeared.

"Sean!" Mary cursed under her breath and spun around, surveying the area. Where in the hell did he go?

Chapter 33
Reckoning

*S*EAN KNEW WHAT to expect, if not where he would end up. The setup was much the same, although he quickly observed that the location was different. He was entrapped by a circle with symbols both inside and outside of it. There were candles in the room just as before, but he didn't see Maggie. He was in part of a condemned building that was due for destruction, he was sure of it. The room he was in was surprisingly intact and actually built into a hill, and he thought he knew where he was. Now what had happened to Maggie? Why wasn't she here?

"Where are you?" he yelled, but he received no answer. *Damn.* He should call to Mary and see whether she can hear him. She was probably wondering where he'd gone, and he knew he was helpless as long as he was in this circle. That could be part of what Maggie wanted, too. Was this just a trap for him? *Or was it one for Mary, too?*

He rubbed his temple trying to alleviate the tension, he hadn't felt that in a while.

"Maggie, where are you?" he bellowed. "Come out and tell me what you want."

Ever so slowly, she stepped out of the surrounding darkness and into the light. She walked around the circle with a measured step and eyed Sean with appreciation.

"You still look good, Sean. How do you manage?"

He growled at her, a sound of anger from deep within him.

She watched him, just a touch of annoyance on her face. "The most inconvenient thing about keeping you there is that I can't touch you."

"Why would I let you touch me?" Sean shuddered in distaste. "You are the foulest, most evil woman I have ever known." He shook his head. "You weren't like that as a child, Maggie. What happened to you? What happened to the girl I was fond of?"

"Her!" Maggie spit out the words as if she were talking about someone else. "She was weak, picked on, imperfect, unloved. No one wanted her; I didn't want to be her. She was an illusion."

"She was my friend," Sean said with so much sincerity that Maggie stopped short then shrugged. "She's long gone, and now you deal with me, a strong, powerful woman who will get what she wants."

"A manipulator, you mean. A weak woman who has resorted to magic and pain to get what she wants."

"Be quiet!" she hissed and waved her hand at him.

He dropped like a stone and curled up as he tried to survive the pain searing every nerve ending in his body. When the pain finally stopped, he crawled to his knees. Maggie stood quietly, watching him, a look of satisfaction on her face. "See, power."

Sean still clutched his side as he stood up. "What do you want? Where's my son?"

"He's in capable hands. I've given him to Paul." Sean groaned. "Oh, don't be so discouraged. He is taking good care of the boy and will do exactly as I instruct him to do, good or bad." The enormity of her words weighed on Sean.

"I'll see you burn in hell if you touch a hair on his head."

"Well, if those are the qualifications, I guess I'm already damned." She sighed, reached for a small silken coin purse on a rickety table behind her, and threw it into the circle with Sean.

Sean swallowed a lump in his throat, afraid of what he would find.

"Go on, open it," she encouraged with an evil smile on her face.

Hesitating, he knelt down and opened the coin purse. He felt his heart clench in fear. Gingerly, as if afraid of hurting what he found, he pulled out a bloody chunk of hair, with a small piece of scalp attached to it.

"My God! What have you done to him?"

"Oh, he's still alive, at least for now." She walked slowly around the outside of the ring. "I'm in no hurry to give him back to you. I'd rather send him to you and Mary piece by piece, but first I have to get her here which means it may be a short while yet." She smiled at him and he wondered if this was a female version of Satan. "I will torture him before your eyes, and slowly destroy the life that you and that whore brought into the world."

"I'll kill you myself before I ever let that happen," he said in a tight voice.

Maggie laughed, a wild, insane laugh, and Sean's heart sank. How in the hell were they going to get out of this? Sean clenched his fists at his side and tried to control his mounting anger so that he could focus and find a way out of this mess.

"Now I want you to do something for me," she said.

"First, why would I do anything for you? And second, what can I possibly do for you from in here?"

"Oh, it's easy. You need to call your slut here. I want to see the happy family."

"No."

"Sean, do you really think it will be that easy?"

"I won't call Mary here to be subject to your perverted sense of justice."

"Such a sense of moral values is admirable, even if they are misplaced." She shook her head ever so slightly. "If I have to persuade you, I will." She turned toward the shadows and gestured at them.

Paul entered the light, holding his little Sean's hand.

"Run, Sean!" Sean called to his son.

The boy looked at him in a strange, calm way. "Why hello, Daddy," he said and leaned back against Paul.

"Hello, Sean," Paul said to the ghost, a vindictive expression on his face, and odd red-rimmed eyes.

"What have you done to him?" Sean snarled at Maggie.

"Nothing bad, just a little spell to calm the boy. He fights less that way."

"What does that mean?"

Maggie smiled, a smile that under different circumstances would have been lovely. "It allowed me to take a sample." She pointed to the bloody locks of hair on the floor by Sean. "And it will make it easier as I slowly kill him in front of you." Her eyes glittered with hatred.

Sean hurled himself against the air, knowing from the last time that something akin to an invisible force field encircled him, but this time his hand made it through. Things today were not the same as they had been last time. He withdrew the hand and kept that information to himself, knowing it had to do with the changes to him this night.

"Call the slut!" she said.

"No."

"I'll kill the boy." Sean looked at his son, who regarded him with calm eyes, as Maggie put out her hand and the boy went over to her. She gently rested her hand on the small boy's shoulder. "Very well," she said, and muttered something short under her breath.

The boy crumpled to the ground, crying in pain.

How could he ask his son to endure this? Taking it upon himself was one thing, but to do this to his boy? He knew it was a trap for Mary, but what choice did he have?

"Stop it! Let him be!" Sean whispered, his eyes bright with unshed tears, "I'll do what you want."

"Good," she said and snapped her fingers. The boy continued to whimper on the floor, still in pain. "Call her!" Maggie demanded. "Call your whore! I want to see her suffer most of all."

"All right, I will." Sean put up a placating hand and calmed himself in order to call Mary. He focused on the task at hand and found it difficult to do what just yesterday had been so easy for him. "Mary, my love, can you hear me? Mary, hear me, please..."

HOLY WATER? NOW, this late in the evening? How crazy was that going to be? Lillie had no idea how she was going to explain this to the kindly old Father Murphy. She and Patrick had rummaged quickly through the items at the pub and come up with some empty wine bottles with corks; they could most certainly hold water of any kind. She hoped the fact that they held alcohol wouldn't taint the holy water, but wine was supposed to be the blood of Christ, was it not? Surely the container couldn't make that much difference, could it? It didn't matter, as she had no time to contemplate anything else. She grabbed the bottles and headed for the church.

Rob and Amy had departed unexpectedly. Rob had said he had a great idea that could help them tonight, and he'd run off toward the Guesthouse with Amy in tow, promising to meet them back at Lillie's house.

Since Cullamore was a small town with virtually no crime, the church was left open for those who might need to seek consolation from God. The time didn't matter. Lillie and Patrick rushed into the church, relieved that there were only a couple of people within, including a surprised Father Murphy. She stopped briefly to do an awkward curtsey before she rushed up to the baptismal font and filled her two empty wine bottles with holy water.

"Lillie? Patrick?" Father Murphy addressed her in a stern voice and with a questioning look.

"Sorry, Father, I don't have time to explain. It's for my nephew."

A brief but awkward silence ensued until Father Murphy spoke again. "Might I suggest that he be baptized in a more traditional manner?"

Under different circumstances Lillie would have laughed. "Yes, father, I will be sure to pass that along to Mary," she said as she finished filling the second bottle and put the cork in it.

The good father gave them a long-suffering look. "Do you two care to explain?"

"We will later, good Father," Patrick said with a respectful bow and followed Lillie as she rushed out of the church and into the darkening night.

"MARY, HEAR ME please, I need you to hear me." His voice was faint, like it was coming in over a distant radio station, not at all like when she normally heard him. She stopped what she was doing and concentrated.

"Sean?"

"Find me, Mary. She has us. If you don't come, she'll kill him..." his voice faded out, and she couldn't hear him at all.

"Sean? Sean!" She muttered several uncomplimentary things under her breath as the cavalry arrived.

"We're ready to go, Mary," Rob said. "Patrick thinks he knows where they might be, so we're going to split up into two cars, since Lillie and Pat know where the hell they're going. You'll go with Patrick, and Amy and I will go with Lillie."

"And we got everything!" Amy said proudly.

That's when Mary realized they were armed with wine bottles, and Rob and Amy were brandishing little Sean's water cannons. How in the hell would they ever manage to stop a witch with wine and squirt guns?

MAGGIE PACED RESTLESSLY around the circle that held Sean. She was more than impatient with the delay and wanted to get started. "Where is she?"

"I don't know. I'm not her keeper!" Sean snapped. "Apparently she has a mind of her own."

"Yes, well that will undoubtedly be her undoing."

"Why don't you bring her here? Or is that beyond her capabilities?"

"No, it's not."

"Then?" The challenge in his blue eyes was obvious. He was hoping if he could push her to do enough, she would run out of power, for surely it couldn't be limitless. "I bet you can't do it. You're a charlatan, not a real witch."

With a snarl of fury, she narrowed her eyes and started chanting. Sean took a deep breath and steeled himself for the pain that would seize on every cell of his now corporeal body and he began to hurl himself against the weakened, invisible wall that kept him contained. Maggie, distracted with her spell, concentrated on bringing Mary to them, didn't notice.

THE SMALL CAR sped out of the town and into the countryside, as fast as Patrick dared to drive. "Where we're going isn't far, but it's out of the way."

Mary chewed her bottom lip, her anxiety starting to show. "You're sure that's where she is?"

"Sure? No, but I'm playing a hunch."

"I don't know you very well, but thanks for your help," Mary said, and she winced.

"What's wrong?" Patrick gripped the steering wheel tightly, scared to death by what they were about to do.

"I feel funny," Mary said, feeling rather like she was going to throw up.

"Funny how?" Patrick worried, knowing that they were getting close to where he thought Maggie was located.

"I don't know." Her vision was blurring as she answered him. "Patrick?" she reached out a hand to touch his arm, but found she couldn't as her vision faded all together, and she blacked out.

"Mary!" Patrick cried in alarm, pulling over. She seemed to be transparent. He reached for her, but she had already disappeared.

"Damn!" he swore under his breath, before getting the car back on the road and speeding off to his destination.

"HAVING A LITTLE trouble bringing her here?" Sean taunted, clenching his jaw because every time his body impacted the invisible wall, he felt like a thousand needles were being shoved into it. "Are you too weak to do that? *Aww*, Maggie, I expected better of you!"

At that moment several things seemed to happen simultaneously. Mary appeared on the floor next to Maggie, semiconscious and groaning as she tried to make sense of her new surroundings.

Maggie screamed in rage at Sean's ongoing insults and turned to face him, her hands gesturing angrily as she cast a new spell on him. Before she could finish her spell, he gathered his remaining strength and hurled himself against the magic wall and screamed as he finally broke through, and Maggie's new spell of all-consuming pain caught him. He groaned as he fought to get up again.

Little Sean suddenly shook his head as if coming out of a dream. "Mom?" he asked, and saw that Mary was in the room. He was going over to her when he saw his father writhing in pain. "Daddy!" he screamed.

THE LITTLE CAR groaned in protest as Patrick slammed it into park and jumped out of it. He looked down the road behind him, knowing that even with Lillie driving faster than normal for her, it might still be a couple of minutes before they showed up. Should he wait for them? He wasn't excited about going in alone, but Maggie had the entire family, and he really didn't want to see any of them hurt. Muttering at the injustice of being put into this unbelievable situation and feeling silly, he pulled out the squirt gun Rob insisted he take with him. How was this going to help?

With a sigh of relief, he pulled out the real gun he had packed and put it behind his back, tucking it into his waistband. He had more faith in that than the holy water.

He stopped and listened outside of the dilapidated building, relieved to hear voices inside, including Maggie's. He had been right—this was where she had taken them. That was good, they wouldn't be running all over hell trying to find them, but there was still no sign of the other car yet. When he heard the scream of the little boy, he stopped pondering what he should do and rushed for the back door.

MARY CLIMBED TO her feet and lunged at Maggie, who only laughed at her as despite her heated struggles she was unable to reach her.

"Do you really think it will be that easy?" Maggie asked.

"You bitch!" Mary snarled.

"Such language! Sean led me to believe you were at least somewhat of a lady, but I can see that he was wrong again. You are far too coarse and masculine to be any sort of lady." She arched an eyebrow at Mary as she sauntered around her.

That's when Mary noticed her son.

"Mom! Mom! Help! Paul won't let me go!" The child was struggling against Paul for all he was worth, but the man wasn't breaking a sweat. He just studied the boy with cold, impassive eyes.

"Are you all right?" Mary almost sobbed with relief seeing her son alive and whole, but she noticed the blood dripping down his face.

"Mom!" he cried, struggling against Paul's tight grip.

"Paul, let him go!" Mary demanded, but Paul only turned a cool gaze on her. That was when she saw his red eyes and knew something was terribly wrong with him.

"He'll not help you. He belongs to me now." Maggie laughed.

Mary felt a chill run down her spine. She looked over to Sean, who was thrashing on the floor, moaning in pain.

"What have you done to him?" she demanded of Maggie.

"Oh, that? Just a minor pain spell. It will keep him occupied while I deal with you."

"I'm going to kick your ass from here to the moon!" Mary screamed.

Maggie shook her head. "You are all such silly children, thinking you can stand up to me and the things I know." She sighed. "I want you both to suffer, so I'll start with the child." She nodded to Paul, who smiled slowly and pulled a knife out of his pocket. "Part of a finger, I think. The smaller the pieces, the longer his torture will last..."

"No!" Mary screamed as Paul held her son in a vice grip and placed his hand on a nearby table.

The boy screamed, cried, and struggled for all he was worth. At that moment Patrick burst into the room, much to everyone's surprise, causing both Maggie and Paul to pause in their actions.

"Patrick? How... unexpected," Maggie said, finding her voice first. "What are you doing here?"

"Why I've... I've come to help you," he said and drew himself up.

"Really? How big of fool do you take me for?"

With her attention now focused on Patrick, the spell keeping Sean in place weakened just enough for him to feel that he could break away from it. Doing too many things at a time must be too taxing on Maggie's abilities, Sean reasoned. He looked at Mary, who was exuding molten anger. If he could get her free, maybe she could do what she so longed to do and kick Maggie's ass, and he really wanted to see that.

Sean ground his teeth together, fighting the pain that seemed attached to his every nerve ending, and stood up. Maggie seemed surprised.

"Such boys. I guess I will have to teach you more of a lesson." She began to gesture when Patrick pulled the gun from behind his back and brandished it, waving it in the direction of Maggie and Paul. It took a moment, but she laughed.

"Patrick, you are even denser than I imagined you. How do you think that can stop me?"

"Like this," he said and, aiming at her heart, pulled the

trigger, releasing the holy water.

She laughed and with a wave of her hand, the bullets bounced off something unseen and fell to the floor. Patrick exchanged a look of horror with Sean and Mary and, having no other options, he pulled out the squirt gun and, saying a small prayer, took aim at Maggie. He pulled the trigger, and Maggie... got wet.

Sean turned to him in amazement. "Patrick, really? Water?"

"Son of a bitch!" Patrick cursed.

"Do it," Maggie gave a nod to Paul, who prepared to cut off the boy's fingertip.

Paul brought the knife down, and the boy screamed. On reflex, using what was currently in his hand, Patrick shot the gun full of holy water at Paul. This time there was a reaction as Paul dropped the knife, howling at the searing pain that burned his back. He dropped the boy, who scrambled away and curled in a ball on the floor, wailing in pain. Paul turned to Patrick, murder in his eyes.

Lillie and the rest arrived at that particular moment and chaos promptly ensued.

"Get the boy out of here!" Sean screamed at them, seeing his son free.

Patrick backed away from demon Paul, only to have Rob step between them, brandishing a water cannon, a huge smile on his face. "Try this on for size," he said and started spraying water over Paul.

Lillie grabbed the boy while Amy stood near the entrance to cover her retreat.

Sean launched himself at Maggie only to feel the spell again. A thousand needles twisted on his every nerve as he fell to the floor. Still, he struggled to his feet.

Mary broke free and tried to control the anger she was feeling, channel it so that it would be useful. She felt an unexplainable burst of power within her as she and Maggie locked gazes.

"I'm tired of you. I will kill you first," Maggie said and, with a move of confidence, gestured a hand at Mary. She blinked in puzzlement as she felt the killing spell deflected.

In a gesture of defiance, Mary threw up her hand at Maggie and the other woman crashed to the ground. Mary tackled her, smashing her fist into Maggie's face. Maggie turned to fight, embedding deep scratch marks across Mary's cheek. Mary punched the Irish witch, knocking her head against the hard ground and, with an oath, Maggie pushed her off. Mary grabbed the witch's long red hair, snapping her head back abruptly.

Paul screamed in agony, smoke trailing from him as he stepped toward Rob, clothes and skin burning off him. Rob kept streaming the holy water with glee, glad beyond belief that the boy had a Super Soaker. Paul collapsed on the floor, his body a bloody and steaming mess.

"I will make you pay for what you've done!" Mary said, every word deliberate as she pummeled the witch. "I hate you! I hate you! I hate you!" She took Maggie down again, but Maggie somehow rolled away from her and got to her feet.

Maggie laughed. "Patrick!"

Surprised to hear Maggie utter his name at this juncture.

Maggie spat blood out of her mouth, and regarded him with a gaze made of ice. "You've always been a dog, so a dog you will be," she muttered something unintelligible and gave him a lethal smile. "See what your new love thinks of that."

Patrick shivered as he felt chills throughout his body and fell to his knees in pain, but after a moment it was gone. He muttered a hundred prayers in the space of a minute. What had she just done to him?

"And you!" She spat on Mary. "Magic! Magic and the need for it will consume you! The more you discover your true heritage, the worse it will be!" She laughed wildly and made an odd gesture with her hand.

"I've had just about enough of you!" Mary couldn't help herself—she hit the witch again and again and again until Maggie could fight her no more and lay helpless beneath her.

"Do we stop her?" Rob asked Sean as they watched for a moment.

"I guess." Sean said in a reluctant voice. "We can't let her commit murder, can we?"

"I suppose not," Rob agreed, and the two of them pulled the furious woman off the now unconscious Maggie.

"My son?" Mary asked as Sean pulled her into his arms. "Where is he?"

"He's safe, he's with Lillie and Amy." He smoothed her hair as she looked into his face.

"Oh, thank God!" Her anger dissipated and, with tears of joy and relief, she buried her face against his chest. "He's safe, you're safe, oh, thank God!" She hung onto Sean tightly.

"*Shh*, Mary, it's okay. Everything will be fine now." He kissed the top of her head as they clung to each other. When she pulled away, he wiped the tears from her cheeks. "Remind me never to make you mad," he said. "You scare me."

She laughed and glared at Maggie's unconscious form. "I'm still pretty pissed. What about her?"

"We'll tie her up, and someone will stay with her until the police come."

"How do we explain Paul?" she said and chewed on her lip. "He's all... *eww*..."

"Well, we'll come up with something."

"But besides that? How do we explain why he was with Maggie?" A brief sadness crossed her face. "I know he was far from perfect, but he didn't deserve this."

"Maybe not, but he wasn't your friend anymore," Sean said and pulled her close. "None of us deserved this. It's Maggie's fault."

She frowned and touched him again, offering him a small smile. "You really are still here."

"Completely," he agreed and gave her a sweet kiss on her lips.

She shivered, nodding at Maggie's form. "What did she mean by what she said?" She looked over to Patrick who seemed normal as always though he was extremely agitated as he spoke with Lillie, no doubt freaked out by Maggie's curse. But Lillie seemed to have things under control. Lillie was speaking to him in soothing tones and he gradually calmed down.

"Can a curse be real?" Mary asked out loud.

"I DON'T KNOW." Sean considered... "It can't mean anything, can it? Probably just the rantings of a lunatic." He gave her a reassuring look. "Besides, we need to go, the lad needs to get to a hospital."

Rob came over to them and grimaced in distaste at the scene around them before he spoke. "Sean, Lillie will take you, Mary, and young Sean to the hospital. The rest of us will stay here to talk to the police and set things straight, or at least as straight as we can make them. Okay?"

"Thank you, Rob."

Mary pulled Rob into a wordless hug, conveying her thanks to him.

"You're welcome," he said and watched as she and Sean departed through the doorway.

Chapter 34
Home

*T*HE TELEVISION WAS on, and Geraldine watched quietly, seemingly undisturbed by everything that had happened that night. She looked up as Lillie breezed into the small living room, Mary and Sean behind her, the boy in Sean's arms.

"Mam, you'll be happy to know that your grandson is going to be fine."

"Yes, he's lost the tip of his finger, and his head needed some stitches, but he'll be fine. Thank God!" Mary said, giving a heartfelt thanks to any deity that might be listening. "He's sleepy from the drugs they gave him." She smiled as Sean entered past her, carrying their son in his arms.

Geraldine got up and stood quietly, looking at Sean, her son, with tears in her eyes.

"I told you he'd save the boy. It's the blue moon."

"Well, were right, Mam. Why do you know so much about the blue moon?" Sean asked curiously.

"I'll tell you before you leave in the morning," was all she would say.

"Damn!" Mary swore under her breath. "I almost forgot." She pulled out the piece of paper Donald had shoved into her hand when the night began. "For your mother," she said and Sean nodded in understanding.

Mary read the incantation that Donald had written out for her, the words of a language she didn't understand were somehow familiar to her, and she could almost feel... something as she finished the mysterious words and gently touched Geraldine on her arm.

The old woman gave a small gasp and would have collapsed if Sean had not been there to catch her.

"Mam!" He lowered her into the nearby chair and watched her in concern as Lillie hurried over to their side.

"Is she all right? What did you do?" she turned to Mary.

"Maggie put your mother under a spell; what I just did is supposed to break the spell."

Geraldine moaned and blinked as she regained her senses and saw three sets of eyes staring back at her. A smile slowly spread across her face as she regarded the three young people.

"Sean! Lillie!" she opened up her arms to her children and for the first time in many years cried tears of joy.

"Mam? Is it you?" Lillie stared in wonder as she remembered the kind woman from her childhood.

Geraldine nodded, still overcome with tears as her children hugged her.

Sean stepped away first and turned to Mary. "Thank you," was all he could manage before pulling her to him in a hug.

When Sean released her she saw that Geraldine was watching her and the old woman reached out her hand to draw her close. She approached the old woman with some hesitation, but Sean nodded in encouragement.

"Mary, I am glad to truly meet you," she said and her face crinkled into a welcoming smile.

"Me too."

"Thank you," Geraldine's voice was sincere as the two women regarded one another.

Sean turned back to Lillie. "Where are the others?"

"Not back, yet," Lille said and bit her lip.

"They'll be fine," Sean said, giving her a fond look as he set his son on the couch and tenderly tucked a blanket around him. "So, you and Patrick?" he asked Lillie with a raise of his voice.

Lillie blushed in embarrassment. "Now, Sean, I know that you and Patrick haven't been on the best of terms for a while, but he really is a different man..."

"He helped us against Maggie, and I'm grateful." Then he asked his sister, "Does he make you happy?"

With a shy smile, Lillie nodded.

"I'm happy for you," Sean said and walked over to enfold Lillie in a fierce embrace, and he hugged her tight until she squeaked.

"Sean!" She protested until he released her. "You seem so real. How can you be here? Can you stay like this?"

"I would if I could. Now that I am dead, it seems I have everything to live for, doesn't it?"

He shook his head and extended a hand to Mary. "*Ahh*, the irony." He walked over to the table and pulled out chairs for each of the women in his life. "Let's sit and catch up while we're waiting for the others," he said.

Mary sat down beside him at the table and never let go of his hand.

TWO HOURS LATER, little Sean slept on his father's lap, as Sean tenderly stroked his son's hair. He marveled that such a perfect little person could exist because of him and Mary. A father—it still sounded strange to him. Strange, but comforting, as though this could restore the part of him that had been lost to bitterness and tragedy, as though this child was the best of both him and Mary. The boy's quiet snores were the sweetest thing he had ever heard. Tired, Mary sat as close to Sean as she could get, taking in his nearness. He pulled her close, kissing her forehead. They were a wonderful family; he wished the night could last forever.

Geraldine, still wide awake startled them all by thumping her cane loudly. "Put the boy to bed. Lillie and I are here to look after him."

"Mam? I don't want to let go of him." Sean stared at her uncertainly.

"Sean, go and be with Mary. Your son enjoys staying here, we're getting to be very good friends," Lillie said with an encouraging smile.

"He'll be here when you get back," she assured him. "Sean, my boy, you can trust your mother."

"Yes, but these are unusual circumstances."

"Let the boy sleep and get out of your chair."

Sean shrugged and did what his mother asked of him.

"You too," she demanded of Mary.

Mary, did as she was told comforted by the warm feeling that now permeated the small house as Sean tenderly placed the boy on the couch where he slept on peacefully.

"Now take her hand." Geraldine stood up and pushed them toward the door, smiling.

He smiled at Mary as he took her hand into his own.

"Now go! But come back before dawn!"

"Yes, Mam!"

His mother pushed them out the door and shut the door firmly.

THE GUESTHOUSE WASN'T close enough, they both thought as they ran to it, hand in hand. When they got to Mary's room, they shut the door behind them and fell onto the bed, oblivious to the world around them, seeing, knowing only each other.

Sean was mesmerized, trying to engrave every feature of her face in his mind, trying to remember not only by sight, but by feel, as he caressed her soft skin.

She leaned forward and they kissed sweetly, remembering the taste of one another, then they kissed again and parted. Slowly they undressed one another, touching everywhere, savoring every moment and every sensation they could share; this might be the last physical memory they would have of one another, so they relished it. When passion finally overtook them, they submitted to their unabated longings with great pleasure.

ROB SMILED TO himself; Amy was nestled contentedly within his arms, and to say it had been a trying day for her was an understatement. His fiancée was having a great deal of trouble believing in things paranormal, and she now seemed surrounded by them. Somehow, Rob didn't think their involvement with it would be ending any time soon. Sean, after all, was a ghost, and Mary was Amy's best friend.

At least Sean's witch of an ex-wife had been taken away. After the police had shown up, the lot of them had managed to frame Maggie rather nicely for both the mutilation of the boy and the death of Paul. It was easier than Rob had expected, and it bothered him a bit that there wasn't any sort of an investigation. He expected resistance, suspicion, more questions, as their story did leave a bit to be desired, but none of that happened.

The police who showed up shared a few insightful looks between themselves, but accepted what was said, gathered the evidence that Maggie was responsible, and took her away, muttering something about psychiatric evaluations. Their analysis was that she would probably be put in an institution for the mentally ill for the remainder of her life. While he could accept that, the lack of thoroughness in a criminal matter was just plain weird. Maybe this whole town was strange; because it certainly seemed to be full of secrets.

Rob smiled as he heard the noises from Mary's room. *Yup, no mistaking what they were doing.* He was glad they could be together, because even if their time together was short, at least they had something. He wished there was a way to bring Sean back permanently, but he had never heard of anything that could make that possible. Much to his surprise, he found he quite liked Ireland and had a great curiosity about the supernatural.

SEAN AND MARY rested together in bed, nestled snugly against each other. The day's events had worn them out, and now they only wanted to sleep. But both pushed sleep away, unwilling to surrender even a moment of their time together.

He held Mary in his arms, softly kissing her hair and breathing in the scent of her. How he had ached to be with her, how he ached for her still. His heart broke to realize their time together was so short, but he praised God for any time with her at all. He had never experienced a miracle until now, and this night with her and their son was priceless. Once he returned to his shadowy realm, he would do what he could to help others and atone for his sins, and he would be a good ghost. Although he was not entirely certain what that would entail, Donald would undoubtedly fill him in, as the bartender seemed to know much more then he was letting on. But for now, he was here with Mary, and every moment was a treasure. He buried his face in her hair and held her tight.

She felt his arms tighten around her and wondered at his thoughts, wondered how it was possible that he was here with her, and said a small prayer of thanks, again, for Sean and for the rescue of their son. She turned so that she could study his face, wanting to memorize every feature. A bemused smile touched his lips as she gently traced his face with her fingertips, but his eyes and the emotions she saw there was what had always kept her captivated. Those clear, blue eyes she wanted to drown in, the eyes that danced with mischief, cried with pain, and now regarded her with a deep and abiding love. How could she have believed he didn't love her when he looked at her like this? God, how she missed losing herself in the blueness of his eyes.

He expelled a long sigh. "*Ah*, Mary. I wish I could make this last longer..." She put a finger to his lips, but he only remained silent for a moment. "Are you really going to stay in Ireland?"

"Can you leave?"

"No, or at least I don't think so. But Mary, you should go," he protested. "You belong with the living. Find a man who will love you like I do..."

"Is that possible?"

"No," he said at last. "No one will ever love you as much as I do."

"Then I'll stay."

"But what will you do? Your life is back in the States."

"I don't know. Maybe I'll finally start that business like I've always wanted to."

"You could. Talk to Lillie." He leaned forward and nibbled on her neck as she squirmed beside him.

"Why?"

"She's taking care of my estate and knows my wishes. You and our son will be taken care of."

"Sean, that's not necessary. . ."

"It is and I'll not waste more time talking about it when we have more important things to do." He kissed her and gestured to himself. "I don't know how long this will last, or even if I'll still be around like before, once this is over..."

"But we just found each other," Mary said.

He stroked her cheek with great tenderness and gently kissed her again. "We have to go."

"Where?"

"To see Mam. She knows more than she's letting on. And I need to see our son, to marvel at the perfect child you brought into the world." He reached for his pants, but was stopped when Mary caught his hands. Curious, he looked at her.

"Sean, it's going to be a long time until this happens again, if it ever happens again." She pulled him close, and he found himself unable to control his longing for her.

"*Ahh*, Mary," he said in a husky voice and succumbed to her urgings as she began to shower him with kisses.

LATER, LITTLE SEAN sat happily between his father and mother as Sean read him a story. Lillie sat across from them, a smile on her face. Mary sighed and saw that the sky was beginning to lighten.

Sean finished the story, closed the book, and kissed his son's cheek, then he picked up the boy and hugged him tightly. Reluctantly, he handed him to Mary.

"I'd better go and say goodbye to Mam."

He left Mary and walked down a short hallway to his mother's closed bedroom door. He knocked on it and put his ear against the door, and he heard a strange noise from inside. Curious, he knocked again.

"Mam?"

He heard a muffled shuffling sound from inside the room, and after a moment, the door opened and his mother, appearing disheveled, peered out at him.

"Mam, are you all right?"

"Fine, just fine." She hastily ran a hand through her gray hair.

"I just wanted to say goodbye..." He stopped, hearing a man's laughter from inside the room.

"Mam?" his eyes widened in shock, and his mother blushed. He was further astounded when the door opened to reveal his father, appearing just as Sean remembered him—mid-forties, healthy, and vibrant.

"Da? My God." He looked in disbelief first at his father and back at his mother.

After a long moment and with a happy smile, Geraldine met her son's gaze. "Well, it is a blue moon..."

"Goodbye, Mam." He smiled and kissed her cheek.

"Take care, son. I love you," she said and kissed him back.

He laughed and returned to the front door, where Lillie walked him outside. They hugged and exchanged a few whispered words and a kiss. With a last squeeze of her hand, Lillie retreated inside the house.

Sean looked at the gray sky, the first rays of sunlight beginning to filter over the horizon. He closed his eyes, already starting to feel a change within himself, and flexed his hand, watching it as it became transparent for a moment. Resigned, he bent down to hug his son, holding him tightly, and when he let go, there were tears in his eyes.

"I love you," he said and wiped away a tear. "Remember, no matter what anyone tells you, I'll always love you." He touched his son's soft cheek. "Will you remember that?"

"Yes, Daddy." The child's sad face looked into his own. "Are you going away?"

"I'm sorry, I have to."

"Will you still talk to me?"

"Of course I will. And I'll always watch over you, even if you can't see me."

The child kissed his father and hugged him, trying to comfort him. "Don't cry, Daddy. I love you, too."

"I love you so," Sean said, squeezing the boy to him tightly.

They embraced, their tears mixing together.

"Maybe we can figure a way..." Mary started.

He put a finger to her lips. "*Shh.*"

"Will you still be around? You're not going to vanish or anything are you?" Her expression was worried.

"I'm not sure, but I think it will be like before."

He bowed his head, aware of his ghostly perceptions again, aware he was losing his physical form and that he was being called back to The Gaelic Moon. He looked at the road and saw that his father stood there, waiting for him to join him.

After a long last kiss, he stepped away from Mary, but they continued to hold hands, maintaining their touch until he was no longer substantial. Sadly, he turned and walked away from her. She watched him, her hands on her son's shoulders, as Sean turned back to her for a moment.

"I almost forgot. Ask Lillie for the box."

"The box?"

"Lillie will know."

He turned away and greeted his father, and the older man dropped a comforting arm about Sean as they began to walk down the road. After a few moments, they simply faded into the morning sunlight.

"Goodbye, Daddy." The boy waved and Mary held him close.

A few minutes later, Lillie emerged from the house, holding a jewelry box in her hand. Silently, she gave it to Mary, who with a forlorn expression, still watched the road where Sean had disappeared. "He told me I should give it to you when he left, to remind you of his love, but somehow I don't think you need a reminder." Lillie took the boy's hand and led him back inside the house.

Surprised, Mary recognized the box in her hand. The last time she had seen it was four years ago, when she had dropped it in the dirt as she had driven away.

IN THE MORNING light, Sean was amazed at how many people he saw outside The Gaelic Moon—people he knew, and others, many he had never seen before. He shook his head, trying to clear it, but kept seeing more people, many in clothing from other time periods. They were all returning to The Gaelic Moon, which stood intact as it welcomed them home. As the spirits approached the pub, they faded into the interior.

"Donald!" Sean clamored trying to draw his attention. "What's going on? Who're all of these people?"

"*Ahh*," he said with a smile. "I was wondering how long it would be before you'd see the others."

"What do you mean? How long? They've been here the whole time? Why couldn't I see them before?"

Donald shrugged. "It takes new spirits awhile to acclimate to their change. So there is no specific time when someone new will begin to see the older ones, but you did take longer than most." He regarded the other spirits. "Some of them will pass on now. Some will stay."

"What about me?" Sean asked anxiously. "What will happen to me?"

The older man offered him an encouraging smile. "What do you want to do? Are you ready to leave?"

"Leave? To where?" Sean shook his head. "Never mind. It doesn't matter."

"Even if it's the gates of heaven that open up to you?"

"With the mistakes I've made? That's impossible."

"Forgiveness and redemption are always possible. You should know that."

Sean's smile faded as his expression grew serious. "I can't go. I don't want to go."

"You'd turn down the pearly gates?"

"Damn straight!"

"Why?"

"You know why. To be with her, with them. Even if it's only as a spirit. Besides, when I thanked God for the Gaelic Moon, I promised to look after them and to be a good ghost." He gave Donald a lopsided grin. "I assume you'll instruct me?"

"I'll be happy to tell you what to do." He winked, but his expression grew solemn. "But there's much to be done, and not all of it pleasant."

"I don't care. As long as I can stay by my family, I'll do what I must."

"That's the spirit!" Donald clapped him on the back and grinned as Sean groaned at his pun.

"But I wish I could be with her again," Sean said glumly.

"You'll get used to it, lad. It just takes time. And it will go faster than you think. One day she'll be able to join you."

"But I want to join her. I don't ever want to leave her."

"I don't have an answer for that," Donald said with a shrug. "But as long as you have unfinished business, you'll have a reason to be around." He smiled at Sean. "Did you ever give her something of yours? A gift perhaps?"

"Yes, a necklace."

"And why did you give it to her?"

"Why do you think?"

Donald nodded in approval and patted Sean on the head. "There's hope for you, yet, my boy. If the gift was given in love, she'll always know when you're near."

He smiled and nodded, feeling his love for Mary flow through him, filling his soul with happiness.

OPENING THE BOX, Mary recognized the necklace Sean had given her so very long ago. And now, after all that had transpired, she knew it had been given to her because he loved her. As she gently removed it from the box and held it in her hand, the light caught it, making it sparkle with a life of its own. She marveled at its beauty. In moments, the sparkle became a warm glow that pulsed within her hand. With a joyful smile, she hugged it to her and knew that somehow Sean would always be with her.

Down the road, the solid image of The Gaelic Moon began to deteriorate. The outline sparkled, shimmered, and finally faded as the sunlight covered it in warmth, and the burned-out structure returned.

Mary watched it from the road and smiled to herself. The world had been set right again and would remain so as long as they had faith in the Gaelic Moon, and after all this time, there was no question of that.

She turned away from the charred remains, knowing her family was waiting for her and that the Gaelic Moon would always be a part of her and Sean. It was part of the bond they shared that would always draw them together.

About the Author

Carol Maschke has a BA in English from Hamline University in St. Paul, Minnesota. She began writing stories as a child. It was a way to fuel her imagination and channel her creative energies into something tangible. She lives with her cairn terrier dogs in Minnesota and competes with her furry friends in conformation, agility, obedience and barnhunt.

For more information on upcoming books and other projects, please visit www.cairnmoon.com.